# The
# Usual Rules

# JOYCE MAYNARD

# The Usual Rules

ST. MARTIN'S PRESS
NEW YORK

www.stmartins.com

Permission to quote from *Anne Frank: Diary of a Young Girl* granted by the Liepman Agency, copyright © 1982, 1991, 2001 by the Anne Frank Funds, Basela, Switzerland.

Excerpts from *The Member of the Wedding* by Carson McCullers copyright © 1946 by Carson McCullers. Copyright © renewed 1974 by Floria V. Lasky. Reprinted by permission of Houghton Mifflin Company and the Estate of Carson McCullers. All rights reserved.

Excerpts from *Goodnight Moon* used by permission of HarperCollins Publishers. Copyright © 1947 by Harper & Row, Publishers, Incorporated. Text copyright renewed 1975 by Roberta Brown Rauch.

Book design by Kathryn Parise

Library of Congress Cataloging-in-Publication Data

Maynard, Joyce.
    The usual rules / Joyce Maynard. — 1st ed.
      p. cm.
    ISBN 0-312-24261-1
    1. September 11 Terrorist Attacks, 2001—Fiction.    2. Brooklyn (New York, N.Y.)—Fiction.
3. Fathers and daughters—Fiction.    4. Loss (Psychology)—Fiction.    5. Mothers—Death—
Fiction.    6. Teenage girls—Fiction.    7. California—Fiction.    I. Title.

PS3563.A9638 U7 2003
813'.54—dc21

                                                                                    2002036754

First Edition: February 2003

10   9   8   7   6   5   4   3   2   1

For my daughter and sons, Audrey, Charlie, and Willy Bethel, whose love for one another shines through even when continents separate them, just as it did when the space they shared was no larger than the backseat of an old Ford station wagon, with a harried mother at the wheel.

All the best parts of the young people in this book came from my life with you.

It's difficult in times like these: ideals, dreams and cherished hopes rise within us, only to be crushed by grim reality. It's a wonder I haven't abandoned all my ideals, they seem so absurd and impractical. Yet I cling to them because I still believe, in spite of everything, that people are truly good at heart.

It's utterly impossible for me to build my life on a foundation of chaos, suffering and death. I see the world being slowly transformed into a wilderness, I hear the approaching thunder that, one day, will destroy us too, I feel the suffering of millions. And yet, when I look up at the sky, I somehow feel that everything will change for the better, that this cruelty too will end, that peace and tranquility will return once more.

—*Anne Frank, in her diary, July 15, 1944*

# The
# Usual Rules

It was a story Wendy knew well, how she got her name.

Your dad wanted to call you Sierra, her mother would begin, because you were conceived in the Sierra Mountains, on a camping trip. Trout fishing, naturally. But ever since I was a little girl, I always said if I had a daughter, I'd call her Wendy.


Her mother loved musicals, the big old-fashioned kind. Growing up in Cedar Falls, the only time she ever saw a show was the annual Lions Club production, but one time they had the real Broadway version of *Peter Pan* on TV, with the actress Mary Martin playing Peter. Having a woman play Peter wasn't as strange as you'd think, because she was skinny and her hair was cut short like a boy.

This was way back. Wendy's mother, Janet, was only five years old at the time. She herself had been named after a singer on her parents' favorite show, *Lawrence Welk*. One of the Lennon Sisters. But even back then, she knew she wasn't a Lawrence Welk type. She was going to be a Broadway dancer. She wanted to play Peter Pan herself. Someday that was going to be her flying over the audience, dancing with the Lost Boys, singing "I've Gotta Crow." Her hair was long but she'd cut it.

She got to New York on a bus when she was eighteen years old. Back home she'd done some typing for her father's insurance office. With the money she'd saved she rented a room in the Barbizon Hotel, which catered to young women who came to New York City from places like Missouri. She went to auditions, but in the meantime she got a job as a waitress at a Chock Full o'Nuts restaurant and a second job, nights, as something called a Peachy Puff girl, selling cigarettes and candy bars at clubs in a little outfit that was basically a bathing suit, with a few ruffles on the bottom. That was where she met her friend Kate. The two of them saved up their money so they could buy tickets to shows. She went without food sometimes, but never musicals.

Janet was a wonderful dancer. They always told her that. But not being able to carry a tune, she was out of the running for featured roles, if any singing was involved.

Her big break was getting to be an understudy in *A Chorus Line*. Not for any of the main parts, but when one of the dancers in the company couldn't go on, Janet did.

The problem was, she got this look on her face when she danced. Hard as she tried, she couldn't change. It's fine to be happy, a casting director told her once. But you keep giving me rapture, and that's a little much.

The audience is meant to be looking at the featured performers, another director told her once. When you're dancing, we end up watching you.

I'll try not to stand out so much, she said.

I don't think you can help it, he told her.


The closest she ever got to an actual role was final callbacks for Princess Tiger Lily in a road company revival of *Peter Pan*. Not Mary Martin anymore.

I think this time I'm going to get it, she had told her mother when she called with the news.

The next day, running across the street on her way to the theater—her last audition, when it was down to just a handful of dancers—a bicycle messenger ran into her. She knew the minute she hit the ground that it was bad. She sat on the curb, on the corner of Forty-fourth Street and Eighth Avenue, crying. A man came out of a stage door, carrying a bunch of tools. A set builder. Hey, he said. You look like you could use a cup of coffee.

That was Garrett. He was working as a carpenter, but he was really an artist. He took her out for dim sum that night. He was very handsome in a way that made her think of Billy Bigelow in *Carousel*. As soon as her ankle was better, they danced together in his loft. East Coast swing.

They fell in love. He painted her. A few months later, he took her cross-country in his truck. Camping mostly, and stopping along the way at places where the fishing was good. He loved to fish, and she actually liked tying flies, or thought she did, she was that much in love.

By then she had started to wonder if it really was what she wanted most, to tap-dance in the back row now and then, nights when somebody in the company called in sick, living in her little one-room apartment, eating her soup alone. She was twenty-six years old. A whole new crop of terrific dancers landed in New York every year, also wanting to dance on Broadway. They were younger than she was, with the kind of fierce ambition she used to have when she first got to New York.

The pregnancy—discovered a few days after they returned from their camping trip—came as a surprise, but not bad news. What do you say we get married? Garrett had said.

From the beginning, Janet had understood that Garrett was something of a Peter Pan type himself. But she had a weakness for lost boys. Even a hit show would close eventually. A tour would end. A marriage and a baby ran forever. That was the hope anyway.

I didn't even have a boy's name picked out, her mother told her. I was so sure you were going to be a girl.

Wendy: the oldest of the children Peter took with him to Neverland. The sensible one, but full of spunk. The one who kept things together for everyone.

Things had been rough in Neverland for Wendy and her two brothers, and the other Lost Boys. They hardly remembered their own mothers, they'd been gone so long, so it was Wendy who took care of them. She did things like mend their shirts, but she also told them stories.

I'd do that, too, Wendy told her mother when they got to this part. If I had a brother, I'd take the best care of him.

Some people might have gotten fed up with a person like Peter Pan. He was so irresponsible, but Wendy was patient. She loved him for the good parts and forgave the rest.

Even though she was this sensible, motherly-type person, there was another side to Wendy. She was an adventurer. She was brave, even when she was captured by the pirates. At the darkest moments, she never gave up hope.

Many times, when she was little, Wendy and her mother had rented the video of Mary Martin playing Peter Pan. When it got to the place where Peter asked everyone to close their eyes and think hard if they believed in fairies, to keep Tinker Bell from dying, Wendy had done it. Yes, I believe, she called out to the television set. I really do.

Of course, everything had turned out all right in the end. That was one of the other great things about musicals, her mother said. The happy endings.

# PART ONE

# New York

# One

Quarter past six. In ten minutes, Wendy would have to get in the shower. Her clock radio came on. A newsman was talking about the elections for mayor of New York City. She switched to music. Madonna.

She went through her new school clothes in her head, thinking up combinations. Her mother said the great thing about the gray pants was how you could wear them with anything, but when she wore them yesterday, she'd felt as if she was playing dress-up. Nobody else in eighth grade had pants like that. She wished she'd gotten the purple-and-green-plaid kilt instead, that her mom said was impractical. Her mom, who owned three different-colored feather boas and red velvet harem pants, a leopard-print cat suit, and a tutu, not to mention all her old Peachy Puffs getups.

Those pants really flatter your figure, her mother said when she put them on yesterday.

Do you think I'm fat? Wendy said. Her mother was a size four, and they could share clothes now, but Wendy could tell that before long, her clothes would be bigger than her mother's.

Of course not. All I meant was they make you look even slimmer than usual.

I'm fat, aren't I? Wendy told her.

You've got a perfect body. Much nicer than if you were one of those stick-figure types. I always wished I had a shape.

In other words I'm chunky, said Wendy.

You look just right, her mother said. Your bones are bigger, that's all.


Louie opened the door partway, just enough that she could see a corner of his face, eyes crusty, thumb in mouth.

Are you dry?

He told her yes.

Positive?

There's just this one little drip but it got soaked up in my sleeper suit, so it doesn't count. He stood there holding Pablo, with the old blue ribbon from when Pablo was new wrapped around his thumb. He liked to twirl the tip of the ribbon in his ear with his free hand while he sucked on the thumb of his other hand.

Just don't get any pee on me, she said.

He positioned himself in the bed so every inch of the side closest to Wendy was touching some part of her. She could hear the slurping sound his lips made on this thumb, and his breathing, slow and quiet, still labored from last week's cold.

One two three four. He was counting the rabbits on her pajama bottoms, though after twelve or thirteen, he usually gave up.

I dreamed we got a puppy, he said. The two of them had been after their parents about that forever.

What kind?

With spots. Little and fuzzy.

Are you going to school again today? he said.

I already explained to you, Louie. I go to school every day now except Saturday and Sunday. Five days in a row, school, and two days home, only probably a lot of times I'll be sleeping over at Amelia's Friday nights.

I want you to stay home with me, he said.

*       *       *

She could hear the shower running in the room next to hers. She called it her parents' bathroom, even though Josh wasn't her real father, only Louie's. It was easier, plus he seemed more like her father than her real one.

You'll be going to school, too, pretty soon anyway, she told him. Thursday is preschool orientation, remember? You might want to work on not sucking your thumb so much. The other kids might make fun of you.

I changed my mind, he said. I don't want to go to preschool after all. I want to stay home and play with you.

Well, I'm not going to be home, she said. And even if I was, I probably wouldn't play that much.

Why?

I'm not in that stage anymore. Once you get to my stage in life, you want to do different kinds of things.

What?

Josh was making French toast. The kitchen smelled of just-ground coffee beans and frying butter. He was playing the *Teach Yourself Spanish* tape. Part one of her mother's birthday present last month. Part two was the trip to Mexico scheduled for next spring, when Wendy was going to stay at Amelia's or possibly go to California to visit her real dad, but she wasn't supposed to count on this. It had been nearly three years since she'd seen him.

Her mother had said they couldn't afford a trip to Mexico, but Josh told her she worried too much. Six months from now, I could get hit by a bus, he said, and boy would you ever wish you'd gone on that trip.

The coffeepot made the sound that meant the coffee was ready. Josh poured himself a cup of coffee. Louie hopped in on one foot. He had taken off his cape now and replaced it with the cummerbund from his Aladdin costume. All week he'd been working on his skipping, and now he was circling the table, making little frog jumps. He hadn't figured out yet how to alternate his feet.

¡Hola, muchacho! said Josh.

Blabbyblaba, Louie said. Where's my cereal?

Josh had already poured it. At your *servicio, señor*.

The voice on the tape was reviewing yesterday's lesson. *¿Donde está la estación central de autobus?* he repeated.

Wendy studied Josh's face as he stood at the stove, holding the spatula. She had been wondering if people looked different right after they had sex, but he looked the same as usual. His hair was going in all different directions, but it always did first thing in the morning. He hadn't shaved yet, and he was wearing the same old green sweatpants and his Yankees T-shirt from last summer's subway series. He wasn't handsome like her father, and he didn't have her father's six-pack that made Amelia call him a hunk when she saw his picture. Josh had curly black hair and the kind of face you'd like to see if you had a problem.

Powdered sugar on yours, miss? he asked. He set down a pitcher of maple syrup in front of her. Heated. She had told herself she was going to cut calories today, but now she poured a pool of syrup on her plate.

Mom up yet?

She's a little tired this morning, he said. I told her she should call in sick, but she said she'd just skip breakfast instead and take a later train.

They had sex all right. Wendy thought so before, but now she was sure.

She was supposed to fill in my field trip permission forms and the one about who to contact in an emergency, Wendy told him. My homeroom teacher said not to leave it to the last day. Also, I wanted to talk to her about my clarinet. They gave me a really crummy rental. I was thinking maybe we could buy one instead.

It wasn't the permission forms that were making the sharp sound in her voice, she knew, or the clarinet, either. She was thinking about the argument they'd had last night about her going to California. She wanted to visit her father. Her mother had said, That's crazy. School just started.

You never let me do anything, Wendy had told her. As usual, Josh tried to make peace.

We'll talk about the clarinet tonight, he said. Meanwhile, I'll sign the forms. Let your mom have an extra ten minutes' sleep.

It's supposed to be filled out by a parent, Wendy told him.

For a second, Josh got a look on his face that reminded her of Louie when he stood at the bus with her that first morning she went off to junior high.

What do you say we give it a try this once, he said, reaching for the form. Father or no father, if you get injured in some knock-down-drag-out volleyball game, I'm probably the one who'll come running down to school to get you.

Watching Josh as he took out the jar of raisins, arranging them on Louie's plate in the shape of a man, Wendy felt crummy for saying what she had. Do you have any idea how lucky we are to have someone like Josh in our life? her mom said to her, times when Wendy treated him the way she knew she had just now. Do you even remember what it was like before he came along? Do you think Garrett would ever put himself out for you the way Josh does?

No.

I don't know why I say the mean things I do, she told Amelia. My parents are just getting on my nerves so much lately. Sometimes these horrible remarks ooze out of me.

Maybe you're possessed, Amelia said. We could perform an exorcism. Amelia had seen a video recently where that happened to a girl, and when they finally held the exorcism ceremony, all this horrible green vomit squirted out of her mouth and her head swiveled around like a cartoon character.

On TV, the weatherman was pointing to a map of New York and saying it looked like perfect weather clear through the weekend. Better grab yourself one last dose of summer, folks. No excuse not to get out and vote today.

Josh had been making her a sandwich. Now he was packing an apple in her lunch bag.

You got Macintosh, she said. I like Granny Smith, remember?

I didn't want raisins, Louie told Josh. I wanted chocolate chips.

We don't have chocolate for breakfast, Lou-man, Josh told him. As for you, Miss Picky, the Granny Smiths at the market weren't any good.

But Sissy gets hot chocolate, Louie said. That's chocolate. Just not in the shape of a chip.

Tell you what, son, Josh said. You eat the raisins, and tonight we'll make ourselves some chocolate-chip cookies. Maybe you can bring in a few extra on Thursday for you know what.

I want Mama to come, too, when I go to preschool, said Louie.

Mama wouldn't miss it, Josh said. That's why she decided not to take the day off today. So she could be there with you Thursday.

Back when her mother first introduced her to Josh, she meant to hate him. She was only seven then. She'd seen a video at Amelia's house around that time, called *Parent Trap*, where a couple of twins whose parents were divorced decided to get them back together, and it worked. Even though Wendy didn't have a twin like the girls in the movie, that was her plan.

She was mean to him that first night at the restaurant. She didn't order anything except water, even though sushi was her favorite. I was just wondering, Josh said to her as she sat there, not even touching the soybeans that she loved, what is your opinion of miniature golf?

She had never been miniature golfing but she always wanted to. There was a course called Dreamland they sometimes passed on their way to Fire Island that her mom said they'd stop at someday, but they never had. Josh took them there, and after that, when Wendy's mother said it wasn't really her type of activity, it got to be something he and Wendy did, on Saturday afternoons when her mom and Kate went to yoga.

They were at Dreamland when he told her about wanting to get married to her mom. I could understand if you aren't too thrilled, he said. I know you've got a dad, and it's understandable that you'd like it a whole lot better if he was with your mother instead of me. But I promise I'll try hard to make her happy. And I'll teach you every single thing you ever wanted to know about jazz.

Which was nothing.


She was the flower girl. All that day, she kept thinking about the *Parent Trap* video and waiting for her real father to come crashing in and say something like Janet, it was all a terrible mistake. Come back to me. What are you doing hanging around with this chubby guy with hair on his shoulders and love handles, when you could be with me?

Even after it was all over, and Josh's mom was hugging her, and she had on so much perfume Wendy could hardly breathe, and saying how she'd always wished she had a granddaughter—even then, Wendy kept expecting something to happen that would make him disappear. But the next thing she knew, Josh was moving his clothes into her mother's room and building a bunch of shelves for his collection of old jazz LPs. Sometimes at night, she could hear them having sex.

Josh was a stand-up bass player. He worked weekends mostly, usually Friday and Saturday nights, and sometimes he'd get hired to play at a wedding, but he was usually home during the day, except when he gave lessons. He loved to cook, and instead of take-out Chinese and pizza, he made them things like eggplant parmigiana and roast chicken with garlic mashed potatoes.

One day he found a box of Duncan Hines brownie mix in their cupboard. He took it into the living room, where Wendy and her mother were watching a video of *The Music Man*.

Janet, he said in a voice that was so serious, Wendy actually worried he was mad. She'd never heard him get mad before. She was surprised at how scary it was, hearing someone who's always nice to you sound angry all of a sudden. Not like her father, who she could remember sounding mad, even though she'd been so little when he left.

Now Josh was holding the box of Duncan Hines in front of her mother, like evidence. I hope and pray this is the last time an item like this ever makes its way into our kitchen. Just tell me it was temporary insanity.

I bought that a long time ago, her mother said. I didn't think I'd ever know anyone who could make us brownies from scratch. I swear I'll never in my whole life buy another box of Duncan Hines.

Then Wendy knew it was a joke, because the look on her mother's face was like some character in a soap opera whose husband just found out she was in love with someone else.

When she said that, he put his arms around her and made a sound like a bear in the forest—a low, happy growling noise, as if he'd just found a tree stump full of the sweetest honey deep in the underbrush. Something about the way the two of them looked at each other like that made it seem as if they were the only two people in the world.

It was Josh, not her mother, who seemed to know Wendy was feeling that way, because he looked up at her then.

Knowing your mother's talents in the kitchen, he said, I can tell the only hope I'll ever have of handing down my secret time-tested brownie recipe is if I teach it to you.

Wendy and Josh melted the chocolate over the double boiler. You melted the butter in with the chocolate. Butter, never margarine, he told her. He showed her how to sift flour and beat the eggs with the sugar till they made a golden-colored froth, and he let her be the one to pour the melted chocolate mixture into the eggs, very slowly, so at first it was part dark brown, part creamy yellow swirls, until gradually the chocolate was all mixed in. Then the flour.

Now for the most important part, he said.

Putting it in the oven?

Oh my God, he said. You have even more to learn than I thought.

He reached for a package of pecans and poured a bunch into a plastic sandwich bag. He took out his big wooden rolling pin.

Josh didn't come with much stuff when he moved in with them. A box of clothes, his string bass, a picture of himself with his sister and his parents when he was around nine, and a stuffed rabbit, also from when he was little. Not a whole lot else. But the rolling pin was his. Wendy's mom never owned one before.

Let's say there's this boy in your class who keeps getting on your nerves, making fart sounds when the teacher isn't looking, he said. Do you know anyone like that?

The thing was, she did.

Or some girl who tells you she isn't going to invite you to her birthday party, and even though she's a major jerk, you really wanted to go because everyone else in your class was going to be there.

This also had happened.

Here's what you do about it, he said. He held the rolling pin over the bag of pecans. He smashed it down with surprising force on the bag of nuts. Not so hard the bag broke. Just hard enough to crush the nuts.

That one's for all the boys who make fart sounds, he said. This one's for snobby girls who won't invite you to their dumb party.

Wendy watched him for a minute. Then he handed her the rolling pin. Your turn, he said. It took her a second to get it.

Ms. Kempner, my gym teacher, she said. Who never picks me for dodgeball. Wendy smashed the rolling pin down on the nuts.

People who are cruel to animals, she said. People who litter. People who sit down on the seats on the bus that are supposed to go to handicapped people and senior citizens. Mom's boss, that makes her stay late all the time. People who give you dirty looks when you go into a store with breakable things, just because you're a kid.

The nuts were crushed enough by this time, but the two of them kept thinking up more reasons to bang the rolling pin.

What's going on in there, you two? asked her mother.

It's not something you'd understand, Jan, he told her. It's one of those things only brownie bakers appreciate.


In the kitchen now, Josh was saying the days of the week in Spanish, but instead of saying them, he was singing, like some performer on one of his old jazz albums. He had Louie's spoon in one hand and he was beating out a rhythm on the counter.

Wendy wanted another piece of French toast, but she didn't let herself reach for it. She poured herself a glass of water. Nice-looking outfit, he said when he finally sat down with his coffee. That's one of the new ones you and your mom got at Macy's, right?

She had changed three times this morning. In the end, what she put on was her old standby from last year, a denim skirt and a sweater. Standing in front of the mirror, she had decided she would give up bread, bagels, and granola bars until she lost ten pounds. There were so many skinny girls in her class now. She weighed 111 pounds, the heaviest she'd ever been.

I bet you're the prettiest one at your whole school, said Louie, patting her hair.

I definitely am not, she told him. Anyway, how would you know? You've never even been to my school.

I have superpowers.

She looked at the clock—Felix the cat, with a tail that swung in time with the seconds. Oh God, it's five past seven, she said.

Why don't you stick your head in the bedroom and say good-bye to your mom, Josh said.

I'm late already, she told him. She picked up her backpack and her clarinet case.

I'm going over to Amelia's after school. Tell Mom to wear the new dress, she called from the stairs.

Wendy had been best friends with Amelia since first grade. In third grade, they'd tied their desks together, until the teacher made them cut the string. They had invented a language nobody else understood. Later they made up all kinds of other things, too. Like saying Bloody Mary ten times very fast for good luck and daring each other to give the cutest boy on their subway train a blue M&M right before they got off at their stop. Mostly, it was Amelia who thought up the stuff and Wendy who went along with it, like when she propped up a picture of Josh's father, who was dead, and they stared at it for twenty minutes without taking their eyes off one time. Wait and see, his lips are going to move, she said, and after a long time, Wendy said, Oh my God, you're actually right.

Last year when Amelia's family got their new apartment in Brooklyn Heights, it felt like the worst thing that ever happened to Wendy.

This morning Wendy rode alone on the bus, as usual, listening to her Walkman. Today the CD was Sade—after Madonna, her favorite. Even though Sade sang a lot about having her heart broken by someone—and Wendy had never had that happen to her—it seemed to her Sade was the kind of person who would understand, even if she didn't fully understand it herself, how it was she could be feeling so confused and unhappy so much of the time, even as everyone around her thought things were going fine. All you had to do was look at Sade's beautiful, mysterious face to believe she knew what she was talking about when she sang about the king of sorrow. *Even the comfort of a stone would be a gain.* How desolate was that?

Wendy looked out the window of the bus, at the men with their briefcases, hurrying down the street to the subway, the women in their business suits and sneakers, a young couple leaning against a phone booth, kissing, teenagers on their way to school, or not. When she spotted a girl close to her age, she always calculated if the girl was thinner or fatter than her. The other thing that had her worried was the uneven way she was developing, so she was still almost totally flat on her right side and rounding out, as even Louie had noticed, on her left. She kept her notebook tight against her chest most of the day for that reason, but today was her first gym class of eighth grade, and already she was trying to figure out a way to change in the girls' bathroom so no one would see.

I would give anything if I could just get out of gym, she said, but only inside her head.

This morning the halls at her school were covered with posters—elections for class officers. Back in elementary school, she knew all the names, but this school was so much bigger. Even though it was just the second week, she already had her routine down. She ate with Amelia and sometimes a boy named Seth, whose voice hadn't changed. She knew the names of people in her classes but doubted many of them knew hers. All around her, people called out to one another, but except for one time when another clarinet player, who sat next to her in band, asked to borrow a reed, hardly anyone except Amelia and Seth had spoken to her so far this year.

At eight-thirty, the homeroom bell rang. Some people lingered in the hall till the last possible minute, but Wendy was sitting at her desk promptly as usual when the teacher came in.

Who's got their permission slips and health forms? she asked. Besides Wendy, there was only one other girl.

The announcements came on. This month's announcer was a girl named Robbie from Wendy's history class. When she was picked to start off the year as guest announcer, she said how perfect was that, since she was going to be an anchorwoman when she grew up.

Okay, guys, said Robbie. Get out your notebooks and write down these dates. Be sure to bring wads of cash to school Friday for the pep squad bake sale. But most important, mark down the night of October twenty-eighth for the absolute best ever Halloween dance, sponsored by the eighth grade. Don't leave it to the last minute to ask someone special to go with you, either. Hint, hint.

Wendy didn't write down the dates. She and Amelia might rent a couple of scary movies that night and color their hair black. Either that or she'd take Louie trick-or-treating around the neighborhood like last year.

She looked out the window. It was a perfect day. She wished she could be outside on her bike. She would put her colored pencils in her backpack and go to Prospect Park and spend the whole day drawing Japanese animation storyboards. She'd go to Ronnie's Pets and imagine she got to pick one of the puppies. She'd go into the city to the Metropolitan Museum—never mind that her mother said she was too young to ride the subway alone—and sit in the room with the Tiffany glass windows and just think.

She'd take a cab to the airport and stow away in a plane to California. And when she got there, she'd call up her dad and say, Surprise, I'm here, and he would come to meet her with this huge bag of almonds from his own personal almond tree in his yard and never mention what her mother had said that one time: Not because you've got a problem but just to let you know, there's twenty calories in every one of those.

In the seat next to her, Buddy Campion, one of the most visible candidates for eighth grade class president, was working on a poster. Wendy's homeroom teacher was doing the annual back-to-school demonstration on the correct method for covering your books with brown paper bags.

People. I want to remind you. We encourage you to decorate your books in a creative manner. But I don't want to see any crude or inappropriate language or imagery on your schoolbooks, and I'm sure I don't need to specify further just what that sort of thing entails.

Wendy looked out the window again. The picture came to her of her little brother in his blue sleeper suit and golden cape, snuggled against her that morning, smelling slightly of pee. She thought about Josh, handing her the brown paper bag with her lunch as she headed out the door. Sade, whispering into her ears through the headphones on her Walkman, "Take me to the belly of darkness."

Call your mom at work, Josh said. You know she hates it when she doesn't get to say good-bye. She thought of Louie, bending his whole head over her plate after she was finished with her French toast and lapping up the last of the syrup. If her mother was at the table, she might have told him no, but Josh laughed. Are you a boy or a dog? he asked.

A dog, said Louie. A karate dog.

Last Thursday, she got a letter from her real father. Why don't you come see me? he wrote. You wouldn't believe my crop of oranges, and the almonds are going to be great this year, too.

Isn't that typical? her mother said. She was talking to Josh, but Wendy heard. All summer he kept putting off the visit, she said, and now that she's going back to school, he tells her to come see him.

She thought about the cabin in California in the picture he'd sent her with the letter, with the cactuses around it and morning glory vines climbing the fence. If she lived in California, she'd eat nothing but oranges off his tree and throw sticks for his dog, and she'd get skinny as Christina Aguilera.

Where did you get your tan? Robbie Gershen would ask her when she got back. Oh, surfing, she'd say. My dad taught me. He lives in California. He's an artist.

She tried to picture her father, but the picture was hazy. It was so long since she'd seen him. We're due for some major father-daughter hangout time. What do you say? he wrote. I'll send you a ticket as soon as you let me know the date.

Even Wendy knew there was no way she could miss two weeks at the start of school, but she asked anyway. When her mother said no, Wendy said she never let her do anything.

You just want me to hate my dad as much as you, she said. You probably hate me, too, because I remind you of him.

Josh took her by the shoulders then—not angry, but firm—with those bass player hands of his gripping her so tight it just missed being painful.

Listen, he said after her mother had walked out of the room. You know that isn't true. Your mom just loves you so much she doesn't want to see you hurt.

Sometimes I wish she'd just drop dead, Wendy told him.


Mrs. Volt was passing out more forms. The revised school dress code, with a parents' advisory concerning midriff tops and guidelines for skirt lengths. At the desk next to hers, a boy named Sean was tattooing his arm with the name of some girl named Cindi. He had made very small cuts in his forearm with a razor blade, in the shape of the letters, and now he was filling them in with ink. Wendy wondered what it would feel like to be Cindi, to have a boy love you so much that he would make cuts in his wrist for you. Josh would probably do something like that for her mother, come to think of it. If she wanted him to. As it was, he just left her Post-it notes all over the place.

She could hear the sound of lockers slamming in the hall. The audiovisual cart wheeled past, and from the cafeteria came the smell of chili cooking. Outside the window, a squirrel ran across an electric line. She could make out the words of the Madonna song that was everywhere at the moment, on someone's car radio. The floor trembled very slightly, the way it always did when the L train went by.

Later, Wendy would think back on that morning, trying to remember every single thing. She would remember the smell of the butter in the pan and the sound of Josh singing along with Madonna, the gold of the sun hitting the roof of the church across the street from their apartment, the woman who had gotten on at her bus stop, talking about some congressman who had an affair. Having to try her locker combination three times before she got the lock to open. The band director calling out to her, I'm betting you're the one clarinet player who practiced over the summer, which she had.

She would list all the things she would do—cut off her hair, cut off her arm, both legs, gain fifty pounds, two hundred, never have a boyfriend, never have anybody fall in love with her for her whole life, stand naked in front of her whole gym class with her two different-size breasts—if she could just return to how it was before.

*Pause,* Louie liked to say when he got up from the couch to go to the bathroom or get a cookie and he didn't want you to do anything until he returned. *Rewind,* he said when he came running back in the room and it looked as if things had been going on without him. Sometimes they'd be watching a video, but he also said it if someone was reading to him, or if they were playing Go Fish or checkers. He thought you could freeze time in real life, same as on a video.

If rewind wasn't possible, then pause. Freeze forever at this moment and never go on to the next, and it would still be a million times better than what happened when she did.

Later, she would consider what she was doing at the exact second it happened. Walking up to the pencil sharpener in front of the room and wondering, as she sharpened her pencil, if anyone was thinking she looked fat. Doodling on the back of her notebook, a Japanese animation-style picture of a girl in an orange jumpsuit with a punk hairdo and a boom box—a picture she would never finish. Opening her binder partway, enough to look again at the picture her father had sent her of the cabin with the cactus. The morning glory vines and the funky green truck and her dad holding the puppy against his chest.

I guess they're still getting the kinks out of our bell system, because it definitely should have rung by now, Mrs. Volt said to them. If it doesn't ring in another minute or two, I'll just send you along to your first-period class.

Then came the voice of the principal on the loudspeaker.

Everyone remain calm, please. We're still trying to get the details. There's been an accident.

# Two

After her father left and they moved to their new apartment, Wendy's mother said she'd have to find a real job. She closed the Pocahontas Dancing School and sold her mirrors and let Wendy keep all the leftover costumes for dress-ups. She bought a suit and navy blue high heels and cut her hair short, and put Wendy in day care.

Wendy could dimly remember those days: the newspaper spread out on the table every night and her mother, with a Hi-Liter pen, marking the prospects worth checking out.

What are those? Wendy had asked the first time she saw her mother dressed up for an interview.

They're called panty hose, her mother said. They're what people with regular jobs wear.

Nights back then, they made soup and snuggled up together under the blue afghan and watched reruns of *I Love Lucy* on Nickelodeon. They had popcorn for dinner a lot.

I don't know how you live with yourself, Garrett. I don't expect anything for myself, but you've got a daughter here, and if something doesn't change soon, she's going to have cardboard boxes for shoes, she heard her mother say on the phone one time. It was late and Wendy was supposed to be asleep, but she lay in the dark, wondering how you keep cardboard boxes on your feet. This was just around the time she was learning to jump rope. She wondered how a person could jump rope with cardboard boxes on.

One day when her mother came to pick Wendy up at day care, she had a bunch of flowers in her grocery bag and she looked happy again.

I got a job, she said. I'm an executive secretary in a giant skyscraper in the city. At the time, Wendy had no idea what an executive secretary was except that it must be good. Later, she learned a few more things about executive secretaries. They worked very hard. They had to buy many pairs of panty hose, and at night when they came home, they didn't feel like making paper dolls or crocheting funny hats or dancing to the *Guys and Dolls* CD. They put their feet up and poured a glass of wine.

For a while she asked when her father was coming home, but then she stopped. The picture that used to be on top of her mother's special treasure case in the living room had disappeared—the one with her mother in the long fairy dress, and flowers in her hair. Can we call him? Wendy asked.

I don't know where he is anymore, her mother said. His phone got disconnected.

Weekends were best because she didn't go to day care. If it was rainy or there was snow sometimes, they'd get under the covers and read all morning. They cut out a picture of Princess Diana from *People* magazine and used a Glue-Stick to attach it to a piece of cardboard from a cereal box, and dreamed up outfits for her that they colored and cut out. Prince Charles didn't deserve her anyway. She was better off without him. They watched old movies while her mother crocheted and went skating at Playland and rode the subway to the city and looked at toys at F. A. O. Schwarz.

The way the game worked, they each got to pick out their favorite Madame Alexander doll that they'd buy if they were rich. Wendy didn't need her mother to tell her they weren't really going to buy anything at that store. Sometimes Wendy would study the faces of the rich girls at F. A. O. Schwarz, who actually got to take the dolls home.

Do you notice how they hardly ever look particularly happy, even after

JOYCE MAYNARD　⇒€　24

they get their doll? her mother said. She had a saying: Treats make trouble. It was amazing how often that applied.

It's more special if you have one doll that you think about a long time before you get her, her mother said. You might wait a whole year, but when you finally brought the box home, you would love her more than you would if you were the kind of person who got a new doll every week.

It's like how I feel about you, her mother told her. You're my one special daughter, who I wanted for a long time.

So if I got a sister sometime, I wouldn't be so special anymore?

You'd still be just as special, her mother said. If I had ten kids, you'd always be the first baby I ever had. Plus, we're the hotbox girls. Nobody else but us knows the dance. She was talking about the times when they put on their *Guys and Dolls* sound track, Friday nights when it was just the two of them, and they did a special number they'd made up to "Take Back Your Mink." Wendy wasn't a good dancer like her mother. Young as she was, she could tell. But she loved their dancing nights.

Anyway, I doubt I'll have any more kids, she said, and she put her head in Wendy's lap. When Wendy asked why, she said it didn't seem like it was in the cards.


Her mother went on dates now and then. Once with a man from work named Tom. At first she didn't introduce him to Wendy, because she said she wanted to check him out first. She met him at the restaurant, instead of having him come to their house, and when he brought her back, Wendy was in bed. So the only one who got to see him was the baby-sitter.

Finally, her mother let her meet Tom. He was tall like her dad, but he didn't have a ponytail, and some of his hair wasn't even there anymore. Wendy couldn't imagine him making artworks or swing dancing. He wore a suit, which Wendy figured was the way the men dressed who you met when you were an executive secretary. When he came over the first time he asked Wendy what grade she was in and if she liked school. The answer was preschool and day care and yes.

For a while after that, Tom used to come over every Friday. Then he started being there on Saturday mornings.

The first Saturday it happened, Wendy went into her mother's room as usual, with the stack of books, and she almost dumped them on his head because she wasn't expecting to see him there. Her mother whispered that Tom had a sleepover, so they should read in the living room instead. When he got up, he had on the pants of the same suit that he'd been wearing when he showed up the night before, and the same shirt, but no shoes. His face was scratchy-looking, and when he came into the living room, her mother set their book down, even though they were in the middle. He also smoked in the house.

Sometime that fall, her mother and Tom went on a trip to Bermuda and Wendy stayed at her mother's friend Kate's house, but when her mother came back, she said she wouldn't be going on trips like that anymore. He wasn't really divorced, she said.

I don't believe men, she told Wendy.

What don't you believe? Wendy asked her.

Anything.

I think the best thing is if I just forget about falling in love, her mother told her. All I really need is you anyway. But sometimes at night in her room, when Kate was over, or when her mother was talking on the phone, Wendy would hear her saying different things. I feel like I'm dying on the vine, she said one time. My problem is that I keep believing the words to songs.

Which songs? Wendy wanted to know. Why was that a problem? What vine was her mother on? But it was the dying part that worried Wendy the most. What if her mother died on the vine? What would happen to her then?

She only saw her father once in all that time. He showed up one Saturday afternoon in early winter. They had just moved all the furniture to the end of the living room, the way they did sometimes when they made up their dances, and they had on Wendy's new favorite CD, the sound track to *West Side Story*. They were at the part where Anita was singing about how great it was in America when they heard the knock, and because the door wasn't locked, he had opened it just as they had their scarves out and they were twirling. Wendy was wearing her nightgown and her mother had on her peasant dress from a show she'd been in when she was young. They had put on lipstick.

You're just as beautiful as ever, Janet, he said. He still had his ponytail and he was wearing a long black coat, with a scarf around his neck, and holding a backpack, which he set on the floor.

For a second when he said that, Wendy thought maybe her mother would jump into his arms and her father might start singing "Tonight" and the three of them would live happily ever after, Wendy and her two original parents. Not dead like Tony and Maria. But that much in love.

You should have called first, Garrett, her mother said. The minute Wendy heard her tone of voice, she knew there would be no more dancing. The next thing her mother did was turn off the music.

I just got in from Maine at five this morning, he said.

There were other days, her mother said. I'm glad Wendy gets to see you anyway.

I wanted to see you, too, Janet, he said.

Here I am.

More than see, he said. Be with.

This isn't the place to talk about that, her mother said. You might want to focus a little attention on your daughter, though.

Look how big you are, he said to Wendy then. You used to be so little.

A year and a half is a long time for a child, her mother said. A long time for anyone.

Can we sit down? her father said. We could go out for Chinese food. A friend of mine is having a party later.

You've got to be kidding, her mother said. No, come to think of it, of course you're not. You haven't seen our daughter in a year and a half and you want to go out and see friends. Wendy wondered if this was the voice she used when she was being an executive secretary.

I was thinking it could take the pressure off a little, that's all, he said. I thought you might like me to take you out on the town. But I'm happy just to hang out here and talk.

We don't have anything to talk about, she said. The time for that has passed.

I was thinking, up in Maine, of all the great camping trips we used to take, he said. Remember that waterfall in Vermont?

At some point, a person has to grow up, she told him.

He looked at her, like he really wanted to know the answer to his question. Why?

You cut your hair, he said to her mother.

Some of us had to get a job, she said.

I was missing you, he said. I was actually thinking there might be some hope for us.

He sounded so sad, Wendy wanted to comfort him, but she knew her mother wouldn't like that. She could see the characters in *Parent Trap* rewinding to the beginning of the movie, where they hated each other, though in this case it seemed like it was only her mother who hated her father, not the other way around, and Wendy didn't understand how her mother could be so mean all of a sudden to someone who kept trying to be nice.

Here, he said. I brought you something. He reached into his pack and took out a fish wrapped in many layers of plastic. I got this in Sebago Lake, he said.

Her mother told Wendy to go to her room and change. Put on your jeans and a warm sweater, she said. You and your father can go out together in a minute.

Put on your fanciest dress, he called out to her, louder than he needed to. Your dad's taking you out on the town.

He took her into Manhattan on the subway. They went to a restaurant in Chinatown, where there were lots of people smoking. They had dim sum. A couple of his friends were there, and they asked her what grade she was in and if she liked school. Preschool. Yes.

After, they walked up Fifth Avenue all the way to F. A. O. Schwarz. When they got to the front entrance, he explained to her how his mother used to take him here when he was her age, and that it was the best toy store in the world. He pointed out the clock with the face on it, with the song that kept playing over and over, and the giant Steiff animals that people like Mick Jagger bought for their kids. He said that as if she would know who it was. She didn't, though later, when she learned the name, she could remember him saying that. They have the most beautiful dolls in the world here, he told her as they rode the escalator up to the second floor. She didn't let on that she knew.

She thought he was just going to play the same game with her, where you pick out the one you'd get if you were rich. But he told her she could have one for real. Any doll in the case, he said. You name it.

So many Saturdays she'd come here with her mother, she knew all her favorites: Meg, from the *Little Women* set, and the princess doll, and the ballerina in the *Swan Lake* costume. There were larger ones, too: Cissette, in her green velvet skating outfit with fur trim and real little skates that hung around her neck, and Movie Star Cissette, with sunglasses and a sparkled evening gown.

In the end she chose her mother's favorite: the gypsy doll with the ruffled skirt and the shawl and one gold hoop earring. It wasn't one of the dolls Wendy liked best, but she was thinking she'd give the doll to her mother. Maybe then her mother wouldn't be so mad at her father.

You could get a bigger one, he told her. It's okay if it's more expensive.

She thought about the old days, the calls in the night. Do you expect your daughter to wear boxes for shoes? We can't live on air.

She studied the face of the girl, a little older than her, who was also picking out a doll from the same case, also with her father, from the looks of it. Also no mother around.

Tell you what, the girl's father said after a long time, when she couldn't decide between Meg and Jo. Why don't we get the whole damn *Little Women* family? He looked like he had an appointment to get to.

A person might have thought the girl would have looked happy then, but she didn't. Her lips were bunched up tight, like the lips on a Madame Alexander doll, come to think of it.

You sure you don't want a bigger doll? her father said again.

No, she said. The gypsy doll is good.

You should have seen the stuff they had back when I was a kid, her father said. Train sets with tunnels and villages and real lights. Castles with knights, and drawbridges that went up and down. I had all that stuff.

Wow, she said, like an actress in a movie. That sounds nice. Even though he was her father, sometimes it was hard to think of what to say to him.

They rode the subway back to Brooklyn, with the big blue box in a bag on her lap. I bet you can't wait to show this to your friends, he said. She knew she never would. They might think she was spoiled.

When they got back to the apartment, her mother's friend Kate was there, instead of her mother. Janet told me to tell you she won't be back for a while and not to wait, Kate told Wendy's father. You got her dinner, right?

It was almost eight o'clock by that time, but he hadn't. Just the dim sum, and that had been hours ago, and anyway, she didn't eat it.

Never mind, Kate told him. I'll fix her a grilled cheese.

Wait, he said. What time is Janet coming back?

She told me to tell you she may be very late, Kate told him. She said to tell you not to be here when she gets back.

For a second, Wendy thought he might get in a fight with Kate about that, and maybe she even hoped he would. He could tell her, I'll just wait on the front steps, then. Or that he'd come back in the morning. Climb the fire escape. That's what Tony would have done to get Maria.

He got down low to the ground then, so low his scarf dragged on the floor, and put his arms around Wendy, but in a stiff, uncomfortable way, like a person in a dance class who's just learning the fox-trot with a partner he's never met.

I want you to write to me, he said. He didn't know she couldn't write yet, except for *Mom* and *cat* and *love*. If you send me a picture, I'll hang it on my wall, okay?

You can come visit me once I know where I'm going, he said. I'll teach you how to fish.

Then he was gone. Later she realized they didn't have his address.

In the morning when she got up her mother had found the doll before Wendy had a chance to show her.

We can put her in our special treasure case, Wendy said. In the living room, with her mother's blown-glass animals and her first prize tap-dancing trophy from when she was in junior high, in the Missouri State Dance Association Contest, and the shoes Gwen Verdon wore in *Sweet Charity*.

That's okay, her mother said. You can keep her in your room. Treats made trouble, just like she'd said.

# Three

They didn't know much, but they knew a plane had crashed into one of the World Trade Center towers. Her mother's building.

In her homeroom classroom, everyone was supposed to remain seated at their desks until someone came for them. Most of the kids had crowded in front of the windows, not that you could see much through the smoke. The air seemed to be filled with snow, though it was actually bits of paper. Some of them small as confetti, but then a whole sheet blew against the window, so you could actually read the words.

Mrs. Volt closed the blinds. Why don't we take this moment to write down all the things in life we're thankful for? she said. One girl who always made the dumbest remarks had asked, Will we get a grade?

It's just for yourself, Hallie, Mrs. Volt told her. Just to help us all remember at a difficult moment how fortunate we all are. After a minute or two, nobody seemed to be following up with their list, not even Mrs. Volt. She didn't offer any more suggestions after that. The top windows that were too high to reach, had been open, and the air was starting to feel smoky. Some people were coughing. In a few minutes the parents started showing up.

One girl in Wendy's homeroom said she had to get out of there. Mrs. Volt said she had to sit back down until someone came for her. I understand how you feel, Jennifer, she said. But we can't just start letting all you young people out on the street until we know someone's there to look out for you. It would be mass chaos.

My dad works across from the Twin Towers, the girl said. I think I'm going to throw up.

The boy making the tattoo, Sean, wanted to find Cindi. She's going to need me, he said. She's got asthma.

A couple of other people started dialing their cell phones, the ones who had them. When one boy finally got through, Wendy could hear him saying, Oh Jesus and Oh my God.

There's people jumping, he said. The fire trucks are melting.

From her desk, a girl named Sandra, who never talked, began to cry. Several people put their heads down on their desks. One girl started getting the dry heaves, but not the one who'd said she was going to throw up. She was already gone.

It's got to be an attack, said Buddy Campion when the word came that the plane hit the second tower. You know what the odds are of this being a simple coincidence? A billion to one.

We've got to get these windows closed, Mrs. Volt kept saying. I need the janitor.

Somebody's mother showed up straight from the gym, still in her spandex. My husband was supposed to be at a meeting over there this morning, but he didn't make it back from Cleveland last night, she said.

Where's a TV set? a girl asked when her cell phone wouldn't work. We have to turn on a TV. The whole city could explode.

There was more, but Wendy wasn't listening. Outside the window she heard the scream of sirens. Plumes of smoke billowed and rose over the East River. From the hall, she heard someone yell, The tower went down.

Parents rushed into the classroom. Kids running. Nobody bothered to gather books into their backpacks. Somebody's Game Boy just sitting there on a desk.

Some of the mothers burst into tears when they reached their children. Mrs. Volt was saying, Everyone keep calm. On the PA, the principal said, I know how hard this is but please stay in your classroom until a family member comes. If you know any prayers, he said, feel free to say them.

The other tower just went down, someone called out from the hall. They're attacking the Pentagon, a boy said. Oh my God, Oh my God, said one girl. This is the worst thing that ever happened to me.

By eleven-thirty all but eight or nine kids had gone home. Of the kids who were left, most stood in a clump at the windows. Wendy stayed at her desk. She wanted to catch sight of her mother's face the first second she got there. She kept her eyes on the door. She took deep breaths, the way her mother taught her back when she was doing her natural-childbirth preparation before Louie was born. If you ever get in a tight spot, Wendy, you should try this breathing. It's not just for having babies.

In through her nose. Out through her mouth. Choose a focus point. The door.

When the familiar face appeared, it wasn't her mother's. It was Josh. Josh with Louie in his arms. Louie in his Aladdin costume, with his thumb in his mouth. Josh still in his green morning sweatpants, unshaven.

Where's Mom. The first words she'd spoken since the news.

It's probably hard for her to get to a phone right now, he said. We need to get back home for when she calls.

They had closed the subways. People were all on their cell phones, but it didn't seem like anyone was getting through. A few steps ahead of her, Josh moved through the crowd like a person who was hypnotized. Louie looked out over his shoulder, staring.

They passed a store with a TV set in the window and a crowd gathered to watch. First there was the head of a newswoman, but the sound wasn't on, so you couldn't make out what she was saying. Then came a picture of the plane flying low toward the tower, and for a second it looked on the screen as if the plane was just flying behind the tower, only it never came out the other side. All you saw was a bloom of flames from the building, and then so much smoke you couldn't even see the tower anymore. The next picture they showed was the other tower, crumbling away from the inside out, like the paper wrapper of those special Italian cookies her mother sometimes brought home in the orange tin, that you could light on fire after you ate them. A poof of flame and then nothing but a little pile of ashes.

As horrible as the pictures were, Wendy wanted to stay on the street, watching the television. They were showing people running away from the towers, covered with ashes and dust, and she wanted to catch sight of her mother. She would be wearing her new red dress they'd just bought at Macy's on their back-to-school shopping trip.

Josh didn't want to watch. We've got to get home, he said. Normally, he had a very calm and steady kind of voice, but he sounded like another person now. We have to be by the phone.

That's Mama's building, Louie said when the TV in the store window started showing the low-flying plane again and the crash. The other tower this time.

Mama's probably out looking for a pay phone right now, Josh said. She never has any change on her.

I'm glad Mama's not at work, Louie said. If she was in that building, she could get burned.

Mama's not in that building, Josh said. Mama got out. She's probably calling us right now.


Usually the stereo was always on at their apartment. Josh playing jazz. Now it was the TV set.

Why do the buildings keep falling down? Louie said. Why doesn't someone stop it?

It's not different buildings, Louie, Wendy told him. They just keep showing the same two. She didn't feel like talking to him, but Josh wasn't answering questions. He was sitting on the couch, raking his hair with his fingers. Wendy sat in the rocker.

You said you couldn't play with me today, Louie said. But you can.

I'll play later, she said. After Mama comes home.

We could make her cookies, Louie said.

Later, she told him. Poppy's not in the mood.

\*        \*        \*

When the phone rang, it was as if someone sent an electric shock through Josh, but only for a second, until he heard the voice. Then Wendy could see his shoulders slump again and he'd tell the person, No, not yet. We have to keep the line open. Sometimes he didn't even say good-bye.

They kept showing the same pictures. The low plane. The crash. The building peeling down to nothing from the inside out. The people running. Firemen. The melted trucks. She wanted them to freeze the picture so she could try to figure out what floor the plane had hit, but maybe that wasn't such a good idea.

The mayor came on but she wasn't interested in that part. They were telling about another plane that crashed, someplace else. It's good you didn't go to California, Louie told her. You could've crashed. It's good Mama wasn't on a plane.

I just remembered she said she might go vote before work, Josh said. For the first time since he'd showed up at her school, his face didn't look so crumpled. She wanted to go with me, but I told her the lines wouldn't be so long if she went early.

Wendy had never heard of her mother going anyplace early, but she didn't say anything.

Look at that, Josh said. You can see lines of people by the pay phones. She's probably having a hard time getting through. She never remembers you can call collect on a local call.

It was sickening, a woman was saying on the screen. There were all these people hanging out the windows, and then they started jumping. I saw two people holding hands.

That's when Josh turned the television off.


Amelia called. I can't talk, Wendy told her. We have to keep the line open.

A friend of Josh's showed up, carrying his trumpet case. I was on my way to give a lesson, he said. I saw it. I wish I hadn't looked up.

Wendy had never seen Josh like this. He couldn't say anything.

You must be going crazy, man, the trumpet person said.

She's just having a hard time getting to a phone, Josh told him.

I bet that's it.

She was wearing these high-heeled sandals, Josh said. They make her feet hurt but she loves how they go with her new dress.

That's what it is all right, said the trumpet guy. The phones are just bad. He left quickly.


Kate came over.

Oh, honey, she said. I know your mom's going to be all right. She's a dancer. She'd be great at getting down stairs.

Remind me what floor she works on, she said.

Eighty-seven. Finally, something Wendy knew. She felt the smallest comfort, having a fact to tell.

Eighty-seven. That's good, Kate said. That's so much better than a hundred and four. If it was me, I'd be tired, but eighty-seven is nothing for your mom.

She almost certainly wasn't in there anyway, Wendy said. She slept late. She probably hadn't even got to the building by then.

Or she was voting, Josh said.


Josh went out. Everyone was saying you couldn't get over the bridge into Manhattan, but he was going to try and check the hospitals.

Wendy fixed Louie a Cup O' Noodles, which her mom kept on hand for nights when Josh was out playing a gig and he hadn't gotten around to making them a casserole. Josh called them Cup O' Nothing, but Louie and their mom thought they were good. He was still hungry after that, so she dumped a pile of raisins on his plate.

Raisins, raisins, raisins, he said. Why does everyone around here keep giving me raisins? I want chocolate chips.

If she could, she would have gone into her room and put a blanket over her head. If there was a place she could have gone, to disappear, or fall asleep for a long time, that's what she would have done, but Louie kept wanting things. TV. A game, but even Candyland felt too hard.

It's nap time, she said, even though it wasn't really. She read him *Sylvester and the Magic Pebble* and his truck book, but not with her usual expression. Automatic pilot was how Josh would have described it, the way some musicians play when they've lost their love of the music. She read him *Curious George,* his current favorite, but he wasn't concentrating.

Where is George's mother anyway, he said? Why doesn't he have a mother? Why doesn't the man in the yellow hat have a wife? Is George's mom a monkey or a person? When is his mother coming back?

Finally he fell asleep, but it was a different kind of sleep from his usual. Wendy lay on the bed next to him for a long time, listening to him breathe. He didn't wake up or call out, but he kept making little whimpering sounds. Whatever pictures he had in his head, they weren't good ones. His thumb never left his mouth.

Josh called. No word, she told him. There was a horrible weight just to the sound of his breathing on the other end of the phone, as if even opening his mouth took too much effort.

Where are you? Wendy said. Why don't you come home?

I'm at St. Vincent's, he told her. There are all these stretchers lined up, but nobody's on them. The doctors are standing around. He started to cry. The only times she'd heard him cry before were when he and her mom got married and when her brother was born, but both of those times had been happy crying.

The only people they're bringing in are rescue workers, he said. I keep thinking there's another place I haven't found yet, where the rest of the people are.

There's other hospitals, she said. Though the sick, throwing-up feeling that had been in her stomach since morning was getting worse.

We should have had a meeting spot, he said, Like it was Louie they'd lost track of—a four-year-old, instead of her mother.

Come home, Dad, she said.


She had the television on for a while, but it was the same news over and over, the same terrible footage of the crashes, the first building caving in, then the second. Often, the phone would ring, but the only voice she cared about hearing was never the one on the other end. We have to keep the line open, she said. Her voice had turned flat.

On the television they were interviewing a fireman with blood all over his face. You don't want to know what it was like, he said. I wish it was me that was in that building, instead of outside watching.

From the doorway, she heard a crying sound—her brother. She could see a wet spot on his pants. He hardly ever had an accident anymore. He was staring at the screen, where the fireman was covering his face in his hands now.

Does God know about this? Louie asked.


Sometime in the night, with Josh still not back, Wendy went into her parents' room, not looking for anything in particular. Just to touch her mother's things.

Her mother had made the bed that morning. She had worn the new red dress. The price tags were on the bed, along with a pair of panty hose she must have put on before realizing they had a run.

There was an issue of *Time Out* magazine with an ad circled for a performance of the Netherlands Dance Theater. There was her "To Do" list that she always kept on her night table. *Louie, karate suit? Special dinner Thursday— order ice-cream cake.* A couple of phone numbers of baby-sitters she wanted to try for the weekend, part of her new plan to leave Wendy free to live her own teenage life. A few scribbled notes: *Vacuum cleaner bags! Coffee! Cover the gray!*

Her bathrobe was hanging on the hook on the bathroom door. On the counter, the red nail polish was out. She had worn the sandals.

Wendy picked up a book, open on her nightstand. *Understanding Your Teenager.* And a thinner volume: Pablo Neruda, *Veinte Poemas de Amor,* in Spanish and English.

She walked through the familiar room as if it were a museum. She didn't have to study the photographs, she knew them all—the one of her mother and Josh on their wedding day; Josh holding Louie right after he was born, his hair even crazier than usual, with the biggest grin. One of her and Louie at the beach the summer before, and another of Wendy by herself, paddling a canoe in Maine.

Wendy had never liked this picture. She wasn't smiling, and her expression was firm, almost to the point of looking mad. The wind had been very stiff on the lake that day, and the canoe had been hard to handle. Josh had wanted to help her, but Wendy said no, she wanted to steer herself. It took forever to get that boat in to shore, but she had done it.

I wish you wouldn't choose that picture to have up, Wendy had told her mother.

I don't need a picture to tell me how pretty you are, her mother said. What I like about this one is how strong you look, how determined you were that day. I look at this and I know you're going to be a survivor.

It was past two when Wendy finally went to bed. With everything that had happened, she still brushed her teeth. She put on her rabbit pajamas from the night before. Nothing else was the same, but her clothes were. She got under the covers.

All day she hadn't cried, and even now, alone in the dark, waiting for the tears, none came. It was as if someone had injected Novocain in the place where crying happened, and all she felt was this horrible gray numbness. She stared at the ceiling, the glow-in-the-dark stars her mother had put there so long ago that they hardly glowed anymore. The poster of Madonna, in her cowboy hat. Her science fair ribbon, First Place. Topic: Why Do Your Ears Pop?

Outside the window, there was an unsettling stillness—no sirens, no planes overhead, just the sound of the late-night delivery trucks. Wendy had been listening for the sound of Josh's key in the door but he hadn't come home yet. Twice she heard Louie cry out, but he'd gone back to sleep both times.

She thought about the night she and her mother had been home in the apartment, watching a rerun of *Grease* on TV. Louie was just a baby then, but he was asleep, so it was just the two of them sitting on the couch, and the words came on the screen, *We interrupt this program . . .*

It was the news that Princess Diana had been in a car accident. At first all they said was "badly injured." Then the news that she was dead.

Her mother had started to cry. I know it's crazy, she said. I never even got to see her in real life. There was just something that made me like her so much. Maybe because she was a single mom, too.

Wendy got up from her bed and walked over to her backpack. She took out her Walkman, still with the same CD in it that she'd been playing that morning, a million years ago. She slipped on the headphones and skipped to number seven, her favorite, the lullaby Sade wrote for her daughter. She climbed back into bed and wrapped the blanket over herself, though she was still shivering.

She had played this one for her mother once, and after that her mother had made her push the Repeat button so they listened to it ten times in a row, at least. She tried to sing along with Sade. "I will always remember this moment," she sang. Off-key, of course. But crying.

For Wendy now, it was like that time in Maine when they had turned on the water at the cabin they rented that summer, and all they got was a choking sound, and air. She wanted to cry, but nothing came out. She thought about Prince William and Prince Harry, waking up in a palace somewhere that long-ago summer morning, having someone (the queen maybe? Prince Charles, who had already broken their mother's heart?) tell them their mother's car had crashed in a tunnel in Paris, and now they would never see her again. She thought of Louie, sitting on her lap, studying the picture in his Babar book, of Babar's mother, lying on the ground, shot by hunters. *But it's just pretend, right, Sissy?* he said. Maria, bent over the motionless body of Tony, in *West Side Story. No no no.* Sade again, asking the moon to protect her daughter as she slept. No moon now.

In English class, they'd had a vocabulary word recently that was new to her, as few of them were—the verb *keen.*

It's a sound a person makes when they're grieving deeply, her teacher said. It might not be loud and dramatic, but it's like the saddest sound you could imagine, the sound a mother might make over the body of a dead child.

Or the other way around, it occurred to her now, as in the darkened room,

in the dim glow of the blue plastic stars, she heard a sound she barely recognized, and because of the strange numb feeling, it took a moment to realize
the sound came from her. She couldn't cry, but she was keening—the same
one word, over and over, though it had been years since she'd actually called
her mother that. *Mama.*

She didn't think she'd fall asleep, but she must have, because then she woke
up and it was morning. For about three seconds, she forgot what had happened, and it was like regular life, but with this creeping memory that something wasn't right.

Josh was in the kitchen. He was wearing the same clothes from yesterday.
He had their photograph albums out and he was turning the pages very
slowly.

We need a picture, he said. We have to make flyers. At the hospitals last
night people were putting them up. I should have thought of that before.

He was staring at a photograph of her mother in Nantucket last summer.
She had on jeans and a T-shirt and her head was thrown back as if she was
laughing. Telling him to quit taking so many pictures probably.

I think it might be better to use one of her in her work-type clothes, Wendy
said. One that's more like how she'd have been dressed when she went to her
job yesterday.

Right, he said, but he was still holding the one from Nantucket. Maybe we
could put two different pictures on the flyer.

Good idea. She put a hand on his arm.

Wendy looked at him sitting there—such a familiar face, but she had never
seen him like this before. This morning, he reminded her of a kid. Like Louie,
in fact. That same lost look her brother had when she read to him the day
before.

It was unnerving seeing him this way. Josh, the one who came running to
her field hockey game when she turned her ankle, carrying a cooler with an
ice pack inside. The one who walked her to the bus in the worst weather,

long after the point where everyone else went by themselves. I just want to see you get on safely, he said. Humor me.

This morning he looked at her and said, What are we supposed to do now?

Her mother was nine years older than Josh. When she met him, she was thirty-four. He was twenty-five. Your friends will think I'm a cradle robber, she said.

My friends will wish you'd robbed their cradle instead, he said.

When I'm forty-five, you'll only be thirty-six, she said. When I'm fifty, you'll be forty-one. I'll be this old wrinkled prune and you'll be this cool jazz guy with young chicks falling all over you.

Please, Janet, he said. It hurts me when you say things like that.

I just don't know what I'd do if you ever stopped loving me this way, she said.

The only thing I don't like about the nine years between our ages, he said, is those were nine years I didn't get to know you.

Sitting at the kitchen table now—same place he had filled out her school forms the day before, and paid the bills, and did the taxes every spring because her mother could never do anything involving numbers—Josh stared at the blank paper. He had started five different versions and ripped them all up.

"Have you seen my wife?" he wrote, finally.

I think maybe we should just write "Missing," she told him.

"Last seen on her way to work at the law offices of Mercer and Mercer, Tower 1, World Trade Center, eighty-seventh floor. Brown hair, hazel eyes. Wearing red high-heeled sandals and a red silk wraparound dress with purple flowers. Any information at all."

The new dress would have blown open a little at the bottom when she walked over subway vents on the sidewalk. Or when a gust of wind came. Wendy could see her mother standing in front of the mirror at Macy's last weekend, trying it on.

It's too expensive, she said.

Get it, Wendy told her.

You don't think it's too daring for work?

You look beautiful.

It would go perfectly with my red sandals. We could share. This dress would look great on you, too.

Wendy knew it wouldn't. Her mother had a waist. Wendy could see her there, twirling in front of the three-way mirror, like the ballerina figure inside her jewelry box, that started dancing when you opened it.

Okay, then, her mother said. You only live once.


A few of Josh's musician friends and Josh's sister, Andy, said they'd help put up flyers. It didn't seem as important anymore to stay by the phone. Kate was going over to the armory to fill out missing-persons forms and then to the Chelsea Piers. She'd heard there were some people they'd found wandering around who couldn't remember their names. A day ago, it would have sounded scary to Wendy to think of her mother like that, but now it would be good news. So what if she didn't know who she was anymore. They could remind her.

Josh had gotten all the way over to Kinko's before he found out he didn't have his wallet, but they let him make copies of his flyer anyway. Everyone who saw them now had this sickening look of sympathy on their faces. Either that or you had to look at them with the same sickening look, because they were printing up flyers, too.


The mother of Louie's best friend, Corey, came over to pick him up. Oh, honey, she said, putting her arms around Wendy. Life isn't supposed to be this hard.

Don't worry about Louie, Corey's mother told them, hoisting his overnight bag onto her shoulder. Leave him with us as long as you need. You know how often Janet helped me out.

Helps, she said.

In the kitchen, Louie and Corey were doing karate kicks with each other. It was one of their usual games, but Wendy had never seen Louie act like this, yelping and lurching and punching Corey in the stomach as if he was drunk.

My mom's in the World Trade Center, but it isn't there anymore, he yelled.

Stop it, Louie, said Wendy.

My mom got captured by space aliens.

You know that's not true, Louie.

She ran away, he said. She fell out the window and nobody caught her. He was spinning in circles now. He was holding onto Pablo by the ribbon and flinging him. He was gasping for breath, and there was drool coming out his mouth. Another second and he was going to fall down.

Everybody's just pretending. My mom isn't ever coming home, he said.

Come on, Louie, Corey's mom said, picking him up off the floor. Let's go get ice cream.

I just got one question, he yelled back over his shoulder as they were going down the stairs. What's a body bag?

Wendy had never seen Josh like this. They were halfway down the stairs before he realized he didn't have the flyers. She had to remind him to stop at Walgreens for tape, and when he got there, the first thing he'd picked up was Scotch tape, when what they needed was duct tape, so if it rained, the flyers wouldn't come right down. But the weather was perfect. There was that anyway.

At least she isn't cold, he said. At least she isn't wet.

One of the jazz guys, Roberto, was covering the Upper West Side. The trumpet person took midtown in the Fifties, and two other guys—sax and drums—headed east. Josh was handling SoHo as far as they'd let you go, and the Village. He wanted to be close to where she was, close as they'd let him go. Wendy was covering Chelsea down to Union Square.

It wasn't hard to know where to put her signs, because already there were so many others. She didn't mean to, but she couldn't help stopping to read them.

Amalia Garcia, shown holding a baby in a pink ruffled dress. "Age thirty-one. Five feet four, 140 pounds. Has a butterfly tattoo on her left shoulder. Any information at all, please call."

Timothy Garvin, Fire Company 237, age twenty-four. The kind of person Amelia would have called a hunk, shown wrestling with his dog on the floor of an apartment somewhere. "Last seen heading into Tower 1. . . ."

Jessica Robards. Twenty-seven. Pictured in her wedding dress. "Has a mole on her right thigh and is wearing a cross with a ruby in the middle. Jess, we miss you!"

The part she hated about putting up the flyers was having people look at you with so much pity. She knew what they were doing, because she herself had looked at people that way in the past—usually homeless people on the street, holding up signs that said I HAVEN'T EATEN FOR TWO DAYS, or HAVE AIDS AND TRYING TO GET HOME.

She would prefer if people didn't know it was her mother on the flyers. But mostly she could tell from the looks they gave her that people understood.

She's so pretty, one woman said. I bet you're feeling mighty worried, a guy said to her. Another man gave her a mimeographed pamphlet of Bible verses. A woman who was taping up flyers of her daughter put her arms around Wendy and said, Maybe they're together.

By two o'clock, Wendy's stack of a hundred flyers was nearly gone. She had saved a handful to put up at Union Square.

When she got there, she saw a few hundred people had gathered—putting up flyers or just looking. Someone had rolled out a bunch of white paper and taped it down on the sidewalk, and now people were kneeling on it, writing poems and messages. There were half a dozen satellite trucks from television stations and a reporter Wendy recognized, standing in front of a camera, talking. Along the fence at the south end of the park, people had been leaving bunches of flowers and notes. There were lighted candles and kids on benches playing music and Hare Krishna people in orange robes chanting. The fence was covered with flyers. By now, Wendy had seen enough of them that some of the faces actually looked familiar.

Have you seen this person?

Yes. On a flyer.

She pulled her roll of duct tape out of her backpack again. Also the scissors.

She cut half a dozen pieces and stuck them on her pants leg the way she'd seen Buddy Campion doing at school last week, putting up campaign posters. She stuck one at the far end of the fence, right next to Amalia Garcia.

By now, it was actually hard finding a spot to stick up her flyers, but she was careful not to cover up even a corner of anybody else's. That would be bad luck.

It was almost four o'clock when she taped her last flyer up at the Twenty-third Street subway station in front of the Flatiron Building. When she was done, she stood there for a moment, reading over the words again: "Red silk dress. Five feet four and a half, 113 pounds. Wearing red open-toed sandals."

She looked at the face of her mother in her suit—a picture Josh had taken of the two of them on Take Your Daughter to Work Day three years ago— and the other, from Nantucket.

She thought about stories she'd read in magazines—about people getting murdered, or getting buried in an avalanche, or turning into a vegetable on account of riding in a car with defective tires or having a leg ripped off by a shark. She hated it about herself, but the truth was that a part of her liked reading those stories. She turned to them first when she leafed through the magazines at Just Cuts or the dentist. She used to study the faces of the people that awful things happened to, to see if there was any clue, when the picture was taken, that something awful would happen to them in the future.

Now the face in the picture was her own slim, beautiful, laughing mother. She knew the face better than anybody's except her own. Only now, for the first time, it struck her that her mother looked different. Not quite like her mother anymore, but almost like someone who used to be her mother. She was always saying what a lucky woman she was, but all of a sudden she didn't look lucky anymore.

Thursday morning neither of them—not Wendy, not Josh—mentioned this was preschool orientation day, the day that Louie had been planning for all summer, trying to decide which of his costumes to wear—the wizard suit or the cowboy or Aladdin. Wendy knew school had been canceled on Wednesday, but Amelia had called to find out if there was any news and let her know school was on again today.

I don't feel like going to school, Wendy said. She looked over at Josh to see if he'd say anything, but he didn't. He was staring at photograph albums again.

Josh's sister, Andy, came over. You can't just sit here forever, she said. Let me take you someplace.

Where?

We could go for a walk. We could go up to the Cloisters and look out at the Hudson River for a while. You could help me wash my car.

He looked at her as if she were a person from another planet. Why would I wash a car today? he asked.

I don't know, she said. I guess you wouldn't.

Andy had heard how they met, of course, but she let Josh tell her again.

It was a gig I almost didn't take, he said. Give me a break—all the way out past Rahway for some dumb wedding where you know you're going to have to play "Up Where We Belong" and they won't even have decent food.

I did it as a favor for Roberto, period. The bass player he'd lined up canceled at the last minute. Not that this was a crowd that was likely to ask for their money back if there was no bass line.

You didn't even bother to press your suit, Andy said. Your other one was at the cleaner's. You had to wear the one with the too-short pants, and the only clean socks you had were white.

White socks, he said. Wendy could see him wanting to take the story slow.

Remind me again what month it was, his sister asked.

April twenty-fifth, he said. It was raining like you wouldn't believe. And we were scheduled to play outside. They'd put a tent up, but I was worried about my bass. I told Roberto I'd never forgive him if my bridge got warped on account of one lousy Rahway wedding gig.

You loved that bass more than anything.

He looked at her for a second. That was true back then, he said.

Remind me, said Andy. Did you meet Janet right at the beginning of the dancing, or near the end?

He wasn't ready for that part yet. First, there was the part about how the bride's father had met them at the entrance to the country club, or wherever it was, and said, Listen, I feel bad about this, but we've come up a little short on the cash here and I'm going to have to cut you guys' pay a little. So maybe you could just play an hour and a half instead of three? Or one of you fellows can sit this one out?

Something about that—this is Roberto for you—made us decide we were going to blow them out of the water that day. Instead of the bargain-basement package they were suggesting, we were going to deliver the best wedding jam ever, God knows why. That crazy rain maybe.

It wasn't really a jazz crowd, he said. We knew that already when the groom told us they wanted "Wind Beneath My Wings" for their first dance. So we played it, and for the first few bars you could even tell that's what song it was, too. Then Omar busts out with this amazing trumpet solo and Frankie comes in on drums and I'm pumping it so hard I think my thumbs might fall off. We follow that with "My One and Only Love," and we don't even stop, just ease right on down into "They Say It's Wonderful." All mellow for a moment, because the bride's dancing with her father now and it's a sweet moment.

Then the groom's got his mom out on the floor, and even though she's what you might call an ample woman, she's a pistol on the dance floor. So we bring it up-tempo and the four of them are rocking it out, which is when everyone else heads out on the floor. This one little brunette in a yellow dress being first out of the gate, of course.

My mom, said Wendy. She hadn't meant to come into the kitchen for this, but she was wanting to hear the story, too. Never mind she knew it better than Pokey Little Puppy or any of those.

After that I didn't even notice if anyone else was dancing, he said. Who could? She had this way of moving on the floor. I must have played a few hundred weddings but I never saw anyone dance like her.

You knew the cat she was with was nobody. He didn't even exist on the same planet. This woman needed a real partner. Small as she was, you knew she had energy enough to keep going all night.

You could have kept up with her, said Andy. Only you were playing.

\*       \*       \*

It didn't even matter that I wasn't out there with her. We looked at each other and that was it. The whole rest of the night, I knew she was dancing for me. Same as I was playing for nobody but her.

It got to the point in the wedding where the bride throws the bouquet, and they ask all the single women to line up in a row. You might think she'd have hung back along the sidelines, not taking it seriously, especially considering there were all these younger types, college girls, junior bankers or something, the kind that probably get a subscription to *Brides* magazine before they even meet the guy.

Not her. She positions herself right in the middle, and you can tell from the look on her face as the bride turns her back to the group and takes aim that she's actually concentrating on catching it. She bends, with her arms held out a little. Slim arms, but I could tell how strong she was.

She always says she'll die before she ends up with those flaps of skin hanging down like her grandmother, said Wendy, then regretted it. The word *die* hung heavy, and they all knew it.

I can just picture it, said Andy.

So the bride tosses the bouquet, said Josh. And it looks like it's heading straight toward one of the junior banker girls. Some blonde in a strapless dress that a lot of the guys there were probably thinking was hot.

Only just when Junior Banker's reaching out to catch it, there's Yellow Dress, stepping out in front of her. Not pushing her out of the way exactly, but close. The bouquet's hers. You can see Miss Junior Banker looking a little put out for about two seconds. Then everyone laughs, and we're supposed to break in with a real up-tempo number so the dancing can start again, but all I can think about is the woman in the yellow dress holding that damn bouquet over her head with this smile on her like she just won the lottery. She wants to dance, but her date's had enough, evidently. He's hanging out with a bunch of guys, talking about basketball, I'm going to guess. That or the stock market. Not that this stops Yellow Dress. She heads out on the dance floor all by herself and starts in with this dance.

They waited for him to say more, but his voice broke. The three of them sat there, nobody saying a word.

*   *   *

The way she danced, he said.

And you had to keep on playing, said Andy. Even though all you really wanted to do was go over and introduce yourself.

But I wasn't worried, he said. Earlier I was. When I first caught sight of her, I'd been cooking up all these different ways I could get to meet her and counting the minutes to the break. But after the bouquet, I knew it would happen. Not that I was ever some kind of lady-killer type. I just knew she was the one, and I knew she understood that, too.

After the last song, he'd packed up his bass, not even with any particular speed, though he could remember the way his heart was pounding. Sure enough, she was waiting at one of the little decorated tables near the podium.

You probably thought someone was giving me a ride home, she said. He had to leave early for some kind of play-off game. He gave me his car to take home.

Not a compact, I hope, Josh said. Some cars wouldn't be big enough to hold a bass, but the ex-boyfriend's was.

They drove back to his apartment and he invited her up. He cooked her dinner, this great stir-fry with a bunch of cumin and coriander, and set a plate of goat cheese and a sliced pear in front of her.

So what song do you want the guys to play for the first dance at our wedding? he asked.


Wendy spent most of Friday watching television again. They were saying the rescue workers were hoping to find air pockets in the rubble where people were alive, but nobody was sounding as hopeful as they did at first.

She couldn't turn it off, even though it made her feel sick, looking at the images of the wrecked buildings, the acres of dust and debris. She didn't want to picture her mother huddled in her sandals and red dress in some dusty air pocket. Better to think of her wandering around New Jersey, barefoot, with her hair flying.

After the Turkish earthquake of 1999, people were known to survive on rainwater in the rubble of wrecked buildings for as long as a week, one of the television reporters said. There had been no rain here. For the third day in a row, they were having perfect, golden weather.

The other news, about the men who had flown the planes, Wendy barely listened to. She knew a lot of people were going crazy about that part, but to her it didn't matter who'd done it. Her mother hadn't come home was all.

Corey's mother called. I just wanted to let you know I took the boys to orientation day and everything went as well as could be expected, she said. Louie's still kind of hyper, but that's understandable. When I picked them up, he wanted to show me his cubby and the play kitchen area. They're having a nap now. He's out cold.

She asked if Josh might like to speak to her. He's not here, Wendy said.

He was doing the rounds of the hospitals again. A lot of families who were missing someone were going over to the armory on East Seventy-third Street to give the workers there hair samples and dental records, but when his sister suggested that, he looked as if he might murder her, and she didn't bring it up again. Some man who'd seen one of the flyers had called to say he'd met a woman at Bellevue who looked just like her mother, but Wendy didn't believe it. He said a bunch of other things—how just as the woman in Bellevue was about to get crushed by some shaft of steel, a bunch of angels had come down and shielded her and now she'd told him she owed her life to the Lord.

Amelia came over after school. It was the first time they'd seen each other since it happened. When she came in the door, she flung her arms around Wendy and burst into tears.

It's the most insane thing that ever happened, she said. If it was my mom, I'd be having a nervous breakdown.

With Amelia, Wendy didn't need to worry about thinking of what to say next, because Amelia kept talking.

How's your dad doing? Horrible, right?

He never goes to bed, Wendy said. He's either doing the rounds of the same hospitals he just finished going to or sitting in the kitchen staring at pictures. My little brother went to stay at his friend's house.

Well that's good anyway.

Wendy wished they could talk about something else, even though she knew it was impossible. How was school? she asked.

Weird, said Amelia. We had this assembly with a priest and a rabbi and some Buddhist-type person and we sang "Amazing Grace" and "God Bless America." Buddy Campion had on a T-shirt with a picture of Osama bin Laden that said WANTED DEAD OR ALIVE, and Hallie Owens had to point out how the Constitution says everyone is innocent until proven guilty and we'd be no better than the terrorists if we all started shooting people before we know the whole story.

Wendy didn't care about this part. She wanted to hear something ordinary, like what was for lunch, or if Mr. Hutchinson had worn those pants of his with the belt halfway up his chest again.

I put up a bunch of flyers about my mom, Wendy said. So far, we've gotten three calls, but nothing real.

There's two other kids that had someone in the towers, Amelia said. One girl had a friend of her mom's that worked on the hundred and second floor. This other kid's older sister's boyfriend was a fireman. But we all agreed your case was the worst.

Josh keeps saying she's probably got amnesia, said Wendy. He says he can feel it, that she's out there someplace.

And how about you? asked Amelia.

I can't feel anything, Wendy said.


All this time, Wendy still hadn't cried. She thought it might be a relief, but she couldn't do it. The dull Novocain sensation that had begun taking hold that Tuesday had overtaken her now. The whole world, everything around her, had turned flat and colorless.

A couple of times she had even gone in her room and closed the door. Told herself, Okay, now let it go. You'll feel better if you cry. Nothing.

Now, though, Amelia was here.

Your mom, she said. Just that. The two of them dropped to the floor, and Wendy let her head fall into Amelia's lap.

Wendy thought her tears might go on forever then. She cried so hard, she couldn't see. She could hardly breathe, and her body, with her friend's arms encircling her, was shaking. She heard sounds come out from a place deeper than she knew was inside. A wail like the sound a ship might make, stranded in the fog, or some instrument that hadn't been invented yet, not brass or woodwind or string, and no note that had ever been played. She remembered the cries her mother had made when her brother was being born, but she'd known that they would only last awhile and when it was over there would be a baby. Now was different: Fleeting pain had not produced this sound. This was sorrow without end.

Even Amelia, as talkative a person as she was, must have known there was nothing to say. The two of them lay on the floor, holding each other, until very gradually the crying slowed to where it was only long, sad sighs. Then, finally, quiet. Even after that, they just lay there awhile.

Maybe we should have some Häagen-Dazs, Amelia suggested. It seemed as good an idea as anything else.


A week before, when the letter came from California, Wendy had called Amelia. My dad wants me to come see him, she said. She had to whisper.

Oh my God, said Amelia. Now you're going to leave and I'll be all alone with Seth at lunch, waiting for his voice to change and watching the pimples spread across his whole entire face.

Probably not, Wendy told her. My mom won't let me go. She says I can't miss school.

Like sitting in some old geometry class listening to Mr. Hutchinson talk about the square root of the isosceles triangle is more important than going surfing in California and being with your blood father, who's only the coolest person in the universe, said Amelia. The truth was, her father had never mentioned surfing, and Wendy knew his real sport, if you could call it that, was fishing.

My mom said this is a really important semester for me to get good grades if I want to apply to Music and Art, Wendy told her, but that's not the real reason. She's just afraid I might start loving him more than her. Which I probably would.

Your mom's not so bad, said Amelia. She's way better than my mom.

You don't know, said Wendy. All she really cares about is Josh and my little brother. I'm just this big old ugly reminder of her old life that was so terrible.

Even as she said this, Wendy didn't exactly believe it.

After the letter came, my mom started in the way she always does, saying all this awful stuff about Dad, like how he just wanted to make himself look good by inviting me out there. She started talking about how she had to sell her stereo to pay for food one time when they were married. Like all that matters is money. I can see why he left. He isn't the kind who cares about material things the way she does.

Your dad is so awesome, said Amelia. She hadn't ever met him, but she'd seen the pictures. I can't imagine my dad doing anything artistic.

He builds houses now, too, Wendy told her. But art's his real passion. Unlike my mom, who gave up her passion to be a dumb secretary, for money.

I hope I never sell out like that, said Amelia. If I ever start, stop me, okay? You, too.


They sat now in the living room, the only light the blue glow of the TV set. They were eating ice cream, which was mostly what Wendy lived on these days, since Josh had stopped cooking or shopping. The thought had actually occurred to her, after Tuesday, that now she was likely to get really skinny. But in fact, she could tell from how her pants fit that she'd probably put on a pound or two.

I guess you wish now you hadn't said all that stuff about your mom, Amelia said.

Wendy couldn't speak.

I'll never tell anyone, Amelia said. Just because you were mad at her didn't mean you wanted a building to fall on top of her. Sometimes people say things. You should hear what I say about my mom.

Wendy had, of course.

Whatever happens, you can't just stop breathing. Your mom wouldn't want that.

Wendy got up and refilled their ice-cream bowls. She changed the channel on the TV, but every station was the same.

I like her hair, said Amelia. They were tuned to NBC now. Maybe we should do ours like that.

I like it too, said Wendy. She put her head on Amelia's shoulder. You know what's so funny, she said. I really miss my little brother.

She dreamed her mother was in an air pocket—air, but no light. In the dream, she was calling out for them to get her, but there was so much rubble and dirt on top of her that no one could hear. Her mother had a package of animal crackers in her purse that she kept for emergencies, like when she was coming home on the bus from day care with Louie and he was cranky.

In the dream, her mother let herself have one bite of a cracker every day. Water was more of a problem, but Saturday it had rained and she collected the drops in the things she had in her purse—the top of her lipstick, a pen cap, her sunglasses case.

Is there anything you don't keep in that purse of yours, Janet? Josh used to say.

Now Wendy was kneeling on top of the mound of rubble, digging with Louie's Pokémon spoon.

You have to take a break, her homeroom teacher, Mrs. Volt, was telling her, but she didn't. Louie was there, too, but all he could do was suck his thumb.

Stop that, she told him. They'll laugh at you in preschool.

Ease up on him, Wendy, her mother said. He's having a rough time.

What about me?

In the dream there were flyers blowing around Wendy with pictures of people on them that she didn't know. Her mother was telling her things— phone numbers of Louie's friends and when he needed his next booster shot. I wanted to take you to see *Contact* on Broadway, she said. I never got around to telling you about sex.

Wendy was calling out that she was sorry about the fight they had at Macy's, when she wanted the kilt. I don't care about kilts, she said. She was sorry she wished gym class would be canceled that day. The list was so long, all the things she was sorry for.

You're the best mother, she said. Just come home.

I wish I could, honey, her mother said. But it's not looking likely. I'm dying on the vine.

*         *         *

It was past eleven. Josh was asleep for once, lying on the couch. She could tell from his breathing. She sat on the edge of her bed and looked out the window at the brownstone across the street. There was a man watching television, and below that room, someone else was also watching television. On the sidewalk, a girl went past on a bicycle, with a bag of late-night groceries in a basket on the back. Ordinary life.

Wind rustled through the leaves of the branches of the tree in front of their building. Soon the leaves would turn color and then fall. When she was Louie's age, she and her mother had gathered the brightest ones and laid them between sheets of wax paper to hang in the window. After that came construction-paper pumpkins and turkeys. Then snowflakes with lacy cutout designs. After they'd made them, they swirled Elmer's glue on the snowflakes and sprinkled glitter on, shaking off the extra into their hair. Their snowflakes, too, she hung in her window, and when the season for snowflakes was done, it was time for the hearts, the four-leaf clovers, the eggs. All the way through the year, till they were ready for the leaves and wax paper again. Josh kidded her mother that there wasn't a week in the whole year she hadn't found some holiday to celebrate.

Wendy dressed in the dark. She jammed a bunch of baby-sitting money in her pocket. Outside, she walked to the corner and hailed a taxi. She'd never done anything like this before, but it was easier than she thought. The driver didn't look surprised to see someone her age riding alone in a cab into Manhattan at night. Maybe it was the times.

She had never been out on her own so late before. If her mother was there, she would never in a million years let her, but that was the thing: Her mother wasn't there.

The streets were quieter than she expected. A couple of homeless people lay on blankets with cardboard over their heads. As she got closer to Canal Street, a parade of army trucks with flags on their hoods rumbled past, hauling loads of broken-up metal. If Louie was here, he'd count them.

The police had blocked off the streets below Canal and West Broadway, but she could see some people getting through. The thing was to look as if you lived there. They were checking people's identification to see their address. Wendy had nothing.

I was walking our dog, she told the policeman. His leash came out of my hand and he ran ahead of me. It surprised her how easy it was lying to a policeman.

Okay, go on through, he said. But next time, you need to have ID.


The air was thicker here. On the news, they called it a burned rubber smell, but Wendy had smelled burned rubber and this was different. She pulled her turtleneck up over her nose and dug her hands into her pockets.

She passed a man carrying a lamp and a suitcase and another carrying a carton of milk, but otherwise no one except the men in orange vests and police. A bus crawled past and let out a dozen people, also in orange vests. Another group got on board. Their faces looked chalky and they sat facing the front of the bus; none of them talking. As the bus pulled away, she could see the fresh group of workers marching in with their shovels.

I was just wondering, she said. A young woman in a vest had stopped to take a drink from her water bottle by the spot where Wendy was standing. You aren't finding bodies or anything are you?

Not much you'd recognize, the woman said. If it's anything human, they've got a priest set up in a tent to say the last rites.

One thing I'll tell you right now, she told Wendy. When this is finally over, I'm going into therapy.


Wendy walked another block. From somewhere in a high-up window she could hear the same Madonna song that had been playing everywhere. From someplace else, the national anthem. A siren wailed. She turned another corner.

At first she couldn't understand what the shape was, spiking up into the night sky against the blue glare of the searchlights. It looked like a giant bony finger pointing toward the moon. A crane maybe. Like the tallest cornstalk ever in some field after harvest time that someone forgot to cut down, and now it was dried up and bent over.

Then she recognized the form. She'd seen it those times she visited her mother at her job, when she and Josh would stop by with Louie, times when they were having a slow afternoon. The giant finger was the base of her mother's building. Not the whole of it, but part of a steel arch, twisted and broken off. Two stories high, maybe more. The only part left you could recognize. Only where the plaza used to be, where just last week Louie had practiced his skipping, there was nothing but a mountain of metal and dust. How high, she couldn't tell at first, until she made out the forms of a couple of men in orange vests in the middle of the vast expanse of rubble. Just dots.

She stood there, looking at the spot, the hole where her mother's building used to be. She had seen pictures of the moon, and a place in the desert of Nevada where they tested nuclear weapons, but she had never seen anything as desolate as this.

The last time she'd been here was with Josh and Louie. They were picking Louie up from day care, and her mother had said, Why don't you stop by the office and take me out for cappuccino after? Her boss was away, and things were slow.

Wendy was used to her brother's costumes, mostly, but that day he'd wanted to dress up as a pirate, with a pair of her mother's boots that were so big he could hardly walk in them. Can't you get him to put on something else, Josh? Wendy had said.

Josh laughed. If you ask me, the world would be a happier place if everyone felt comfortable enough to put on pirate hats and capes when they felt like it, he said.

Louie had also stuffed in his pocket a velvet bag his mother had given him, that some makeup came in. On the elevator going up, he passed out stones he had gathered in the bag. Wendy stood as far away from him as possible, but it was hard to act as if you didn't know someone, when you were in an elevator together for eighty-seven floors.

Her mother took them into her boss's office. Wendy just wanted to get out of there, before anyone saw her brother in his pirate costume, but Louie had sat down in the boss's special chair and spun around.

Oh, miss, he called out to their mother. Miss. Is the report ready?

One of her mother's coworkers had stuck his head in the door then, and her mother introduced them all. This is my daughter, Wendy. My husband, Josh. When she got to Louie, the man had said, This one's the dancer, right? We've heard all about you.

Her mother and Louie had a routine they did, from *A Chorus Line*—"One, Singular Sensation." When they did it back home in the living room, they each had their own hat and cane, but here in the office of Mercer and Mercer, her mother had used Mr. Mercer's umbrella. Louie had located a golf cap.

Looks like we'll be seeing this one on Broadway one of these days, Janet, the coworker had told her.

Wendy plays the clarinet, her mother said.

All Wendy could do was shoot her a look.

There had been no music at their house since Tuesday morning, but on the one-week mark, she woke up in the night and heard the album her mother and Josh were always playing late at night. *Clifford Brown with Strings.*

She got out of bed and went into the kitchen. Josh was smoking a cigarette.

I didn't know you smoked, she said.

I gave it up the night I met your mother. She said she had a rule—she'd never kiss a smoker.

You shouldn't start, she said. Mom would hate it if she knew.

Some people have started acting like the situation's hopeless, he said. They're having memorial services. I got a call to play at one.

What do you think?

I try not to think, he said. If there was anything I could do, I would. The sickening thing is that there isn't. Having to sit here, waiting. Knowing this could go on forever.

So what are we supposed to tell Louie? When do we go get him?

Louie's probably better off over at Corey's for now, Josh said. The song on the record was "Laura"—another of the ones they used to dance to in the kitchen. For all the days since her mother had disappeared, Wendy had felt a strange new awkwardness about hugging Josh, and he must have felt something similar, as if maybe, putting their arms around each other, one or both of them would break. Now, though, she leaned her head on his shoulder and patted him. When she did, he wrapped his arms around her. They just stood like that, nobody moving, for a long time.

Maybe it would be good if you started playing your bass again, she said.

He looked at her as if he wasn't sure what music was anymore.

I was thinking I might call my father, she told him. She thought if she said that, Josh might finally do something, but all he said was, Good idea.

# Four

He had written his phone number in his letter. She reached for her desk atlas to find out what time it would be in California. Nine-thirty.

Hey, said the voice. It was a little scratchy. Cell phone.

Is this Garrett DeVries? This is his daughter speaking.

She could hear voices in the background. It's my kid, he called out to someone. More voices.

I'm calling from New York, she said. I guess you know about what happened here.

I was meaning to call and make sure you were okay. Your school's nowhere near that place, right?

On the other side of the river.

Still, it's got to be pretty bad just being there.

It hadn't occurred to her that he wouldn't know. She hadn't had to tell anybody before.

Yes.

So how's school going? he asked. Rough start, I guess. She could hear him say, I told you I had a kid.

We had Wednesday off.

60

Well, there you go. No news is all bad.

The reason I called, she said.

Quiet down, Bobby, he called out. Sorry about that. The crowd's a little rowdy here. In the background she could hear country music and the sound of glasses clinking.

So when are you coming to see me? he asked. You got the letter, right?

Maybe on one of my vacations, she said. Right now, it's the start of school and everything. I'm in band.

She just wanted to get off the phone now. She couldn't even remember why she'd thought it would be a good idea to call.


Let me guess, he said. Your mom put the kibosh on you coming out to visit, right?

Not that so much, she said.

Just remember you're fourteen years old now, babe, he said.

Thirteen, but she didn't say it.

You have a say in your own life.

My mom, Wendy said. She didn't want to cry, so she stopped talking.

A different song was playing now. A woman singing about how you can take this old frying pan. A voice called, You in this round, Garrett?

My mom worked at the towers, she said. She didn't come home.


She thought when people were divorced as long as her parents, they probably didn't care if the other one disappeared. Her mother, for instance. From how she talked, Wendy could imagine her mother might have been almost happy if a building fell on her father. But now all he could say was, Oh my God, oh my God.

Josh thinks she might have been hurt and lost her memory, she said. Some people say there's sure to be people waiting to get dug out from the air pockets.

Oh my God, he said. I can't believe it. Quiet down, you guys.

Things are a little strange here right now, she told him.

Your mother and I, he said. I never expected.

I should probably go now, she said. I think my little brother needs something.

I've got to think. His voice sounded hoarse.

So I guess we'll be in touch, she said. What's the weather like there? She didn't know why she said that. Just to stop him from saying Oh my God over and over probably.

We had our rough times, he said. The thing is, we really used to love each other.

I guess I better go, she said.


She was in her mother's closet one time, looking for dress-ups, when she found the painting. Even at five years old, Wendy knew it was of her mother. She wasn't wearing any clothes except a scarf around her shoulders and her hair was still long. She was standing in front of some mountains, with a river at her feet.

Your dad painted that, her mother told her. We were really young then.

By this time he was gone, and the only time his name came up was when her mother had something bad to say about him, usually to Kate. It was hard imagining her ever looking out at him the way she did in the painting, with a smiling mouth and no frown lines in the space between her eyes.

We should hang this up in the living room, Wendy said. We could color over the bare parts.

She thought it was beautiful, but she was also thinking about the boyfriends who came over now and then to take her mother on dates and how it might be embarrassing if they saw her naked.

I don't think so, honeybun, her mother said.

Wendy wanted to know why. Her mother looked so pretty in the painting. Like Ariel in *The Little Mermaid*.

Bad memories, she said. I'd throw this painting out, except that I don't think you should ever destroy someone's artwork.

We could give it to a museum, Wendy said. Sundays, she and her mother went into the city a lot, and sometimes after the polar bears in Central Park, they went to the Met.

They might not think he's quite as great an artist as he does, she said.

\*      \*      \*

It wasn't hard remembering the fights because there'd been lots of those. Jesus Christ, Janet. If what you cared about so much was a microwave oven and health insurance, you should have married a damned banker.

They must have thought she couldn't hear them when *Mister Rogers* was on, because they always seemed to have their worst arguments at five o'clock, right around the time he was taking off his sweater. But Mister Rogers spoke very quietly, even with the volume up. She'd be curled up under the blue afghan in her TV chair with a plate of Ritz crackers and peanut butter and a glass of soy milk, but she could hear them in the bedroom, even though the door was closed.

You make it seem like there's something sick about wanting to be sure your child can go to the dentist twice a year and take a few swimming lessons.

Who said she couldn't go swimming? All I did was bring home one lousy tube of orange paint.

I don't recall hearing you ever did without much when you were a kid. Seems to me I'm talking to the person who used to get daily private tennis lessons every summer.

Maybe it was doing that shit that made me understand how little it all adds up to. Not to some people, I guess.

She couldn't make out what her mother said then. Just the sound of crying. On TV, Mister Rogers was telling Audrey it was time for the trolley to come. Then came the jingle of the bell, and sure enough, he was right.

I wonder what Trolley's got with him today, said Mister Rogers.

From the bedroom, the other voice. Her mother's. You care more about going fishing with your friends than your own child. Maybe I might like to make art, too. We've got a child here to think about.

Looks like Prince Friday might have gotten a new balloon for his birthday, Mister Rogers said. A beautiful shade of blue.

But I want the red one, said the prince. And then her father: Who'd want to stay home with a person who's always ragging on them?

Oh, now I get it. It's all my fault.

People can't always get what they want, Prince Friday, Mister Rogers was saying. But it's all right to be disappointed now and then. What do you think, Mister McFeeley?

You know what, Garrett? Her mother, crying. You break my heart.


They were in their green car with no roof, driving somewhere in the country. Wendy was very young.

It's not safe having her on my lap, Garrett. She should be riding in a car seat.

When was the last time you saw an Alfa with a car seat, babe?

Slow down at least.

What about you, Wenderina? You want the wind in your face?

She didn't actually, but she knew what he wanted her to say.

Faster! More!

They were heading someplace outside New York City. Her grandmother's house, with the piano, and the olden days cart, with the tea set on it, which she used to serve special cookies that came from England. Wendy stuck her hand out the side of the car and let the veil on Wedding Belle Barbie flap in the wind.

At her grandmother's, she slept in the room that used to be her father's. There was a picture over the bed of a man on a horse that her grandmother said her father made when he was a little boy.

Your father was supposed to go to art school in Rhode Island, her grandmother told her. Before you came along.

Give it up, Mother, he said. I've got my artwork right here. He meant Wendy.


On their way back home, driving fast on the Hudson River Parkway, she accidentally dropped her Barbie out the side of the car. She wanted to go back, but her father said they couldn't.


He had a show of his paintings. Not in New York City, but someplace a little ways away, where you had to ride a train. She and her mother put on long skirts. Her mother dabbed perfume on Wendy's neck.

You can wear this, she said. Her purple boa.

Her father came in the room. He must have shaved, because he had the special smell he always had after. She rubbed her face on his smooth cheek. He looked handsome as a prince.

Nobody else's daddy knows how to draw dinosaurs like you, Wendy said.

Too bad nobody wants to buy paintings of dinosaurs. Her mother talking. She was laughing, but her father wasn't.

Will you ever quit, Janet? he said.

He had another show, someplace upstate this time. He was gone a week, setting things up. He told her mother not to hassle with coming to the opening. I'll be home in two more days anyway, Janet, he said. Dance our girl around the room for me, and tell her there's a treat waiting for her in my bag.

Times like that, when he was coming back from one of his trips, she and her mother would decorate the house. One time they made paper chains they hung from the ceiling and put on their long dresses. They worked out a dance routine to "Under the Sea" from *The Little Mermaid*.

Another time, the two of them hid in the closet to surprise him. They waited so long that time, Wendy's arm fell asleep and their hairdos got mussed up. After a long time waiting, her mother said they'd better get out of the closet.

Something must have come up, she said. By the time he finally got home, Wendy was asleep, and when she woke up in the morning, he was gone again. They'd had one of their fights.


The time he went to New Jersey, her mother had the idea they should show up and surprise him. They put on their dresses again. They had to take a train from Penn Station to Trenton, and from there a taxi to his motel. Her mother got the key from the front desk. I'm his wife, she said.

Whatever, said the guy at the desk. Wendy had made her dad a card with a flower taped on the front.

At first when they opened the door, she thought they'd come to the wrong room, because there was a naked woman lying on the bed. Hard to make out her face in the candlelight, but she was no one they knew. Then they saw his boots with the alligator skin on the toes and they knew they were in the right room after all.

Excuse me, her mother said. When she said that, the woman sat up and started grabbing for her clothes, but not before Wendy noticed she had a rose tattooed over one of her breasts. At the time, Wendy had never seen a tattoo before.

That tattoo was one of the things she kept asking her mother about later—why the girl had the flower on her front. Maybe because there were so many big things she knew she'd never figure out that night, it seemed like the one question she could ask where a straight answer might still be possible.

I guess she thought it would be pretty, her mother said. They were in the taxi, going home from the train station, and rain was coming down faster than the windshield wipers could keep up with it.

Right around when the woman was pulling her dress over her was when her father came out of the bathroom. Also naked although he had a towel around his waist. His hair was wet.

After that came a lot of yelling. Somewhere along the line, the woman on the bed put on the rest of her clothes and went away. Her mother picked up the painting that was leaning against the table and kicked it so hard, her foot broke through the canvas.

I'm sorry, Janet, he said. It didn't mean anything. I didn't really care about her. It was just this thing that happened. You're the one I love. God, what was I doing?

You were screwing up our life, that's what.


When she woke up the next morning her mother was throwing their stuff in garbage bags and boxes—piles of clothes, CD's, the videos of their favorite musicals. Her top hat and dancing cane from *A Chorus Line.*

My tea set's breakable, Wendy whispered. She watched her mother fling her shell collection in the bag. Then her sweet potato vine. Not my Pound Puppy, she said. You're scaring him.

Sometime before lunch, they had all their stuff packed up, and they loaded the bags in the trunk and the backseat of Kate's car. They stayed at Kate's apartment for a long time, while her mother found their new apartment.

At first she didn't ask any questions about her father, but finally she asked when they were going back home again. Never, said her mother.

You said everyone deserves a second chance, Wendy said.

Maybe they do, said her mother. But not a one millionth.

# Five

Josh was in the kitchen. For the first time since Tuesday, he was cooking, which seemed like a good sign. He was chopping carrots and celery, and the smell of onions and garlic was coming from the stove.

I called my father, she said.

He stopped chopping.

He didn't know what happened, but now he does.

You still thinking you might want to go see him? Josh asked her.

Not really. I just wondered if it might feel better talking to him.

I can understand that. If my dad was around, I'd probably want to call him up, too.

The picture came to her then of Garrett, as he was in the photograph he'd sent her, standing in front of the cabin with the morning glories. The picture Amelia said made him look like Josh Hartnett. She tried to imagine him as a person she'd tell her problems to, but couldn't.

Josh was wearing the same sweatpants he'd had on the day it happened. He must have changed sometime since then, but he hardly looked as though he had, and his hair was sticking up like Louie after his nap. The only famous person he looked like was one of the Three Stooges maybe.

So what do you feel like doing now? he asked her.

She looked at him standing at the cutting board with his shirt hanging out and a piece of carrot peel on the front. His arms were outstretched like a conductor, only what he held was just a paring knife. It felt like one of those moments on *Who Wants to Be a Millionaire* when the person's up for the million-dollar prize. He's made his guess but he's not that sure about the answer and Regis is saying, Is that your final answer, and everyone's waiting to see if he's going to go for the million or play it safe, only in this case nothing good was going to happen whatever you chose.

We should go pick up my brother, she said.

Louie was on the floor with Corey coloring when they got there. He didn't look up when he saw them.

I already know, he said. You didn't bring my mom. His voice was husky and his shoulders were hunched over his coloring book, as if everything that mattered in the world was on that page.

We don't know where Mama is yet, Lou-man, Josh told him. But we figured it's time for you to come home. He had pulled himself together for this.

I want to stay here, Louie said. He had not stopped coloring, though the marks he was making on the paper were only scribbles, back and forth.

You've been here a long time already, Josh said. Corey's mom needs a break. Plus, your sister and I miss you too much.

I don't miss you guys one tiny bit, he said. I like it better here.

Josh got down on the floor next to him. I don't believe that's true, he said. But even if it is, you need to come home.

You haven't even told us about preschool, Wendy said. What's your teacher's name?

Mrs. Nobody, he said. Brown crayon, back and forth.

Listen, Lou-man, Josh said. He wrapped his arms around Louie now and picked him up, but Louie was wriggling to get loose. I know you're worried about Mama. But you're coming back with us now. It's not open to discussion.

Before, Louie had only struggled a little. Now he was thrashing in all directions. He tore the page out of the coloring book and ripped it in bits that he threw at Josh. He kicked so hard his shoe flew off. I hate you, he said. Get out of here. I wish you'd fall out of a building.

You don't mean that, Josh told him.

I'll play with you, said Wendy. We'll dress up.

I don't care about playing, he said. Foot. Arm. Foot again. His legs pedaled in the air like a cartoon character who's gone off a cliff but kept running. His hands flailed out in all directions and he was yelling, Buttface. Poophead. Penishead. Diarrheabreath.

Corey ran to the kitchen and came back with a Popsicle, but Louie was past caring. Corey's mom, Cheryl, stroked his back. For a second it looked as if he might bite her.

We're leaving now, son, said Josh.

I'll call you, Cheryl, Josh said over the sound of Louie's yelling. One of us can come back later for his stuff.

Whatever works, Corey's mother told him.

Hard to imagine what that might be.


On the stairs going down, Louie was still kicking, but not as hard anymore, and his breathing was coming steadier. I hate you, he said again, but not as fiercely as before. When they got to the second flight of stairs, he seemed to have run out of words. By the time they got out the door of Corey's building, his body was nearly still.

A girl at my school said all the people got buried under the building, Louie whispered. My teacher said to be quiet but the girl said her mom said all the people got turned into bits of dust and the reason everyone's wearing masks is they might be allergic to dead people.

They were standing at the bus stop. A bunch of flyers were taped along the enclosure—some Wendy had never seen before and a few familiar faces.

Suddenly Louie's body lurched back so hard he nearly fell out of Josh's arms. A long, low moan rose from him and that sound again, keening. A couple of people around them looked up as he called again, more piercingly, *My mama.*

It was her face on one of the flyers, with part of the tape starting to come undone. Flapping in the breeze. *Desperately waiting. Please call.*

*     *     *

I don't know if this is crazy considering everything that's going on, Amelia said. But I was thinking we could head over to the Virgin megastore after school and listen to CD's.

They hung out at the listening stations for half an hour. Then they tried on jeans. Neither one of them had any money, but Amelia wanted to see how she'd look in a pair of spandex hip-huggers. After, they went out for smoothies.

I talked to my dad, Wendy told her. He didn't know my mother worked in one of the towers.

It struck her when she said it, that in ten days of thinking about almost nothing else, she had hardly spoken the word *mother*.

So how did he take it? Amelia asked her. As usual, no response was necessary. She kept talking.

He was grief-stricken, of course, right? They were probably one of those couples that have this passionate attraction that lasts forever, it's just too intense for them to actually live together like normal people, like Sean Penn and Madonna. But now he realizes she was the love of his life.

I think maybe it just caught him by surprise more than anything, Wendy said.

I bet it felt good talking to him anyway, Amelia said. Like maybe now is the moment you two guys will find your way back to each other.

I don't know, Wendy said. It was like I was talking to some stranger. He forgot how old I was.

He was probably just in shock, said Amelia. Being an artist, he'd be the supersensitive type.

Really the one that's in the worst shape about everything is Josh.

You don't think he's going to have some kind of a breakdown, do you?

Until Amelia said that, the thought had not occurred to Wendy, but now she imagined what would happen if Josh couldn't take care of things anymore. More even than her mother, he had become the person she counted on to keep things steady.

At least you still have your real dad, Amelia said.

# Six

When they were little, in third grade, Wendy and Amelia had this game they liked to play called Pennsylvania. Not a game exactly. All you did was talk about all the things you'd do when you grew up. Starting with how they were both going to live in Pittsburgh, Pennsylvania, in side-by-side houses, so they could see each other every single day for their whole life. Neither one of them had ever been to Pennsylvania, but they liked the sound. They were going to marry two incredibly cute boys who were identical twins, so their kids would be cousins, and they'd spend all their vacations together. They'd go to Disney World, and a town in Delaware Amelia had driven through one time that had the best miniature golf Amelia had ever seen only her father wouldn't stop.

Some of the other places they'd go were Paris, Hong Kong, the Grand Canyon, a mall Amelia had heard about that had an actual wave pool inside, and Universal Studios in Hollywood.

Mostly, all Wendy had to do when they played Pennsylvania was listen, because Amelia thought up most of the things. They would go on *Jeopardy* and win the hundred thousand dollars, for instance. With the money they won, they would buy their husbands sports cars, and a moped for themselves, and go to a spa and get a home-entertainment center in one of their houses.

No need for both to have them, because they were such good friends. Amelia wanted to have one whole room in her house with nothing but wigs in different hairstyles and colors. Wendy would get a dog and every kind of art supply in Sam Flax. The rest of the money they would donate to charity.

Now that they were older, they didn't play Pennsylvania much anymore, but every now and then Amelia would still start in. When we're in Pennsylvania, let's have our own restaurant that only serves desserts, Amelia said. How do you like Jasmine Francesca for a name for my daughter? She liked Sade for a girl, too, but most people wouldn't pronounce it right.

They were walking along Union Street, on their way to the library. Usually, they only went there after school, but it was a Saturday. This was only the second time Amelia had been over since Wendy's mother disappeared, and it had been so depressing being in the apartment, she'd said, let's go to the library. They were passing a fire station, Engine Company 342. Piles of flowers had been left out in front and a row of photographs of missing firemen, with a candle burning next to each of them.

Look at him, said Amelia. The man in the picture was probably around twenty-two or twenty-three. In the picture, he was grinning, and you could see he had a dimple, but only on one side. He had naturally curly red hair.

That's the handsomest person I ever saw, said Amelia. That's who I want to marry in Pennsylvania.

Billy Flynn was his name. The pile of flowers next to his picture was particularly large, and there were a bunch of smaller photographs of him, too. One with a group of young women, all shorter than him but with the same smile, and another of him holding a snowboard.

He was at the Twin Towers, Amelia, Wendy said to her. I don't think he's going to be going to Pennsylvania with you. Even if he wasn't a ton older than us.

Nobody had ever made up rules for Pennsylvania, but they both knew you didn't question anybody's plans for what they were going to do there.

They may find him, Amelia said. Look at him with the snowboard. He's exactly the kind of person that would find some hidden secret passageway out of the rubble. He'll probably lead all these other people to safety. Your mom maybe. Then we'll get to meet him.

They stood there for a while looking at the pictures.

He doesn't look like the kind of person who'd be dead, said Amelia.

I know what you mean, said Wendy. But lots of people don't.

Anyway, Amelia said. The girls in the picture are obviously his sisters. But maybe he's got a brother for you.

You are so crazy, said Wendy.

You never know, said Amelia. She took hold of Wendy's hand and they walked to the library.


Apart from Amelia, there was nobody Wendy felt much like seeing. Her grandmother, with the tea cart, had been pretty much out of the picture since the divorce, except for one time years ago when she'd been passing through the city and took Wendy and her mother out for lunch at a place she called her club. Now she just sent a card every Christmas, along with her annual gift of a white cotton blouse that had Wendy's initials monogrammed on the pocket, each one size bigger than the year before.

Josh's mom had been calling a lot, but she lived in Florida and was afraid of flying, particularly now, so they hadn't seen her.

Her mom's dad had died when Wendy was just a baby, and her mom's mom was too sick to travel all the way from Missouri, but her aunt showed up from St. Louis. Just for a day. Her mother and Aunt Pam had never gotten along that well, and in the years since she and Josh had been together, Wendy had only seen her twice. She brought a box of candy for Wendy and said she needed to talk with Josh alone.

You know I'd take her if I possibly could, but with my job, it's just not possible, she could hear Aunt Pam telling Josh. As if Wendy would want to go live with her. As if Josh would want her to live anyplace but here.

With some people, this would be the moment Josh would start talking about amnesia and air pockets, but with Aunt Pam, he just sounded tired. That's fine, Pam, Wendy heard him say. I understand.

Josh's sister, Andy, came over every day or two, usually with food, and one time she brought scissors and cut his hair, which was an improvement. She made a pot of tea for herself and Wendy and told her about her therapist, who was great with kids. I could set up an appointment, she said, but Wendy said she was okay.

The woman whose apartment was underneath theirs stopped over with a cake and a book she said had helped her when her mother got breast cancer.

There were strangers, too, people who'd gotten their number off the flyers. Most of those were a little crazy: a woman who said she could locate a person's spirit if she could touch one of their shoes. Another woman, who said she'd noticed a pattern to the names on the flyers. An unusual number started with J.

I would disconnect the phone, Josh said. Only we have to make sure she can reach us.

Kate called. Let's go someplace and talk, she said to Wendy. I know I'm not actually part of your family, but your mother and I have been friends for so long, I feel as if we're related.

More and more lately, Wendy found herself feeling like a person in a play who's trying to remember her lines. She knew it was her turn to talk now and that she should say something about how Kate felt like a part of her family, too, which was even true, but nothing she could say now seemed to matter.

I know you probably don't feel like eating, Kate told her. But I'm taking you out anyway.

Kate showed up, wearing the sweater Wendy's mother had crocheted for her, even though the buttons didn't line up with the buttonholes. She had made them some kind of soup. Kate was a terrible cook, but Josh said, This looks good. Wendy could tell from the way he was talking that he was also acting in a play, a different one.

Listen, Kate told her when they were outside on the street. I'm trying hard to imagine what your mother would tell us right now. I think it would be that you've got to go back to school and start having some kind of life without her, and even if it feels totally crummy, after a while it will start to get a little better. I don't know how myself, but I have to believe that. She put her arm around Wendy.

Kate took her to a manicure place she and Wendy's mom used to go to sometimes on Seventh Avenue.

This is a nice mindless activity, Kate said. The Korean woman reached for Wendy's hand and placed it in a soapy bowl. Wendy realized this was the first person she'd been around in two weeks who didn't say one thing about the

World Trade Center. The woman just sat there working on her cuticles. Wendy felt as if she was someplace far away, wandering in a field of wheat. She forgot all about where she was until the woman said something Wendy couldn't make out that must have meant her nails were done.

Wendy studied her hands. It was the first time she'd ever had a manicure, so it didn't even seem as if they belonged to her, but when she saw her hands, her chest tightened and an awful wave of memory and sadness washed over her. Laid flat on the white cloth of the manicure table with their round moons and pink polish, her hands looked exactly like her mother's.

At school, nobody said anything about her mother, but it was clear everyone knew. When she walked into homeroom, Mrs. Volt took her aside. I want you to know you should feel free to do whatever feels best for you right now, dear, she told Wendy. Anytime you need to take a few moments and be alone, you can go down to the nurse's office or just sit in the library. We're all rooting for you.

Some people may find gym class a helpful outlet, she was saying. But if you'd rather not play volleyball at this point, everyone will understand if you sit out PE. Three weeks ago that would have been her dream. Now she just looked at Mrs. Volt and said, That's okay. I don't mind volleyball.

In English, they were reading one of her mother's favorite books, *The Diary of a Young Girl*, by Anne Frank. Originally, they were supposed to read *Lord of the Flies* first, but Mrs. Gardner was saying she'd decided everyone could use a little different tone at the moment.

I thought it could be helpful to everyone to read about a young person who managed to maintain this tremendously hopeful, optimistic spirit through another very dark time in history, she said. Maybe through Anne's words we can all find some comfort and inspiration for the heartbreaking times we're living through today.

Buddy Campion interrupted her. But all that time this girl was writing her upbeat stuff, he said, she didn't actually know she was going to die, right? What I want to know is, was she still talking about how people were basically so great when they herded her into the concentration camp?

Some of us who haven't been as diligent as you in keeping ahead of the reading assignment might appreciate it if you didn't give away the ending of the book, Buddy, Mrs. Gardner said.

Yeah, right, he said, but only loud enough for the people who sat in his row to hear.

At lunch, she sat with Amelia and Seth, same as always, though Hallie Owens had joined them, along with a girl Wendy didn't know, a very serious-looking person wearing a T-shirt with a hand on it holding a bunch of flowers.

Hey, Wendy, Hallie was saying. Tanya and I just wanted to invite you to join our Unitarian Youth group, if you're interested. We're having a rally Sunday about how violence is never the answer to solving problems, and it would be really great to have some people there who had, you know, a kind of personal take on the situation.

There's going to be a spaghetti supper afterward, Tanya said.

I don't know what my plans are at the moment, Wendy said.

Seth looked up from his tuna melt. That homework in history killed me. How'd you guys do? As usual, his voice shifted octaves partway through his sentence, but Wendy was glad just to hear someone talk.

His face flushed.

I didn't mean killed, he said. But, like, bad.

I didn't have my book home with me, Wendy said. I'm way behind.

I don't think you need to worry, Hallie said. She reached across the table as if she was going to take one of Wendy's hands, but patted her sleeve instead. All the teachers said people in your situation should just go with the flow for a while.

Wendy looked at her sandwich, trying to imagine what it would mean to go with the flow. She saw herself on a raft, bobbing along a river someplace. Crowds on the sidelines, rooting for her.

Nobody said anything for a couple of minutes. After awhile, Tanya and Hallie picked up their trays to go. Well, it was great talking to you, Tanya said. Me, too, said Hallie. I'd really like to get to know you better.

Amelia had been cutting her tangerine peel with her fingernail into the shape of a person. After the girls left, she walked her tangerine-peel man across the table toward Wendy and made him talk in a squeaky voice.

I'd really like to get to know you more, the tangerine peel said. It's just so fascinating having a friend whose mother got killed.

The second she said it, she gasped. Seth looked up from his sandwich. Oh my God, said Amelia. It just came out.

It's okay, Wendy told Amelia. She felt relieved that someone said it, finally.

It was Saturday, raining hard, the sky gunmetal gray. Normally, Josh would be watching cartoons with Louie, but he had gone down to the armory with her mother's hairbrush and her dental X rays—the thing he had said, at first, he'd never do.

Louie wasn't allowed to watch TV unsupervised anymore, because you never knew when they were going to break into the programming with some piece of news, and it was never good.

Louie was in the family room, eating his cereal. Nobody had gotten around to turning on the lights. Josh had taken the batteries out of the remote control so he couldn't turn the television on. Now he sat there in his elf costume, with his cereal bowl set on the tray table they used to put their food on, video nights, when Josh had a gig and their mom let them eat their meals with a movie. His back was strangely straight, as if he was balancing a book on his head, and he was holding his spoon in midair. The way he was sitting reminded Wendy of squirrels you'd see in the park—the way one would freeze halfway up a tree, or in a patch of grass, and lock its eyes on some random spot for long seconds, before it got back to whatever it was doing before.

Come on into my room, Louie, she said. I'll read to you.

She'd told him to bring a pile of books into bed, the way her mother had done with her when she was little. They had already read *Katy and the Big Snow* and *Cloudy with a Chance of Meatballs* and *Curious George*. Now he wanted *Goodnight Moon*.

Don't you want a more grown-up book than that, Louie? she asked. Their mother used to read *Goodnight Moon* to him way back, when he still slept in his crib.

I want this one. He put the old familiar book in her hands. They were in her bed now. He adjusted his body so he was curled up against her tight. She started reading.

"In the great green room there was a telephone and a red balloon," she began. "And a picture of the cow jumping over the moon."

As she read the words, he placed his finger on the part of the picture she was talking about, the same way their mother had taught her to do when she was very little. When she got to the part about the quiet old lady murmuring hush, Louie put his finger up to his lips the same way Wendy used to when she was little. She'd forgotten how her mother always did that on this page.

"Goodnight room," she said. "Goodnight moon." She looked over at her brother then because his finger wasn't on the moon. His thumb was in his mouth, was part of it, and his hand was busy twirling his ribbon.

But also she saw now that he was crying. He was crying so softly that if she hadn't looked at him, she wouldn't have known.

"Goodnight comb," she said. "Goodnight brush."

She had begun to cry also, and for a few seconds the two of them just sat on the bed, looking at the picture. The rabbit in the rocking chair. The glow of the table lamp. Out the window through neatly drawn curtains, the moon.

Goodnight nobody, he said when a minute had gone by that she didn't speak. Goodnight mush. Do you think Mama is ever coming back, Sissy?

I don't think so, Louie, she said.

# Seven

Days passed, and less happened than a person might have expected. There were still flags everywhere and streets blocked off downtown, but when you were standing at a crosswalk waiting for the light to change and you picked up a piece of someone's conversation, it might be about whether the Yankees were going to make it to the play-offs, and not the way it had been a few weeks earlier, the same one thing over and over. People were going into stores and coming out with shopping bags, and smoking cigarettes and buying lottery tickets and looking at the cheap watches the men sold on the street. There were Halloween costumes in windows, and pumpkins. Things are finally getting back to normal, Wendy heard a woman say to her friend as they stopped to look at winter coats in a window.

For a second, Wendy felt like grabbing her arm and yelling, Are you crazy? But instead, she just stopped to look at the coats, too. She wanted to be around people who actually felt things were back to normal, or acted like it anyway.

Life goes on, the woman looking at the winter coats had said to the friend. To Wendy, that was the strangest part: people going on with their lives, making comments like the friend's, that she couldn't stand the kind of coat that only had a pocket on one side.


When she was little, Wendy had never understood how it was that you could be walking down a street in the city and see some homeless person sitting there with a sign that said HAVEN'T EATEN IN THREE DAYS and you just walked right past them. The person might be lying on the sidewalk in a way that made you wonder if they were even alive. Shouldn't we check on him? she used to ask her mother. You'd think so, her mother said. But this is New York. That's how life goes here.

Now look. Three thousand people had said good-bye to their families and gone off to work one day and never came home. To Wendy, it would have seemed more understandable if, walking down the street, you saw people ripping out their hair, or lying on the ground, pounding the cement. She could have understood it better if they were running through the city, scream-ing, or swinging baseball bats into store windows, or going up to total strang-ers and grabbing them by the arm, saying, My husband disappeared! This person was my only child! I need my mother!

What seemed craziest was all of this regular, ordinary-looking behavior: shopping, talking about some brand of car, going to school. Business as usual, they called it. Behaving, out in the world anyway, as if nothing had changed, when the truth was, not one thing was the same, like everyone was in on this big show. Sometime when she was sleeping or off putting up flyers, they'd handed out the instructions about how people should behave. She was still trying to figure out what the rules were now.


Who knew what a girl was supposed to look like who had a mother for thirteen years of her life and then all of a sudden one day she didn't. Now that she was that girl, she knew the answer. She looked just like anybody else. Same as the people looked normal on the flyers that had mostly fallen down by now. Same as Anne Frank did, whose diary she had been reading in English and whose face she studied every time she picked up the book. Same as those kids at Columbine High School whose pictures she had also looked at long and hard, in *Time* magazine, after they'd gotten shot by those two boys. Same as the two boys who had shot them, for that matter. It turned out that horrifying things could happen to ordinary-looking people. Unimaginable things could happen in the most regular places.

One thing Wendy had learned from carrying on her own normal-looking behavior for a month now—pushing her tray along the line in the cafeteria, working on her geometry proofs, buttering her toast: You never knew who else was doing exactly the same thing—which people were really okay, and which ones only looked like it, even though they could just as easily go jump in front of an oncoming subway train as step inside it for a ride to the next station.

Nothing was as it seemed—that was what she understood now. You could be riding across from a person on the bus and never know that just four weeks ago her sister, who she used to talk to on the phone every night, called her up on her cell phone and said, Listen, this building's on fire and it doesn't look like I'm getting out, so I just want you to know I love you. There could be a regular-looking man sitting on the A train, carrying a regular-looking bag, and you'd never know that he'd gotten married last summer to this woman he'd been in love with since they were sixteen years old, and they had returned from their honeymoon just after Labor Day, a trip they'd saved up for all year—and she'd gone back to work, and a week later she didn't come home for dinner, and she still hadn't. You wouldn't know that what he was carrying in the bag was her hairbrush and a piece of her fingernail he'd found on the floor of their bathroom, hoping to match her DNA with pieces of bodies they'd found in the mountain of rubble where her building used to be.

There could be a person like Louie, who'd be climbing the ladder to the slide when you went out on the playground at school to take him home at the end of the day, calling out, Hey Sissy, look at me. And you'd never believe that a few hours before, when his father had been tying his shoes, he had looked up, with his eyes wet, and asked, If a bus ran over me and I was dead, would I get to see my mama then?

Or Wendy herself, on the phone with Amelia, talking about the outfit a girl named Jessica Overbeck had worn to school the day before, until Amelia had said, Got to go. My mom's calling. Just that—nothing more than the thought of a mom saying it was time to get off the phone—was enough to change everything, take her from normal to crazy in about two seconds.

Sometimes it was a flash flood. Other times it came on like a slow-building rainstorm, the kind that gives you enough warning you might even have time to get inside before the clouds burst. Once it started, though, there was nothing to do but let the sorrow pound you like the most powerful current, the strongest waterfall. When the sorrow hit, small losses came crashing over you in one suffocating torrent.

The picture came to her of the time she and her mother had decided to crochet themselves matching hats, and Wendy's came out with a funny pointed nub on the top, but they wore them anyway, all that winter, when they went skating. She saw her mother wearing hers, with the goofy red-and-white pom-pom, doing her pretend ice-dancing routine to the hokey music at the Rockefeller Center rink. She didn't really know any figure-skating moves besides the bunny hop; she just made a lot of arm movements.

Their *I Love Lucy* nights, the two of them curled up under the afghan with the popcorn. Lucy and Desi were married in real life, her mother told her. But they got a divorce. I wonder if it made Lucille Ball sad afterward, watching these old shows from back when they were still together.

The time they made Ukrainian Easter eggs. Sticking the pinholes in the two ends of the egg, her mother putting the egg against her lips to blow out the inside part, watching the yolk come shooting out the bottom, her mother swallowing a little raw egg and spitting it out, and then making their designs in wax, dipping their eggs in the dye baths, first one layer of wax, then another, until the great moment when the design was finished and they could rub off all the wax and watch the patterns they'd made come through. Only Wendy had gripped hers so hard that, after all her work, the egg had cracked. She had cried then, and her mother had said, Never mind. We'll make another one. And they had, too, even though they'd been working on their eggs all morning already.

Floodwaters now. More pictures coming at her than she had time to collect even, they rushed by so quickly. Catch it, catch it. Don't let that one get away.

The time they were reading *The Secret Garden* out loud, and every time they got to the end of a chapter, Wendy had said, Just one more, which wasn't even necessary, because her mother didn't want to stop reading either, and in the end they stayed up till midnight and finished the whole book. The two of them under the covers, crying so hard at one point, her mother had to stop reading to blow her nose.

The time, walking home from preschool, she and her mother had found a pair of mannequin legs on the sidewalk in front of a store. They'd been thrown out, probably because a piece of one of the feet had broken off, but otherwise the legs were perfect. Her mother carried them home on the subway, while Wendy had taken their bag of groceries. The whole way, everyone they passed—even the kind of people who normally looked mad all the time—had smiled at them. When they got back to their apartment, they'd propped the legs up in their living room and set a potted African violet on the top, and her mother had put stockings on them, which they changed periodically over the years—sometimes purple, sometimes fishnet; one time, bobby socks and high heels. They were always on the lookout for the top half of a mannequin to go with the legs.

Lying in bed, with the floodwaters rushing over her, the picture came to her of the time she and her mother had taken a bus all the way to Cape Cod. From there, they'd taken the ferry out to Martha's Vineyard and checked into a rooming house. They rented bikes—Wendy had only just learned how to ride, but the bike paths were flat enough that it was no problem—and they'd gone on a carousel where if you grabbed hold of the brass ring, you got a free ride, and her mother did. In the end, they must have ridden that carousel ten times in a row. They had thought up names for their horses—Galahad for her mother's, and hers she named Happy.

That night, sitting on the patio of the restaurant they'd chosen because you could get a whole hamburger meal with a drink included for $5.95, she had seen her mother looking over at the family sitting at the table next to them. The mother and father were drinking piña coladas, and the three kids also had expensive drinks in fancy glasses. They looked as if they weren't having any fun at all, like their whole vacation was just one big inconvenient chore.

Wendy had recognized (young as she was, she had seen this) a sad look on her mother's face, and she had said, I bet all the husbands in this restaurant wish they were married to you. Her mother was always the prettiest one, and she was so much more fun than those grumpy-looking mothers, on vacation with their husbands, who were always complaining about the food or the service or yelling at their kids. Wendy's mother was just so happy they'd found their great little rooming house for twenty dollars a night, and the best hamburgers ever, cheap.

Only Wendy knew how much she would have loved it if instead of her five-year-old daughter across from her at the table—or in addition to—there had been some man who loved her, and the two of them were drinking one of those drinks with a parasol, and he reached across to hold her hand.

Sometimes when Wendy let herself start thinking about her mother, it would be memories of whole days that came to her: the birthday party—second grade—where her mother had taught her and a bunch of her friends how to do the Charleston and Kate had made a video of them in their flapper outfits. Their trip out to St. Louis to visit Aunt Pam that one time, when Aunt Pam had tried to convince her mother they should move to Missouri, it would be lots cheaper, telling her, Maybe it's time you faced the facts, Janet. New York is for people with money and prospects. You keep acting like you live in *Brigadoon*. Who do you think you are—Princess Diana?

The plane ride on the way back, her mother said, I don't think my sister ever liked me all that much. Not crying, but close.

It could be the smallest things that hit her. The way her mother always got hiccups when she ate raw carrots, and how Wendy would think up ways of scaring her, so she'd get over them. The first time they rented Rollerblades, Wendy sitting on the bench at the Chelsea Piers while her mother laced up her skates. Her mom singing along with the music they were playing, but off-key, as usual. Wendy whispering to her, Not here.

Memories of her mother and Josh. The scrapbook she kept with all the Post-it notes he left for her. The time Wendy came home unexpectedly after she was supposed to be on Fire Island with Amelia's family, except Amelia's parents had gotten into a fight and they had all come back early. And when she walked in the door, there were sounds coming from her parents' bedroom, even though it was the middle of the day. And when her mother had come out in her bathrobe, her hair was messed up. And a little after that, her mother came into her room and sat down on the bed next to her.

Listen, she said. I know right now the whole idea of sex doesn't make any sense. You probably hate thinking about it. But anytime you start feeling uncomfortable about having parents who make love, I want you to remember how uncomfortable it would be if you had parents who didn't want to anymore.

Amelia's, for instance, though she didn't say that.

She could picture the street corner where her mother's dancing studio used to be her big dream—where there was some kind of furniture repair shop now. You a dancer? a man had asked as her mother stood there that day, moving out the last of her things. Not really, she said. I used to be.

My mom was in *A Chorus Line* on Broadway, Wendy told him.

She saw her mother dancing then—not in the Pocahontas Dancing Studio anymore, but in the living room with Josh and Louie. The four of them swirling around the room while some corny record played, of polka music, or one of Josh's old R and B albums, or the soundtrack from *Crazy for You*. First Wendy danced with Josh, and her mother danced with Louie. Then her and Louie, her mother and Josh. Stop looking at the floor, Sissy, Louie told her. Young as he was, he was a better dancer than she was, a natural. Once he didn't have his mom to dance with anymore, Louie lost interest. Then the two of them would just watch their mother and Josh. He dipped her so low her hair fell back and grazed the floor. They were out of breath, and Josh's hair was going in a million directions, but they didn't stop.

She thought of the day, on one of their Sunday drives to the country, they'd stopped in a little town in upstate New York where there was a bed-and-breakfast for sale, and Josh had said, Suppose we left the city, came out here, and ran this place? The whole drive back home, they'd talked about how it would work. Wendy was going to have a dog, and stand at the front desk greeting the guests. Louie said he'd count the money.

What could I do? her mother had said. I'd be a terrible waitress.

You'd be the most important part of the whole operation, he said. You'd keep us happy.

She wanted to remember everything, and yet she couldn't bear to. Once you lowered your raft into the rapids, there was no steering anymore.

I never understood before, she heard Josh saying one night when Roberto had stopped by, how precious everything was.

# Eight

Wendy and Amelia were walking to the library past Engine Company 342, as usual. The bouquets of flowers that were always piled there were now starting to look a little withered and dried up. The pictures of the firemen and the flickering candles were gone.

He's not here anymore, said Amelia. They'd studied his photograph several times by now, so Wendy knew right off who Amelia was talking about—the handsome one she wanted to marry in Pennsylvania.

There was a fireman out in front, washing his truck. I guess nobody ever found Billy Flynn, huh? asked Amelia.

The fireman set down his cleaning rag. You knew Bill? he said.

You could say that, Amelia told him. As long as Wendy had known Amelia, she'd never gotten used to how her friend could do this stuff.

Well then, you know what a terrific guy he was. That Tuesday was his day off. He just drove down there to lend a hand. I've talked to three people now that told me they never would have got out of the towers that day if it wasn't for him.

That's the kind of person he was, said Amelia. One time, my cat got stuck in this place on our roof. He carried her down on his back.

Come on Amelia, Wendy said. She usually got a kick out of Amelia's made-up stories, but this one made her uncomfortable.

I suppose he had a girlfriend, Amelia said.

All the women loved Billy, the fireman said. But nobody in particular. You probably know how he was about his sisters, though. Not to mention his mom. Sun rose and set.

Tell me about it, said Amelia.

Wendy looked at her. Amelia, she said.

Listen, the fireman told her. They're having a Mass tonight at six-thirty at St. Catherine's in Queens. If you're interested, I'll give you the address.


In the old, normal days, Wendy could never have just gotten on a train to Queens and not gone home for dinner or called, but now she doubted Josh would notice. Amelia called her mom and said she'd been invited to Wendy's for dinner.

They took the train to 182nd Street and walked from there. This is my first funeral, said Amelia. I wish I had on something black.

Your jeans are navy blue, said Wendy. It's close enough.

They could tell from a block away they were getting near the church, there were that many people. Dozens of firemen in their uniforms, but regular people, too. They were gathered in bunches on the sidewalk in front of the church. Never saw a guy play center field with so much heart, Wendy heard someone say. He'd do anything to catch a ball. I was in love with him since second grade, a woman was saying. Changed my oil every three thousand miles like clockwork, whether I asked or not. Taking his grandmother to Mass. Sister's baby's baptism. Coaching Little League. Poker night. Always cried at this one Garth Brooks song. His dog. That old Camaro. Playing air guitar.

The seats were all taken, but they squeezed into the back of the church. In the front, there was a solid wall of flowers and a flag, but no coffin. The familiar photograph was there, but a bigger version. Also a baseball glove and a fireman's hat. Candles everywhere and the smell of incense.

After the organ music stopped, the priest came to the pulpit and started talking. Wendy had wondered if anything he said might apply to her situation, but it was all about Jesus, and she had a hard time concentrating.

There was a prayer. Most of the people in the church seemed to know all the words, but Wendy and Amelia didn't. They bowed their heads anyway, but Wendy opened her eyes and looked around the room after a few moments to see what everyone else was doing. A lot of people were on their knees. She could hear bits of words, people whispering softly. *Heavenly father. Eternal life.*

A woman came to the front. Her dress was bright green, not black, and she was pregnant—at the stage where it looks as if the baby could pop out any second. Wendy recognized her, even from a distance, as one of the women Billy Flynn had his arms around in the smaller photograph she and Amelia used to study in front of the fire station.

My little brother was the kind of person who would do anything for a friend, she said. Not just friends, either. Even someone he never met. Which is what he was doing on September eleventh.

Someone he helped that day told me that after he got her out, she said, Don't you think you'd better get away from the building yourself now? And he just smiled at her and said, Not while my buddies are still inside.

She started to cry then, and another woman, who was wearing a beautiful white dress and looked a lot like her, but not pregnant, took her arm.

We just want to say, she said. Our family. The loss. Ever get over it. Know he would have wanted. Life to the fullest.

There were others. A couple of firemen, with stories about fires they'd fought with Billy, nights at the station house, a pair of lucky boxer shorts one of his sisters had given him for Valentine's one time, a fishing trip.

A woman talked about her son, who had cerebral palsy but still got to play on Billy's Little League team. A man in a wheelchair told about how Billy used to deliver newspapers as a kid on 174th Street, and how he'd always stick a Tootsie Roll in with the Sunday edition.

His dad. There we were with five daughters, and then along came this boy. Well, you can imagine. All his life, all my son ever wanted was to be a fireman.

From the church Wendy could hear the faint, soft sound of people crying. When they started playing the Garth Brooks song, about a river, Amelia began crying, too.

There was another prayer, then another song, only this time everyone stood up to sing. "Morning Has Broken" was the name of the song. Wendy knew the tune from an old album her mom had from back in the day. Josh used to call it a remnant of her cornball phase, from before he taught her to love jazz, so she only put it on when he was off playing a gig. One time when her mother was listening to that album, Wendy had looked over at her and saw tears streaming down her face. Don't mind me, her mom said. Certain songs just bring back memories.

By the time they'd finished singing "Morning Has Broken," Wendy was crying, too. There was silence then, and people slowly began getting up. Only just when everyone thought the Mass was over, there was one last thing. At first, Wendy couldn't figure out where the voice was coming from. Then she understood it was a tape someone must have made, just fooling around, playing over the speakers at the front of the church. Even though she'd never heard his voice, she knew it had to be Billy.


He was telling a story about a fish he tried to catch one time. When the people in the church heard his voice, they stopped wherever they were. Some just stood there. Others sat back down.

This fish, he said. Let me tell you about this fish. This was a fish that, if he spotted your line in the water with a good-looking piece of bait on it, he'd take a nice hefty morsel, leave the hook, and tie what was left of that baby into a bow with a note that said, *Better luck next time.* This fish should've had a Ph.D. from Harvard, he was so smart. This fish could have pitched for the Yankees.


The story of the fish went on awhile. The thing was, Billy caught him.

Long story short, he said, when he finally got that sucker up in the boat and he was taking out the hook, Billy made the mistake of looking the fish in the eye.

This is a goddamn—excuse me, Mom, darned—striped bass we're talking about, mind you. Ugly sucker. But wouldn't you know it, he gives me this sorrowful look, like I'm his long-lost friend and how could I do this to him? And I'm thinking about how great he's going to taste, grilled over the coals with a little lemon. And a tall, cold one to wash it down. And then I look into those sorrowful eyes. His mouth is practically talking to me, and I can almost hear him say, One more chance, Bill. How about one more chance? Damn if I don't toss him back in the lake before I change my mind.

There was a sound of laughter on the tape. A couple of other people laughing, too, but the sound of Billy Flynn's laughter was the loudest, and it was filling the church, mixing with the sound of people crying, and other people laughing, or doing both. The laughing was still going when Wendy and Amelia made it out onto the street, where it was dark now.

I guess it's not all that likely we'll ever really live in Pennsylvania, Amelia said.

Probably not.

Somebody told me Pittsburgh is this really ugly city anyway, she said. They told me North Carolina is lots nicer.

Or Vermont.

Do you believe any of that stuff the priest was saying about him being in heaven? Amelia asked her.

I don't know. How about you?

I never did before, said Amelia. But it would be too awful to think somebody like Billy Flynn just turned into dust and that was it.

They walked back to the subway station. Ever since the eleventh, Wendy had hated going in the subway because of all the pictures of missing people there. They were mostly gone now, and the ones that were left, she didn't look at anymore.

Are you guys ever going to have some kind of service for your mom? Amelia asked her. Not to be pushy. But maybe it would make you feel better. Not a lot, but a little.

It seems like it might be a good idea, Wendy said. But I don't think my dad's ready for it.

Well, if you do have one, you should wear some really pretty dress like that sister had on today, Amelia said. Only not white. Blue maybe. That's a really good color on you. Or yellow.

They got on the train.

＊　　＊　　＊

Josh was sitting at the kitchen table when she came in the door. Not cooking or listening to music, and not looking at photograph albums, for once. His hair was standing up in all directions again. Do you have any idea how worried I was? he said.

He put his arms around her. The strength of him, maybe from all those years of lugging the bass around, always felt good. The other thing about the way Josh hugged you was how he didn't do it just for a second and then let go, like a lot of people. He stood there a long time holding on.

I was going crazy, he said. What in God's name were you doing?

I didn't think you'd notice, Wendy said.

Ten o'clock and my daughter's not home, and you don't think I'll notice? Who do you think you're living with here?

It's just that lately you haven't been paying much attention to things, Wendy said. When she said that, his face changed from angry to sad. She almost wished it would have stayed angry.

I know, Josh said. You're right. I'm sorry. Just never do something like that again, okay?


Poppy, Louie called out from the bedroom. Where are you? He wasn't really awake, it was just something he had started doing in the night. For a while there, he was calling out Mama, but for the last few weeks the only one he had called for was Josh.

I'm here, Lou-man, he said. You can go back to sleep.

Your brother was upset, too, Josh said. He didn't want to go to bed till you came home.

I'm sorry, she said. Everything's been— Whatever the word was to finish her sentence, she didn't know it.

They sat at the kitchen table, with the pair of salt and pepper shakers in the middle that her mom had bought at a yard sale. From the front, they looked like a bride and groom, with the bride all pretty and the groom handsome. But when you turned them around, the bride had turned all chubby and her hair was a mess, and the groom had a big beer belly sticking out over his pants.

So would you still love me if that was me? her mother had asked.

I'll get back to you on that, he told her.

Amelia and I went to Queens, she said.

Queens, huh? Happening place, Queens.

We went to a memorial service. There was this fireman.

I see. He didn't ask how they came to know a fireman. Stranger things had happened recently.

They played his favorite music. His family told stories about him. It was nice. Afterward, they had a tape of him talking. He sounded like a really great person. Even if you never met him before, you kind of felt like you knew him.

I know how that can be, Josh said. I've played at a few services like that over the years.

He fixed them each a mug of hot chocolate. He took the dispenser of whipped cream out of the fridge, that he always kept there. Not Reddi Wip, but the real thing. You do the honors, he said.

She squirted the whipped cream in their mugs. His first, then hers. Here, she said. She squirted an extra dollop on his chin. Let's see what you'd look like with a beard. Because you've practically got one now anyway.

He reached his hand to his face and licked off the extra. Think we could drown our sorrows in this stuff if we ate enough of it? he asked her.

She studied her spoon.

Not enough whipped cream in the world, huh, Wen?

Roberto called tonight, he said. He wants me to play a gig Tuesday.

So what did you say? she asked him. She hadn't seen him pick up his bass in close to a month, since her mother disappeared.

I said I had to check with you. I'd need you to pick Louie up from school.

I could do that, she said. I don't have anything special Tuesday.

Well then, okay, he said. Someone here had better start bringing home the bacon, right?

At this service, they sang a song from that old record Mom loved. Cat Stevens.

Nobody ever said your mother was perfect, he told her. It was the first time Wendy had heard Josh talk about her mother in the past tense.

It made me think about what music we would choose, she said. If we did something like that.

Not just yet, okay, Wen? he said. I just can't let myself believe she isn't coming home. If I did, I don't know how I'd go on living.

It scared Wendy hearing him talk like that. Wendy had been trying so hard to keep from feeling that way herself. It was as if she'd fallen overboard, and she'd been working at pulling herself back into the boat, and when she finally managed, it turned out the boat had a giant leak.

You want to just give up, he said when he was able to speak. Only you have to keep going. You still have to get up in the morning and pour the cereal in the bowls. You keep on breathing, whether you want to or not. Nobody's around to tell you how it's supposed to work. The usual rules just don't apply anymore.

He was still talking, but she wasn't even sure if it was to her.

When it started, he said, I thought nothing could be worse than those first days. And it wasn't only us, but everyone else you'd see, wandering around like they'd landed on a whole different planet. Instead of just dealing with your own heart getting ripped into pieces, wherever you looked you knew there were other people dealing with the same thing. You couldn't even be alone with it. Like you're out in the ocean and the undertow catches you and you start yelling for help, but then you look around, and all around you in the water for as far as you can see, there's all these other people flailing, too.

He sat there for a moment, shaking his head.

You keep getting up in the morning and knowing this will continue for maybe ten thousand more mornings. You wish you were the one who died. How much better would that be?

\*　　\*　　\*

She knew about that feeling he was talking about, that nothing made sense anymore. That you couldn't think of one hopeful thing.

The idea that he wanted to be dead, though, that part was new. At her worst moments these last six weeks she never wanted that. She wished the world would disappear plenty of times. She wished there was a place to be where she didn't have to think anymore, where the pictures stopped coming at her. But dead, never.

It was like this thing she and Amelia would get into sometimes where one of them would say, Whatever you do, just don't think about the word *philodendron*. Or the pimples on Seth Coglan's forehead. Or Mr. Hutchinson having sex with his wife. Then the one thing you could think of was that.

She didn't want to think about how it was for her mother after the plane hit. But she did. Especially at night.

One girl at school, Stacey, had made a scrapbook of photographs cut out from magazines, everything related to the Twin Towers. She'd shown it to Amelia one day at lunch. Someday I'll give this to my kids, she told Amelia. It's like being at the Kennedy assassination, or Columbine, but bigger.

When Wendy set her tray down on the table, Stacey put the scrapbook away fast, and kept saying, Oh my God, I'm such an idiot.

Catch you later, she said. I love your jeans, Wendy. Same ones she always wore.

Even though she didn't look at the scrapbook, Wendy had seen plenty of pictures. The worst ones being the people jumping out the windows. But others, too.

Sometimes she couldn't help studying them, looking for a flash of red—a glimpse, under some piece of rubble, of one of the uncomfortable red sandals. Other times, she pictured her mother sitting there at her desk, with the framed pictures of her, Josh, and Louie next to the phone, and the orange juice can pencil holder Wendy made back in first grade. Everything she didn't want to think about then, she did. Her mother looking out the window, seeing the plane heading for the building. The flames afterward and the smoke. People trying to find someone with a cell phone that worked so they could call their families one more time to say, I love you. Good-bye.

Now, in her bed, it was happening to Wendy again—the images she dreaded, flashing through her brain like the most horrible slide show ever.

Once, when she was little, and they were going past the Metropolitan Museum after the zoo, her mom had taken her hand and they'd walked to the top of the steps. The two of them tap-danced down, like Shirley Temple and Bojangles Robinson in *The Little Colonel*. They'd watched that movie so many times, her mother knew all the steps.

Now, whether she wanted to or not, she saw her mother's slim legs running down the stairs from the eighty-seventh floor. She would've taken off the sandals. Dancer's feet. Red nail polish.

Her mother would have been thinking about the three of them as she ran. Her, Josh and Louie. I was beaming you a message, she said to Wendy the day she had to give her John Adams report in front of the class. Did you feel it?

There in the blackness of her bedroom, Wendy went back over those minutes in homeroom that Tuesday morning, wondering if there had been a message coming in to her from her mother. If there was, she missed it.

All she could see was her mother running, her feet barely touching the steps, more flying than running, it seemed to Wendy now.

The thing about a dress like this is, the skirt always flaps open when you walk fast, her mom said that day in Macy's when she was trying it on in front of the three-way mirror. What I really need to do is sew a snap on the inside.

Never mind the skirt flapping open. Just get out of there, Wendy called out silently, when the picture played in her head of her mother flying down the stairs, and for the smallest moment, she let herself forget that it was already over. For that fraction of a second she saw her mother's flight from the building like some sports show Josh and Louie were watching live on TV, an event whose outcome remained in question, where you could call out instructions to the players.

*Just run!* she called out. *Never mind if you drop your shoes. Just get out of there.* As if she still could.

Whatever the actual moment was that did it—the building tumbling down, some explosion, or after, out on what used to be the plaza, some huge slab of metal crashing down like an actual lightning bolt—she didn't let herself imagine that part. When the picture started coming to her, she clicked ahead, so what she saw instead (this was awful, too) was her mother trapped some-place under all those tons of metal, calling out to them. Her mother, who didn't even like staying in an elevator too long—didn't like any space, she said, too small to dance in.

Maybe there was someone with her. One of those people whose face Wendy had studied on the flyers in Union Square. The grandma with the add-a-pearl bracelet with Kerri-Robert-Bernadette on it, whose navy blue pocketbook had a broken strap. The sisters who made pastries at Windows on the World, last seen carrying a crate of eggs off the elevator. The man in the business suit who was wearing Christmas Tree socks, even though it had only been Sep-tember, because he was always such a nut about Christmas.

Two animal crackers left in her purse. Half of one. Only the box.

Stop it, she told her brain. *Don't think about this.*

Another picture, but no better. The mountain of wrecked metal. The mountain of dust. The workers digging, and the cranes, the people with masks on, the burned-out fire engines and cars, the trucks hauling away load after load of rubble from the wasteland that, from what she could see on TV, never seemed to get any smaller, as if the more rubble they dug out, the more rose up from the center of the earth.

And somewhere under it all, her mother, but not in any form they'd rec-ognize her. Like something that would happen to a bad guy on Louie's Saturday-morning cartoons: Vaporized. Dust. Or less than dust. Somewhere lay the gold ring Josh had given her, with the words he'd had inscribed for her, *More Even Than Music*. Somewhere, her house keys that she was always losing, but really gone this time. Somewhere the gold compact her grand-mother had given her that she said would be Wendy's someday, but it wouldn't.

Somewhere in the pile under the shards of melted computers and tele-phones and file cabinets and computer discs and air conditioners and inter-com systems and water coolers and Xerox machines and red sandals and every other color of sandals and every other kind of shoe, under the shredded remains of business suits and briefcases and raincoats and car keys, gym bags and diaper bags and bag lunches and half-finished books, business cards and

charge cards and postcards and anniversary cards and maybe somewhere even
a love letter, or one word from one, or maybe just a question mark, somewhere beneath a million other pieces of paper and metal and plastic and—
her brain would settle on this image whether she wanted it to or not—pieces
of bone, too, flesh and bone, somewhere in there was a scrap of a scrap of a
photograph of her own self, under the Christmas tree, smiling, with her baby
brother in her arms.

At first when she heard the music, she actually supposed it was part of her
slide show, her dream was so real. It was the Cat Stevens song her mother
used to play all the time when Wendy was little, and the two of them would
take out the scarf collection and dance—but only when Josh wasn't around,
because he said that album was drek. Wendy could remember lying in her
same bed in this same dark room, but long ago, with the stereo set on Repeat
so that one song played over and over. She could see her mother sitting in
her nightgown with her glass of wine, or more likely spinning across the floor
as the record played, scratchy from so much use. "Oh very young," came the
voice. "You're only dancing on this earth for a short while."

She could hear the lyrics again now. Clear as she heard them, Wendy
thought it was her dream, but it was real, coming from the living room, and
for a second her heart exploded. For a moment there she thought her mother
must be back. How else could this music be playing?

Half-asleep, she got out of bed and made her way down the hall. There
were no lights on. The music was louder now, and it pulled her down the
hall, though there was another sound coming from the living room, the sound
of weeping.

She saw him then, though it was hard to make him out with no light
except for what came in through the window from the street. Josh, sitting on
the floor by the stereo, his head in his hands, his shoulders heaving.

# Nine

She had just started third grade when her mother told her she was going to have a baby. You said it wasn't in the cards, Wendy said. But it was after all. Wendy was so excited she could hardly stand it.

The baby wasn't coming till March. Wendy asked how many more days so often, her mother made her a chart to cross them off. When Wendy saw how many days were left to cross off, she said she could never wait that long. You'll see, her mom said. The time will fly.

She went to the doctor with her mother and Josh and listened to the heartbeat with the stethoscope, and when there was an ultrasound, she got to see that, too. Looks like you've got yourself a boy this time, Janet, the doctor said. How could he tell? Look, said her mother. That's his penis. Just a speck on the screen. *A brother.*

Later came the kicking, the bump on her mother's belly where one of his feet stuck out, different places at different times. This one's a gymnast, I think, her mother said. Either that or a tap dancer. She said maybe they should call him Jimmy Slyde, after her favorite tapper, but Josh wanted Louis, after his all-time-favorite jazz musician.

One time when they were reading together on the couch, her mother set the book down. Listen, she said. When Wendy laid her head against her mother's belly, she could hear a soft rhythmic sound, muffled but steady as breathing. He's got the hiccups, just like me, her mother said.

If Wendy wanted to carry the baby around, she'd better build up her muscles, her mother said. Most babies weigh seven pounds at least, she told Wendy. Could even be ten. When they bought a ham or a roasting chicken, a seven- or eight-pounder, she'd put it in Wendy's arms when they got home, and for a few minutes Wendy would haul the piece of meat around the apartment, imagining it was her brother. One time when Josh's mother was visiting from Florida and they explained what Wendy was doing, she said she didn't think that was a good idea. What if Wendy dropped the baby? Nine years old is just too young, she said.

Wendy studied Josh's face when his mother said that, to see what he'd say.

Wendy's no more likely to drop the baby than Jan or me, Mom, he told her. Less, probably.

Come to think of it, I'm not so sure you're a safe bet, he told her, grinning. Too much mah-jongg, not enough weight lifting. Then he had inspected her upper arms; she had on one of those golf jackets she liked to wear with the matching pants. Nope, he said. Our daughter's definitely got you beat.

Josh read every book about babies and childbirth. Sometime that winter he stopped taking gigs outside the city, in case her mother went into labor. It's still two months away, honey, she told him.

You just don't know what could happen, he said. I can't risk missing this.

Her mother went into labor on a Saturday night at the end of February. Josh woke Wendy up. Listen, he said. Your mom thinks you'd do best going to Kate's house, because it could be a long wait, but if you promise to be patient, you can come to the hospital with us.

She had her backpack ready, with markers and paper and a bunch of books and art supplies and the scarf she'd been making for her baby brother on her Knitting Nancy.

They'd chosen a special birthing center that let big sisters be at the birth. There may be some moments while he's getting born I'm going to look like I'm practically dying, her mother told her. That's just how it goes when babies are born. It might seem scary but it only lasts a little while and it's definitely worth the hard part.

They held her hands. Josh on one side, Wendy on the other. They did the breathing with her when the pains came. Josh rubbed her back. Wendy put ice chips in her mouth. When the midwife finally told her mother she could start pushing, the two of them made the sounds along with her like they were the ones having a baby.

I see the top of his head, Josh told her.

One more push, the doctor said.

After all the waiting, time finally flew. Once the top of his head pushed into the air, the rest of him—neck, shoulders, arms, belly, legs—whooshed like someone at a fair coming out the tunnel at the end of the flume ride. Josh's hands were there to catch him, his big bass player's fingers circling air first, then baby.

Her naked brother, with the cord still attached, was pink as the inside of a conch shell and covered with something white and creamy, and his fingers looked as if he'd been in the tub a long time. His face was bunched up and wrinkled, but he opened his eyes right away and when he did the person he looked at was Wendy. Josh was crying. After they cut the cord, he had handed the baby to a nurse, who wrapped him in a blanket so only one foot was showing, kicking just the way it had all those months they were waiting. From inside the blanket Wendy could hear the sound of crying, not the mouse squeaks she had expected, but a big, deep yell, like the kind of person that gets his way. Josh had his arms around her mother, kissing her. Our little boy, he said.

Louie. He even has lips like a trumpet player.

Hello, big sister, her mother said.

Later she gathered that people expected her not to like her baby brother. She'd be at the market with her mother, with Louie in his front-pack, and some woman from the neighborhood would stop to admire the baby. Then she'd look anxiously at Wendy and say something like, I bet he cries all the time and drives you crazy, right? Wendy wondered why the woman would think that. Actually, no, she said. When he cries, I comfort him.

Your baby brother probably doesn't know how to do anything, one woman said to her, as if this would cheer her up, as if she needed cheering up in the first place. Isn't it wonderful you know how to do so many grown-up things? All he can do is lie in his crib.

My brother can do tons of stuff, she said, and she bent over him in his infant carrier to get a quick whiff of his head. He can burp and sneeze, and if you rub this certain place on his belly, he laughs every time.

They were in the park having Popsicles when the mother of a boy Wendy sometimes played with when she was younger, Oliver, came over. She also had a baby in a front-pack who looked around the same age as Louie.

I bet someone's nose is just a little bit out of joint, am I right, Janet? she said. She spoke the words, as if she was talking in pig Latin.

All those years of having a certain person all to herself, and then along comes Mr. Buttinsky. I can sympathize, because you-know-who has been hell on wheels ever since the new baby came along. We're back to wetting our bed, if you follow me.

At first, Wendy thought her mother's friend meant she and her husband had started wetting the bed. Then she figured out that Oliver's mom was talking about Oliver. He had always been a little babyish, so she wasn't that surprised.

Times like these, her mother usually cut the conversation short. Wendy's just wonderful with her brother, she said. We'd be lost without her.

*Lost without her.* Her mom and Josh, wandering in a forest like Hansel and Gretel, but with Louie in the front-pack. Calling out, Wendy, Wendy, where are you? We're lost without you.

Of all the things I ever got to do, she told her mother on the way home, being a big sister is my favorite.


The first word Louie said was Mama. The next was Sissy, his name for her.

Louie worships the ground Wendy walks on, Josh told his sister, Andy. You should see him in his infant seat, propped up on the table, following her every move. When she's been gone all day, I take him to pick her up at school. A whole block before we get to the building, he's waving his arms and yelling, Sissy.

For a long time he was too young for Wendy to play with much, but he never minded when she dressed him up, even if it was in a girl outfit for one of her plays. Sometimes he was the king, propped up in his infant seat with a construction-paper crown she'd made him. Once he could crawl, she and Amelia pretended he was a monster, come to overtake the kingdom. Then he could talk and they gave him lines, but only a few. They taught him to say, Marry me, Your Highness and Cut off her head. They made him capes and swords and gave him a mustache once, made out of the cotton from a bottle of aspirin, stuck on with tape, and he hardly even cried when they took it off.

Wendy's mother could only take two months off work after Louie was born, so Josh was the one who took care of him most of the time, and it was always Josh who picked Wendy up at school. Sometimes he was Classroom Parent, when he could find someone—another mother—to watch Louie.

What do you mean, *another* mother? Wendy's mother said.

I spend so much time on the playground with the mothers, he said, sometimes I forget I'm actually a dad.

But a dad who knew all the different brands of disposable diapers and which ones had reusable tapes, a dad who could name every character on *Sesame Street*. If I ever get to the point where I know which Teletubby is which, do me a favor and shoot me, he said.

Nights when her mother came home, over the dinner Josh had made them, he'd fill her in on their day. A bird landed in front of Louie at the park and he made a tweeting sound, Josh told her. We climbed the ladder to the slide and went down, and he loved it. Wendy taught him how to clap. Josh taught Louie how to beat out a rhythm in four-four time. Then he was riding a tricycle. They went to see the dinosaurs at the Museum of Natural History, and Louie knew practically all the names.

Much more interesting than my day, her mother said. All I did was take dictation.

I love this, Josh told her. I can't believe I waited all this time to find out how great it was. Nobody ever told me.

Your dad, Wendy's teacher said one afternoon when he was picking her up. I never saw someone who was better with babies. Louie was walking a little by this point and Josh had taken him over to the cage to study the fifth-grade hamster.

He came into her class one time to teach them about the bass. Some people think the bass isn't that important, he said, because bass players don't play the melody. Then he played them a tape he had of Roberto and Omar doing "Brown Eyed Girl," but without the bass line. Then he put the tape on again, only this time he picked up his bass and played along.

Which one sounds better? he asked them. Everyone agreed it was the one with him playing. After that he let everyone in her class try making notes on the bass, and he didn't even say anything when one boy, Jason, got paste on the wood. Before he left, they all said they were going to be bass players when they grew up.

Times like that, Wendy never said he wasn't really her father. Same as she never called Louie her half brother. Somebody else did now and then—Aunt Pam, for instance. The word had an unfriendly, tightfisted sound to it, like a person who's splitting the cost of a candy bar right down to the penny. Wendy had to ask her mother what that meant. Half a brother.

Some people have this crazy idea that you have to have come from the same parents to be brother and sister, her mother said. But we know all that matters is we're in the same family now.

So what would happen if your mom and Josh ever got a divorce? Amelia asked her one time. Who would get Louie?

I would, Wendy said. But anyway, she wasn't worried. Anybody could tell her mom and Josh were going to be together always.

# Ten

We need to do something for Halloween, Amelia said. The boys are going to ask all those dumb girls like Robbie to the dance, and we'll end up standing around or going to the water fountain every three minutes.

The year before, in seventh grade, they were dice, and in sixth grade they were Spice Girls, but what can you expect out of sixth graders?

A million girls were going to be Britney Spears, but Amelia said that was just to have an excuse to get around the dress code and show their belly button. Wendy wouldn't have wanted to show hers anyway, particularly now, on account of all the ice cream she'd been eating.

You are not one bit fat, Amelia said. You're just going to be more of the Jennifer Lopez type, and I'm more Jennifer Love Hewitt.

So we could be them, Wendy said. Just joking.

You wait, Amelia told her. In another couple years when your chest evens up and I'm still all flat, I'll be dying of envy. Wendy still had her problem with one breast developing faster than the other. Amelia was the only one she told.

Ricky Pasiello had planned to have a Halloween party and invite a bunch of people from their class to some club his dad belonged to, and then go home and have a haunted house, but his parents decided it wasn't a good year for that, so instead he was just taking a few kids to see *Scream 3* and then have them sleep over at his house.

Like we would ever have been invited to the party anyway, Wendy told Amelia.

You never know, Amelia said. Actually, I think Ricky likes you. He just pretends not to notice us, but really he does.

He's a very good actor, Wendy said.

Hallie Owens said she was spending Halloween night collecting money for the Red Cross. Buddy Campion said he was going to be Osama bin Laden, and Mrs. Volt said, Inappropriate, Buddy. She jerked her head in the direction of Wendy, as if she was trying to send him a subtle message.

We could all go to *Rocky Horror Picture Show* in the Village and dress up like the characters, Seth said. Seth was one of those people who knew every single word in the movie and said them along with the characters.

We have to take Wendy's little brother trick-or-treating and then baby-sit, Amelia told him, because Seth was getting on their nerves. But once she said that, it was their plan.

As much as he loved dressing up, Wendy wasn't sure if Louie would be into Halloween this year, but he was. Every day when he came home from preschool, he'd be talking about what he wanted to be, only it kept changing. First a karate guy. Then a wizard. Then the Pokey Little Puppy. Then a robot. Then a karate guy again.

The amazing thing is, the actual night of the thirty-first is the full moon, Amelia said. That makes the whole thing ten times as intense.

Louie had been sitting in the kitchen with them, coloring, when they were discussing it. Halloween's magic, right? he asked her.

Kind of, Wendy said. Some people think strange things happen that night. But you don't have to be scared. We'll be with you the whole time.

Are ghosts real? he said.

I never saw one, Wendy told him.

Some kids in my class said ghosts are real.

Maybe if you went to a cemetery, Amelia told him. But you won't have to worry here.

Josh had a gig that night. It was only the second time since her mother disappeared that someone had called to have him play at a party, and at first he wasn't going to take the job.

Halloween's a crazy-enough night on a regular year, he said.

You should go, Wendy told him. Amelia and I will stay with Louie, and we won't go anyplace except around the neighborhood.

No subways, he said. Not the parade in the Village.

We'll rent a couple of movies, that's all, Wendy said. We won't even put them on till Louie's in bed.

Amelia wanted to see *Carrie,* and *Rosemary's Baby.* My mom says those are classics, she said.

Louie had gone back to the robot idea. They had put together a robot costume for him with a bunch of cardboard boxes spray-painted silver and some flexible air-conditioning duct tubes Amelia found in the basement of her building to go over his arms, but when they put the colander on his head, he started to cry. He said he didn't want to be a robot after all.

With all the costumes in his collection—his wizard suit and his cowboy chaps and his tiger tail and his golden cape and his pirate hook hand and the little checked suit their mother had got him one time at the Goodwill that they called his Fred Astaire get-up—when it got to the actual time to dress up, Louie couldn't decide on anything. In the end they put on his Spiderman pajamas, only with shoes on and a jacket, because it was starting to get chilly.

He didn't want to wear the jacket. If all anyone sees is my pajama bottoms, they won't even know I'm Spidey, he told her.

You can tell them, Wendy said. Plus, you can act like you're crawling up walls.

How?

Pretend.

Wendy and Amelia decided to put on witch costumes for taking him around. Amelia's was a black leotard with a cape she'd found at the Salvation Army. Wendy had planned to wear a long black dress she'd gotten for her aunt Andy's graduation party for becoming a paralegal last year, but when she tried it on that afternoon, it was too small.

I bet there'd be something in your mother's closet, Amelia said.

\*　　\*　　\*

Wendy hadn't been in her mother's room since the day it happened. She figured she had to go there sometime.

Louie was watching a special, *Charlie Brown and the Great Pumpkin*. Amelia opened the door.

Her mother used to give Josh a hard time about the way, when he took his pants off, he'd leave everything on the floor, like someone who'd melted, and all that was left of him were these two scrunched-up pants legs with a couple of socks coming out the bottom and a pair of boxer shorts inside.

Now there were many days' worth of dirty clothes scattered on the floor. On the side of the bed where he slept, the sheets were bunched up and wrinkled, and a half dozen empty glasses lay on the floor by the bed.

The bureau though, with her mother's makeup and the photographs in their silver frames, was just the same as always. Her mom's earring tree. The picture of her mom and Josh on their honeymoon in New Orleans, standing in front of the Louis Armstrong statue. A framed drawing Wendy had made for Mother's Day last year in Japanese animation style—a picture of this superhero mother in a hot-pink jumpsuit with thunderbolts up the sides. A set of belly-dancer castanets Josh had given her one year, that she actually learned how to use, and an ankle bracelet.

She opened the door to her mother's side of the closet. Amelia was standing next to her.

Remember, Amelia said, they're just clothes.

Her mom had always said she liked dress-ups better than regular clothes. She had to have a few of those for work, naturally—her gray suit, and a blue one that Josh said made her look like a flight attendant. She had one black skirt and a couple of dresses she called the Secretary Collection, but the rest of the closet was full of her other stuff, from before she got her job, or for times when she and Josh went out on the town.

Wendy fingered them one by one: her gypsy skirt, her *West Side Story* dress and a leopard skin–print cat suit and a Chinese silk jacket trimmed with fur. The yellow dress she'd worn to the wedding where she met Josh. She had an actual tutu someone had given her, bought at a fund-raiser for the New York City Ballet.

Nobody else's mother had things like these in her closet: a pair of silver pants with a matching silver belt, that she wore with a gold leotard; a skirt made out of a fabric that looked like fish scales; an actual rhinestone crown— and she wore it one time, too. There was the black dress Wendy remembered, full length, with just the right sleeves for a witch, the kind that hang down like dripping icicles.

Your mom had the coolest stuff, Amelia said.

Wendy slid the dress off the hanger and pulled her shirt over her head. She stepped out of her pants. Even with a friend like Amelia, she pulled in her stomach and held the front of the dress against her unevenly filled bra.

Look at this, Amelia said, studying the cosmetics. White powder. We could make ourselves really pale and put on dark lipstick. Wendy could hear Lucy's voice lecturing Linus in the other room. She pulled the black dress over her head and slid her arms into the sleeves.


Wendy never knew when it was going to hit her—some little thing that sucked her down into the undertow. It happened now, standing in her parents' bedroom in her underwear, the dress halfway over her. She felt her throat tighten, and the bones in her knees seemed to go soft, and when she tried to breathe, the air seemed to sting.

She felt dizzy. She wondered if this was how it felt to be drunk. She thought she might drop to the floor. She heard a voice say Mom before she realized the voice was hers. She was on her knees, with her head still buried in the fabric of the dress.

It was the perfume that had hit her. Months since her mother had put on this dress, her scent clung to the fabric still. For a moment, it was as if she was there in the room. Wendy wished she could stay in this spot forever, just breathing her in.


One good thing about Amelia was how she understood moments like this, and didn't try to fix everything. She kept rummaging in the closet, commenting on the clothes, as if there was nothing strange about her friend lying there on the closet floor with her face buried in the fabric.

I've got a dress like that, too, she said finally. I can never find the head hole.

Wendy pulled the dress the rest of the way on. Her breathing was coming evenly again, though there were still tears in her eyes.

She looked at herself in the mirror. Her hair had gotten longer in the last month, and in the shadowy room, standing among the piles of dirty clothes, she actually did look like a witch. She raised her arms out to the sides and let the fabric hang down.

And as for you, my little pretty, she said. As suddenly as the wave of grief had hit her this time, it had passed over. She could hear her brother calling her.

My show's over, he said from the doorway. Can we go trick-or-treating now?

Before they went back in the living room, Wendy reached for the bottle of aftershave on Josh's bureau and patted some on her neck and arms. If you were going to smell like one of your parents, it was better to smell like the one who wasn't dead.


Louie was sitting by the door with his jacket on and his goody bag in his hands. They had safety-pinned the cape of his Spiderman pajamas on the back of his parka to make his character a little more recognizable.

Out on the street, things were a lot quieter than on other Halloweens. They passed a couple of ghosts, a Power Ranger, and one princess, but nobody's costume looked scary, and fewer decorations were up. The moon had not yet risen, but the night was clear, and though the air felt cool, it was a good night for trick-or-treating.

They went to the building next door, where Wendy knew the doorman.

Who do we have here? he said to Louie. A pirate?

I'm Spiderman, Louie told him.

They took the elevator to the top. We can work our way down the stairs, Amelia said, and then she stopped herself. Oh my God, she said. I wasn't thinking.

It's okay, said Wendy. That's what we always do.

They went to four apartments on the twelfth floor, then walked to the eleventh. One woman gave them little American flags instead of candy, and a man in the other apartment told them to be careful as he sprinkled Hershey Kisses in their bags.

These are totally safe, but why should you trust me? he said. For all you know, I could have loaded them with anthrax.

At the tenth floor, they got mini Almond Joy bars and Tootsie Roll pops. On the ninth, more American flags. Louie was dragging.

Other years, when she and her mom and Josh had taken him around, they couldn't get him to go home, he was so into it. Now they had to remind him to say Trick or treat.

At the eighth floor, he asked if they could go home now. Sure, Louie, Wendy said. But we hardly did any trick-or-treating.

I thought it was going to be magic, he said. I thought ghosts would come.

I told you we didn't need to worry about ghosts, Louie, she said.

She looked at him, bundled in his jacket, with the bottoms of his pajamas stuck into the tops of his work boots and one side of his cape drooping down in back where the safety pin had come undone. He was not sucking his thumb, but probably only because he didn't have his hands free.

I wanted there to be ghosts, he said.


After they got him into bed, they fixed a pot of hot chocolate. I always wanted to see this movie, Wendy said. She was looking at the picture of Carrie in her prom dress on the front of the box. The actress playing her had blood dripping down her face and her hair was a mess, but Wendy was thinking how thin she was and wishing she could look that way.

I brought over something else for us to do first, Amelia said. I was saving it for a surprise.

She reached into the shopping bag she'd brought over to carry her costume. She pulled out a beat-up box. My mom's old Ouija board, she said. She's had this since way back when she was our age.

Amelia set it on the table. My mom said this board actually told her one time that she was going to live in New York and have a daughter with brown hair. Not only that, but this other time when she was having a sleepover with a friend of hers, the friend's dead grandmother sent her all these messages about how she needed to break up with her boyfriend because he wasn't a safe person to be around, and the next year he got in a car accident and died. She probably would have been killed, too, if they hadn't broken up. Either that or permanently paralyzed.

Wendy looked at the board, the rows of letters and the little plastic piece in the middle that was supposed to move around all by itself and spell out the messages. Or not all by itself. Controlled by spirits.

You never know how strong the power will be, but sometimes you can actually talk to the dead, Amelia said. If you want to.

At first, they did easy things. Are you a good spirit or an evil one?

Good.

How are you feeling tonight?

Fine.

How old do you think we are?

The plastic piece wobbled between thirteen and fourteen, but Amelia's birthday was just one month away and Wendy's soon after, so that made sense.

Spirit, we would like to contact a person my friend has been worried about tonight, if possible. We'd like to know how she is.

Are you sure?

Amelia looked at Wendy.

Yes.

The two of them held hands tightly over the plastic piece for a moment before asking the question. You should do it, Amelia told her.

I am looking for a lost parent, she said. She didn't know why, but she had a hard time saying the word *mother*.

There's someone I need to reach, she said. Someone who went away.

Sure you want to hear? Not always good news.

I know.

Outside the window, the moon had risen over the city. A siren sounded. In the apartment across the way, a man and a woman were watching television dressed in monster suits, but without the masks. The candle flickered from inside the smiling face of Josh and Louie's jack-o'-lantern, making an orange glow, and from the kitchen came the smell of chocolate.

It would be better knowing than wondering.

Louie called from the bedroom, Sissy, where are you?

I'm right here, Louie, she said. You can go back to sleep.

Is Halloween over?

Soon, Louie.

It's just us here?

Just us and Amelia.

She waited a minute to see if he'd go back to sleep. Silence. She turned back to the Ouija board.

I hope we didn't lose them, Amelia said. Sometimes it's a problem when the spirits get interrupted.

They closed their eyes and put their hands back on the game piece.

Are you there? Amelia asked.


They heard a knock at the door. Trick or treat, the voice called out. She wasn't expecting anyone, but the voice sounded familiar in a way, though she couldn't place it.

Even though Josh had told them never to do this, they opened the door. Her father stood there. Garrett.

# Eleven

They offered him hot chocolate. He said he'd been traveling all day from California. Major flight delays on account of all the airport security. I wanted to get here way earlier and take you out to dinner, he said.

That's okay, she told him. We were out trick-or-treating before anyway. Taking my little brother.

Oh, right, Garrett said. What's his name again?

Louie. Like Armstrong. This is Amelia.

I've heard a lot about you, Amelia said. She sounded like her mother.

So where's the guy? Josh.

He's working tonight. We're baby-sitting.

Good for you, he said. I remember when you were little how tough it was coming up with a good sitter. Your mother and I would want to go out to a party or something, but we never found anyone, besides her friend Kate, she felt she could trust you with. So I'd end up going alone. That probably wasn't a very smart idea, looking back.

How are things in California? Amelia said. I always wanted to go there.

She sounded like Rosie O'Donnell interviewing some celebrity sitting on the couch next to her.

Well, maybe you will, he said. Now that you'll have a girlfriend living there.

Wendy didn't know what he meant. Every time we make this, I always burn my tongue, she said, setting down her hot chocolate. I always want a sip before it cools down. When Josh fixes it for us, he puts real whipped cream in.

She had started to say my dad instead of Josh, but she stopped herself. Just saying his name, though, gave her a strange tugging sense of missing him. She pictured him off at the party in the city in his rumpled performing suit, bent over his instrument, plucking out the bass line of "I Get a Kick out of You" that nobody knew was so important unless the notes weren't there anymore. When he said good-bye that afternoon, he looked worried. I shouldn't have said yes to this gig, he said.

What I meant is, I want to take Wendy home with me, Garrett said. To California. Strangely enough, he was talking to Amelia, rather than to her.

I've given it a lot of thought. Still to Amelia. As if she was in charge. For a second, Wendy wondered who this person was—with her name—that her father was telling Amelia about.

What do you mean? she asked.

I've been thinking it would be good if you came to live with me now. Under the circumstances.

I live here, Wendy told him.

You have up till now. Hardly anybody stays in the same state their whole life anymore. When I was a kid, we moved all over with my dad's company. We didn't move up to the Greenwich house till after the divorce.

I have school, she said. My friends are here. My little brother.

We'd think of it as a trial period, he said. You could see how you like it.

He reached over to touch her arm, just barely.

I know it's a shock, he said. You've been through a lot. You're holding up better than a lot of people would; I can see that. But this is the kind of time when it's good to have your dad around.

He ran a hand through his hair, but differently from how Josh would.

Garrett's hair was longer and fine-textured, not the brushy kind that stood up all over the place. It was mostly gray and tied in a ponytail. Even with his lined face, he was still handsome.

I'm sure that's what your mother would have done if you'd been living with me and something happened where I wasn't around anymore.

Wendy knew she never would have been living with him in the first place. Not if her mother was there.

I have Josh, she said. We're managing all right.

Or maybe they weren't, but she couldn't see how moving to California would make it better.

Amelia was twisting her hair while they were talking. This is intense, she said. Maybe I shouldn't be here.

I can see why you and Wendy are such good friends, he told her. You're a really perceptive person.

I can just go home, said Amelia. When it's late like this, my parents like me to take a cab. She dug into her pocket and took out a ten-dollar bill.

We were having a sleepover, said Wendy. We were going to watch a movie.

Amelia could come out too, to visit, he said. We could go camping at Yosemite.

Listen, Wendy told him after Amelia had left the room. I might like to come visit sometime. But I can't move away anyplace. I live here. Not to mention the fact that Josh would never let me.

Don't get me wrong, Garrett said. I'm sure he's a great guy, and it was probably really good for you having the kind of stable setup you get when there's two parents and a little half brother. But the situation's different now.

He's just a plain brother, she said. Not half anything.

He looked around the room. She wondered if he was looking for the painting of her mother naked that he made when they were young, but nothing would be familiar to him here. Louie's bike with the training wheels, that Josh had just started teaching him to ride Labor Day weekend, and then stopped. The electric bass he sometimes fooled around on. The art table with Wendy's colored pencils and the wooden mannequin Josh and her mother gave her for her birthday the year before to help her with her action drawings, and the mannequin legs she and her mother had gotten out of the trash, still holding a plant, and dressed in bright green patterned tights. Her clarinet and the music stand. Louie's trucks.

Your grandmother talked to a lawyer, he said. The air in the room seemed to change when he said it.

I'd never get into all that legal bullshit, but if we did, your stepfather wouldn't have a leg to stand on. All that would happen is he'd spend a lot of money for nothing, because if I know your grandmother, she wouldn't quit. You should have seen what she was like when she took my father to court, when I was your age.

It's not like Josh would be stopping me from leaving, she said. I'd be stopping myself. I don't want to move away. More than any other moment since the day everything changed, she wanted her mother there.

He must have seen the look on her face, because he got up from where he'd been sitting and sat next to her on the couch. If it was Josh, he'd have put his arms around her, but Garrett reached out his two hands, one on each side of her head, and held them there.

I know this is hard for you, he said. The thing is, you're fourteen years old. You're confused. The world looks crazy to you at the moment.

He still had her age wrong. But the rest, she could believe.

All my things are here, she said. I'm in the middle of a bunch of projects at school. I'm in band.

I bet Josh will ship out your things once we get back to California, he said. I've heard they have schools out west, too.

Amelia, she said. She's my best friend.

He did put his arms around her then. He had long arms, and his chest was a lot thinner than Josh's, so she could feel where his rib bones were. He smelled like the inside of a store she and Amelia went in sometimes where they sold crystals and dreamcatchers.

Josh sounds like a great guy, he said. But the fact is, he's probably having a hard time managing to take care of things, with Louie and his job and everything. He'd never say it, but it'll be a big load off him, too, if you come home with me.

She thought about what she'd heard Josh tell his sister on the phone the other day, and what he'd said that night when she came home from Billy Flynn's funeral—the hollow, throwing-up feeling she'd gotten, listening to his words, and realizing he felt just as lost as she did. Maybe more so.

I honestly don't know how I'm going to take care of these kids, he'd told his sister. It's just too much.

He'd told Wendy, that night, he wished he was the one who died. You keep on breathing, he told her. Whether you want to or not.

She was tired all of a sudden, and her head felt fuzzy. She knew she didn't want to go away, but she was having a harder time remembering why it wouldn't be a good idea. Sometimes, she knew from living with Louie, parents did know best what their child needed, more than the child did. She felt dizzy and a little sick. Mostly what she wanted was to go to bed.

You were probably too young to remember, he said softly. But your mother and I had a lot of really good times, too. Those first few years after we met. I wouldn't trade them.

She just went off to work that day like a regular morning, Wendy said quietly. We kept thinking she'd call.

The waiting must've been hell, he said. I wish I'd been here.

I was late for school that morning. I didn't even say good-bye.

Then she said the other part, that she hadn't spoken out loud the whole time. How she'd said she wished her mother would drop dead. How they'd been arguing about her going to California to see him. That's what she was telling her mother she wanted, and now she could do it, but she didn't want to anymore.

It's okay, he said. She knew you loved her. Kids say all kinds of terrible things to their parents. You should have heard some of the things I said to my mother as a kid. Not just as a kid, either. Last week, as a matter of fact.

I never thought anything could happen like this, Wendy said. Nothing can ever be okay again in my whole life.

He stroked her hair and pressed her head against him, and though she didn't want to, she began to cry.

You think that now, he said. But it will get better. California will be good for you.

She thought about the photograph he'd sent her, that she kept tucked in her binder. The morning glories. The cactus plants. The puppy.

I know how hard everything is for you right now, he said. You're going to have to trust me on this. I'll do everything I can to make this work out.

It would just be a trial period, right? she said. I could always come home again if I wanted.

You could, he said. But you might also end up feeling like you were home, with me.

There's Louie, she said.

He's still got his dad, Garrett told her. His real dad. It's different for him. Wendy looked at him squarely then. His blue eyes, which she saw for the first time resembled hers.

I'm your father, he said. I'm the one real parent you have left. You need to be with me now.

What's your dog's name? she asked him.

Shiva, he said.


She didn't hear Josh come in, but in the morning when she got up he was already up and making breakfast. Waffles.

How did it go last night? she asked.

Fine. How did you and your brother make out trick-or-treating?

At the last minute, he didn't want to wear the robot suit, she told him. He went as Spiderman. After all that talk, he wasn't really into it. We were home by seven-fifteen.

Sometimes that's what happens. Too much buildup.

Amelia brought over movies, but we didn't get to them after all. She decided to take a taxi home.

He looked surprised. You two have a falling-out?

It wasn't that, she said. She had been trying to think of how to tell him. She had this idea maybe she should write it on a piece of paper and hand it to him. But she got the words out.

My father came over.

From California? Just showed up?

His flight was delayed. He wanted to get here earlier.

You knew about this before?

It was a surprise.

He turned his back and dipped the measuring scoop into the flour bin. Two cups. Slowly, he reached into the fridge for the maple syrup and set it on the table. Until they met Josh, her mother always bought Aunt Jemima. I have so much to teach you, he told her. This could take years.

So, was it good to see him? I assume he's coming back to see you some more while he's out here? You two getting together after school? There was a tightness to his voice.

He said he wants to take me back to California, she said. My grandmother talked to a lawyer.

And how do you feel about that?

She was quiet. She thought about what Garrett had said, that Josh had more going on than he could handle right now.

I don't know, she said. I told him I'd miss you and Louie.

And don't you imagine we'd miss you? His voice caught. We've still got a family here. Even if one person's missing.

I don't know what to do, she said. I don't want to go, but he said he knew what was best for me. He said he's the one parent I have left.

The one parent, huh? What do you call me?

He had sifted the flour so it formed a mountain in the familiar Fiesta Ware bowl. Now he was measuring the baking powder. Now he was sprinkling in the salt. He opened the refrigerator and took out two eggs and the carton of milk, that he set on the counter. He turned around and faced her.

He stood there, looking at the eggs—one in each hand—as if he couldn't remember how they got there or what he was supposed to do with them. The way he looked at the eggs, they might have been meteorites that fell out of the sky, or the ball of dirt and fur and microscopic crumbs of bone he'd dug out of one of Louie's pockets that time, after one of their hikes in the country, that turned out to be owl droppings. He looked that bewildered.

What do you call me? he asked again.

I call you Josh.

# Twelve

Amelia was waiting for her at her locker. I can't believe he just showed up like that, she said. Just when we were asking the Ouija board for a message. Your dad is the coolest person.

Josh said he should have called first. He said a considerate person doesn't just knock at your door at nine-thirty, after you haven't seen him for three years, and say, Hello, I'm taking you to California now.

California, said Amelia. You are so lucky.

What am I supposed to do without you? Wendy said. You're my one real friend.

It's not like I'm exactly thrilled, either, Amelia said. I'm just trying to think what's best for you. My mom said it might be a good thing for you to get a change of scene.

What about school? I'd have to start in at a whole new place in the middle of the term. I wouldn't know anyone.

You could create a whole new identity, Amelia said. You might even be popular.

The other thing is my brother, she said. He's having a hard enough time dealing with our mom.

You know little kids, Amelia said. One minute they're crying because their truck broke, and the next thing you know they're eating a Popsicle.

It's not like this would have to be forever, either, Amelia said. You could go out there and see how you like it. You could think of it as a getaway. Like when my mom goes to a spa.

Wendy could use a getaway. She could be anyone she wanted in California. Nobody would have to know anything. Not even that she came from New York, or what happened to her mother. She wouldn't have to go through every day with people giving her their sympathetic looks. As far as they were concerned, her mother could be off on a business trip. On tour with Madonna, one of the dancers on the Drowned World Tour. And then there was the other part she had been thinking about. How much easier it would be for Josh without her. It was different for Louie. Josh was Louie's real father. Same way Garrett was hers.

I'd probably come back at Christmas, she said. If not before.

And we'd talk on the phone. I'd make my parents give me a ticket out there to see you, February vacation. If you're still there.

I might look totally different by then, Wendy said. She was thinking that in California she'd probably get very thin, like Sissy Spacek in *Carrie,* eating all the organic vegetables in Garrett's garden. She might streak her hair.

So when would you leave? Amelia asked.

Two days, she said. Longer than that and she might change her mind.


Louie, she said. He was curled up under the blue afghan with his wings strapped over his shoulders. *Mister Rogers* was on—one of the few programs they still let him watch. He was holding Pablo and sucking his thumb, with the ribbon in his ear, like always. Nobody was trying to get him to stop these days.

I need to talk to you, Louie, she said. Maybe we should turn off your show.

I got to see how it turns out, he said.

It's kind of important, she said. But I guess you can keep the TV on.

She wrapped one arm around his back so he could snuggle in closer. He leaned against her shoulder, still sucking hard on the thumb. She bent down and smelled the top of his head, the way she had when he was younger. It was fainter now, but he still had that sweet baby smell that had nothing to do with any brand of shampoo.

I'm going away for a while, Louie, she said. I'm taking a trip on an airplane.

No, he said. You'll crash.

They don't let that happen anymore. They're much more careful now. They only let good people get on the planes.

When are you coming home?

I'm not sure. I might have to be gone awhile.

Will you bring me a treat?

Sure. She should have been happy that he seemed to be taking it okay, but his not minding that much made her sad.

So it's just going to be you and Poppy here for a while, she said. But I'll call you up, okay?

Maybe she was imagining, but she thought she could feel his body stiffen. His head shifted toward the screen, where Mister Rogers was explaining how to sharpen pencils. Louie hadn't taken his eyes off the TV set the whole time she'd been talking with him, but now more than ever his gaze stayed locked to the screen.

Okay, he said, not really listening.

You know you're my only brother in the whole world, right? she said. And who's your only sister?

You. They'd been through this before.

And even if I'm not around, you know how much I love you, right?

Yup.

I guess I'll go pack now, she told him.

He didn't say anything. From where she stood in the doorway now, she could see him still sitting there, just the back of his head, hair slightly matted, with one of Pablo's ears draped over his shoulder like one of her mother's boas and his feet, in their Ernie slippers, curled under him. She could see from the back of his neck that he needed a haircut. Scraggy curls hung over the collar of the sweatshirt he made them put on him every day, even though he'd outgrown it, that their mother gave him.

Louie sat perfectly still on the couch, facing the television screen. The soft, lulling voice of Mister Rogers talking about something—she didn't even know what. Nothing moving except the two fingers of the hand he used to twirl the tip of frayed blue ribbon in his small pink ear.


Kate called.

Josh told me what your father did, she said. I won't even call him your father. Garrett. Because as far as I'm concerned, your real father's Josh.

It's okay, Kate, Wendy said. I have things worked out. I'm just trying it out for a little while.

The same tired feeling she'd had the night before was back. She didn't feel like talking about it. Better just to go.

And what about Louie? asked Kate. How's he supposed to deal with losing his mother first, then his sister?

When I told him he didn't seem all that upset.

He doesn't understand, Kate said. He thinks it's like when his dad goes on some gig upstate.

I'll come back and visit soon. Or just come back, probably.

I just can't believe you're actually letting Garrett do this, she said. I don't want to bad-mouth him, but he was never the most responsible person.

Maybe he's changed, Wendy said. He said he loved my mom a lot. He said he knew he made mistakes.

Oh, great. What a breakthrough, said Kate.

I don't mean to be rude, Wendy told her. But I should go pack.

You know what your mother would do if she knew? Kate said. Then, before she knew what she was saying: She'd die.


Wendy was in her room packing when Josh came in.

Listen, he said. I've been trying all day to figure out what a person's supposed to do in a situation like this. Not a person. Me. I want to do the right thing here.

You do everything fine, she said. You practically always do the right thing.

I used to think that, he said. Everything in my life made total sense for the longest time. I didn't ever have to sit and ask myself what to do about the people I loved. I just knew, like breathing.

She had been taking T-shirts out of her drawers when he came in. When Josh went on road trips, he brought her back shirts with corny sayings on them. Now he picked up one of them, from some diner in Syracuse.

I remember that night perfectly, he said. We finished playing just after midnight and stopped in for burgers. I called your mother from the pay phone and sang her this old Fats Waller number. "Your Feet's Too Big."

She had really small feet, Wendy said.

I know.

She was taking papers out of her desk. A stack of photographs from last summer. A list she and Amelia made one time of every type of ice-cream flavor they'd ever tasted. A report she'd written back in fourth grade on polar bears, her favorite stop at the Central Park Zoo. Her first clarinet songbook. A tally she and Amelia had kept from second grade through sometime in sixth, where they made an X every time they cracked an egg, making cookies.

Now, though, he said, I never know anymore. It's not something you're prepared for, having a person you thought you'd be spending the next fifty years with walk out the door and never come back.

You thought you had this great life, and in one minute the whole thing disappears. It's not even like you did anything wrong that you can blame yourself about. It's this totally random thing that happens, but once it does, you wonder what any of it actually meant. If something like this could happen, you wonder about everything else. It isn't just now that looks so screwed up; it's everything.

You start wondering if anything that you thought was real actually was, or if the whole thing was all some kind of a joke. Why it makes sense caring about anything else ever again. You don't know what to do.

I don't know what I'm supposed to do now, either, she said. I guess I figured going to California would be different anyway. I already know what it's like here, and it's not very good.

I keep thinking maybe I'm supposed to stop you, he said. I try to imagine what your mother would have me do. If it was me the way I'm used to being, I'd pile you guys into the car and we'd just start driving someplace. Go up to New Hampshire and spend a few days hiking in the White Mountains or going on amusement park rides. Play about a million holes of miniature golf, till I was sure he was gone.

Only me the way I used to be, in the life we used to have, this never would have come up in the first place. And me now, I just don't feel that sure I can do any better than some guy in California who hasn't dropped in for a visit in three years. He may be a screwup, but who's to say I'm any better, staring out the window, trying to decide if I should go to the grocery store or back to bed?

I would tell you you can't go with him. I would tell you it breaks my heart to see you walk out the door, not to mention what it could do to your brother. But everyone here is heartbroken anyway. Maybe your best shot is getting out of here. Maybe the shame of it is that there isn't some guy from California or Maine or South Dakota or God knows where to come along and take your brother away, too.

She didn't want to look at him. Wendy hadn't realized it until then, but up until that moment, she had believed that Josh would stop her from leaving. She might tell her teachers she was going away, and take her clothes out of the closet and pack them into suitcases, pack up her drawing pencils, take her Madonna poster down off the wall. She might even get as far as the airport. But at some point, he was going to come crashing in like the Dustin Hoffman character in her mother's all-time-favorite movie in the nonmusical category, *The Graduate*, and bang on the glass. Get her out of there, just as Simon and Garfunkel started playing "Mrs. Robinson." Garrett hadn't stopped Josh from marrying her mother, as she had once believed he would, but it had seemed reasonable to suppose, given everything she'd known about him, that Josh would stop Garrett from taking her away now.

Not until this moment did she realize it was actually going to happen. Tomorrow morning, she would board a plane for Sacramento, and by nightfall she'd be walking into the house of a man she hardly knew, who called himself her father, and everything she'd known or loved best in her life up to this moment would be gone, and whatever was coming next, she didn't have a clue.

# PART TWO

# California

# Thirteen

Garrett lived in a town called Davis, a little outside of Sacramento. Wendy asked him if the Golden Gate Bridge was nearby. That's San Francisco, he said. But I'll take you there one of these days.

When she pictured him in California, she'd imagined a little cabin off in the middle of a field, facing out at the ocean, with a sleeping loft and plants in macramé holders and crystals hanging in the window—like a picture she'd seen of a place where her parents had lived in upstate New York one summer when she was a baby. She imagined artworks all around, and the smell of incense and bread baking. But he lived in a regular house, with neighbors on both sides, and a couple of shrubs in front and a cement walkway leading up to the door.

Inside was an old leather couch and a La-Z-Boy chair and a TV set, also a stereo, and a coffee table with magazines, and those were the regular kind, too. *Time* and *TV Guide.*

There were some tools and fishing equipment leaned against a wall, and a painting over the couch, sort of abstract, but she could make out the figure of a man and something that looked like a boat.

I like that, she said. I draw a lot, too.

I don't make as much art as I used to, he told her. The job and all.

He did carpentry work. Framing mostly, but he could build cabinets, too, when people wanted them.

The things you do to pay the bills, he said. He had opened the curtain of a window that looked out into a little backyard. There was a barbecue and the orange tree she'd heard about in his letter.

The puppy from the photograph, part black Lab, part retriever, was older now. His neighbors had been looking after Shiva while Garrett was in New York, so the first thing he did when they got back to the house was go next door to pick her up. I always wanted a dog like this, she told him. Some people wouldn't like it when a dog licked their face, but Wendy did.

He opened the fridge. Here, he said. See what hits the spot.

It was nothing like their refrigerator back in Brooklyn, with half a dozen different kinds of cheeses and the crisper drawer crammed full of vegetables that her mother used to complain were always more than they needed. You never know what you're going to feel like, Josh used to say. Could be cold roast chicken. Could be a bagel with cream cheese. A person has to be prepared.

Here there was a stick of beef jerky and a package of sliced turkey breast. Store-bought tomato sauce. A couple of eggs. Margarine. Never trust a person with margarine in their fridge, Josh told her once.

Stop giving our daughter these ideas, her mother said. The first thirty-five years of my life, that's all I ever had.

Our daughter.

Wendy was still standing in front of the open refrigerator. Nothing strikes your fancy, huh? he said. Can't say I blame you. But I was saving the best for last.

He opened the top door, the freezer. A half dozen different Healthy Choice dinners were stacked inside. Take your pick, he said. The sky's the limit.

In the end, she settled on a couple of Oreos. That's genetics for you, he said. I love these things, too.

He had fixed up a room for her. It must have been his workroom before, because there were still boxes stacked in the corner with papers and a few more tools and art supplies. But he'd put an India-print spread on the bed and a vase of flowers next to it. He'd set a stuffed lion on the pillow.

It was mine when I was a kid, he said. Of course, you're old for that kind of stuff. I just thought you might like a little homey touch.

He set her bigger suitcase on the floor at the foot of the bed. In a day or two, we can set you up with whatever other stuff you need. You probably like music, right?

Yes.

We'll head over to Circuit City and get you one of those portable CD players. Just don't tell me you like rap okay?

She hadn't pictured herself this way. Actually playing music in some room other than the one back home. Hanging her clothes up in this closet next to the box of tools.

No, she said. I listen to jazz mostly. But I like Madonna and Ani DiFranco and Sade.

He left the room. When he came back, he was holding something—a very old photograph of her mother, from when she had long hair. Pregnant, from the looks of it.

Janet kept most of our pictures, he said. I only have a few.

She looked at the face in the picture. Her mother wasn't exactly smiling. She had a puzzled sort of expression. Wendy wondered if even then they had been arguing.

We had different ideas about a lot of things, he said. She was more the type to want to settle down and make a home. I never believed in traditional family structures. It always seemed to me like most people's problems start with their parents. I wanted things to be a little looser, hands-off. Like the whole world was your home, instead of just one place.

Didn't you like your mom and dad? she asked him.

Garrett made a sound a little like a laugh, but not really. Let's just say I might have been better off raised by wolves, he said.


She should have been tired, considering the time difference. But after he left her, she lay in the dark room and couldn't sleep. He had said he'd take her around tomorrow, show her downtown Davis, all three streets, and then take her over to her new school so she could see it. One friend of mine in particular is looking forward to meeting you, but that can wait, he said. You might want to adjust a little first.

She thought about her room at home in New York, with the posters still up. "Sailor Moon" and the framed *Playbill* from when her mother took her to see *Guys and Dolls* on Broadway. In her mind, she moved down the hallway past the bathroom to Louie's room. She knelt beside the bed.

Louie, she said. Are you sleeping?

I dreamed I was driving a cement mixer, Sissy. But I'm awake now.

Want me to get in with you?

Yes.

She lay there in the dark with him. He snuggled against her the way he liked, like they were making an electrical connection and all the surfaces had to be in contact to work. She could feel him adjusting his body to curve in alongside her better. She draped her top arm over him and rested her hand on his round belly through the fleece of his sleeper suit.

What do you want to talk about? he said.

I don't know, Louie. How about you?

Trucks, he said. Which one would you want, a dump truck or a street sweeper?

How about we talk about farm animals instead? I'm not in the mood for trucks.

If you could have any animal, what would you pick?

A dog, she said. He knew this already. A Boston terrier.

I'd want a pig.

They're cute at first, she told him. But have you ever seen how pigs get when they're older? Really fat and ugly and covered with mud.

Not the pig in *Charlotte's Web*. I like him.

He was a great pig all right. But I don't think they're all that good. Plus, they'd track mud in all over the place, and Mama would hate it.

Mama isn't here anymore.

Poppy, then. He has enough work to do without cleaning up after a pig.

Sissy? he said.

Yes, Louie.

Did you know I can make a pig noise?

No, Louie. Let's hear.

He used to just say, Oink, but now he snorted. That sounded just like a real pig, she told him.

Sissy? he said.

Yes, Louie.

After Charotte had her babies, she died, didn't she? At the end?

Yes, Louie.

But the baby spiders were okay. They had Wilbur anyway.

Also each other.


In the morning, because they didn't have much food in the house, Garrett took her out for breakfast. She had a grapefruit, something she never ate at home. She hadn't told him, but she was going to eat all different things in California, so when she went home, they'd barely recognize her. You can create a whole new identity, Amelia had said.

Don't you want something else? he asked. English muffin? Pop-Tart?

She said she never ate much for breakfast.

They drove down E Street so he could point out the landmarks: the other diner he sometimes went for breakfast, the bar he and his buddies went to after work sometimes to play a round of pool. Not that I'll be stopping in there now that you're here, he said. We'll be doing the bonding thing.

They were sitting in the cab of his truck. Shiva rode in back, with her head facing the wind and her tongue out. Wendy was worried that she might jump out, but Garrett said she never would. This is one loyal dog, he said.

I always wanted a dog, she told him. My mom and Josh didn't think we had room.

Speaking of her mother now, even in that small way, left a sad little hollow feeling in Wendy. She had been thinking about her mother just about constantly in New York, but she realized as she said the words that an hour or two had gone by today in which she hadn't thought about her. She should probably feel guilty about that, but she also liked it that she could forget for a little while, or put it out of her head anyway.

When they got back to the house there was a message on Garrett's machine from Josh, wanting to be sure she'd gotten there safely. She knew she should call him back, but she wasn't in the mood. She wasn't sure she wanted to hear his voice yet, least of all Louie's. They're probably out now anyway, she told Garrett. I'll get back to him later.


I'll drive you to school, Garrett told her on Monday. He made the announcement as if it was no big deal, starting in at a new school two months after the start of the year.

The junior high was a long, low, flat building. Nothing like the way schools looked in New York City. There were playing fields out back, too, and a parking lot full of cars, and a sign that said, HOME OF THE HOLO COUNTY REDBIRDS.

She had worn her jeans, same as she did to school back home, and a heavy sweater. She wasn't expecting it to be so warm, but she had nothing underneath but her underwear, so she had no choice but to keep the sweater on.

Remember, he told her, it's always a little weird at first, anytime you start off in a new place. You have to give things a little time.

They went to the office. If it had been her mother and Josh, they would have made a bunch of calls ahead of time, talked to the guidance counselor, tracked down parents in the know to find out who the best teachers were and which ones to avoid. But she could tell this was the first time Garrett had talked to the principal.

One thing she was grateful for: He didn't mention what had happened. Only that she was moving here from New York.

So you were there on September eleventh? the principal asked.

We figured it was a good time for my daughter to get out of New York, he said, like it was some kind of joint plan. They'll be sending her records along.

That was it.

They set her up with a schedule pretty much like the one at home. This is a big school, the principal told her. You might feel a little lost in the crowd at first. Just remember, we Redbirds are a friendly bunch. Before you know it, you'll be a real California girl.

\*     \*     \*

In English, they were reading "The Lottery," a story she'd read with her class back home. The assignment was to write a three-hundred-word essay on whether or not, if you'd been in that village that day, you would have picked up a stone like the people in the story, and why.

When the bell rang, a girl who'd been sitting next to her asked where her next class was. I'm going to geometry, too, so I can show you, she said.

You come from New York—huh? she said. It must have been so unbeliev-ably crazy being there with all those dead people everywhere.

Wendy didn't say anything.

So, the girl said. You want me to tell you who the cutest boys are?

Then it was gym. She didn't have sneakers with her, so the gym teacher told her she didn't have to change into a uniform this time. You can just wear your jeans today, she said. You can play right wing.

The teacher gave her a field hockey stick and some shin guards and told her what to do if the ball came her way. You don't want to try to be some big hero and make a goal, the teacher told her, as if she ever would. Just pass it to your teammate and work on blocking your opponent if she's bringing the ball up your side of the field.

Her position was on the far side of the field, just to the right of a little brook. From where she stood, she could look across a long, low, flat expanse of land, past the school, to a housing development and some kind of wheat fields and, beyond that, low hills against the horizon. It was just 9:30, but already the sun was beating down hard. Wendy imagined what Amelia would say if she could see her standing here with her hockey stick.

The two players in the center of the field started off. The girl from the other team got the ball and ran with it partway down the field, toward the opposite goal, before passing it to a player on the opposite side from Wendy. From there, the girl moved nearer to the goal. She took a shot and missed.

The game went on like that for a long time. Sometimes the ball came back up the field again, but never very close to Wendy, except one time when it rolled right toward her and she just stood there. Another girl on her team ran up from behind and took it.

Wendy felt as if she was watching the game, not playing. Not really watching, either. Just standing in her spot next to the place where the little trickle of water flowed past. Four feet over and she'd be off the field completely. She stepped slightly closer to the sidelines to see whether anyone noticed. They didn't.

There was a bunch of brush by the streambed. Not brush exactly, but a pile of old athletic equipment covered by a few weeds.

A person could just step across this stream and be off the field. A few more steps and she'd be in the housing development, instead of school. In five minutes she could be out on the road.

She walked over a little more. Down at the far end of the field, most of the players were bunched up around the goal. Even the ones who weren't there seemed totally focused on the spot. Wendy jumped over the stream. Hardly a jump at all, it was so narrow.

She climbed up over the other side of the bank. She was standing in a pile of old netting and what might have been track and field equipment. She looked back over her shoulder again, but nobody was noticing. She walked over to the sidewalk, toward a row of identical houses. She was walking faster now, like a person with a destination, instead of someone just moving her feet around.

A woman was running toward her with one of those baby joggers. Off in the distance now, she could hear the dim sound of yelling on the field. She realized she still had her hockey stick in her hands, and set it down. Unbuckled the shin guards and laid them neatly next to the stick.

Wendy walked a long time. After a while, the road came out onto a highway. There was a sign for downtown, so she went in that direction, and after a while more, she spotted a restaurant where her father told her they could get a good steak. Next to that was a bookstore.

It was a small bookstore. There were some tables near the front with new books, but farther back was a used-book area and a couple of comfortable-looking old chairs. Wendy studied the shelves. She found a used edition of Anne Frank's *The Diary of a Young Girl*. She took the book off the shelf and sat down in one of the chairs.

When she left her old school, she was nearly finished with the book, but she opened it now to one of the earlier sections, back when Anne Frank had just moved into the annex, when she was still thinking the war would be over soon and she could go home. Back then, it had almost seemed cozy and nice, the way everyone in the family was gathered in close, stocking up the pantry, having their meals with the other family. Their friend Miep stopping by with news from the world outside and special treats like fruit or jam. Back then Anne thought it was a problem that her mother didn't understand her that well. Nobody had any idea yet how bad things were going to get.

Wendy flipped back to the front of the book and studied the familiar photograph of Anne Frank some more. Anne also worried about how she looked, though Wendy thought she was pretty. Not like the kind of girl who would get picked for cheerleader, but like someone she and Amelia would want to be friends with. Anne didn't say much about her breasts, but it was possible she might have had exactly the same problem as Wendy, one growing faster than the other. One thing she did talk about was the angry feeling Wendy had all the time, where even the people she loved got on her nerves, and she said mean things to them, even though she loved them and wasn't really a mean person.

"I'd like to scream 'Leave me alone,'" she wrote. " 'Let me get away, away from everything, away from this world.'" Oh yes.

So many times, reading the diary, Wendy felt like crying out loud, Me, too. All these years later, in a different country and a different world, long after the girl in the photograph had turned to dust, the words she'd written could have been coming from Wendy's diary, if she kept one. Including the inconsistencies—the way, one minute, Anne would be writing in her diary how she was filled with hopefulness and affection for the people around her, the way that, even in those terrible times, she managed to view her life as an adventure and to see beauty all around; and then how, a page later, she would be sobbing with rage and despair.

Wendy read for a long time, long enough that she got to the part where the diary stopped and there was an editor's note explaining how Anne had died in a concentration camp just one month before the Allied troops defeated the Nazis and liberated all the prisoners. If only she could have held on a little longer.

Wendy thought about her mother. What if she was two steps from the door when the building gave way? What if she had made it to the street, but a piece of falling metal hit her just as she was about to reach safety? What if she'd been lying somewhere under the rubble just as a group of rescue workers made it to her spot with their shovels?

By the time Anne Frank died, her mother and sister were dead already. Probably knowing that made it harder for her to keep going. After a while you'd think, What was the point? Wendy reread, then, Anne's line about believing people were basically good and thought about Buddy's remark that she'd written before they took her to the concentration camp. He was a jerk but he had a point. She also wondered if Anne still believed people were basically good by the end.

The editor's note went on to say how only one person in the Frank family had survived the concentration camp—Anne's father. She wondered what it was like being him after the war, knowing his whole family was dead. And then getting a visit from their friend Miep Gies after all that time. And Miep saying, Look, here's the diary. I found it after the Nazis took Anne away. I saved it for you.

Anne's father had put the diary away for a while. He couldn't even bear to read it at first, and when he finally did, there were parts he didn't like, so he kept those separate and didn't show them to anyone. The first time the diary was published, and for a long time after that, only the parts he wanted were kept in. The parts where Anne talked about being angry at her mother he took out. Also some parts where she talked about her body, about sex even.

Why did parents think they could control their children that way? And only pick the parts of their kids that they wanted, telling them where they had to live, the people they were supposed to like and not like. Her parents had done that—first her mother, saying you can't go with your father; then Garrett saying you need to come with me. By then she didn't even know herself what she wanted or felt.

She turned back to the beginning of the book again to check what year Anne Frank was born. She was the same age Wendy was now when she started writing her diary, but if she was alive, she'd be an old woman now, older than a grandmother. She might even be dead. Sooner or later, she would have died, whether there were Nazis or not. So maybe by the time enough years passed and it got to the point where you were going to die anyway, it wouldn't matter if something terrible happened to you when you were young. Things could finally be almost like normal, and it would seem as if nothing bad had happened.

But things still wouldn't be normal. Because even now, sixty years after Anne Frank had died at the age of fifteen in Bergen-Belsen concentration camp, things hadn't evened out. Anne had never gotten to fall in love with anybody good, just that one boy in the annex. She never got to get married and have children or write all the other books she probably would have, knowing her, or know that her diary would get published and that millions of people were going to read it and she'd be famous. There were all those places she would have seen that she didn't get to, and music she didn't hear, because when she died, it hadn't even been written yet. Movies she would have loved. Parties and dresses and pets and times with her sister and her friends. She of all people, who loved life so much, and got to experience so little of it. And there would still be all those others—or one anyway, her father—who had to spend the whole rest of their lives never getting over missing her.

Fifty years from now, Wendy's mother might have been a ninety-year-old woman, just getting around to dying. Most of those other people in the World Trade Center that day might have lived to be very old, too, if not dead, even Billy Flynn, though it was hard to picture him as anything but young and handsome.

Wendy must have sat in that chair in the used-books section at the back of the bookstore longer than she knew, because when she looked up, it was getting dark outside.

You're welcome to stay as long as you like, said the man who'd been at the counter in front when she came in. I was just wondering if you'd like a cup of tea.

There was a pot with hot water on a little table, along with the kind of herb teas she liked from home, with pictures of fruits and flowers on the boxes. She chose Raspberry Zinger.

Most people your age are in school on a Monday afternoon, he said when he handed her the mug.

I'm a home schooler, she told him. It just came to her to say that, as if she was Amelia.

Smart idea, he said. Probably no better education to be had than the one you'll get from reading.

That's what I decided, she said. She liked the idea that home schooling would have been her decision, not someone else's.

You were really off in another world there with your book.

She showed him the cover.

I read that one years ago, he told her. Maybe after that one, you'll try *The Autobiography of Malcolm X,* for something a little different. It's great, too.

She realized then that maybe she should buy something, only she didn't have any money, except for a couple of dollars Garrett had given her for lunch.

I'll probably come back and buy something later, she said.

It's not a requirement for hanging out here. You're welcome in the store anytime.

I'll definitely be back, she said. Home schooling like this, it's good to get a change of scene now and then. It sounded like something Amelia would say. Or the kind of girl who ate half a grapefruit for breakfast and nothing else, then walked off a field hockey field in the middle of PE class.

My name's Alan, he told her.

Kitty, she said, the diary fresh in her mind. I guess I should head home now, she told him. My family's expecting me.

Anytime, he said. If you ever feel like a job, I'm always looking for help shelving used books.


She found Garrett's street without any trouble. It was close to five when she got there, but his truck wasn't there yet. She let herself in. Took out her drawing pad and sat on the couch. She was working on a picture of two girls running across a field. The field looked a little like where they played field hockey at Amity Junior High, with the wheat fields in the background and the hills on the horizon, but the girls were nothing like field hockey players. She drew them in her usual Japanese animation style, with skintight outfits in bright colors and legs twice as long as normal people and small, delicate heads and crazy, wonderful hairdos.

Sometime around six o'clock Garrett and Shiva came in. Shiva came right over and licked her.

So, he said, setting down his tools. How's eighth grade treating you so far?

Fine, she told him.

If it was her mother, she would have had a million questions. Josh, too. But Garrett just unfolded the paper and turned to the sports section. You're probably a Yankees fan, right? he asked. In which case we might have a few tense moments when the new season starts next spring.

I don't actually follow baseball that closely, she said. Josh loved the Yankees, but she didn't mention that.

Well then, he said. There's still a chance I can convert you over to the Giants. He'd been studying the sports page but now he looked up.

You're going to be a lot taller than your mother, he said. You've got a totally different bone structure from Janet. More the statuesque type.

My mom was a lot skinnier than me, she said.

I was just thinking what it was I was going to call you, he told her. I was thinking I'd call you Slim.

# Fourteen

Wendy had always been the kind of person who followed directions. As far back as preschool, she'd never gotten into trouble. She hardly ever even turned her homework in late.

Riding the subway alone to Queens or taking a taxi to lower Manhattan in the middle of the night would be things she couldn't have imagined. Let alone what she was doing now. Just not showing up at school. Not even being worried when she did it, that she might get into trouble.

Now she knew what real trouble was, and everything looked different. Once you crossed the line, she discovered—where you realize you don't have to be good all the time, and you aren't scared anymore of things like teachers not liking you—it was easy to go to the next step. Madonna was that way, it occurred to Wendy—and now she wondered if that had anything to do with Madonna's mother dying when she was young, too. The thought came to her—crazily—of Babar, leaving his jungle home and heading to Paris, meeting the old lady, buying his green suit, having all those wild adventures he never would have had, back in the jungle, if the hunters hadn't killed his mother that day.

\*      \*      \*

On her way to school Tuesday morning, she asked Garrett to drop her off a block from the parking lot. She waited for him to drive away, then took a bus into Sacramento. She walked around for a while. She went to 24 Hour Fitness, where they were offering a complimentary workout session. She spent an hour at Macy's trying on perfumes, and after that, she got a makeover at the Estée Lauder counter from a girl who didn't seem to think twice about putting all that foundation and mascara and lip liner on a thirteen-year-old.

She rode the escalator to the second floor and tried on shoes, and by the time she was done, she was hungry, so she went to an outdoor café next door. Since she was still eating only fruits and vegetables, she ordered a salad. Before going back to their house, she stopped in a bathroom at a gas station to wash the makeup off.

The next day, she took Garrett's bike and rode around Davis, past the university dorms and out to a field for a picnic of grapes and a banana. It was close to three o'clock by the time she got back to town. She stopped in at the bookstore.

Hey, said Alan. I was afraid you'd forgotten about us. I set aside another book I thought you'd like.

It was called *The Member of the Wedding*, by Carson McCullers. She settled herself in the chair in back, and he brought her some tea.

Your parents must be pretty progressive people, he said. Leaving your education up to you this way.

They don't really believe in traditional family structures, she said. So many of the worst problems in people's lives come from their parents. They trust me to take care of myself.

So how's it going?

Fine, she said. You have any kids?

One. He's autistic. He lives in a group home up north.

Do you get to see him much?

Oh sure. I drive up every Tuesday. He's older now, nineteen. He's actually a lot happier than when he lived with his mother and me. When we first took him up there when he was fourteen, it was awful. But things are better now.

I have a brother, she said. He doesn't live with me, either.

Some kind of custody thing?

Not exactly. She thought for a moment.

You know how they have to choose someone to be the next Dalai Lama? she said. Some really special little boy with amazing powers, and once they find him, they have to take him away to start his training? That's my brother. He's only four, but already they know. They spotted him when he was only two.

It came from a story her mother told her once. They had gone to hear the Dalai Lama give a speech in Madison Square Garden. They picked him out when he was really little, her mother said after it was over. He had to leave his mother and receive special training up in some very isolated mountaintop temple.

I would never let them do that with Louie, Wendy had said. She was only nine or ten then. Louie was still in diapers. I don't think you need to worry, her mother said. They usually find the person a little closer to Tibet.


I thought they usually found the person in Tibet, Alan said.

That's true, she said. We were traveling there. On a vacation. My parents thought it would be an educational trip. But we weren't bargaining on the search team wanting my brother.

Your parents just let him go like that?

It was a rough decision, she said. We all talked about it a long time, and my parents decided it was important not to hold my brother back. They believe in letting their kids make their own decisions about life. We go see him every year though, and when he becomes the Dalai Lama, we'll always go hear him when he comes around to give his speeches.

Alan seemed quiet. I see, he said.

She thanked him for the tea. I should probably be heading home, she said. But next time I'll help you put away books, if you want.

I'd say both the children in your family have unusual gifts, said Alan.

*     *     *

Nights at Garrett's, he defrosted a couple of Healthy Choice dinners and put on a record. The music he listened to was different from what she'd listened to back home—old rock and roll albums from back when he was young, and rhythm and blues, and tons of reggae. Sometimes he brought home a video or they watched the Discovery Channel. She sat on the couch with him sometimes, drawing, with Shiva's head on her feet. Sometimes, sitting there, she'd think of home, her mother and Josh, and Louie. The odd thing was that sometimes she didn't.

Most mornings, on his way to work, Garrett would drop Wendy off near the school. This corner's good enough, she'd tell him. I can walk from here. After he pulled away, she'd catch a bus back into town. Some days, she'd ask to borrow his bike in the morning.

Pedaling along the bike paths of the university or out along the highway, with the sun on her shoulders and the smell of cut grass in the air, the world felt like a blank canvas, the day stretching out in front of her like a long, flat field.

I thought I'd teach you how to tie flies, Garrett said. Come spring, we can go fishing in the Merced River. He took out a box with drawers full of special hooks and wire and feathers. They sat there working on their flies from six-thirty till close to eleven, not even talking, except when he gave her instructions now and then.

You have a lot of patience, Slim, he said. Sign of a good fisherperson. I taught your mother how to do this one time, he told her. She liked it at first, but she got tired of it. You know how she was—she could never sit still that long. That's a dancer for you.

I'm not a very good dancer, Wendy told him. I'm terrible, actually. She said it as if this wasn't a big deal to her.

Never mind, he said. Your mother was lousy at fishing.

Wendy studied the fly she'd made, a collection of feathers with a bobbin attached, and a piece of sparkly filament. If her mother could see it, she'd turn it into an earring.

I like doing things like this, she told him. It's like drawing or playing clarinet. You concentrate so hard, everything else in the world goes away.

She called Josh and Louie before Garrett came home, so she could be private.

I figured you might be too busy to call back right away, Josh told her. I wanted to give you a little time. But every day I wanted to call.

I'm fine, she said. It's different from how I thought but it's okay. She didn't want him to think she was too happy, but she didn't want to upset him, either.

So how's school? In the background, she could hear Louie calling out, Let me talk. You'll get your turn, Lou-man, Josh told him.

School's okay, she said.

How about the kids? You spot any potential friends?

One maybe, she said. Alan.

Potential romantic interest or just a friend?

Just a friend, definitely, she said.

How about your clarinet? They have a decent band? You make arrangements yet to rent an instrument out there?

I decided to take a break, she said. I'll look into it soon.

Don't leave it too long, he told her. It'll feel good to start playing.

You should talk.

We have a gig again Saturday, he said. Things are picking up a little in the city. Kate said she'd stay with your brother.

How about just playing? she asked. In the old days, Josh never let one day go by without spending a few hours on his bass.

Maybe in a while, he told her.

She didn't need to ask if there'd been any news about her mother.

Sissy. A small voice on the other end. Last Christmas, Josh had gotten them walkie-talkies, and they'd tried them out on the street. Louie sounded as if he was on one of the walkie-talkies now, and drifting out of range.

Hey, Lou. I missed you.

When are you coming home?

Not for a while, Louie. Remember how I went away in an airplane? And just like I said, nothing bad happened to me.

It's time to come home now.

Maybe in a while, Louie.

Now.

She could picture just where he was. In the kitchen, on the high stool at the counter, where he liked to sit while Josh fixed dinner. She could tell from the sound that he was eating carrot sticks.

What did you do in preschool today, Louie?

Nothing.

I don't believe you. There had to be something.

Peed my pants. Pooped on the floor.

You're just joking. You don't do those things. You're a big boy.

My teacher threw paint at me. There's a mean girl in my class that puts worms in your sandwich.

You're making up this stuff, Louie, she said. Poppy would never let your teacher throw paint at you.

She could hear him sucking his thumb, and then Josh's voice saying, It's long-distance, Lou-man. We'll talk to Sissy again soon. Then Louie saying, One more chance. I can talk regular now.

Sissy, he said, softer now.

Yes, Louie?

Some people say magic isn't real, but it is, right?

I don't know, Louie, she said. Sometimes, maybe.

That's what I told them.

She could hear him on the other end, breathing, and Josh telling him to say good-bye.

You weren't supposed to go away this long, Sis.

I'll call you again soon, Louie, she said.

Say good-bye, Louie, said Josh.

Wait, he said. There's something else.

You can tell Sissy next time, Josh was saying in his firm voice.

So we'll give you a call in a couple of days, Wen, Josh said. In the background, she could hear Louie crying. Then Josh saying, I know how hard it is to say good-bye. What do you say we put on our coats and go find ourselves some pigeons to feed? We'll call Sissy again in a day or two.

One thing, Josh, she said.

I'm here, Wendy.

It's not like it's so great here, either. I just thought I'd see what it felt like.

And what does it feel like?

Like I'm hardly even the same person.

Don't change too much, he said. I liked the old you.

Saturday morning, Garrett told her they were going for a ride. Carolyn wants to meet you, he said.

Who's that?

My girlfriend.

She lived on a dirt road a couple of miles out of town. When they pulled up in front, Wendy recognized the cabin from the photograph he'd sent her. There was a car in the yard that looked as if it hadn't gone anywhere in a long time, and another one not much better. There was a sign that said PALM READINGS, and another that said CACTUS PLANTS FOR SALE.

Shiva knew the place. She was out of the truck before Garrett had come to a full stop. A woman came out.

She looked around the same age as Wendy's mother. She was tall and large-boned, as her mother would put it. More friendly-looking than pretty, with freckles and a strawberry blond braid down her back and jeans with holes in the knees.

It's about time you brought her by, she said.

We've been busy.

She looks like you, Garrett, she said. But prettier.

You sure have a lot of cactus plants, Wendy said.

You could say it's my obsession, Carolyn said. Can you believe I started with one measly ninety-nine-cent cactus from Albertson's Market six years ago?

They're beautiful, Wendy said. She was telling the truth. Funny how she had started considering, in the last few days, whether what she said was real or made up, because so much of it was made up.

I'll give you the tour, Carolyn said. The ones in here are very sensitive to water. One rain shower and they'd be done in. So this is the indoor garden. Outside, you've got your hardier varieties.

Wendy studied one of the larger plants, a perfect globe, covered in spines. There was a smaller one next to it that looked like the ruffle on the bottom of her mother's gypsy skirt, with a tall fan of spears and little teardrop bits coming off the sides. I never knew how many different kinds of cactuses there were, she said.

Honey, you couldn't even count them all. In the yard alone, I've got a hundred and twenty varieties, and I'm just a beginner. I meet people at the cactus shows with six, seven hundred different species in their collection, and they can tell you every one. Cactus people—they're a different breed of fish.

I was thinking you were giving us breakfast, Car, Garrett said. Or should I run into town and pick up some doughnuts? Not that this one would have any. Slim here eats like a bird.

I made corn bread, Carolyn said. You ready for coffee?

Carolyn only had two chairs, but they brought in a stool from the garden and Garrett sat on that.

California's a lot different from New York, I bet, she said.

Wendy realized Carolyn was the first person she'd met out here who must know about her mother. Now she was waiting for Carolyn to say something about that, but she didn't.

I come from Iowa myself, she said. Flat. But not as hot as here.

I've been in New York all my life, Wendy said. Till now.

I'm thinking you're a Gemini, Carolyn said. Or a Capricorn.

Capricorn, Wendy told her. She didn't know much about astrology, but Amelia used to read their horoscopes out loud over the phone. *Look for career advancement opportunities in the early part of the week,* she'd say. *Romantic prospects bring confusion best resolved by taking things slow.* Think they're talking about Buddy Campion's desk being moved next to mine? she said.

It's the eyes, Carolyn said. Capricorns always have deep, clear eyes. Unlike your father, for example. His are opaque. You never have a clue what's in there. Just as well maybe.

You're looking good, Car, he said. He stroked her shoulder. When they'd first pulled up, he'd kissed her, but nothing particularly romantic. Not like Josh kissing her mom after they hadn't seen each other for a few days. Or even just one.

I wasn't wild about him showing up at your family's apartment the way he did, she said to Wendy. I thought he should call you first, or write.

Wendy might have said that Josh agreed but she didn't.

The thing about your father is, he means well, even if he might not do things the best way.

She's doing great, he said. Enrolled in junior high and everything. On a basketball team.

Field hockey, Wendy said. Just in gym class. She didn't want to talk about school.

I hated gym, Carolyn said. I remember when I was your age, trying to figure out how I could get to the locker room first so I could dress in private, without all the other girls seeing me. I was so modest.

I guess you got over that one.

Shut up, will you, Garrett? Don't you know anything? Like I said, he means well. And in answer to your remark, mister, most girls thirteen years old are more modest than forty-three-year-old women.

My daughter's fourteen.

I'm thirteen actually, Wendy said. I was going to tell you.


She doesn't have any kids? Wendy asked him as they were driving home.

Can't. Some kind of problem. I never got into it with her.

How long have you known her? she asked.

Three years? Four maybe.

She's nice, Wendy said.

Carolyn's what you might call a no-nonsense gal, Garrett said.

Nobody needed to point out it would have been different with Wendy's mother. My problem is, I still believe love should be like all the songs, her mother used to say.

Has grandma met her?

Wendy hadn't seen her grandmother on her father's side for a couple of years anyway, and then just briefly. But she could remember those visits to Connecticut well enough to know what it would be like having her grandmother pull up in front of the dead car, and the nearly dead car, and the palm-reading sign. Getting the cactus tour.

My mother? Not on your life, he said. First off, she's never been out here. And if she did, the last person I'd want her to meet would be Carolyn. For Carolyn's sake, among other things. Your grandmother is still waiting for me to get back into the game of tennis, and have a show of my paintings in some gallery in Newport.

But that's not what you want, right?

My mother wasn't the type to consider what I wanted, he said. It was more what she wanted for me. Or what she wanted for her, that I might provide. As I mentioned, I'm not a big fan of the extended-family concept.

She keeps sending me these white blouses with my initials stitched on, Wendy said. I never wear them.

Join the crowd, he told her. She still sends me shirts from Brooks Brothers for Christmas.

Parents, he said. The best you can hope for is that their children get away before the parents do too much damage.


They rented a video—*Traffic*. Michael Douglas played a judge in charge of stopping drugs in America, but his daughter was taking cocaine and sleeping with her boyfriend. Michael Douglas thought she was this good student who never did anything wrong. There were other parts in the movie about drug dealers in Mexico that she didn't follow too closely. The most interesting thing was the girl. Wendy watched as she took out a lighter and heated up drugs on a spoon. One second after she sniffed it, she looked like every problem in her brain had floated away.

Wendy wondered if she'd get into drugs now that she was a dropout. She never would have thought about that before. Who knew anymore? It looked sort of tempting, the way the girl drifted off into this happy mood every time she sniffed the stuff on the spoon. Wendy knew the movie was supposed to be showing you how bad it was to take drugs, because the girl also got so desperate to have drugs, she started having sex with all these guys. But the part Wendy kept thinking about was how the girl didn't care about anything once she took the drugs. How every worry went away. Being stoned might be terrible, but maybe not as bad as thinking about your mother being dead all the time.

The guy's not very tuned in to his kid, is he? Garrett said. The mother in the movie knew she was on drugs, but Michael Douglas didn't have a clue.

I guess he was really busy with his job, Wendy said. Talking with the president and everything.

Still, he said. He should have paid more attention, right?

I guess so. She reached for the popcorn. She had told Garrett that she didn't like butter on it, even though, with Amelia, they used a whole stick.

That might be true of me, too, he said. Not paying enough attention. I know I haven't been doing the greatest job these last few years.

It was okay, she said. She could have said but didn't that up till now she had her mom and Josh.

I didn't have the best role model, he said. My father was always off working when I was a kid. Either that or playing golf. When he came home, all he wanted to do was read the paper and drink his martini. He liked it if you won a tennis tournament, but other than that, I was never all that sure he would have noticed if I just didn't show up.

That must have felt bad.

One thing it does is set you free in a way, he said. There's nothing holding you back. I took off when I turned eighteen, and never felt anything pulling me back. The whole thing made me my own person.


Anne Frank had said something like that when she was describing how she felt about her problems getting along with her mother. "I've emerged from the struggle a stronger person," she wrote. ". . . There's only one person I'm accountable to, and that's me."

I'm not saying I'm so much better at it now, either, Garrett was saying. On the screen, Michael Douglas had discovered his daughter sitting on the toilet, taking drugs.

I want to do better, Garrett said.

It made her uncomfortable hearing him talk this way. With someone like Josh, who was always talking about his feelings, it wouldn't seem so odd, but with Garrett, it was different. You could tell he'd be more comfortable talking about trout lures or the designated-hitter rule.

How do you like the popcorn? he asked.

It was microwave. Another thing Josh said they should make a law against, along with margarine and Minute Rice. At home, they had an old-fashioned popper with a crank you turned while the kernels were popping. Josh used some special oil and more butter than her mom said was good for them.

Great, she said. She put a hand under the blanket and felt her stomach. Almost flat.

That Catherine Zeta-Jones, he said. She even looks good pregnant.

# Fifteen

It was Sunday.

With her mom and Josh, if there was a day Wendy didn't have school and neither one of them was working, they'd nearly always head out on some special family outing. They would go to a museum or the zoo, or take a road trip.

Josh had a thing about amusement parks. They knew all the roller coasters within driving distance of the city, but now and then he'd hear about some new ride, and they'd have to go try it. Her mom hated scary rides, and Louie was still too little to meet the height requirement. It's up to you and me, Wen, he'd say. Let's test-drive this baby.

They'd buckle themselves in while her mom and Louie stood at the fence.

The first couple of times she went on a roller coaster with Josh, she was scared and only went to make him happy, but then she started loving them, too. For one thing, he held on to her so tight she knew nothing bad could possibly happen. If it gets really dicey, start singing at the top of your lungs, he said. There was this Fats Waller song, "Choo Choo Cha Boogie." That was their favorite for roller coasters. But sometimes they sang old Beatles songs, the early period.

He taught her to put her arms over her head when they went down the loopiest parts. He kept his around her. She'd be reminded of that sometimes now when Garrett gave her a hug. She'd think how differently Josh hugged her. Garrett's way of putting an arm around her—just one, not two—was casual, not really holding on so much as draping his arm across her shoulders, as if it just happened to end up there.

One time, they'd driven all the way to Connecticut to pick apples. They stopped at a farm where you could watch them make cider and doughnuts.

I'm not sure I'm happy I saw this, her mom said. Now I know how greasy they are. But even after standing in front of the machine, watching the circles of dough dropping into the deep fat and bobbing along like corks in a stream—just like in "Homer Price and the Doughnut Machine"—she still ate half of one. Josh and Wendy and Louie had two apiece.

They checked out the animals in this barnyard next to the doughnut operation that Louie loved. This farm didn't have that many animals, just a few of each kind for the little kids. There was another area where you could pay five dollars and make a scarecrow by picking out old clothes from a big heap and stuffing them with straw, with stuffed panty hose for the head. On the way back to the city, driving along Route 684, with her mother and Josh in the front seat and the scarecrow in back with her and Louie, the four of them sang "We Ain't Got a Barrel of Money." They sang "Old MacDonald" all the way from Brewster to White Plains, with every animal Louie could think of, even zoo animals. None of them knew what sound a lemur made, or a platypus, so they made them up.

Sundays with Garrett in Davis were quieter. He stayed in bed later than other days, and when he got up, he spent a long time reading the paper. You fix yourself some cereal yet? he asked her sometime around ten-thirty.

I had a grapefruit and some eggs, she said.

She was thinking that they'd probably go for a hike or something, but around noon, when nothing had happened, she saw it wasn't like that here. She was working on drawing a comic book, the adventures of a girl named Zara, who looked like this nerdy, loser kind of person with thick glasses and boring clothes, but after her parents went off to work in the morning, she changed into a purple-and-orange jumpsuit and went off on adventures. The comic book was called *The Secret Life of Zara.*

Sometime in the afternoon, Garrett said he thought he'd cruise over and see Carolyn. You want me to leave Shiva here or take her with me? he asked Wendy.

She can stay with me, Wendy said. She liked it that Shiva followed her around. She felt like some character in one of the movies she used to love when she was little, *Old Yeller* or *Sounder.*

Catch you later, he told her. She heard his truck drive off.

After he left, she looked in the refrigerator. There was a can of tuna fish half used up and a hunk of cheese. She took a slice of the cheese, even though she was mostly trying to avoid dairy products. She knew from her daily inspection of her body in the bathroom mirror that her shape was changing.

Shiva loped over to her. Wendy gave her a little tuna fish and put water in her bowl. She picked up the cordless phone and took it out into the yard, where her father had a couple of chairs set up next to an old birdbath with an oven rack on the top, that he used for a barbecue. She dialed Amelia's number.

Finally, Amelia said. I've been practically dying here, I missed you so much.

Me, too, Wendy said. It had surprised her that she hadn't been missing Amelia more, but the minute she heard Amelia's voice, she did.

Tell me everything, Amelia said. Is your dad's house the coolest ever?

Not exactly, Wendy said. It's okay. I'm sitting in the yard right now. There's an orange tree in back, and you can see these hills that are sort of like mountains. He has a great dog.

Orange trees. I hate you. Do you realize it's forty degrees here? Is your dad around? she said. Can you talk?

He went over to his girlfriend's house. They're probably having sex.

Is she mean or nice? She's jealous, I bet. Because you're like a reminder of your mom, that he really loved best all these years. You coming back just points out what was missing in their relationship probably.

She's nice, Wendy said. She has a cactus collection, and she guessed my sign.

And he's so incredibly happy to be back together with you after all these years, right? Like the father in *The Little Princess.*

When they were little, they had watched that one together with her mother a million times. They still liked to act out scenes from Shirley Temple movies sometimes, only changing the words—to make Shirley like a Valley Girl or someone from Brooklyn.

He's more of the laid-back type. It's strange, after dealing with my mom and Josh all this time.

Everyone at school was talking about you, Amelia said. A girl in seventh period started a rumor you had a nervous breakdown and had to go to a rest home. Hallie Owens said she didn't blame you. She said just seeing some of the stuff they showed on CNN was enough that her parents put her in therapy. I told them you were fine. Having a getaway.

It's completely different here, Wendy said. People don't even talk about what happened very much. Nobody here even knows where I was before, except my father's girlfriend.

There's a new boy in our class, Amelia said. They had to close down his regular school for a while because it was in SoHo, and his family's apartment got covered with dust, so now he's living with his aunt and coming to our school. Wait till you hear his name. Chief. His actual name on his birth certificate is Chief. Which fits, because he is awesome.

Have you talked to him?

The other day I ate lunch with him and we had this intense conversation about God and if he exists why something could happen like the World Trade Center. Chief was saying he thinks everything in the world is part of a giant plan, even if you don't understand it at the time, because we're like ants in this anthill and our whole planet is actually just one tiny speck in some cosmic game.

He sounds a lot different from Seth, Wendy said.

Yesterday we went to the East Village after school and picked out the tattoos we'd get if we could.

But you won't really, right? They had a pact they were going to get a tattoo together when they turned sixteen. Matching roses.

My parents would kill me. But I could get it someplace they wouldn't see. The problem is, it costs forty dollars, and most places need a permission letter if you're under sixteen.

I guess you really like this kid, huh? said Wendy.

It's not like with you of course, Amelia said. I could never talk about the things we do. But for a boy, he's definitely awesome.

How about you? she said. What are the kids like out there?

I don't know any that well, Wendy told her. I'm not actually going to school here.

What do you mean? Your father's letting you stay home?

He doesn't know. I just stopped showing up, and nobody did anything. I take bike rides and go to the mall. Friday was really warm, so I went over to the campus of the college here and sat on the lawn and listened to this bunch of people playing drums. There's a bookstore where the owner lets me sit and read as long as I want, and he gives me herbal tea for free.

You might want to watch that, Amelia said. He could be one of those pedophile types like on the Internet who are on the lookout for really young girls to become their sex slave.

He's nothing like that, Wendy said. He leaves me alone pretty much. Most people do here. Even Garrett. It's kind of strange after being home, where everyone was so concerned all the time.

So do you like it? Amelia asked her.

I don't know, Wendy said. She wanted to tell Amelia the other part. Amelia was the one person who'd understand.

I make up stories, she said. Like you, but more. I tell people things that never really happened. One time I ordered food at a restaurant and didn't pay. I told this one woman on a bus that I'm a child prodigy who got sent to UC Davis to study astrophysics. The man at the bookstore thinks Louie's going to be the next Dalai Lama.

I wish I was there, Amelia said. Other than Chief coming to school, it sucks here. Everyone's stressed out all the time, waiting for some bomb full of chemical weapons to go off. There's men in rubber suits checking all the letters. Louie'd probably want to dress up as one for Halloween if it was now.

It's not exactly great here either, Wendy said. Just different is all.

You think you'll be home by Christmas? Amelia asked. We could dress up in wild outfits and go skating at Wollman Rink. We could take your little brother. Or Chief might have a friend for you.

I don't know what's happening, Wendy said. It's like my whole life is a movie I'm watching.

Just don't have a breakdown for real, okay? It's happened to some people. My mom told me the therapists in Manhattan are all working overtime.

I'll be fine, Wendy said. The hardest part is missing my little brother. Josh, too. And you, naturally.

Tell me about it.

Amelia, she said. One interesting thing.

What's that?

I'm getting thinner. I'm not anorexic or anything. I'm just changing is all.

Well, I'm exactly the same as before, she said. Flat as a board.


You are so brave, Amelia said. If it was me, I don't know what I'd be doing now.

I better go, Wendy said. This probably costs a fortune. Hearing Amelia's voice like this was making her miss home a lot more.

Say hi to your dad for me.

Your parents, too, she said. Amelia said their special good-bye code from their old made-up language back in fifth grade: Spice Girls forever.

Michael Jackson is a pervert. What you said back.

The whole time they were talking, Wendy had been in the backyard, sitting in one of Garrett's old lawn chairs. She had been studying a parade of ants carrying crumbs of toast, one crumb at a time, across the bricks of the patio to their anthill home. In the orange tree beyond, a couple of hummingbirds were hovering beside the blossoms. Shiva had found a sunny spot to sit and lick herself, but now she was asleep.

Wendy walked back in the house. She went to her room. She opened the top drawer of her bureau. She took her mother's dress out—the one from Halloween, that she kept in a plastic bag, separate from all the other clothes—and lifted it to her face.

She breathed in deeply then, as if she were diving to the bottom of a reef, looking for conch shells, and this one breath would have to last her till she made it back to the surface again. She filled her lungs with the scent of her mother's dress. She kept her eyes closed, waiting for a picture of her mother to come to her, the way it had the first time she smelled the dress.

In those early days, after that first terrible one, Wendy had only to close her eyes to see her mother's face or hear her voice, but the image of her had started to grow less clear. The edges were blurring. What came to Wendy now, when she held the dress to her face, was no longer a picture or a sound—more of a feeling. Her mother no longer seemed like this separate person, with clothes and shoes and hair, a voice, a way of walking, a job, but like a piece of herself now, a piece still forming.

The thought came to Wendy that a person didn't just die in a single instant, but gradually, in stages. She had begun to lose her mother that day in September, but it was still happening, a little at a time, as if her mother had been on a little boat that was very gradually drifting out to sea, or holding on to a balloon that kept on rising till you couldn't see it anymore. And even as her mother faded out of sight, someone else seemed to be coming into view: a new and unfamiliar girl.

# Sixteen

Monday, after Garrett dropped her off on his way to work, Wendy took the bus into Sacramento again. She didn't even know where she was headed. When she saw the hospital sign, she decided to get off.

Even then, she didn't have a plan. Maybe she'd bump into some little kid Louie's age in a wheelchair with a terminal illness and she'd read to him. She could volunteer to be one of those people who take the trays into people's rooms. There might turn out to be some old grandma type of person—not a grandmother like Garrett's mom, but the kind who bake cookies and tell stories of the olden days.

She studied the buttons on the elevator. Cardiology. Intensive Care. Oncology. Fifth floor was Obstetrics and Gynecology. Also the neonatal unit. She pushed five.

There were a couple of women in hospital gowns walking up and down the halls, holding their bellies. Wendy knew from when Louie was born that they were in the early stages of labor.

She walked farther down the hall. There was a glass window, and inside the room were rows of cribs, lined up like seats at a theater.

If Amelia was here they'd choose their favorite. Or make up names for the babies, or imagine what each one would be when they grew up. One of them, a baby with a blue ribbon on his crib, at the far right in the front row, looked like her geometry teacher back home, Mr. Hutchinson. A girl next to him had a full head of black curly hair—so much it even stuck out from underneath the little hat they'd put on her.

It had been a long time since she'd seen babies this little. Not since Louie was born. She'd forgotten the funny spastic way they flailed their arms and legs around, like they were punching in the dark. Even at this stage, though, Louie had started finding his thumb.

She imagined Louie back home on those mornings snuggled up in the bed next to her, sucking his thumb hard and a little guiltily, knowing he was a preschool boy now. Like he was trying to get whatever good thing it was out of that thumb before he had to go to school, where he would try hard not to let the kids see him do it. First thing in the morning, his thumb always had a wrinkled look, as if he'd been in the tub too long.

Sissy, he said. Is it true God sees everything?

I don't know, Louie. What do you think?

Then he'd be watching even when I poop.

He probably has more important things to do, Louie. There's a lot of people to keep track of.

Do you think he knows where my mama is?

I don't know.

Because if he did, he should tell us. So we could go there.

A girl was standing next to her in front of the baby window. She was wearing a bathrobe and paper slippers, and though she was a skinny person, her stomach looked a little pooched out. She had stringy hair and her front teeth were crooked, but with her mouth shut she was a little bit pretty.

None of them's yours, right? she said.

I'm just visiting, Wendy said. She must really have changed for someone to imagine she could be some baby's mother. Not that this girl looked old enough either.

Mine's the second on the left, second row, she said. Walter Charles.

Wendy couldn't see him that well but she said, He's really cute.

I wasn't going to keep him but I am, the girl told her. My mom kicked me out of the house. She said she knew if I kept him she'd end up taking care of him, but she's wrong.

If he was mine, I couldn't give him away either, Wendy said. You'd always wonder what happened to him.

That's what I thought. Plus, he's the first person I ever met that's just mine.

Wendy thought what Garrett might say if he were here. That children didn't belong to their parents. They had to be free.

One thing's for sure, the girl said. My boyfriend's history.

Lots of people have kids without a father, Wendy said. When I was little, it was just my mom and me, and we did fine.

My name's Violet, the girl said. How old are you?

Almost fifteen. I just look young for my age.

I'll be seventeen next week, she said. I guess he's like my birthday present, huh?

It sure will be fun when you get to take him home, Wendy said. If it was me, I'd just want to put him on my bed and look at him the longest time.

You could come over sometime, if you wanted, Violet told her. I'm not living at my mom's house anymore. I rented a room in town. I had some money saved up from my job.

Don't you go to school?

Not anymore.

Me neither, Wendy said.

What's your name, anyway?

Kitty.

You could hold him if you wanted. Once I get him home. They're letting us out right after lunch. Only problem being they have this rule that you can't leave without some family member going along with you, and my mom's not speaking to me.

I could pretend to be your sister, Wendy told her.

That's what I was thinking, Violet said. I always wanted a sister anyways.

Wendy waited in the sunroom while Violet checked out. She picked up a magazine and read about no-muss, no-fuss summer fun desserts. The magazine was from July. She thought about where she'd been in July—New York mostly, but that was also when they took their trip to Nantucket. A million years ago.

Violet came out. A nurse was pushing her in a wheelchair, and she had Walter Charles wrapped in a blanket in her arms. She had on sweatpants and slip-on sandals.

I can walk fine. It's just the rules, she said.

So this is your sister, said the nurse. I was picturing someone older.

They rode the elevator down to the curb. A taxi was already outside waiting.

Well, here you go, said the nurse. Don't let her tire herself out, okay, honey? the nurse said. You need to get a car seat, she told Violet.

They got in the back.

Man, said Violet. I thought I'd never get out of that place.

Walter Charles made a squeaking noise from inside the blanket. I think he's hungry, she said. My mom said I'd wreck my boobs if I breast-fed him, but I read in my baby book that it's a ton healthier for your baby than if you give him a bottle.

Don't you want to be private? Wendy asked. The driver can see in the rearview mirror.

I'll never see him again, said Violet. Anyway, some cabdriver seeing my tit is the least of my problems.


Violet's building was in a not-so-great part of town next to a gas station. The good part is that anytime you need to make a phone call or buy chips, it's handy, Violet said. They walked up to the third floor, taking it slow. Wendy was carrying Violet's overnight bag, along with the diapers and the starter kit they'd given her at the hospital.

It was just one room, but with one of those mini refrigerators in a corner and a hot plate. There was a mattress on the floor, and a shelf with a boom box on top and a pile of folded clothes. There was a brand-new crib and a table set up with a box of Huggies and diaper wipes set to go, and a TV and a beanbag chair. There was a poster of a couple of kittens playing with a ball of yarn, and another one of Madonna, the same one Wendy had, with the cowboy hat.

I love her, too, Wendy said.

She had a baby a little while ago, and she got right back into shape, said Violet.

Here, she said. Let's take a look at him. She carried Walter Charles over to the mattress and laid him down. She picked a spot where the sun was coming in the window.

I bet that feels good to him.

She unwrapped him slowly, like a present. First the blanket, then the little undershirt with the snap in front. I always hated it when I was little and my mom pulled my shirt over my head, Violet said. I still remember the feeling.

She bent his arms through the holes, first one, then the other. They looked as if they could snap off. Don't worry, Wally, she said. I'm here.

Then it was just his bare chest and his diaper left. Wendy hadn't expected his legs to be so skinny. He still had the booties on but they were too big. The air against his skin, even though it was warm, seemed to make him shiver.

He wriggled on the mattress, waving his arms like a bug trying to right himself. His mouth was making little sucking sounds, as if he was looking for something—Violet's nipple, probably. You could see the rise and fall of his chest, his lungs filling with air, a single blue vein in his forehead, where the skin looked almost translucent. The beating of his heart even, faster than regular people.

We can take off his diaper, said Violet. It was as if they were thieves, sneaking in someplace they shouldn't.

He wasn't even wet, but they took the diaper off anyway and looked at him. His tiny penis was red-looking and sore from the circumcision, and white where the nurses must have put cream on him before he left the hospital. Wendy knew about that from Louie. There was a piece of plastic clamped onto the last inch of his umbilical cord.

They said the dead skin will fall off in a few days, Violet said. When it does, I'm going to put it in his baby box with all the other keepsakes, so I can show them to him someday when he's grown up. She hadn't taken his hospital bracelet off yet. I have his footprint, too, she said.

Tomorrow morning when you wake up, do you think you'll remember right off that he's here or forget? Wendy asked her.

I sure hope I don't forget, she said. It seemed like my mom forgot all the time. Even when I was like fourteen, it was like she didn't always remember she had a kid.

Sometimes when I first wake up, I forget things for a second, said Wendy.

It must feel pretty strange. That you're just sixteen and still you're a mom.

I thought it would be weirder than it is, having him, said Violet. But once you actually have the baby, everything changes. You started out being this person that all they care about is getting the coolest jeans at the Gap, and all of a sudden you start wanting things like a musical mobile to hang over the crib and a stroller with good tires so the ride won't be too bumpy for your kid.

What made you change your mind about giving him away? Wendy asked her.

There were these people in San Francisco that were supposed to take him, she said. A lawyer I met from an ad introduced me to them. The wife was one of those people that wanted to wait till she had her career and a bunch of money before she decided to have kids, and by the time she was finally ready, it was too late. She and her husband wanted to know a whole lot of stuff about my family background and how tall I was and if anyone in my family ever had mental problems, but I still figured it would be good for the baby, going someplace where they could buy him nice things and send him to college and stuff.

I was listening to this song one time. You like Led Zeppelin?

She went over to the boom box and turned it on. The volume had been set really loud. Walter Charles looked startled. Violet turned it down.

"Babe I'm gonna leave you," the singer was saying.

For a few bars, the song was slow and almost pretty, like something Wendy could imagine her mother liking, but then the guitars got really loud and the drums started crashing. You could tell from the words that the singer wasn't talking about leaving a baby; he was talking about leaving a woman. The point was, someone was leaving and somebody's baby was going to be left behind.

Violet was holding Walter Charles while she listened to the song, dancing with him, as much as a person could dance to a song like that. His head flopped over a little. From the look of her, Violet hadn't held too many babies.

I was thinking I was going to do all this stuff, she said. A friend of mine knew this person that could set me up working at Disneyland. Then I started wondering if there was anything I could do that would end up being more important than doing a good job raising my kid. Not like my mom did with me.

I just wasn't all that sure that these people in San Francisco with all the money were going to care about him the right way, she said. They kept on wanting to know things like my IQ and if I had a weight problem or pimples.

Your mom should be the type of person who loves you no matter what you're like, Wendy said. Even if you aren't all that smart or cute.

That's how a mom should be, definitely, Violet said. My mom keeps telling me what a loser I am. I'd never say something like that to Walter Charles. It would be nice if he had a dad, too, but he'll have me anyways.

And he might have a dad sometime, Wendy said. Like my mom. When I was seven, she met this really great guy, and he was just like a dad to me.

So where is he now? Violet asked. If he's such a great dad, why'd he let you drop out of school?

For a second, Wendy couldn't think what to say. Violet was right. She had never met Josh, but even she could tell a good father would never let a thing like that happen.

He died, Wendy said. He was on one of the planes that crashed into the World Trade Center.

Oh my God, said Violet. I can see why you'd be shook-up. How's your mom taking it?

I don't like talking about it, if that's all right, said Wendy. But that's why things are a little unusual at the moment.

Listen, said Violet. You can come over here and hang out with Walter Charles and me anytime.

They sprinkled some baby powder on him and picked out a fresh shirt, even though the old one was clean. Then they put on a fresh diaper. They tried to think if there was anything more they needed to do but they couldn't. Violet laid him in his crib and he fell asleep.

He sleeps a ton, she said. I kind of wish he'd be awake more often, so I could do stuff with him.

They listened to the rest of the Led Zeppelin CD, and after that, they looked at a magazine article Violet had about the Madonna tour.

It says she has twenty-three different outfits for the show, Violet said. And every single night she performs one of her concerts, she throws one of her special custom-made hats into the audience, and the person that catches it gets to take it home. Imagine if it was you.

Someone would probably pay a thousand dollars just for that hat, Wendy said. In the magazine article, it said if you wanted to see Madonna on the Drowned World Tour, tickets cost three hundred dollars apiece.

But listen to this, said Violet. Those people in San Francisco? They were going to pay ten thousand dollars to adopt Walter Charles. And still I decided to keep him. They had all that money, but they don't have anything as special as him.

I think you made a good decision, said Wendy.

It's the one thing I have, Violet told her. I never had a family before. Now he's it.


When Wendy got home, Garrett was already there. We knocked off early today, he said. Lumber shipment didn't come.

He was out back, putting charcoal in the birdbath. I thought I'd make us a little barbecue tonight, he said. Carolyn's coming over.

Sounds good, Wendy said. Shiva was sniffing her right in the place she'd been holding Walter Charles when he spit up a little on her lap.

Good day at school? he asked.

The usual, she told him.

He unwrapped a packet of meat and sprinkled barbecue sauce on it. Hope you worked up an appetite out on the playing field. I've got us some sweet porterhouse steaks here.

I might not eat a whole one, she said.

I guess Shiva can figure out what to do with your leftovers, he said. He looked at her.

You wearing baby powder, Slim? he asked.

I sometimes put it on after my shower, she told him. I like the smell.

It was bringing back memories, he said. You know how smells do that sometimes. I was remembering when you were a baby, if you want to know the truth.

Wendy thought about a picture from their old album, of her mother looking very young, and holding Wendy, wrapped in one of the goofy-looking buntings she crocheted back then. Wendy had seen this photograph a hundred times, but for the first time, she imagined who the person must have been taking it: her father.

Just so you know, he said. Your mother and I were happy then.

I could read your palm, if you feel like it, Carolyn said.

They were sitting in the backyard, waiting for the coals to get hot. Garrett was inside boiling potatoes.

Sure, said Wendy. She wondered what would have happened if someone had read her mother's palm on the tenth of September. If they had, would the person have seen anything in her mother's hand? What if she did and she said, Whatever you do, don't go to work on the eleventh. Stay out of the towers.

Does it ever happen that you look at somebody's hand and you can tell something bad's going to happen to them? Wendy asked her. Like you look at their lifeline and it stops in about three more days?

It's not like that exactly, Carolyn said. It's more likely to be a case where you can tell what the danger areas might be, and you talk about those with the person.

There was one time, though, she said. There was this guy I knew. I was reading his palm, and the lifeline just stopped, right at the place where you'd expect it to branch. Instead of a line for love and prosperity and health and all that, there was nothing but smooth skin.

What did you do?

I asked him what his plans were for the next few days, she said. White-water rafting down the American River, he told me.

You raft much before? I asked him. I was stalling for time. Trying to think how I should handle it.

Never, he said. But I'm going with my son, and he's been plenty of times. You could tell he was really proud of the kid. Nineteen years old. Training to be a river guide.

Listen, I told him. I've never said anything like this before. But you shouldn't go.

But if the lifeline stops like that, could you do anything about it? Wendy asked her. Isn't it something that's already set up, that you can't change?

That's what I was thinking, Carolyn told her. But you've got to remember that I don't know everything, either. I'm still figuring out how it all works myself. It's a lifelong process.

So he didn't go?

He went, she said. On the second day the two of them were on the river and they opened up some dam upriver without telling people and it made the water three times as fast and higher than usual. The commercial rafting companies weren't even putting in on the American that week. But this guy and his son had their own raft, so they didn't know anything about it.

And the man drowned?

They got him out. It was the son who didn't make it. But the father was destroyed after that from what I heard. Started drinking really bad. Then his wife left him.

If you saw something bad on my lifeline, would you tell me?

Honey, I think the bad part already happened. The part from here on is likely to be better.


This was the first time Carolyn had referred to what happened back in New York.

But that man in the raft, Wendy said. First one bad thing happened. Then it just got worse from there.

He was a different type of person, Carolyn told her. The give-up type. Like a fern. You're sturdier. More of a cactus-type girl.

How can you tell?

Because you're sitting here talking to me, she said. Some people would just lock themselves in a room and make the world go away. You're still out here living.

How're those coals looking, you two? Garrett called out.

Another ten minutes, I'd say, Carolyn told him.

So let's see what you got, she said.


I'm looking at the family line, Carolyn told her. It's full of love. Lots of good things there.

That's my future?

The funny thing is, it's like I see two different figures looking out for you, but from different places.

Maybe one was her mother. From someplace, who knew where. In the sky or under the rubble—she wasn't sure. She was thinking that, but she didn't say anything.

There's all this male energy, Carolyn said. It's from your father house, but it's coming from two different directions.

Wendy wished Carolyn could tell her something about her mother. You see a woman anyplace? she asked.

There's this one, and she's coming your way. But I'd be on my guard with her if I were you. She's not a very positive force for you.

Garrett walked out into the yard just then.

Hell, Carolyn, you scare me sometimes, he said.

What are you talking about, Garrett? My hair that bad?

That woman heading our way who my daughter needs to watch out for? he said. My mother called this afternoon. She's coming out here for Thanksgiving.

# Seventeen

Alan was right that she'd like the book he gave her, *The Member of the Wedding,* by Carson McCullers. The girl in it, Frankie, was around Wendy's age. She lived in a little town in the South with her father and a black cook with only one eye. Her mother had died when she was born. She wanted to run away from home and have adventures. She also made up stories—not because she was a dishonest person, just so she'd have a different life that she liked better than the real one. Her older brother was getting married, and she kept thinking he was going to take her along with him and his bride. Wendy knew right away that this would never happen.

One thing she liked about Frankie was how, like herself, Frankie had felt a terrible and unexplainable contrariness overtaking her the summer she was twelve.

"This was the summer when Frankie was sick and tired of being Frankie," the author had written. ". . . It was the year when Frankie thought about the world. And she did not see it as a round school globe, with the countries neat and different-colored. She thought of the world as huge and cracked and loose and turning a thousand miles an hour."

If Wendy had read that page a year ago, she wouldn't have understood how Frankie felt. Then September happened and the planet she lived on had seemed more like a meteor, spinning and falling.

Hey, Kitty, how's tricks? Alan asked when she leaned Garrett's bike up against the front of his store. I was just boiling water for tea.

For the first time since she'd been in California, she'd been thinking it would be nice if she had a clarinet out here. Not to play the pieces they'd been working on at school for the Christmas concert back in New York, but a couple of the jazz numbers Josh had been teaching her. If she started playing clarinet again, maybe Josh would pick up his bass.

I was working on my clarinet, she told Alan.

Clarinet, he said. Now that you say it, I can see you with a woodwind instrument. Clarinet goes with your personality.

Josh used to tell her that, too. Any kind of person you meet, he said, there's an instrument that suits them. Could be nothing more than the triangle or a harmonica, but there's a piece of the band someplace in everybody, even the tone-deaf types who couldn't clap along with "Jimmy Crack Corn" to save their life.

Your brother, for instance. He'd be baritone horn. Loud and a little bit of a grandstander, breaks right into the action and stirs things up. Class clown. Your mother's more of a flute type. Dancing over the surface. Light as air. You, clarinet, right on the money. Low and thoughtful and crucially important to the sound of the band, without making a big show about it. Playful at times. Very subtle and deep.

And what's a bass player? she asked him.

Steady and loyal, he said. Doesn't carry the melody, doesn't have to be the star, but he's always there holding things together. Some people think it's the drummer, but really it's the bass player who's the heartbeat of whatever group of instruments he's playing with. Slow and steady, keeps on pumping. And handsome, naturally. Did I forget to mention that part? Same as you clarinet people are beautiful.

Yeah, right, she said.

You don't know it yet, but you're going to be a knockout, Josh told her.

*      *      *

Now that I know you like the clarinet, Alan said, I have the perfect piece of music to play for you. He was at the front counter, where the cash register and the CD player were, flipping through discs. She figured maybe he'd have Woody Herman, Josh's favorite, but the CD that he chose for her was classical.

Old Wolfgang Amadeus, he said. The clarinet concerto. You know it?

He brought the tea to her reading spot in back. She was just sitting there listening to the music. She thought Josh would like it as much as she did, even though this was nothing like jazz. For a moment, she felt a great hollow yearning for him to be sitting there with her, sipping his hot chocolate, tapping out the beat or playing imaginary bass in the air the way he always used to.

I'm up to page seventy-four of that book you gave me, she said. It's one of the best books I ever read.

I thought you'd like it, he said. The girl in the story seems a lot like you. Good imagination. She spends a lot of time on her own, too. Walking around, thinking. Not enough people do that, in my opinion.

I could give you a hand putting books away, she said. If you still need help.

Do I ever. I bought out a guy's whole library yesterday. Don't know what to do with them all.

He gave her a box of paperbacks. Just find the right place in the alphabet and squeeze them in the shelves where you can, he said. More or less in order is good enough.

She worked a couple of hours. Except for finding spaces to put the books sometimes, it wasn't a hard job, and she liked the way the alphabetizing occupied her mind. Every once in a while as she was shelving, she'd stop and flip through the pages, so her afternoon became an interesting kind of grab bag of sentences and fragments of stories. A book on how to train a puppy written by a bunch of monks. A book about understanding the hidden messages in dreams. Vegan recipes. A collection of poems by a man named Rumi.

Now and then when customers would come in, she could hear Alan talking with them in the front, discussing some book they'd read or taking a special order.

How's Tim? a woman asked him.

The usual, he said. I was up visiting on Tuesday. Sometimes it's hard to know if he even notices I'm there, but I like to think he does. For Linda it's just too difficult, though. She hardly ever comes with me anymore.

I can still remember him as a very little boy, the woman said. Jumping on that trampoline and talking about dinosaurs. You wouldn't have known anything was wrong.

First three years nothing was, he said. You don't realize how precious certain things are that you took for granted. Then they're gone and what you wouldn't give for one hour with that kid you used to take on the back of your bicycle, naming every single fact about the stegosaurus.

It's probably harder on you than on him, the woman said. It's like the people who got killed in New York. For them, it's over. The people who suffer are the ones they left behind.

# Eighteen

It never seems like you have any homework, Garrett said. Not that I want to start being your policeman. Just curious.

There are lots of study halls, she said.

A few days after she stopped going to school, she had typed a letter on Garrett's old Smith Corona, as if it was her father writing, to say there'd been a change of plans. "My daughter will not be residing in the area after all," she wrote. It wasn't hard to forge her father's signature.

She hadn't fully expected the letter to work, but a few weeks had gone by and nothing had happened, so she figured the school had bought her story.

It's probably not the most challenging educational institution going, Garrett was saying now. I'm betting that when your grandmother gets out here, she's going to want me to check out some damn private school, someplace where you can finally put all those white monogrammed shirts to use. But it's probably not the worst thing in the world to have a little time right about now just to take it easy and coast.

Right, she told him. The less said the better.

*　　*　　*

She's flying into San Francisco Tuesday night, Garrett said. I figure we can give her a day on her own to do some shopping, then drive down to meet her Thursday morning. She's taking us out for a holiday meal at the Fairmont Hotel. We'll stay over, and head back Friday.

I haven't seen my grandmother in years, Wendy told him. One time when she was going on some cruise, my mom and I met her for lunch in the city, but that was awhile ago.

She's probably not as bad as I make out, he said. She's just one of those people who always leaves you with the feeling you've disappointed her. The only two people I can think of her talking about with any enthusiasm or affection were Mamie Eisenhower and Rod Laver.

Who are they?

The wife of a president from fifty years ago, and her all-time-favorite tennis player, he said. The rest of us just never measured up.


Even from down on the street, Wendy could tell that Walter Charles was crying. She climbed up the two flights of stairs and rang the bell.

It's open, Violet said.

She was sitting in the beanbag chair, trying to nurse him. Her shirt was unbuttoned and her hair was a mess. The TV was on and her baby book was open on the bed. She looked as if she hadn't slept in a long time.

I don't know what's the matter, she said. Whatever I do, he keeps screaming.

When my brother used to cry like that, my dad had this thing he'd do where he'd walk him around the room, making jazz rhythms in his ear very softly, Wendy told her. She reached for Walter Charles and put him over her shoulder, and tried to sound like Josh doing his bebop routine. She could feel the baby's body relax against her own. He was still making little worried noises, but less desperately.

I've been losing my mind, Violet said. He was doing that all night. I was starting to think my mom was right and I should have signed the papers after all and let the rich people in San Francisco have him. I don't know one thing about how to take care of babies.

You probably just need a change of scene, Wendy said. That was the same thing Amelia told her back in New York. Come on, Wendy said. Let's get his diaper bag.

At Macy's they took turns trying on clothes. They didn't have any money, but it never hurt to pretend.

None of my shirts fit anymore, Violet said. I could probably get a job at Hooters if my stomach would just flatten out. I wish I was like you.

Wendy hadn't realized how much thinner she'd gotten until she tried on the clothes. The strange thing was, she hadn't even been thinking about it as much as before. It just happened. She wasn't even starving herself now.

Violet didn't try any tops. She was afraid of milk dripping out of her breasts onto the fabric. Sometimes that happened, especially when Walter Charles cried.

It's an automatic thing, Violet said. Like my body just knows I'm his mother, and I don't even need to think about it. They said in my book that it's this animal instinct. I wish my brain knew as much as my tits.

They got a Cinnabon to share, and a Diet Coke. Sitting in the food court, which was crowded with mothers pushing strollers, they compared the babies.

Walter Charles is definitely the cutest, Wendy said.

You should have seen his dad, said Violet. Everyone said he looked like Brad Pitt.

I used to shoplift, Violet told her, reaching for the last piece of Cinnabon. But I don't anymore.

Did you get caught?

I just decided to quit when I knew I was having a baby, she said. I wanted to be a good role model. But sometimes when I go into stores, I pick out in my head what I'd take if I was still doing that stuff.

Thinking it doesn't really matter, Wendy said. Everybody thinks stuff.

You probably never stole anything in your whole life, Violet said. I can tell. It just goes to prove what I was saying about role models. Your parents kept you on the right track.

My little brother stole a Matchbox truck one time, Wendy said. When my mom found out, she made him go back to the store with her to return it.

He was scared they were going to put him in jail, but she told him they didn't do that to four-year-olds.

He must be so sad now, Violet said. Missing your dad. At least you two have each other.

Sort of, Wendy said. Just thinking about Louie made the hollow feeling come back.

People always think that just because kids are little, they don't take things so hard, Violet said. Me, I remember every single bad thing from when I was little. At least when you're older, you can get out in the world and talk to your friends. Go to the mall. When you're little, you're trapped.

This guy I know has a son who was fine until he was three, and then he turned autistic, Wendy said. I'd die if that happened to my little brother.

It probably won't, said Violet. But I'd definitely keep an eye on him.


Your brother's started hitting at school, Josh said. Nobody's making a fuss about it, but I'm worried.

What does he say when you talk to him about it? Wendy asked him.

He says the kids are mean to him. He says they hit him first. I don't think I believe it.

Maybe it's just a stage. Maybe he saw some show on TV that got him started. Maybe someone in his class teases him about his costumes.

He doesn't want to go over to Corey's anymore, either. He says he doesn't like Corey's room.

Does he talk about Mom?

Not anymore. When I bring up her name, he says he hates her. I've got him scheduled to see a therapist on Tuesday.

What does he say about me? she asked him.

He wants to know when you're coming home, Josh said. He was silent for a moment. I don't know what to tell him.

Garrett's mother's coming next week, she said. The one with the lawyer.

Josh sounded tired all of a sudden. Just do what you need to take care of yourself, Wen, he said. We'll figure out our end of things here.

\*     \*     \*

So where are you going for Thanksgiving? she asked him.

Kate invited us to her mother's, and my sister's having some friends over to her place, too, he said. My mom wants us to come to Florida, but that's definitely out. I don't know. We might just sit this one out. Hang around the house, watch the *Sesame Street* Thanksgiving special like a couple of wild and carefree bachelor guys. Heat ourselves up a couple of TV dinners.

If you ever see me buying one of those, he'd said to her mother one time when they were out shopping together and they passed the TV dinners in the frozen-food case, just have me committed, and make sure no sharp objects are within the vicinity. Because you'll know for sure I've lost my mind.

# Nineteen

Her mother used to say, when Wendy asked her to explain the divorce, that she and her father fought all the time. Living with Garrett, that was hard to imagine at first. Whatever she did or didn't do, he never had a problem. She could leave the butter on the counter, and not just the butter but a whole pile of dishes, and her socks on the floor—no problem. Living with him, it was almost like the two of them were roommates. She didn't have to eat a green vegetable every day. It would be great if you could get around to feeding Shiva, he said. That was pretty much it.

Slowly, though, it was beginning to occur to Wendy that even Garrett's easygoing way of acting could get on a person's nerves.

Nobody could ever have accused her mother of being easygoing. Her mother was on duty twenty-four hours a day, noticing everything. Wanting her to do better.

With her mother it would have been, Do you think we're your servants here? I can't believe a person could be so incredibly inconsiderate that she couldn't even think to put one crummy dish in the dishwasher before going off to the movies.

Does it ever occur to you? her mother said. I spend nine hours a day in this fluorescent-lighted office, typing, while you glide around with your friend, trying on sweaters and thinking up names for your imaginary pets, and you can't even be bothered to pick up the three lousy groceries I asked you to bring home?

Thinking about it now—all the times she should have helped out, but didn't, how selfish she used to be—made Wendy feel sick. In the past, she had believed her mother was unreasonable, having all these expectations for her behavior. Living with Garrett, she almost missed them. She could do what she wanted now. But sometimes she wondered if it meant he was nicer, or just that he didn't pay enough attention to notice.

I didn't mean to be thoughtless, she said to her mother one time.

Hardly anybody ever means to be thoughtless, her mother said. That's the whole idea about thoughtlessness.

There was this time, just last spring. Her mother wanted to see a matinee of the Mark Morris Dance Company at the Brooklyn Academy of Music and Josh had a gig. I need you to watch your brother, she said.

Most of the time it wouldn't have been a big deal but that day it was. A boy in Wendy's class named Jasper Sandstone had been telling everyone about the new home theater they'd installed in his dad's apartment on the Upper East Side and a bunch of kids from their class were supposed to go over and watch a movie and have pizza and listen to music. There was this one record from back in their parents' day, Pink Floyd, *The Wall*, that was supposed to be unbelievable when you listened to it in surround sound.

I'm really sorry you have to miss it, sweetheart, her mother said. I tried three other people to baby-sit. Kate got me these tickets for my birthday, and we've been planning this for weeks.

I'm always taking Louie, Wendy said.

I'll make it up to you another time, her mother said.

Oh, right. Like you'll take Louie and me to *Disney on Ice* or something. Woo woo.

*     *     *

Times like this, Wendy, she said. She said this very quietly, which was the worst. I wonder what I did to raise such a selfish, ungenerous daughter. I wonder if I even know you anymore.

When she said that, Wendy actually felt scared. What if she really had turned into this awful person? Maybe it was true. Everything about her family was getting on her nerves. Even Josh, who was always so easygoing. Louie, for sure. He didn't even seem that cute anymore.

I'll go to *Disney on Ice* with you, Mama, Louie said then. Even if Sissy doesn't want to.

Sissy was just feeling a little upset, Lou-man, Josh said. He'd been in the other room, putting on the suit he wore to gigs, but now he came out, in his shirt and tie and rumpled pants—the too-long ones, not the too-short ones—and put an arm around Wendy. She brushed it off.

This family makes me sick, she said. Nobody here knows one single thing about how it feels to be me.

After they left—Kate and her mom to the dance performance, Josh in the van with Roberto for their gig—it was just Wendy and Louie, eating the grilled cheese Josh had made them. We're going to have so much fun, just wait and see, Sis, Louie told her. When we play Candyland I'll let you win.

Amelia couldn't believe it when she came over and heard Wendy couldn't go after all. Do you know how many people would die to get invited over to Jasper Sandstone's? she said.

We didn't exactly get invited, Wendy said. Seems to me you told him we were going to be at this modeling tryout you were invited to in his neighborhood and maybe you'd stop by after with a couple of the other models.

He was happy, she said. The more the merrier, he said, if you recall.

And what if we had showed up and it was just us and no models? Wendy asked. You still think he'd have been so thrilled?

This is why you don't get invited to parties, Wendy, Amelia told her. You get too negative.

So they went anyway. They put Louie in an outfit like he'd been trying out for a commercial and slicked back his hair with gel. We tell them he's this kid we met on a cereal commercial, Amelia told her. They'll probably want his autograph.

Where do you get this stuff? Wendy said. And how are we supposed to explain it when he calls me Sissy all the time?

Okay then, he's your brother. Your brother that's been making an ad for Raisin Bran.

I don't want to go on the subway, Louie told them. I like it here.

It's just for a little while, Louie, Wendy said. It'll be fun.

It's fun here.

More fun. There'll be pizza.

I had grilled cheese already. I'm full.

Louie, Amelia said. If you come with us, I'll get you a treat.

What?

It's a secret. You'll find out after. But you have to be very good. When we get to the big boy's house you can just lie down someplace and take a nap. That would be the best thing. And afterwards, if you promise not to tell your parents, Wendy and I will get you this awesome treat.

I hope it's a Matchbox, he said. That or Pokémon cards.


It turned out there were only two other people at Jasper Sandstone's. Both boys.

One was a boy Wendy and Amelia had never met, named Travis, who had rainbow-colored braces. Hey, he said. I thought you told me there were models coming over.

I didn't say model whats, said Jasper. He was holding some kind of Coke drink that must have had liquor in it because there were a bunch of bottles of Jack Daniel's and Absolut vodka and things like that out on the counter. No parents around.

Who's the midget? Travis asked.

My brother, said Wendy.

He's been working on a commercial, Amelia told them. Raisin Bran. With the money from the residuals he's probably going to have enough to buy the whole family Jet Skis.

So, kid, Jasper said. Tell us your lines.

My sister's getting me a treat after, he said. I bet it's going to be a Matchbox.

You ladies care for an aperitif? Travis said. He had a bottle of Dr Pepper in one hand and a bottle of Johnnie Walker in the other.

No thanks, said Wendy. To Amelia she said, Let's get out of here.

The movie's just starting, Jasper said. You only missed a few minutes but you'll probably figure it out.

It was a horror film called *Child's Play*, where a doll named Chucky comes to life and starts killing people. One girl was dead already, but one of her arms was still lying on the floor. The doll had the kind of eyeballs like the Madame Alexander dolls at F. A. O. Schwarz. Chucky's eyelids opened and closed, and he had fake-hair lashes and staring glassy eyeballs, but other than that he looked nothing like Cissette or any of those other dolls Wendy and her mother used to look at on their pretend doll-shopping trips.

I don't like this movie, Louie said. I want to change the channel.

You should go to sleep, Louie, Amelia said. I think it's nap time.


I really think we need to take him home now, Wendy said. Amelia wasn't paying attention to her. Travis was asking her if he'd seen her in an ad for the Gap.

That's you in the blue bikini top and the cutoffs on the billboard over on Forty-third Street, right? he asked her.

I don't think so, she told him. They haven't put mine up yet.


On the way home they bought Louie two Matchboxes: a snowplow and a '57 Thunderbird convertible. When they were back out on the street he said he wanted the Formula One racer instead, but Amelia said, That's life.

Her mother was already back when they got to the apartment. We just took him out for a treat, Wendy said. Amelia and I wanted to get him a couple of cars.

Her mother, still in her dress-up clothes, looked like she wasn't necessarily buying it but Louie was so tired, he just lay down on the couch and fell asleep.

I myself never feel a need to put on eyeliner and mascara when I go out to Walgreens, her mother said.

Was the choreography good? Wendy asked her. She knew Mark Morris was her mother's favorite and if they could just get talking about that it would be a good idea.

The man is a genius, she said. If I was twenty years younger, I'd do anything to dance in that company. I can't imagine anything more rewarding.

As opposed to being a mother. As opposed to living with them in this little apartment, heating up Josh's casserole and scraping cheese off the grilled-cheese maker.

She was sitting at the kitchen table with a glass of wine, studying the program. There's one dancer in his company that's just two years younger than me, she said. Of course she's been dancing with Mark Morris since she was twenty. It's not like she sits at a desk Monday through Friday, typing up memos.

Always before, even in the old days, when times were hard, Wendy had always seen her slim, light-footed mother as glamorous and beautiful. That afternoon, sitting there in her *West Side Story* dress with the belt that showed off her twenty-three-inch waist and her red leather high-heel boots that she'd resoled a couple of times, they were so old, her mother had looked a little sad and worn.

Amelia had to go. You'd better take a cab home, Wendy's mother said. I don't like to see you going home on the subway after dark. She handed Amelia five dollars.

I don't mind the subway, Amelia said. But she took the money.


That night, Louie woke up crying. By the time Wendy got to him Josh was there already.

Chucky's coming to get me, he said. And the boy with the rainbow braces.

Who's Chucky? Josh said. Is this someone from day care?

He makes people's arms come off, Louie said. They fall in the garbage disposal.

Chucky's not here, Louie, Josh said. He went away.

I saw him, Louie said.

Her mother was standing in the door to the room now, her hair wild and her bathrobe half on, half off. She stared straight at Wendy.

You and Amelia took your brother to that boy's house today, didn't you?

There was never any point lying to her mother.


Once Wendy started thinking about all the things she regretted, she couldn't stop. Riding Garrett's bike in the hot, dry air of Davis, out along the flat expanse of wheat-lined highway, the pictures of her mother and her kept coming back to her, like buildings she passed along the road. Diner . . . gas station . . . avocado stand . . . fight with mother.

She wanted to bring the other mother back. The one who stood there in the fitting room at Macy's with her when they bought back-to-school clothes. We have to get you these pants, honey, she said. You just look so great in them.

I have to warn you, she said, when Wendy put on the pink angora sweater. Every time you come near me in this, I'm likely to have to give you a hug.

Then the shoe department—always her mother's big weakness. I think we could get you a pair with heels this fall, what do you say? Your have such nice long legs. Let's try on these boots just for fun.

And after, in the little coffee shop they went to for cappuccino and a milk shake. What would I do if I didn't have you for my daughter? If I spotted you here having a milk shake with some other woman, I'd have to kidnap you.

All my life, this is what I wanted. A smart, funny, beautiful, wonderful daughter just like you to try on shoes with.


Pedaling along the highway, sweat dripping down her neck, it was the other images that came to her: discount jewelry store . . . car dealership . . . health club . . . fight with mother. The horrible moments filled up her brain.

There was the time when her mother announced they were driving some- place in New Jersey to see farm animals.

Have you even noticed I'm not six years old anymore? Wendy said. Did it ever occur to you I might not want to spend every Sunday for the rest of my life driving around hick towns with you and Josh, sitting in the backseat with Louie, looking out for eighteen-wheelers and making cow noises?

We do other things, too, her mother said. When we go to amusement parks and you ride on roller coasters, your brother mostly just watches. She didn't sound mad as much as hurt.

Oh, great. That's really my idea of a perfect way to spend my Sunday afternoons. Going on rides with my mother's husband.

She had never called him that before.

I thought you liked going on rides, her mother said. I thought our family day was important to you, too. You forget all those years we never had anyone to go out exploring with.

Ease up, Jan, Josh said. Somewhere in there he'd come into the room. Now he put his arm around Wendy, but not too tightly.

We've been a little selfish, he said. Just because we want to spend Sundays with Wendy doesn't mean that's what she wants to do. I'm probably the worst offender here.

There were just so many years I missed out on, Wen, he said. I guess I was trying to make up for them.

There, her mother said. You satisfied now? Here's the guy you want so much to get away from. Your own father walks out on you flat, and along comes Josh, who hadn't exactly been in desperate need of some seven-year-old daughter. He was having a pretty great life without us, as a matter of fact. And all he wants to do is spend as much time with you as he can. So you kick him in the teeth for it? This is the guy who sold his saxophone to buy you that bicycle.

Stop it, Jan, he said. Wendy hardly ever heard him talk that way to her mother. You're laying it on too hard. I didn't even play my sax anymore.

The point is, your coming along was the luckiest thing that ever happened to us and she's complaining about it. You should have seen her father. Or the person who called himself her father.

Kids are supposed to complain about their parents, he said. I should feel flattered. If our daughter started saying how thrilled she was to hang out with us all the time, we'd know she must be doing crack cocaine behind our backs. Either that or she was a hopeless loser.

Our daughter.

Tell you what, he said. Why don't you bag the Friendly Farm picnic this afternoon? But keep next Sunday open, because there's an amazing concert of Brazilian drummers up in Harlem, and I want you to hear them. You can bring Amelia if you want. You'll be the only ones in your class cool enough to know about Oladum.

They went to New Jersey without her. Amelia was busy that day, so Wendy stayed home and drew for a while, then watched a movie. By the end of the afternoon she was actually missing her family.

When they got back around seven-thirty, it turned out they'd stopped at some flea market on the way home and bought her this great set of plastic Beatles figures with bobbing heads from the sixties. This was her *Hard Day's Night* period.

Mama said they were too expensive, but we got them anyway, said Louie.

Hush up, Lou-man, Josh said.

She set the figures on the table to study them. They were wearing matching blue suits and ties with identical hairdos except that Ringo had the mustache. Louie bobbed their heads.

I was a Paul girl, her mother said.

You would, Josh told her. Wendy likes John the best, right?

This was true.

So, he said to her in a British accent. What do you call that haircut? They had only watched the movie together maybe seven times.

Arthur, she said. Without missing a beat.

Sometime back, more than a year maybe, her mother brought up the idea of Josh formally adopting her. We haven't seen Garrett in a couple of years, she said to Josh. Just one crummy visit from his mother that time, to eat cucumber sandwiches and find out if I've made plans yet for Wendy's coming-out party.

I don't need any legal formalities, Josh said. It's enough knowing we're a family.

I'm just thinking about if something happened to me, her mother said. Not that I'm planning to cut out on you. But you never know. It's a risky business being an executive secretary. You never know when I might trip on my dictaphone cord and break my neck. Or my boss might just flip out one day and start wildly flailing that putter he keeps in his office. I'd be first in the line of fire.

I don't want them to hit you with a golf club, Louie said.

Mama's just joking, Josh told him.

You should be more careful, Janet, he said. That kid can pick up what we say from three rooms away, even with the *Magic School Bus* video going and his sister working on her scales full blast.

Nothing bad's going to happen to me, Louie, she said. I was just talking to Poppy about your sister.

We'd have to serve Garrett some kind of papers, Josh said. I wouldn't want to get him all riled up. It could start something.

You don't know Garrett, she said. He's too fascinated with his own life to come tearing out here to fight for legal rights to his daughter. Try taking his truck away from him, that might be a different story. Touch his tackle box and you're looking for trouble. Let him hear about some reggae festival and he's there. But his daughter? I don't think so.

Still, he said, I'd just as soon not risk it. Besides, if anything ever happened to you, the rest of us would have to run off to Alaska and wait for the wolves to come get us.

I don't want to go to Alaska, said Louie.


But it was Wendy who'd come out of her room then. I can't believe you two, she said. Plotting behind my back to wipe my real father out of my life.

I wasn't plotting, her mother said. I was just trying to be practical and consider what would be best for you if anything ever happened to me. And it wasn't Josh who was thinking any of this. It was me.

You'll never stop hating my father, Wendy said. Just because things didn't work out with him, you expect me to hate him like you do. You want to erase him from my life because you erased him from yours.

That's not what your mother was saying, Josh said. But I think we should leave this topic alone. It wasn't a good idea.

Oh, fine. Never mind the part about sneaking off and signing all these legal documents to cancel out my real identity. We'll just keep going the way things have been, pretending the first four years of my life never happened. She was holding her clarinet at the time. Now she was shaking it.

Why don't you imagine for a second what it would be like if you weren't around all of a sudden, Josh, and some other guy came along and wanted to adopt Louie? He's four years old, too. Seems to me you're fairly important in his life. Don't you think he'd mind if Roberto or Omar or mom's boss or somebody decided to make him *their* kid?

I never said it was a good idea, Josh said very quietly. Let's just drop it, okay? I'm sorry. He turned back to stirring something on the stove.

Oh, Wendy, her mother said. You break my heart.

# Twenty

She was out on the highway somewhere. At a gas station, she found a pay phone and took out the calling card Josh had given her. It wasn't even noon yet, but back in New York, Amelia might be home from school by now. This was their early day.

What's the matter? asked Amelia. You sound funny.

I was just thinking about my mom. How mean I was to her.

You weren't mean, Amelia said. Nobody's perfect.

The dumb thing is, I'm way nicer to my dad out here and he hardly did anything for me up till now.

That's probably the point. He wasn't around enough for you to get mad at. That's how dads are. My mom says it's totally unfair.

But I was mean to Josh, too, she said.

Well, Josh, sure, said Amelia. But the thing about Josh is, he's kind of like a mom, too. In a guy version.

She told Wendy about how her family was going to her aunt's for Thanksgiving. The Saturday after that, she was going to a hockey game with Chief. Hockey, can you believe it? I told him I was crazy about hockey. Now I've got to read up on it on the Internet or something.

What gets into you? Wendy asked her.

I am such a total liar, she said. Sometimes I probably don't even know myself what's true.

I know the feeling.



The baby was crying again. So was Violet.

I want to be a good mother, she said. I just can't figure out how.

He's at a difficult stage, Wendy told her. He's probably got colic or something. Maybe you should take him to a doctor.

Maybe next week, she said.

Walter Charles was very red and his voice sounded hoarse, like he'd been crying for a long time.

I'm not sure you should wait till next week, said Wendy. He could have something wrong with him. I don't think they charge you anything if you go to one of those clinics.

I can't, said Violet.

What do you mean? Wendy said. I'd go with you.

It's not that, said Violet.

Then what?

This one time yesterday, when I was at the end of my rope and he just wouldn't shut up, I hit him. It left a mark.



Her mother had hit her once. Just a couple of months ago, in fact. After the letter came from her father.

You are just so bitter, Wendy said. You can't ever forgive him for one dumb thing he did a million years ago. Like you never screwed up.

It wasn't one dumb thing, her mother said. It was everything.

Oh, right, I forgot, Wendy said. My father was the worst person who was ever born. You should have married Adolf Hitler instead. You should have married that guy who murdered all the little boys and ate them. That would have been better.

Stop it, her mother said. Just go to your room before this gets any worse.

That's what you want, isn't it? You think if I just go away, you won't have to think about the truth. If I shut up, you can stick to your own nice easy version of the story, instead of having to consider the possibility that maybe my father wasn't such a monster after all. You just turned him into one in your own sick, bitter brain, after all these years of hating and not forgiving him. It was too hard to believe the truth.

You don't know the half of it, her mother said. I could tell you a lot more, but I love you too much to hurt you that way.

You think saying all this doesn't hurt me? Telling me I'm not allowed to visit my own father? You've done an incredible job protecting me from how much you really hate my dad.

Her mother had started to cry then. If you think it was easy, she said. Sometimes I'd hear him on the phone with you, telling you things, and want to scream, but I didn't say anything. All that stuff he filled you with, about wishing he could be with you. Like I was the one who was keeping him from being a father to you. Like I'd put a fence around the entire borough of Brooklyn to keep him from coming here.

No, you were just the one who listened in on our phone conversations, I guess, said Wendy. Her voice no longer yelling. Ice.

You probably read my diary, too, right? The part where I talk about how pathetic it is—you finding some young guy who follows you around like a dog, to make you feel like you're so great after all. Instead of the bitter, angry, sick, controlling dried-up person you actually are.

If Josh was there, he would have stopped them. But Josh was gone, with Louie. It was just the two of them now, and even if Wendy had wanted to stop, which she did, actually, she didn't know how. She had grabbed hold of her mother's shoulders.

Wendy and her mother were close to the same size, and soon, she'd realized, she'd be bigger. She dug her fingernails into her mother's skin. Thinking about it now, she could picture the marks.

How can you do this? her mother said. She was balled up in her chair, with her hands over her face. How can you protect him and punish me? Do you have any idea of how hard it was for me to take care of everything on my own all those years?

How could I not know? You reminded me enough.

Wendy had been yelling so much, her voice was hoarse, but she couldn't stop. She felt her heart pounding, saw the red, ugly, wrecked look of her mother's face, twisted up with crying, and still she couldn't stop.

Maybe my father didn't make all the sacrifices you did. But he doesn't hold it over my head and make me feel guilty all the time, either. He's happy just accepting me the way I am, without reminding me all the time how great he is and what a terrible person you are.

Her voice was hoarse, but still she kept screaming.

Which, incidentally, he never said one single time. Maybe that's what real love is.

Slap.

Oh my God, she said. I can't believe I did that.

But you did, didn't you?

Violet, she said. The apartment smelled like fish sticks. That and cigarette butts and overflowing diaper pail.

There are places you can go. People can help you. I'm not sure where, but we could find out.

You don't know anything, said Violet. If I told them what happened with Walter Charles, they'd take him away faster than my old boyfriend could hot-wire a car. That'd be the last I ever saw of him.

Not necessarily, Wendy said. I think people would understand.

Yeah, right. You just think that because you grew up in Neverland. Let me tell you something. When I was three years old, my mom's downstairs neighbor reported her to CPS, and the next thing you knew, they were putting my brother and me in a foster home. I got to go back home six months later, but my brother never did. Somebody told me one time he was living in a juvenile center in Fresno, but I sure never saw him again.

But you have to do something, Wendy said. You can't keep sitting around all day in this apartment listening to Walter Charles cry. It's bound to happen again, and next time could be worse. Babies are really delicate. Especially their heads.

There's this kind of breathing you could try, Wendy told her. You close your eyes and think of the most peaceful place you can imagine and breathe very deeply, and then you hold it in a long time before letting it out. Never mind if he's crying while you're doing it. He'd do better lying in his crib crying than having you pick him up and start shaking him.

I'm trying to think of one peaceful place, Violet said. The hot tub at the Ramada Inn on I-5 maybe. My boyfriend and me sneaked in there one time.

My dad was always driving us out to the country, to places like New Jersey and Connecticut, Wendy said. He had this thing about picking fruit. Apples, blueberries, strawberries, grapes. Then we'd take it all home and make jam.

I never knew you could make jam yourself, Violet said.

We had a whole shelf of jars in our pantry, Wendy told her. My mom used to say if she lived to be a hundred, we'd never get through all that jam.


Wendy stopped at the bookstore on the way home.

Got a bunch more books in this morning, Alan said. If you feel like another shelving job.

I don't have a lot of time today, Wendy said. I was actually thinking I'd look for a book.

You finished *The Member of the Wedding,* eh? he said. Talk about a heart-breaker.

I haven't quite gotten to the end yet, she said. But I need this other kind of book. She found her way to the child-care section. There was a book called *What to Expect When You're Expecting,* and a book by Dr. Spock. There was the book Violet had, with a picture of some doctor in a suit on the cover. A bunch of babies were sitting around him on the floor, and one particularly cute and pudgy baby sat on his lap. From the looks of them, their mothers weren't having problems slapping them or putting water in their formula when they ran low on food stamps. The mothers who had those kind of problems didn't have money to buy that many books probably.

I was wondering if you had anything about child abuse? Wendy asked. It's for a friend of mine.

He didn't speak for a moment.

Child abuse, huh? he said. I don't think I have anything like that in stock.

I'm doing a research paper, she told him. For my home schooling.

There are people who help kids out when they have that type of problem, he told her. He was talking slower than usual, and his voice sounded low and serious. I could find you a number to call.

It's not me, she said. This is just for my paper.

I thought you said it was for a friend.

That, too, she told him. It's a paper I'm writing with a friend.

Let's see what we can find, he told her.

Great, she said.

One more thing, Kitty. Anytime at all, you know. You could come talk to me.


Garrett's truck was just pulling in the driveway when she got back. Carolyn invited us for dinner, he said. She's made vegetarian lasagna or some damn thing.

No rush, he told her.

It was in the shower that she noticed her other breast was growing. They weren't quite evened out yet, but close. She was taller, too, she realized, and she had definitely thinned down. Her hair reached her shoulders now, long enough that she could pull it back.

If her mother could see her now, she'd be surprised. *I told you how nicely you'd fill out.*

Wendy imagined what she might look like ten years from now, or twenty.

Ten years from now, her mother might not even recognize her. Already she was different, but the day would come when she'd be this person her mother had never seen. There would be other people—someone like Carolyn or Alan, or even Violet—who had known her longer than her mother ever did. The day would come when Louie would not even remember anymore the sound of their mother's voice.

Our mother had this thing she did where she pretended you were Fred Astaire and she was Ginger Rogers and she got you this little top hat, Wendy would tell him. She used to make you a man out of pieces of pickle, stuck together with toothpicks, for your TV-watching snack. Sometimes, on the way out the door, she'd scoop up a handful of glitter that she kept there and toss it in the air, over our heads, so all day when we walked around places, we sparkled.

Tell me another story, he'd say.

She stepped out of the shower and dried herself off. Put on her too-loose jeans and a T-shirt, studying herself one more time in the mirror first. Symmetrical, almost.

You know what, Slim? Garrett said when she came out of her room. I never used to think so before, but you're starting to look like your mother.

They were celebrating a new job Carolyn had gotten. Some company was putting up an office building outside Sacramento, and they wanted a low-maintenance cactus garden. They'd hired Carolyn.

So now you've got to part with some of your precious darlings, Garrett said. Think you can handle it?

That was a problem all right. There were cacti in her collection—her sea urchin cactus, that she'd gotten at a show in Arizona; the Seven Stars one of her sisters had brought her; the Scarlet Ball she'd dug up on a camping trip to Death Valley with Garrett—that were almost like children to her, she said.

And then once people see the garden you've got going, you're going to start getting more jobs like that, said Garrett. Before you know it, there's going to be a damn traffic jam out in front of your place, people wanting to buy cactus plants off you, and you'll be sitting there bawling your head off, watching them go. Nip the problem in the bud's what I say. Tell them right now at the get-go you've changed your mind. They're better off with petunias and marigolds.

What I might just do is make a trip out to that farm up in Chico tomorrow and buy a bunch of new stuff, she said.

Sounds like a plan, said Garrett, but I've got to stay home and work on the truck.

You can come along if you're interested, Wendy, Carolyn said.

They took the backseat out of Carolyn's old Valiant station wagon to make more room for the plants. Wait till you see this place, said Carolyn. The way some women get when they walk in a shoe store, that's how I am when I'm at Harvey's Cactus World. She threw a couple of shovels in the back in case there were any specimens they'd need to dig up, and two desert garden reference books with pictures of arrangements she particularly liked.

If you want to bring headphones, I won't feel offended, Carolyn told Wendy when she picked her up. It's not like I expect you to make conversation the whole way. I'm just happy for the company on the drive.

Wendy had brought her Walkman and a couple of CD's—Ella Fitzgerald and Louis Armstrong together, and Sade, *Lover's Rock*. She had her book with her, too, in case she got tired of looking at the cactus plants.

They rode in silence for a long time, past flatland and hills. They passed a place where there had been a bad fire a few years before, Carolyn told her—a stretch of five miles or more covered with the black stubs of trees. They could see a little faint sign of green starting to push through the ash.

Look at that, Carolyn said. It's finally coming back to life.

They passed a valley with row after row of windmills, all turning at different speeds, depending on the angle the breeze hit them. Those are beautiful, Wendy said. Like an artwork.

Garrett always says the same thing, Carolyn told her.

There are art galleries in New York City where they show things like pictures of this bridge some guy wrapped in fabric, Wendy said. He spends thousands of dollars just to get pictures of the wrapped-up building, and then after a few weeks, they unwrap it. One time, this rich woman paid Josh a bunch of money to stand next to this garbage dump with his bass playing this piece of music she'd written, while a lot of her friends sat around listening. Afterward, there was wine and sushi.

I think Garrett misses that kind of stuff sometimes, Carolyn said. There're hardly any artists out here. Not even bad ones. He really closed out that part of his life when he came out here.

He didn't sell his paintings much when we lived in New York, Wendy said. It probably got pretty frustrating for him. That was one of the things my parents used to argue about.

I can understand where your mother was coming from, she said. If I know Garrett, he'd have been wanting to go out with his friends all the time or off on some camping trip, leaving her home to take care of things.

She was right. You probably didn't even need to be a palm reader.

The reason it works for us, Carolyn said, is because I don't expect too much of him. That's all well and good for me. We don't have kids. All I've got is a bunch of cactus plants. It would be different if you had a kid with a person like that.

Wendy fingered her Walkman. She would have put the headphones on, but she got the feeling Carolyn wasn't done talking.

I did have a kid one time, she said. It's not something I talk about much, but your father knows.

A boy or a girl? Wendy asked her. She wanted to start with an easy question.

Boy, Carolyn said. I was eighteen at the time, living on my own in Modesto. Guy I was with at the time would make Garrett look like Ward Cleaver.

Wendy didn't know who that was, but she figured she should, so she didn't say anything.

I gave him up for adoption, Carolyn said. He'd be twenty-five years old now. Is, I just don't know where.

Wendy thought about Violet. The rich couple in San Francisco wanting to know her IQ score. The Led Zeppelin song. "Babe I'm Gonna Leave You." Violet saying, He's the one thing I ever had.

Did you ever regret it?

Oh, plenty of times. Not giving him up so much. But being in the position where I didn't have much choice.

I have a friend like that, Wendy said. She was going to give her baby up, but she decided to keep him.

I wish her luck. Some people can manage it. I'm glad I was at least smart enough to recognize I couldn't.

Maybe someday he'll come back to you. Some people who are adopted track down their birth mother when they get older.

Maybe he will, maybe he won't, she said. It would be one great day if he did. But I don't kid myself. I'm not his mother anymore. I was for nine months and a day, but that's all. His mother's the one who raised him. Best I could be is someone like a caring friend who might happen to look a little like him. If he's unlucky.

Wendy wanted to ask more. Why Carolyn never had any other kids—later, when she might have been ready for it. Garrett had said she had some kind of problem where she couldn't, but Wendy wondered if that was really it. Or maybe Carolyn had been like her mother back before she met Josh, saying how it probably just wasn't in the cards.

The thing about cacti, Carolyn had told her. They're tough little devils. They live on dirt mostly. It's harder than hell to kill a cactus. But just because they've got all these spines and they aren't likely to keel over and die doesn't mean they don't appreciate a little babying and know-how. They're tough, but they've got needs, just like every other living thing. You have to pay attention.

An hour must have passed where they had said nothing. They were still on the highway. It was getting very hot. High desert.

Later I got to realizing I probably would have made a decent mother for someone after all, Carolyn said. It's all a matter of timing. When the opportunity comes along, and there's this person you really should be loving and taking good care of, you might not know how. Then all of a sudden, you're ready. Only they're gone.

Wendy's mother used to say it was a risky business talking to any woman who didn't have children about why. Even Kate, her best friend in the world, kept her cards close to the chest on that one, she said.

What if you couldn't have had children? Wendy asked her mother one time. Then you could've been a dancer. You could have joined the Mark Morris Dance Company.

Maybe, her mother said. I might have had a really great life without kids, too. If I could have just stopped feeling sad about not having any kids around long enough to enjoy myself. Which I never would have.

But we messed up everything for you, Wendy told her. First me and then just when you might have gotten back on the track, along came Louie.

How lucky can one woman get? her mother said.

*     *     *

I'd never in a million years try to pretend I was some kind of mother figure to you, said Carolyn. But I want you to know if the day ever comes when you need a woman around for some reason, you can give me a try.

Wendy was thinking about the bruise on Violet's baby, and worrying about Louie turning autistic, and Amelia starting to like Chief more than her maybe. The grandmother coming who was always disappointed by everyone who wasn't a tennis star or a First Lady. Wendy didn't even have any of those white monogrammed shirts to wear to Thanksgiving dinner at the Fairmont Hotel.

Most of all, she worried about the terrible things she'd said to her mother and how she could never say she was sorry now.

You probably have tons of other people you'd want to talk to before me, Carolyn said. If not out here, in New York anyway. And, of course, there's always your father. But just so you know, if the situation ever comes up where you need a woman to talk to, I'd do my best.

The strange thing was, when she had a mother to talk to about the things that upset her, she hardly ever did. In the old days, it had seemed as if her worst problems all had to do with her mother, so that wasn't exactly the person she'd have gone to.


Terrible things were happening to the girl in *The Member of the Wedding*. She had met a soldier in a bar and pretended to be older, and he believed her. He took her up to a hotel room and tried to take her clothes off. She bit him. Then she hit him over the head with a pitcher and ran out of there. She might even have killed him, but she didn't know if she had, she got out of there so fast.

Wendy couldn't stop reading, even though she knew it would give her a headache, reading in the car. This was one of those situations where you didn't want to know what would happen next, but you had to keep reading and find out.

And it got worse. When Frankie got to her brother's wedding, where she thought he was going to take her away with him after, she realized it wasn't going to happen and she went crazy. When her brother and his bride were driving away for their honeymoon, Frankie had flung herself on the ground and yelled, "Take me, take me."

Wendy almost wished she was that kind of person, the kind who would have a breakdown, like the kids at her old school thought she'd had, instead of the kind of person she was, who keeps on going no matter what she feels like. A cactus girl.

"Frances wanted the whole world to die," it said in the book. This was right near the end, when everything was going wrong. "She was against every single person, even strangers in the crowded bus, though she only saw them blurred by tears—and she wished the bus would fall in a river or run into a train. Herself she hated the worst of all, and she wanted the whole world to die."

Wendy had felt like that in New York City, after the day it happened. When she was walking around putting up flyers, but knowing how totally pointless it was by the time she got to the bottom of her stack. Looking at the faces of all the other people, feeling like one little drip of misery in a whole ocean of more. She had wanted the world to disappear, and her in it.

"You think it's all over," the black cook told Frankie after the big scene she'd made at the wedding, "but that only shows how little you know." Here was this girl who had done the most humiliating thing a person could do. Her mother was dead and her father never paid any attention to what was really going on, and she didn't have any friends—not to mention that she might have murdered someone, though he probably deserved it. And still her life kept going.

That must be a good book, Carolyn said. They were heading toward the mountains now.

It's about a girl my age, Wendy said. It was written a long time ago, but the feelings are just the same.

I should read more myself, said Carolyn. I'm always meaning to, but there just never seems to be any time. Except for garden books and tarot.

A friend of mine has a great bookstore, Wendy said. We could go there sometime. Then she realized he'd call her Kitty and wonder if Carolyn was the mother of the boy who was going to be the next Dalai Lama.

Or I could bring you a book, if you told me the kind of thing that would interest you.

Things I don't know about, I guess. How people live in other countries. Stories of people who do things like go to Africa and live with gorillas. Some civilization on another planet. Good vegetarian recipes. It wouldn't be some love-type book I'd want, probably. Those never feel totally real to me.

Maybe I'll just borrow that one when you're finished, she said then.

They were on a smaller road now. We're almost there now, she said. Wait till you see this place.

It would have been easy to miss, if you didn't know the way. There was only a very small sign that said HARVEY'S CACTUS WORLD, and one of those wooden cutouts of a woman's rear end bending down, where all you could see was her enormous butt and a couple of shoes sticking out the bottom. There were some pots of cacti hanging up and some larger ones planted in the ground, but the real collection was out back, Carolyn said.

She pulled up in front and took out the shovels. They were the only ones there. A man came out of the house.

Look what the dog brought in, he said. Long time no see.

I've actually got cash in my pocket today, Harvey, she said. I got hired for a landscaping job, if you can believe it.

Let's see if anything strikes your fancy, he said.

They walked out back. It was nothing like the places Wendy used to go with her mother and Josh in Connecticut, farms where everything was lined up in rows. Or the place where they went to cut their Christmas tree. Maybe there was an order to how Harvey had things arranged, but if so, Wendy couldn't figure it out. There were cacti everywhere. Large and small. A million different types.

He took them into a long, low structure with plastic nailed on the roof and wooden tables set up for the cactus plants. There were markers with the names of the different varieties stuck in the dirt. Staghorn cholla. Hedgehog prickly pear. Buckhorn. Beavertail. Some of them were very beautiful and symmetrical—spheres and spikes and egg-shaped cacti with bright pink blossoms coming out the sides. Others looked like some horrible skin condition, like Seth's face after the worst breakout ever. Like a vegetable her mother found at the bottom of the crisper drawer one time, with so much mold growing off it, you couldn't even tell anymore if it was a zucchini or a yam. Still think we don't keep enough produce on hand, sweetheart? her mother said to Josh, holding it up, but with one of her rubber gloves on.

Can I take it to school? Louie asked.


These are so ugly, they're beautiful, Carolyn said.

Wendy could see her point. And not just ugly but strange. Like there was a whole other way for a plant to be, a whole other direction for things to grow besides straight up or across. It would never have occurred to you before, like the usual rules for plants just didn't apply to cacti.

Finding what you were looking for? Harvey asked. Carolyn was already over in another corner, digging.

You know me, Harvey, she said. When I think about heaven, I picture cacti there.


The car was so full by the time they were done, Carolyn had to put a couple of plants on the floor in the front. Don't let the prickers get you, she said to Wendy. She laid a piece of cardboard over the spines of the sharper-looking one to protect Wendy's feet, since she was only wearing sandals.

I wish my little brother could see that place, she said. She'd never mentioned Louie to Carolyn before. He'd want to take out his trucks and make roads in the dirt and play that the really weird cacti were space aliens. He'd set up his cowboy figures in the dirt and have them all talking to one another, having these crazy battles with plastic cocktail-pick swords.

The picture came to her now of Louie, in the sand at Nantucket last summer, making the voices for all his different action figures. The funny thing was that sometimes, even when he didn't have a single toy with him, or one cocktail pick even, he'd still make those voices. He could carry on an entire conversation with half a dozen characters, just sitting there alone, with nothing but a pebble in his hand or a twist-tie from his sandwich bag.

I bet you miss him a lot, Carolyn said.

Sometimes I forget all about him for a while, she said. Then other times I'll remember, and I just want to see him so much. Maybe it's partly because there's a little boy around his age in my book, she said. John Henry. He's a pain, but he's actually the only real friend the girl has besides the cook.

Wendy turned to the page where Frankie was lying in her bed with John Henry beside her, the way it was with Louie, nights when she read to him and he'd fall asleep partway through the book. Now she read the words aloud to Carolyn.

"She lay in the dark and listened to him breathe, then after a while she raised herself on her elbow. He lay freckled and small in the moonlight, his chest white and naked, and one foot hanging from the edge of the bed. Carefully she put her hand on his stomach and moved closer; it felt as though a little clock was ticking inside him and he smelled of sweat and Sweet Serenade. He smelled like a sour little rose. Frankie leaned down and licked him behind the ear. Then she breathed deeply, settled herself with her chin on his sharp damp shoulder, and closed her eyes: for now, with somebody sleeping in the dark with her, she was not so much afraid."

Just reading the words out loud like that, she felt a sharp little stab. Like a cactus spine in her throat.

# Twenty-One

This time she told Garrett she was headed into Sacramento, it being Saturday. I can take the bus, she said.

You meeting up with some friends? he asked. He was lying under his truck working on some belt he said was giving him trouble.

One friend, yes, she said. A girl I know.

She figured he wouldn't ask for details, and he didn't.


Violet was sitting on the beanbag chair, watching TV when she came in. Walter Charles was in the crib. He wasn't crying, which was a good sign.

Check this out, Violet said. The topic on Maury today is "I Hate My Mom's Boyfriend." This one girl was saying she never had sex with her mom's boyfriend, but her mom didn't believe her, and the funny thing was, it seemed like the thing that made the mom madder than anything was the idea that her daughter stole her boyfriend.

I didn't have sex with that fat slob, the daughter was saying. If I was going to have sex, I'd choose someone a lot better.

The mom kept saying, That's the thanks I get, and calling her daughter a tramp. The daughter kept saying she was a virgin.

You wait, Violet said. If I know Maury, the next thing they'll do is haul her off backstage to take a lie-detector test.

Sure enough.

Don't let them do it to, you idiot, Violet yelled at the TV screen. It's a setup.

Maybe it's a good thing, Wendy said. Maybe it'll just prove she's telling the truth.

The kid's always wrong on shows like this, Violet said. Don't you ever watch Maury? It seems like the whole point of the show is to make whatever poor sucker he's got in the chair that day look like the biggest jerk in the world. If you ask me, they might as well tell the kids that go on that show right at the beginning, when they first come out, to pull down their pants and show the audience their naked behind, because basically that's the idea.

There was a commercial then for a company that helped you pay off your credit-card debts, then one for a machine to flatten your stomach.

I could definitely use that one, Violet said. This kid totally wrecked my body.

When they came back from the commercial the girl was all done taking her lie-detector test. The mother who said her daughter was lying came back out to be there when they announced the results. Then out came the expert.

Okay, Doctor, Maury said. We're ready for your scientific analysis. Is Shannon a virgin? Did she have sex with her mom's boyfriend?

The lie-detector expert said the girl was lying.

Big surprise, said Violet.

Up until this point, the mother had been sitting on the couch like a person waiting for an appointment, but when the doctor told about the test results, it was as if someone sent an electric shock through the seat cushions.

They probably tell them to go totally apeshit like that, Violet said.

Wendy would have thought the mother would have a thing or two to say to the boyfriend then, but the person she yelled at was the girl.

You little slut! she yelled. They bleeped out the slut part but Wendy could tell that was what she was saying.

I knew it all the time, when you started wearing those tube tops, the mother told the girl.

If tube tops are supposed to be a sign a girl is balling her mom's boyfriend, all I can say is there's a whole lot of girls on Maury doing it, Violet said. Tube tops are practically all they wear on this show. I think they have a room backstage full of nothing but tube tops for the girls to put on before they come out onstage.

The girl started to cry. I didn't do it, she said. He wanted to, but I said no.

Come on now, Shannon, said Maury. You'll feel better if you level with us. You and your mom can't start the healing process until you get out of denial and face the truth. I want you to tell Mom you're sorry for letting her down. Sorry for lying to her.

What about the mom? Violet said to the television. What about how she let her kid down, going out with some creep that would sneak into her kid's room at night and ball her? Why is it only the kid's fault?

Maury was down in the audience now, sticking the microphone in people's faces. One woman was saying how she lied that way to her mother one time when she was young, and now she knew how wrong she was but it was too late. Her mother got cancer and died.

I want to tell Shannon from personal experience that she should shape up before it's too late, the woman said. What did she think was going to happen if she wore that type of getup around the house?

The audience clapped.

What did I tell you? said the mother. Didn't I always say you were sending the wrong message?

Just because I look hot doesn't mean I wanted to have sex with Bobby, the daughter said.

Shannon, Shannon, Shannon, said Maury. I want to see you look Mom in the eye and tell her you're ready to change.

They've got three minutes left till the end of the show, Violet said. They always try to end on a positive note.

The lie detector doesn't lie, the lie-detector expert said.

Facing up to your mistakes is the first step, Maury said. Just tell your mother you're sorry.

Say it, someone called out from the audience. Then a whole bunch of people.

You can do it, Shannon, said Maury. He was leaning close to her with the microphone, like he was offering her a lollipop. It'll feel so good. *So good.*

It'll feel so good, Violet said, like she was Maury, but her voice had a harsh, bitter sound. I bet that's the same thing the mom's boyfriend told her. Right before he stuck it to her.

The mother was looking at the girl. Her arms were crossed in front of her big droopy breasts. She looked like she knew she'd won. Not the kind of look Wendy had ever seen, or could imagine, on her own mother's face.

I'm sorry, the girl said but in a small, flat voice. She didn't actually say sorry for what. Sorry she went on this show maybe. Sorry she was ever born.


They showed us a documentary at school one time, Violet said. About these prisoners of war that got locked up by enemy forces and after they tortured them, they made the prisoners be in a video to send home to America. On the video, they were saying all these great things about the people that were keeping them prisoner, but they had that same look on their face, like they were already dead.

And what else, Shannon? Maury was asking the girl on the couch. Wasn't there something else you'd like your mom to know?

The girl looked confused, as if she actually wanted to give the right answer now, just to have it over with, but she wasn't sure what the answer was.

And I'll never do it again? she said.

That must not have been what Maury wanted. He was still leaning in very close, pushing that microphone into her mouth practically.

You know what I'm talking about, he said in his low, sexy voice.

And I'm sorry I let you down? I shouldn't have lied to you? I should've listened to you? I'm a loser?

The audience started clapping again, louder now. Watching them, Wendy thought of that short story she'd read in English class back in Brooklyn. "The Lottery." The part where the townspeople pick up the stones and start throwing them at the woman.

Okay already, she said. Maybe I let him do it. I had sex with him, okay?

But it didn't look like she'd hit it on the money yet, from Maury's standpoint.

You want to tell your mom you love her, don't you, Shannon?

And what do you say, Mom? said Maury. Don't you want to give your little girl a hug?

Maybe she did, maybe she didn't, but the mother unfolded her arms.


From the crib, Walter Charles made a noise like he was waking up. Violet didn't say anymore that she wished he wouldn't sleep so much. It seems like I just finished putting him down, she said.

Maybe we should take him outside, said Wendy. It's a nice day out.

You know what scares me? said Violet. That mother. That I could actually start being like her someday.

You never would, Wendy said. You love him too much.

But sometimes, said Violet, I just wish I could run away. Sometimes I want to be my old self again. Walter Charles won't shut up, and I just want to turn him off, only with a baby, you can't.

That's the good thing about Maury Povich, she said. He may get on your nerves, but you can always change the channel.

# Twenty-Two

The main thing to remember with my mother is just to let her do the talking, Garrett said. They were in his truck, driving to San Francisco. He had shaved and put on a shirt that had a man on a horse stitched onto the pocket holding something that looked like a field hockey stick. Garrett's hair was tied back in a ponytail, and there was a suit jacket hanging from a hook on the back of the truck cab. Wendy was wearing the gray pants she'd bought with her mother on their back-to-school shopping day, though they were so loose now, they were practically hip-huggers, and blue-and-white-striped blouse they'd picked up at Goodwill, but some famous brand.

She'll want to know if you belong to any clubs, Garrett told her. My mother has always had a thing about clubs.

I could probably make something up, Wendy said.

Go for it, he said.

The landscape changed as they headed south. In Davis, the land was mostly flat, but as they got closer to San Francisco there were hills and it was a lot greener. If you like green, just wait till the rainy season, he said.

They were driving alongside water now—the bay, he told her. Great clouds of mist rolled in over their car from the hills above the highway. When the mist cleared, they could see the towers of the Golden Gate Bridge rising up out of the top of the clouds. First, just the top parts showed through, then the whole bridge. Like what a person might imagine it was like entering heaven.

They were outside her grandmother's hotel earlier than he'd expected. Ten o'clock.

This is not necessarily good news, he said. It gives us three hours to kill before we eat. He gave the truck keys to a man in a uniform in front of the hotel. You got the feeling they didn't see trucks like this here very often.

Wendy and her mother and Josh had gone to a hotel once for a party, but this one was fancier. There was a flower arrangement as tall as a person in the lobby, and the kind of carpet her mother used to say made her want to kick off her shoes and run around barefoot. Men carrying trays with a single drink on them moved across the room as if they were riding Hoverboards. You could tell just from the shopping bags the women carried that whatever was inside them had cost a lot of money. The children all wore blazers and velvet dresses.

This is my mother's idea of how people should live all the time, Garrett said. Gilt furniture and ready access to room service.

There was a special telephone for placing calls to people's rooms. When he picked up the receiver to let her grandmother know they were downstairs, Wendy realized she hadn't called Josh and Louie that morning, even though she'd meant to. She thought of them on the living room couch together in their pajamas. Josh would have made popcorn. Maybe they'd decided to go to Kate's mother's after all.

We'll be right next to the fountain, her father said into the phone. Like if he didn't tell her she might not recognize them.

I'm sorry to trouble you, sir, the doorman said to Garrett. But we're having a little problem with your vehicle. It seems to have stalled out.

Must be the damn belt again, Garrett said. I hate to do this to you, Slim. But you'd better wait here on your own for your grandma. I'll go take a look at the truck.

*   *   *

Wendy's grandmother looked older than last time and smaller than she expected, but she had the same mouth. If you were drawing it, all you would need would be one line straight across the bottom part of her face.

The elevators are very slow here, she said when she got to the spot where Wendy was standing. She said it as if Wendy might have been the one who built them.

Wendy had been wondering if she should hug her grandmother, but once she saw her, she knew the answer.

So, her grandmother said. You've definitely grown. What grade are you in now?

Eighth, Wendy said. She actually had to think a second, it had been so long since she'd been at school.

I don't suppose there are any good private schools up where your father's living.

I just got here a few weeks ago, Wendy said. We haven't talked about it.

Your father, she said. Where might he be?

He had a little trouble with his car, said Wendy. Better not to say *truck*.

Some things never change, said her grandmother. I suppose he'll join us eventually.

I brought you a present, her grandmother said. It was still in the Lord & Taylor bag. Gift-wrapped. She handed it to Wendy like a parking ticket.

I meant to send a thank-you note for the shirt last Christmas, she said. My mother was always reminding me.

Children don't seem to write thank-you notes anymore the way they did in my day, said her grandmother. I guess we have to look to the parents to ask why that might be.

Wendy looked in the direction of the door for Garrett, but the only person she saw coming in was a girl around her age in a navy blue skirt and kneesocks, and a white blouse like the ones her grandmother had sent her. She could tell her grandmother would like the other girl better.

How are things in Greenwich? Wendy asked.

Not very good. Ever since this September business, nothing seems to be working very efficiently. The person who was supposed to install my new bathroom hasn't been able to get the tile in from Italy. A friend who was going to visit from Palm Springs decided to postpone her visit.

That's too bad, said Wendy.

This must have been difficult for you, too, she said after a minute.

Garrett came through the doors. He looked as if he knew she'd be having a hard time.

Mother, he said. He put an arm around her shoulder and brushed her cheek with his face. How was your flight?

Terrible, of course, she said. I left three hours to get through the security at the airport, and I still wasn't sure I'd make my plane. They picked me to be the one passenger whose bags had to be totally unpacked and inspected.

I guess you look like a particularly scary kind of person, he said. It was supposed to be a joke, but the truth was, she did.

I can tell you I did not appreciate having these people handling my personal belongings and laying everything out on the counter for all the world to see, she said.

Don't tell me you brought that racy underwear, said Garrett.

Her grandmother ignored him. They start serving the meal at one-thirty, she said. That gives us time to take a walk around Union Square. Maybe Wendy would like to see the store windows decorated for Christmas.

She might be a little old for that, he told her.

Well, all right, Garrett, she said. What do I know? Some people continue to take an interest in Christmas decorations even when they're significantly older than your daughter, however.

I was thinking we might take a taxi over to the Japanese garden, he said. I'd drive us, but we seem to be having a little car trouble.

It still amazes me, she said. The interest people take in Japan.

How so? he asked her. Mostly, it seemed as if every word her grandmother spoke was exactly what he'd expected to hear, but when she said that, he looked genuinely curious.

Considering the war, she said. Pearl Harbor and so forth.

That was almost sixty years ago, Mother. Some of us have started to get over it.

Fine, fine, she said. Make a joke of it. Hundreds of American servicemen lost their lives in that attack. Upstanding young men defending our country.

*　　*　　*

The taxi took them through Golden Gate Park to the place where the Japanese garden was. Her grandmother decided to stay in the cab and wait for them. No sense wasting the admission charge.

Garrett was right: Wendy loved the gardens. There was an archway at the entrance, like something out of a Japanese house. Inside, a series of walkways wound among flowering trees and water gardens. They walked over a little bridge and leaned over, looking down on a pool full of water lilies. He handed her a penny.

You never know, he said.

She thought a second. No point wishing for the things that were truly impossible. She wished that Josh and Louie, wherever they were, were having a happy time.

I warned you about her, he said.

I guess that's just what happens when people get old.

That might explain it now, he said. The only problem is, she was like this forty years ago.

She must have been in a good mood sometimes, Wendy said. On Christmas or something. Didn't she have some special hobbies?

Wendy was thinking about her mother's face when she got home from the Mark Morris dance performance that time, how excited and happy she'd looked. But so many other times, too, too many to count. On Martha's Vineyard that day they rented the bicycles. At Louie's day-care group last June, watching their play, *The Story of a Tooth*. Rollerblading with her along the West Side Highway near Battery Park. Dancing with Josh in the kitchen.

Let's see, he said. My mother always liked getting her hair done. She used to say the great thing about sitting under the dryer was that nobody came along and bothered you.

There was a teahouse in the Japanese garden, where you could sit and order tea and little Japanese crackers. Wendy thought how nice it would be to sit there and look out at the ducks, if her grandmother wasn't outside waiting for them.

We'll come back another time, he told her. When it's just the two of us.

That would be good, Wendy said.

You think she's a piece of work, he said. You should have met my father.


So, Wendy, her grandmother said when they were back in the cab. What clubs do you belong to at school?

Stamp collecting, she said. Also cooking.

Your grandfather used to collect stamps, she said. Maybe it runs in the family. I'd give you his collection, but I threw it out a long time ago.

I also belong to the Cactus Society, Wendy said. It just came to her.

Cactus Society? And what might that be?

Wendy looked at Garrett. He wasn't having a problem with this, clearly.

We study various species of cactus and trade specimens, she said. Sometimes we go out in the desert and collect cactuses—cacti, I mean. We bring shovels and camp out overnight.

You should see the stuff they bring back, Garrett said. One cactus Wendy collected on her last trip was actually carnivorous. Took out a piece of my dog Shiva's tail just like that, fur and all.

Not only that, said Wendy. But on that same trip when I got the meat-eating cactus, my teacher got bitten by a rattlesnake. He would have died, but this girl in our club knew the antidote. She sucked the poison out with her mouth, and spit it out before she had a chance to swallow any.

Things have changed since my day, her grandmother said. I belonged to Girl's Junior Tennis and the Daughters of the American Revolution. Of course, those were the days when young ladies still wore gloves and took dancing lessons. I don't suppose you take dancing lessons, Wendy?

Actually, I do, she said. Belly.

That would be ballet, her grandmother said.

No, belly. You know, with bells and those little clapper things you put in your hands, and harem pants?

When you've got it, flaunt it, right, Wendy? Garrett said. His hair was starting to come out of the ponytail, and she could tell he was having a hard time not laughing.

It's a very ancient art, Wendy said. It goes all the way back to Genghis Khan.

It's interesting that we should be talking about ballet dancing, her grandmother said. Because as it happens, I had a little surprise in store. I got the three of us tickets to see *The Nutcracker* tonight with the San Francisco Ballet. Thinking of how your mother cared so much about dance.

Wendy didn't know why, but it made her uncomfortable when her grandmother mentioned her mother. She had almost been having a good time for a minute there, but then she wasn't anymore.

That sounds great, Wendy said. I love ballet.

The meal was served buffet-style. They'd set up a row of tables in the hotel dining room with turkey, and also ham and roast beef and a bunch of vegetable side dishes and a centerpiece involving a pilgrim and an Indian and a lot of chrysanthemums, and a cornucopia with American flags coming out where you'd expect to see fruits and vegetables. At another table, there were pies, every kind you could think of—also chocolate mousse and carrot cake and silver trays with cookies and candies in the shape of turkeys. Wendy couldn't believe it when her grandmother came back with her dessert choice, strawberry Jell-O.

Rich food doesn't agree with me, she said.

Wendy had chosen pumpkin pie and a smaller slice of pecan.

Some of us don't seem to be thinking much about our figures, she said.

For the love of God, Mother, she's thirteen years old, Garrett said. Couldn't you wait till she was at least fourteen before you get to work on totally annihilating her self-esteem?

I should have known it was too much to expect that the three of us might spend a holiday meal in each other's company without some of your snide remarks, Garrett, she said. Not that I'd expect much consideration from you, but I might have hoped you'd consider your daughter's feelings.

I do consider my daughter, he said. I consider her feelings plenty, actually. More than you appear to, making a bunch of idiotic complaints about airport delays, when the kid's mother just died.

Under the table, Wendy gripped her napkin. She could see her grandmother's face crumple. Her hand, halfway to her mouth, looked thin and old, with its clanky bracelets and age spots. The Jell-O on her spoon trembled.

I'm sorry to do this in front of you, Slim, he said. But there's a limit.

First, Mother, you call me up and tell me how important it is to fly out to New York and get my daughter. She should be in the *bosom of* her family, you say. The bosom. Right. Nice cozy place that turns out to be.

Wendy didn't want to, but she couldn't stop looking at her grandmother. It felt as if all the air had suddenly been sucked from the room.

We'll hire lawyers if we have to, you say. She belongs with us now. And just who is this *us* anyway? The ladies at your bridge club, once they check on her background first, to make sure there isn't any Jewish blood in her, like you were always wondering about her mother? Sign her up for Miss Porter's School, so she can learn how to fold napkins and do the fox-trot at her coming-out party when she turns sixteen? And maybe, if you do the job right, turn her into as dried-up and small-minded a person as you someday?

He wasn't yelling, but people at the tables next to him had started to look up from their meals. Moments like this, his mother said, I could swear you were your father.

He was the smart one, Garrett said. He knew enough to get away.

In the end, it was just the two of them, Wendy and her grandmother, who attended the ballet. Garrett said he'd pass. Give the extra ticket to some homeless person, he said.

He told Wendy he was going to stay at an old friend's over in the Mission. Your own hotel room at the Fairmont all to yourself, he said. Not too shabby.

He said he'd pick her up in the morning. I don't like leaving you to your own devices this way, he said. But if I stuck around, I might just strangle her.

The odd thing was that once it was over, her grandmother didn't seem much different. A little quieter maybe.

The present she'd bought Wendy at Lord & Taylor turned out to be a smocked dress. Wendy didn't know they still made them in her size. You can wear it to the ballet, her grandmother said.

At least nobody would know her there.

If there's one ballet I don't ever have to see for the rest of my life, it's *The Nutcracker,* her mother used to say. When I think about all the children who get dragged off to see that thing year after year as their introduction to dance performance and come away convinced they'll never attend another ballet. No piece of repertoire ever set the cause of ballet further back than that piece of sentimental junk.

Don't feel you have to be inhibited on our account, said Josh. We want you to be free to express your uncensored opinions.

The Christmas ballet her mother loved, Wendy knew, was the Mark Morris version, *The Hard Nut,* with the skinny cross-dressing maid in black toe shoes and the party guests dressed up in sixties clothes, and Mark Morris himself— the only man she might have left Josh for, her mother used to tell him— dressed up as some kind of Indian swami in a veil. When the Sugar Plum Fairies came out, the whole stage filled with sparkles. Much more interesting than some old tree they crank up to the ceiling every year, her mother said.

They'd gone to see *The Hard Nut* two times, and this year, even though the tickets were expensive, her mother had been planning to take Louie. Maybe Kate would take him now. Except that it would only make them all sad.

Going to see *The Nutcracker* has always been a tradition for me, her grandmother said. The hyphen mouth was back. Wait till you see what happens to the Christmas tree at the end.

She bought Wendy one of the special five-dollar programs, even though she didn't ask for it. This will be a keepsake for you to show your friends, she said.

I notice the girl playing Clara is actually a year younger than you. That just goes to show what a person can accomplish with a little stick-to-itiveness and discipline.

My mother was Clara four different times, Wendy said. This was actually true.

Of course, a lot can happen between adolescence and middle age, said her grandmother. Just look at your father. You should have seen him as a young person. The artistic talent. He was supposed to study at the Rhode Island School of Design. Not to mention where he could have gone with his tennis.

What do you think happened to him? Wendy asked. For a second, she imagined that she was some old lady having tea with her grandmother, exchanging stories about their sorry, messed-up children.

This falling in love business, said her grandmother. It's not all it's cracked up to be.

# Twenty-Three

Alone in her hotel room, Wendy folded the smocked dress and stuck it in a drawer of the bureau. Maybe the next person who stayed in this room would want it.

She ran a bath. It was a deep tub, and there were little bottles of bath gel and a shower cap. She lay in the water for a long time, her head leaning back against the porcelain of the tub. She wished again she'd thought to call Josh and Louie, but now it would be too late in New York.

When she got out of the tub, she put on the white terry-cloth robe that had *Fairmont Hotel* stitched on the pocket. She flipped through the room-service menu. Josh had taught her about room service one time when she and her mother went with him to Syracuse for a gig. Pick a dish, any dish, he told her. All we have to do is pick up the phone and they bring the food right to our room, and they only charge three times the usual.

Now she picked up the phone and made her voice sound low, more like a grown-up. This is room five sixteen, she said. We'd like a dish of cashews and a Coke as soon as possible. And if you have raspberries, those would also be good.

The raspberries came with whipped cream on the side. The bill came to twenty-one dollars, but all she had to do was sign her name and write down that she was adding five dollars for a tip. Josh had taught her that, too.

She took off the bathrobe and put on her pajamas. She climbed into the large bed and set the tray next to her. It turned out there was also a piece of chocolate on her pillow, wrapped in gold foil.

She piled up the pillows and opened her book. She only had a few more pages left in *The Member of the Wedding*.

It was the night of the wedding where Frankie had thrown herself in the dirt, begging her brother and his new wife to take her with them. But they had driven away without her. Frankie was back home with her father now, but she'd made a plan. She was going to run away. She was going to catch a train someplace, and wherever it was headed, that's where she'd go.

Wendy folded back the remaining pages of the book, not to read them, just to count how many there were. She wished there were more. She reached for a handful of cashews—twenty calories apiece, but she never counted any-more—and took a slow sip of Coke.

In the book, Frankie wrote her father a farewell letter. "I told you I was going to leave town because it is inevitable," she wrote. "I cannot stand this existence any longer. . . . Please Papa do not try to capture me."

Wendy reached for a raspberry. She imagined what Garrett would do if she ran off on a train someplace. Would he chase after her in his truck? She thought about the soldier in the hotel room who had tried to take Frankie's clothes off. What she would do if some man burst into her hotel room and tried to take her pajamas off? She wondered if she could hit him over the head with the Coke bottle.

She put one hand on the breast that had started growing recently and tried to imagine that it was someone else touching it. Not any of the boys she'd met, but someone she didn't know yet. She undid the top two buttons of her pajama top and looked at her chest. I always wished I had a shape, her mother'd said in the fitting room at Macy's.

Outside her room, Wendy could see the lights of San Francisco. This city was a lot different from New York. The buildings weren't as tall here, and there was more sky. From the window, she could see a corner of the bay and a bridge, not the same one she and her father had crossed that morning, but another one, stretching across to some other city. Over there is Berkeley, Garrett told her, as if she would know what that was.

That island is Alcatraz, where they used to keep the most dangerous prisoners. You can take a boat out there and go inside the prison cells. Out of all the prisoners kept there over the years, there wasn't a single one who successfully escaped. A few who tried swimming to shore were never found, but more than likely they drowned in that freezing water. Some people would rather die trying to get out than just sit there.

Eighty-seven floors. *Run.*

Frankie's father was asleep when she tried to run away, so she had been able to slip his wallet out of his pants pocket without him noticing. She was going to use the money to live on while she was on the lam, starting with buying the train ticket, but it turned out that he only had three dollars and a few cents in his wallet, and she knew that wasn't enough.

At first Frankie was thinking she'd hop a freight. Then she realized that would be too hard.

She was still figuring out what to do when the police found her. When she got to that part, Wendy felt a clutch at her stomach, as if she was the one running away. She wasn't even sure if it was a good thing that Frankie had tried to leave. Maybe she was really too young and should have stayed home with her father after all. Probably it wouldn't have worked for her to be off on a train to Chicago all by herself. Still, Wendy registered a stab of regret that Frankie wasn't even going to make it out of Alabama after all.

"The world was now so far away that Frances could no longer think of it," Wendy read. "She did not see the earth as in the old days, cracked and loose and turning a thousand miles an hour; the earth was enormous and still and flat. Between herself and all the places there was a space like an enormous canyon she could not hope to bridge or cross."

She lay there a long time, reading and rereading that part and thinking about what it meant. She knew when she read the words that was how it had been for her after her mother disappeared—waiting for her to come back and coming to the slow, awful realization that she never would. The feeling she'd had first, of panic and horror, the world spinning out of control. And how, in the days and then weeks that followed, the numbness had set in to replace it.

The world had flattened out for her then, until it seemed as if it wasn't just the towers that had been leveled and the space around it turned to rubble, but the entire landscape for as far as she could see or ever hope to travel— a flatness you couldn't escape on a bicycle or a car even, because the faster you pedaled or drove, the more the flatness extended, farther in all directions, oozing out, eating up whatever lay in its path, so that as far as you could see, and beyond even, lay nothing but more of the same.

For Wendy, that September, colors had faded till there was only gray. Smells disappeared except for the one terrible lingering scent she had breathed in that night she traveled to lower Manhattan to see the wreckage for herself, a smell she couldn't get out of her lungs after that, whether she inhaled or not. Maybe somewhere, someone was playing instruments, but music also seemed to have left the planet—the only note remaining being the sound of one long, low, wailing siren.

In September, everything she loved—songs on the radio and clothes and flavors of ice cream and types of dogs, leaf piles and roller coasters and skating, and Japanese animation movies and sushi and shopping and the clarinet and splashing in the waves at Nantucket with her brother—had melted away, not gone maybe, but this was almost worse: still there, but robbed of any capacity to give pleasure, like a soup with so many ingredients that, in the end, it tastes of nothing, like what happens when you mix all the wonderful colors of paint and it turns out that together what they add up to is brown.

Reading that section of *The Member of the Wedding,* Wendy understood how Frankie felt that night. She also knew that she herself didn't feel that way anymore. That like small green spikes pushing through the black of a burned-out mountainside on the way to Harvey's Cactus World—or maybe not even spikes of green yet, just the barest blush of color—something had begun to grow back in her. The earth was taking shape again; color was returning. She wasn't any less sad. In fact, maybe she was more so. But she was alive again.

Wendy took another sip of her Coke and unwrapped the chocolate. She was only one page further in the story, but all of a sudden it was a year later, and Frankie was thirteen. She had a friend now. They were planning to travel around the world when they were older.

Wendy was just starting to feel happy about how much better things seemed for Frankie now, almost as if Frankie getting a friend and planning her big trip meant that a hopeful future might be waiting for Wendy, too.

One thing was disturbing her, though, as she read through the final pages of her book. Where had the little boy gone? Where was John Henry, the one who reminded her of Louie? A thirteen-year-old girl definitely wouldn't want to be hanging around with a little boy, playing card games all the time, the way she had when she was younger, any more than Wendy felt like playing Candyland with Louie anymore, but something in the way the final pages of the story were unfolding gave her a certain sense of dread.

Then she knew why they weren't hearing about John Henry anymore. One minute, she was reading how John Henry had gotten a headache the year before. Four sentences later, it turned out he was dead.


Wendy was stunned. She didn't know that anything she read in a book could hurt that much. She reread the words, in case she'd got them wrong. It was as if someone she actually knew had died and, just as she would for someone she had known, she felt herself begin to cry.

It was past eleven, but she wasn't tired. She got out of bed. There were a few cashews and raspberries left, but she wasn't hungry. She reached into her overnight bag and took out her clothes—jeans, a T-shirt, and, because the weather was cooler in San Francisco, a sweater and socks. She laced up her sneakers, stuck her room key in her pocket, and went out into the long hallway, heading toward the elevator.

She imagined what her mother would say if she could see Wendy now— alone in a hotel, heading out into the night. She could almost hear her mother's voice. *Not safe, not safe.* Never mind. Nothing was. Once the worst had happened, a person could do anything.

There was nobody else around, just a few other room-service trays like hers lying on the floor next to the rooms where they'd been left. One had a rose on it in a silver vase and a bottle of champagne. There was still some left in the glass. She bent down and took a sip, then gulped down the rest.

Wendy considered the possibility that someone might stop her, but nobody did. One of the men in uniforms in the lobby opened the door for her even. Then she was outside in the night air, with the whole of the city sparkling below.

Except for their trip in the taxi to the park, and then going to the ballet with her grandmother, she didn't have a clue where anything was in San Francisco. She just started walking.

You could tell this was a fancy neighborhood, but within a few blocks, the buildings changed. There were bars and clubs with signs that had pictures of naked women on them. She passed a man with a shopping cart that had all his stuff in it, and a woman who had two different shoes on and not a whole lot of teeth.

Hey there, Cookie, a man said. Got any change for cigarettes?

I'm sorry, she said.

Late as it was, a lot of people were up, though there were some sleeping, too, wrapped up in blankets on the sidewalk, and others had just a piece of cardboard box laid over them.

She walked some more—a person in a dream. She was using the other bridge she'd seen as her marker, heading toward it. In a few minutes she'd reached the bay.

There was a long, wide street running along the water's edge and a bunch of low warehouse-type buildings, closed up. In one place where the sidewalk widened out, a group of boys were skateboarding. Not like the boys she saw in New York, who mostly just skated to get around. These boys were doing fancy moves and tricks. She stopped, not right where they were but a little ways back to not get in the way.

One of the best skaters was a boy a few years older than her probably, in big pants you'd think wouldn't stay up and no jacket, even though the night was not just cool now but cold. He was skinny, but surprisingly muscular under his T-shirt, and his thin face had a haunted look. He had the kind of dark beauty guys like the Backstreet Boys tried to have on the pictures on their trading cards, only with this boy the look had seemed to have come from someplace real.

He was doing amazing things—sliding his skateboard down a railing, flipping it, and landing so smoothly, you wouldn't know his board had ever left the ground. She watched him tear along a smooth stretch of concrete at the top of a bunch of steps, not even slowing down when he got to them, just sailing out over the air, crouching down, touching the tip of his board before making contact with the concrete at the bottom and then moving off like a leaf in a stream—that smooth, but faster.

*Sweet,* one of the older skaters called out to him. I saw somebody land that one in San Jose. Kid's probably sponsored by now.

When they took off, their wheels made a whirring sound. She thought of *Disney on Ice,* the show she went to with her mother and Josh and Louie last winter. The part at the end where Mickey and Goofy and the Seven Dwarfs all came out at once, whizzing past one another and jumping over things.

She stood in the shadows for a long time, watching the skateboarding boys. She imagined what it would feel like if she could skate like that. She could ice-skate, and she and her mother used to Rollerblade on Sunday mornings, but all she ever did was go along the path with all the other skaters. The thing about these boys was how they broke out on their own, the way they defied fear and common sense, and gravity.

She thought about the ballet performance she'd seen that night, the perfectly choreographed snowflake dancers, the Sugar Plum Fairies, the totally unsurprising moment when the giant Christmas tree had risen up to fill the stage as the audience applauded, perfectly on time, almost as if they, too, were part of the choreography. And later, in the lobby as they filed out, the audience members, in their holiday clothes—even a few teenagers the age of this boy and herself, in their blue blazers and velvet dresses, carrying on as if this were just one more holiday season like all the others they'd celebrated, with the identical clothes and music and dance steps.

As if the worst thing that could happen to a girl was having her nutcracker break. As if the idea of somebody sleeping under a piece of cardboard on the street or a seventeen-year-old girl getting hit by her boyfriend and having a baby all by herself, or an airplane crashing into a skyscraper—somebody's mother going to work and never coming home, or a hundred people's mothers never coming home, a thousand fathers, or sisters, or brothers—was just some other fairy tale, the kind nobody made ballets about.

There was a time when Wendy was one of those people who believed the world was a safe place, where the bad things only happened far away. She had supposed she knew, more or less, how life was going to go, and that even the hard parts would be things like having to convince her mother to get a puppy or let her go to California, or getting into the High School of Music and Art.

In the old days, Wendy had believed that there was a set of rules your life followed, the main one being that certain things, like your family and the world you inhabited, were never going to change. Her parents had stood as fixed on the landscape as the lions on either side of the steps to the New York Public Library, or—she might actually have thought about it this way once—the Twin Towers at the base of Manhattan. Your mother simply disappearing, and your father, your original father that you barely knew, taking you someplace three thousand miles away to live this whole other life with him, was as impossible as putting the rain back in the sky.

From the looks of them, the skateboarding boys had stopped buying into the rules a long time ago, if they ever had. From what she could tell, they almost certainly had not spent the afternoon eating turkey from a silver platter, or their evening at a place like the San Francisco Ballet, in the sixty-five-dollar seats.

At this very moment, in fact, one of them—a kid they were calling Crash— had evidently spotted a police car, and now they were scattering in all directions, tearing down the pavement, past the ABSOLUTELY NO SKATEBOARDING sign.


The picture came to her again of *Disney on Ice*.

Admit it, Janet, Josh had said to her mother, putting an arm around her as they were making their way out of Madison Square Garden after. All through that last number, you were wishing you had one of those Cinderella getups.

Just the wand maybe, her mother said. I already have a tiara.

If it was me, I'd want to be Mickey, Louie said. He wanted to know where the characters went after the show was over. If they got on the subway, same as him.

It's really just a man in a Mickey Mouse suit, Louie, Wendy told him. All afternoon, she'd been feeling irritable, starting with noticing that her jeans were too tight, and wondering why she ever said yes to joining her parents and Louie at the ice show. It was one of those moments she hated herself, when she could feel herself becoming mean and angry for reasons that probably had nothing to do with her family, they were just the only ones around to blame.

Didn't you notice how Mickey's eyes never moved? she told her brother. That's because it's a man in a mask. He probably goes out after the show and drinks a whole bunch of beer. He probably goes home and yells at his kids.

I'm not sure your brother needed to hear that theory, her mother said. She and Josh had been holding Louie's hands, one on each side, so he could jump up in the air and swing.

If that's what you want, she said, to have my brother growing up believing that some stupid cartoon characters are real, go for it. Just don't blame me if he gets totally depressed later when he finds out the truth about life.

She slowed down so they'd be ahead of her. She was going to pretend she was by herself. Looking at the three of them up ahead, her mother and Josh, with Louie swinging between them, she had this urge to disappear. Slip into a doorway, round a corner, get on a train. It might be another ten minutes before they'd even notice she was gone. She could be on her way to the East Village by then. Or anywhere, just away from the rest of them. Without her, they were a perfect little unit, singing "Heigh-ho, Heigh-ho" off into the sunset.

She had not run away. She had ridden the same train they had back to Brooklyn—just in a different car, though even then she had to ask Josh for fare money. When they got back to the apartment, she had gone into her room and slammed the door without saying anything. She didn't even know why she was feeling so miserable. She put on Tori Amos, took out her drawing pad, and made a picture of her mother with a ridiculous grin on her face. Then she scribbled all over it. Then she ripped it into pieces without feeling any better.

She didn't even say good night to her parents that night, though Louie had knocked at her door to say, Sweet dreams, the way he always did. When he asked if she'd come snuggle with him, she said, Another time, Louie. Later, her mother must have slipped a note under her door, because it was there in the morning when she got up.

*Precious Wendy—*

   *I know it doesn't seem as if we understand a single thing about how you're feeling these days. I don't expect I can make you feel any better. I just wanted you to know that I'm not so old I can't still remember a few things about being thirteen years old. The best I can tell you is, nobody stays thirteen forever. Though I'll just add, I have loved you madly, every single age you've ever been, and expect the trend to continue.*

   *Like it or not, your mom (the only one you'll ever have!)*

The night was chilly now, much cooler than in Davis. Wendy had found herself a spot along the pier a little ways down from where she'd watched the skaters. She sat on the wall, looking out at the lights across the bay.

Hey, he said. It was the skinny skateboarder. You're the one that was watching us before, right?

You're really good, she told him.

You skate?

Just Rollerblades.

We don't use that word around here, he told her. But I'll excuse you this time.

He sat down next to her. Some nights I feel that way, too, he said. Like crying.

You live here? she asked him.

I don't live anywhere, he said. I'm on the road. How about you?

I used to live in New York, but now I don't.

New York, he said. Bad scene there, man.

I know, she said. My mom was in one of the towers.

\*   \*   \*

His name was Todd. She told him hers, the real one. Also about Josh and Louie and Garrett.

So now all of a sudden this guy comes along wanting to be all fatherly, huh? he said. Making up for lost time?

It's not like that exactly. My father's a kind of hands-off type, but he's doing his best. I call him Garrett, not Dad.

It's got to feel weird for you, coming to a whole new place, Todd said. It would be different for someone like me, who's used to their family being screwed up.

I didn't want to come out here with him at first, she said. Then I figured there wasn't anything else so great back home, either, so I might as well.

If it was me, man, I'd miss my brother the most. I've got a brother four years older. As far as my family goes, he's the one good thing.

Todd liked the part about Wendy not going to school. He called it the bomb, which turned out to be good.

Here, they tell you they're doing all this stuff like checking up on whether you're doing drugs and if you turned in your homework on time, but they don't even notice when you don't show up for a month.

I wrote the principal a letter, she told him. I forged my dad's signature.

What do you figure will happen when this Garrett dude finally finds out? When there's supposed to be high school graduation and you have to break the news you stopped going to school in eighth grade?

I don't think about the future much, she said.

Join the club.

They sat on some wood pilings, looking out at the bay. The moon was up, just a thin slice, but it was reflected in the water. They could see the lights of another city, across the bay. Oakland, he told her.

Where's your family now? she asked him.

I have a dad in Pennsylvania. My real dad lives in Texas, but I never met him, he said. My mom's in Cleveland, but before that, we lived in Rhode Island and Delaware and South Carolina. It's been two years since I saw my brother.

My best friend, Amelia, and I always used to have this plan of moving to Pennsylvania when we grew up, she said. We were going to live in Pittsburgh.

You might want to rethink that plan, said Todd.

Your mom must be upset about you taking off, Wendy said. Did you call and wish her a happy Thanksgiving?

Not exactly, he said.

I bet she's always getting after you to wear a helmet when you skate, right? asked Wendy. That would be my mom.

I don't have one of those type of moms, he said. My mom's the type, if I was wearing a helmet, she'd tell me to take it off.

# Twenty-Four

You shouldn't be out alone at night, Todd told Wendy. Particularly in this neighborhood. I'll walk you home.

She pointed up the hill. I'm staying at a kind of fancy hotel at the moment, she said.

He stepped on his board, but not to ride. He kept one foot on the sidewalk, pushing himself along. When they got to the hill, he put the board under his arm.

When my parents split up, the idea was that my mom would get Kevin and I'd live with my dad, he told her. She must've gotten first pick. I was really little then. Second grade. Kevin was in sixth. We used to call ourselves the Ultra-bros.

My little brother and I have this song we sing in the car, "Side by Side," she said. It's kind of corny but he's only four.

After the divorce, I hardly ever saw Kevin anymore. When I went to visit my mom, he'd be checking in with Dad. Ships in the night, he called us. Sometimes the only place we actually saw each other was some truck stop where they'd trade us off.

I couldn't stand it if it was like that with Louie and me, she said. It occurred to her then that in a way, it was.

*      *      *

Across from the Fairmont Hotel was a park, and beyond that a very large church. Todd told her it was a cathedral. I always wanted to try those steps on my board, he said, but there was always someone around.

They crossed the park. He took the steps two at a time. When he got to the top, he set down his skateboard a few feet back and then started to build up speed. Wendy stood at the bottom.

She imagined how it would look here on Sunday mornings, with all the people dressed up, going inside. This looked like the kind of church where there'd be a choir and a huge organ, candles, and maybe boys in long robes swinging incense as they walked down the center aisle.

Todd was heading for the stairs now, the railing. She held her breath.

Todd got most of the way down before his back wheels clipped the handrail. His board stopped in midair while his body flew forward, then down. He lay there for only a second before he jumped up, cursing. Wendy could tell he was hurt, but he was walking in tight circles, shaking one arm.

You should sit still, she said. In case you broke something.

I'm okay, he said. I just don't want it to be my collarbone.

His arm was bleeding, and one pants leg was ripped. He lifted up the back of his T-shirt. The skin was scraped away, but that was it. Nothing's broken, he said.

You need to clean that up, she said. It could get infected.

It's not as bad as it looks, he told her. I'll wash it off in the all-night Denny's.

You can come back to my hotel for a minute, if you want.

She thought about the girl in *The Member of the Wedding* and the soldier trying to take her clothes off.

Jeez, he said. I can't even remember the last time I had a hot shower.

*      *      *

When they got to the hotel, the doorman wanted to see her room key. My brother and I were just out for a walk, she said. It's our first time in San Francisco.

I hope you went up to Coit Tower, he told her. That's the best view in the city.

When you pick a hotel, you don't fool around, he said in the elevator.

She opened the door to her room. The cashews and raspberries were still sitting on the tray on the bed. Help yourself, she said.

He took a handful of cashews. Midnight snack, he said.

She gave him a towel. He closed the bathroom door. In a minute, she heard the sound of water running.

She looked around the room, at his skateboard leaning against the fancy gold wallpaper, her book, the empty Lord & Taylor bag, and the program from *The Nutcracker*. From the bathroom she could hear the shower running and Todd singing "God Bless America," which people were playing so much these days, but in this funny joke way, like the type of singer that would perform someplace like a bowling alley. Then he was doing another number, as if he was that blind Italian singer she'd seen on TV, Andrea Bocelli, but with made-up Italian. Anyone who knew her would say she was crazy, inviting this boy into her room.

She turned on the television and found MTV. They were showing the Madonna video. Her hair made her look like some woman in an Italian painting. If Wendy could be anyone in the world, it would be Madonna.

The water stopped. In a couple of minutes, Todd came out, wearing the Fairmont Hotel bathrobe. Don't worry, he said. I'm not going to try anything funny. I just thought it would feel good to put this on for a second. I never had a bathrobe.

That's okay. She handed him the bowl of cashews.

This is the life, he said.

Even though his mom liked Kevin a lot more than Todd, she'd gotten fed up with Kevin, too. The minute Kevin graduated from high school, he was out of there. Todd didn't find out Kevin was gone until sometime in the fall, when he finally called home, hoping to get his brother when their mom wasn't around. She answered instead.

You're about three months too late, she said. He took off. Darned if I know where.

He must've left me some kind of message, Todd said. He wouldn't just leave without giving me some idea where to find him.

Wherever your brother was going, she said, it's doubtful he's got an address.

That was a year ago September. Todd had been looking for Kevin ever since. Everyone he ran into, he'd show Kevin's picture and ask, You ever see this guy?

My brother always had this idea he wanted to be a snowboarder, Todd said. Even though he was never the most coordinated person. I've been thinking that he might have headed out west. Tahoe area maybe, or the Rockies.

It's really something, how you don't give up, Wendy said.

He's my one brother.

Here's my brother for you, he said. When I was younger I was really into baseball. The problem being, I needed someone to take me to the games. At this point I was back living with my mom for a while, on account of my dad got this girlfriend that hated kids. But just because my mom let me come back, she wasn't exactly the type to bring Kool-Aid to games and sit in the stands with the other mothers.

So Kevin brings me. I'm maybe twelve years old at the time. He's sixteen, and there's sure to be other stuff he'd rather be doing with his Saturdays, but he signs the permission slip like he's a grown-up, in cursive. Rides the bus with me to the park every Saturday and sits on the bleachers through all my games. After a while, I've got a few hookups with this other kid's dad, where I could probably have got there without him, but he still came to every game just to watch. When I got a hit, I could always hear him cheering like a maniac.

We saw this movie on TV one time when we were little, *Swiss Family Robinson*, about a family that gets shipwrecked on this island with no other people around. They build a tree house, but not just a normal tree house. This place has all kinds of rooms and lookout spots and there's a swinging bridge to get to it, and pulleys to bring their food up to them.

I saw that movie one time, too, Wendy said.

So he gets the idea of us building a house like that someday, him and me. When we're in bed at night, that's our thing we do.

We were just little, right—five and nine, maybe? But we made all these plans about how it was going to be on our island. Like one night we spent the whole time just talking about how we'd make a secret room with a trapdoor to store our stuff in, or another time we made up this imaginary meal with all our favorite foods. Kevin was always saying it would be nice to have a mom at our tree house, if she was like the mom in the movie, but I figured we'd be better off just the two of us, nice and simple. What do you need a mother for? I said. If all she does is tell you to pick up things and brush your teeth?

Sometimes it's important to have someone like that around, Wendy said. Even if you might disagree with what they tell you. It was strange, hearing herself tell him this. She knew how differently she'd felt in the past.

What a person really needs is more of a sidekick, he said. Someone who can tell you you're full of it, but in a nice way. When you've got a brother like that, you're never totally alone. There's always someone on your team.

I know plenty of people who don't feel that way about their brother, Wendy said. I know people who can't stand their brothers.

They don't have a brother like Kevin is all, he told her.

I've got a great brother, too, she said. Louie. Just the sound of his name in the room made something happen to her voice. She could see him in his bed, with his tiger tail pinned on his sleeper suit, and Pablo under his arm. She wondered if he dreamed about her sometimes.


It was almost morning now. You probably want to get to bed, he said.

Where do you sleep? she asked him.

A guy I met skating's been letting me crash at his place, he told her. I'm only here temporarily, anyway.

You're heading up to Lake Tahoe from here? she asked. In case Kevin's there?

That was the plan.

\*     \*     \*

She wrote down her phone numbers—both of them, Davis and New York. If you end up in my town someday, you could give me a call, she said. I've got a pretty flexible schedule.

Me, too, he said.

Where are you going to spend Christmas? she asked him.

All I know is, not Cleveland, he said.

If you're out here, give a call, she said. My dad and his girlfriend have a pretty relaxed policy. Nobody should be alone on Christmas.

# Twenty-Five

After Todd left, Wendy couldn't get to sleep. It was five o'clock in the morning, but in New York, it would be eight. She dialed her old number. Josh picked up.

I was going to call yesterday, she said. But there was all this stuff going on with my grandmother.

The grandmother, he said. I forgot about her.

Yeah, well, my dad probably wishes he could. Then she wished she hadn't said that.

So you had a big old family-style Thanksgiving? Josh asked.

It was kind of quiet, she said. Just the three of us. How about there?

We were going to hang out here, but Kate kept getting after me about coming over to her mother's place, and I thought it might be good for Louie, so we went. She's a terrible cook, but she'd invited a bunch of nice people, and your brother seemed to enjoy himself.

How's the hitting going? she asked. Did you take Louie to that therapist?

He spent the whole time playing with blocks, Josh said. A hundred dollars an hour, not that I'm about to argue if it does any good. When she asked him about his mom, he said she was away on a trip.

How about at school?

He hasn't hit anyone lately, Josh said. He just isn't very sociable. He never wants to go over to Corey's anymore. All he wants to do is watch TV and play with trucks.

Can I talk to him? she asked.

Louie, Josh called out to him. Your sister's on the phone.

She could hear them talking, but she couldn't make out the words.

Of course you do, Josh said. Come on, Lou-man. You can watch TV anytime. It's long-distance.

More talk. Then Josh was back on the line. I guess he's not in the mood right now, he said. He's in the middle of some show.

I really wish I could talk to him, Wendy said. I think it would be a good idea.

Me, too, said Josh. I tried. I just can't budge him.

I'll call back another time, she told him.

Sounds good. He sounded distracted and tired.

Josh, she said. I miss you. Not just Louie, but you, too.

Oh, Wendy, he said. I miss everything.


Garrett came to pick her up a little after ten-thirty that morning. Wendy hadn't heard from her grandmother at that point, so she'd stayed in her room, drawing and watching MTV, and eating her room-service toast.

We should say good-bye to her, right? Wendy said.

They rang her room. She told Garrett she wasn't feeling that great, so she'd just say good-bye over the phone. The turkey didn't agree with her.

What does? he said, but only after he set the receiver down.


Garrett had gotten the truck going. So what's it going to be, Slim? he asked as they pulled away from the hotel. Pair of tumbling tumbleweeds, loose and free in the city? We could go check out the hippies in the Haight or do some big-time tourist thing like ride the cable cars. Or go over the bridge and see the beach and the giant redwoods.

The redwoods sounded good. She'd had enough of city life for a while.

They drove along the water, where she'd been the night before, though she didn't tell him that. The Embarcadero, he called it. She saw a bunch of skateboarders, but not Todd.

There were crowds of people gathered around. Everyone seemed to be looking at the sky. Then they heard a sound like a rocket, and for a second all she could think was, Another attack.

They looked up. There were five planes—not the kind regular people ride in, but fighter jets—streaking across the sky over the bay in a formation, like migrating birds, but fast as bullets.

Is it war? she asked him.

I forgot, he said. I even read about this. It's the Blue Angels. They're these fighter pilots who go around the country putting on air shows to get people excited about joining the military.

As he said it they passed back overhead, so low that for a moment she couldn't hear him. The crowds on the pier were cheering.

The Blue Angels broke out of formation then, fanning out in five different directions. In a funny way, it reminded her of an old movie she'd watched with her mother one time, starring this woman who had been famous a long time ago, not for acting so much as swimming. They must have set the camera up above a giant swimming pool with a bunch of other very good swimmers in matching bathing suits so you could see the patterns they made in the water. That's what I want to be when I grow up, Wendy had said.

There might not be a whole lot of job openings for synchronized swimmers these days, Josh said. But far be it from me to get between a person and her dream.

The Blue Angels were about a million times faster than Esther Williams and her team. But there was something graceful and wonderful about them, the way they corkscrewed over the bay, looping in and out around one another like a pod of dolphins. Wonderful and terrible at the same time.

The picture came to her of the plane that day. She imagined it shooting straight as an arrow into her mother's building. The passengers inside looking out the window, seeing towers instead of sky. The man at the controls steering straight toward the building. The look of fierce and deadly conviction on his face.

Then suddenly, the sky was empty. The Blue Angels were nowhere in sight. You couldn't see anything but the streaks in the sky from their last fly-over. Several minutes had gone by with no sign of the planes. You could see people milling around a little uneasily on the pier, scanning the horizon in different directions, listening. Nothing.

What do you think happened? she asked Garrett. How can five fighter jets just disappear?

Another minute passed. An uneasy feeling came over her, similar to how she'd felt reading those last pages of *The Member of the Wedding*, when she realized that John Henry no longer seemed to be around.

Wendy saw herself and her mother crouched on the floor of their little closet when she was little, back when her mother still loved her father and she and her mom had waited for him to get home from the art opening he'd gone to without them.

I bet he'll be home any minute, her mother said.

He's going to be so surprised when we jump out in our beautiful dresses, Wendy said.

She saw Josh sitting on the couch, his hands pulling at his hair, eyes fixed on the silent telephone.

She thought about the sidewalk in front of St. Vincent's hospital that day, that she'd seen on television—the rows of empty stretchers and the rows of emergency medical people in their white jackets, waiting for ambulances with nobody inside.


What if the planes crashed? she asked Garrett. What if instead of fanning out like a flower, the Blue Angel pilots had got it backward and all five shot into the center, their paths leaving only a shower of spark and flame, a fireball of exploded fighter planes?

I don't think so, Garrett said. But he sounded a little worried.

They heard a roaring sound, and like cowboys galloping in over the hill, they were back, but from five different directions.

They're okay after all, she said.

Nothing ever happens to the Blue Angels, Garrett said. They're not allowed to crash. It's a rule.

\*      \*      \*

The parking lot was full at Muir Woods, so they had to pull the truck over to the side of the road. There were lots of tourists with cameras, and a couple of tour buses.

The good thing is, most of these people won't walk in more than a couple hundred feet before heading back to their bus, he said.

He was right. Once they'd walked farther down the path they had the place to themselves.

Wendy had never seen trees like these before, so big, a whole family could be holding hands and still not be able to get their arms around the trunk. They towered over her, not quite blocking the sky, but almost.

They had walked beyond the paved path to where it was just wood chips and moss. The air had a sweet, moist smell, and they could hear the sound of water running over the rocks in the stream alongside them.

When you come here in spring, you can see salmon spawning, he told her. You could just reach your hand in the water and pick one up, not that I would. I like to give my salmon a fighting chance.

They came to one of the largest trees. The trunk was charred, as if it had been burned, but it was still alive.

That's another thing about these trees, he said. Even when they burn, it doesn't kill them.

So they live forever?

A long time anyway. Eventually, even redwoods die. Like that one over there.

She studied it. The diameter of the trunk, lying sideways, was taller than her father. This one's probably been down since before you were born, he said. Maybe before I was. It takes a long time for a tree like this one to rot away.

Young saplings had begun to grow up around it, though. Another couple hundred years and they'll be high as the mast on a sailing ship, he said. I always think it's kind of reassuring, knowing that long after I'm dead and gone, these trees will be here.

They started to climb up a steep embankment. They hiked for a long time. At one point, they had to climb down a little ladder that had been attached to some rocks in a ravine. At another point, it got steep again and the walkway was very narrow, with a drop-off so sharp, Garrett took her hand.

They got to the top of a hill, and all of a sudden the horizon opened up and they were standing in a clearing with a vast expanse of deep blue water dead ahead. Fifteen more minutes and they were rolling up their pants legs and putting their feet in the Pacific Ocean.

Cold, huh? he said. You think because it's California, it's going to be warm, but it's easier going in the ocean in Maine than it is at Stinson Beach most of the time. It's beautiful here, but if you're looking to swim, you can't beat the East Coast.

Nantucket. Collecting shells with Louie to string into a necklace for their mother. Josh rubbing suntan oil on her mother's back. Tuna sandwiches from the cooler, and brownies they'd made the night before. Driving home late that night, Louie asleep in his car seat, his head leaning against Wendy as she and her mother and Josh sang old Beatles songs. And later, as they made their way down the West Side Highway, the last few miles to home, her mother looking into the backseat and turning to Josh. I don't need anything else, she said. Beyond what's in this car.

Wendy and her father had come out at the road now, the stretch of Highway 1 that turned into the main street of Stinson Beach. They sat outside at a table in the sun and a waitress with very long gray hair brought them lemonade and hamburgers. Wendy was hungry after the long hike, but after a few bites, she realized Garrett hadn't touched his burger.

After all these years, you'd think it wouldn't get me down anymore, he said.

What?

Seeing my mother, he said. Forty-eight years old, and I still get disappointed that she isn't this other person I would have liked to have for my mother. Crazy, huh?

Not really, she said. She wondered if Todd would be like that thirty years from now. Still wondering why his mother always liked his brother best. And

Violet, and that girl on Maury Povich. She wondered which was worse, having a good mother and losing her, or a bad one who stayed around long enough to grow old.

Maybe if I'd had one of the good type of mothers, I'd still have found something to be mad at her about, he said.

I know I let you down, too, he said. My mother was right about one thing probably. I was a major fuckup as a father.

It's okay, she said, not exactly denying it.

Not only that. I screwed up where your mother was concerned, too. She was one terrific girl. I just wasn't ready to handle all the responsibility. Sometimes it's not till the person's gone that you notice what a big space they were filling up, he said.

Like the bass line of a jazz ballad, she was thinking. The notes that only come to seem important when nobody's playing them.

Other things come along eventually, he said. It's not like there's this hole that stays empty forever. It's just different. Carolyn, for instance. She's a wonderful woman, too.

I know.

It's not like you end up being lonely and sad the rest of your life, he said. You can be happy again. It won't always hurt, losing someone. It's just there.

# Twenty-Six

Alan was unpacking a shipment of books when she got to the bookstore. Here's one for you, he said. Seeing as how you're on a run of juvenile narrators. It was called *The Butcher Boy*.

Story of a young boy living in Ireland, he said. People do unspeakable things to him. He only has one friend, and then that person goes away, too. His mother dies. It's a pretty dark story, but I'm thinking you can handle it. I'd like to think this is the kind of story that couldn't ever happen, but the truth is, it probably could.

It was hard to think of starting another book so soon after *The Member of the Wedding*. She almost felt as if she needed a certain grieving period for the boy, John Henry, but she took the book from him.

About that other issue, he said. The child-abuse question. I've been doing a little research for you.

You didn't need to, she said. After she'd left that time, she'd gotten worried what he might do. Suppose he reported her to the authorities as a victim?

I got the name of a person you could talk to, he said. For your friend.

She's doing a lot better, Wendy told him. She had forgotten for a minute there that it was supposed to be a research paper.

I see.

I know what you're thinking, she said. You're thinking it's really me and that my parents hit me or do bad things to me or something. But actually, that isn't even my real problem. That really was a friend. I have a whole different problem, actually.

First of all, she said, my name isn't really Kitty.

Then she told him the rest.

I was thinking you might like to take a trip with me, Alan said. Since evidently you aren't on this intense home-schooling schedule after all.

Dorothy's coming in to take care of the shop this afternoon, he told her. I'm driving over to Modesto to see my son. Maybe you'd like to come.

Tim's nineteen, he said, but in most ways, he's like a little boy. My wife has a hard time seeing him, even now.

What does he like to do? she asked him.

Go to the Laundromat.

Alan had saved up all their laundry. When they got to the place where his son lived, he took a big bag of dirty clothes out of the trunk, that he carried in with him. Also a tin of cookies and a box of Legos.

There were five or six little kids out on the porch, sitting around a table with mounds of clay. A bunch of teachers—more teachers than kids maybe—were helping them turn the clay into shapes, but mostly it seemed to be the teachers who were making the shapes. The kids were just watching, except for one boy with glasses, who was talking nonstop.

The sinking of the *Lusitania*, May 1915, he said. One thousand one hundred and ninety-five people died. The sinking of the *Titanic*, April 1912. Death toll: fifteen hundred people.

Every time I come here, he's doing something like that, Alan said. The kid's an encyclopedia.

They walked down a hall with lots of artwork on the walls. They got to a room with a sign on the door that said TIM AND BRIAN. Alan knocked.

It's your dad, Tim, he said. He waited.

He needs a minute or two to get used to the idea, Alan told her.

I brought a friend today, Tim, he said through the door. Wendy.

More waiting.

So we're coming in now. First me, then Wendy. She's a girl. Like Picabo Street.

Who's that? she asked.

This champion skier he likes, Alan said. He watches a lot of downhill skiing on television. She's a lot older than you, but to him, it's the same.

Picabo Street is the only American skier to win a World Cup downhill championship, he said. A voice from the other side of the door: Picabo Street eats Wheaties for breakfast.

We're coming in now, Tim, he said. I think you're ready for us.

He was standing up, facing the door, like a person waiting for a bus. He had a turtleneck sweater on, though it was hot in Modesto, and long pants belted high over his waist, the way Mr. Hutchinson did, back at her old school. His hair was cut very neatly. You could see he shaved, but apart from that, he seemed years younger than nineteen. He could almost be handsome, but he had a slumped-over way of holding himself, like he was afraid his head might bump the ceiling. She'd never seen bluer eyes.

This is my friend Wendy, Alan said. She helps out at the store sometimes. He hugged the boy, even though Tim didn't hug back. Wendy thought of her grandmother, the stiff and uncomfortable way she had greeted her son. Even though Tim just stood there, it seemed that Alan must have made a decision a long time ago just to hug him anyway.

I thought you said you brought Picabo Street.

I said she's a girl. Like Picabo Street. Except I don't think she skis. Right, Wendy?

No, she said. I like to ride my bike, though. And I used to Rollerblade.

Tim walked over to a little table in one corner of the room with a bunch of Legos on it. He was building something, but not like the kind of constructions Louie made with Corey, or used to anyway. It looked like a perfect replica of some famous building, although she wasn't sure which.

This is really good. What is it? Wendy asked him.

Did you bring cookies? he asked his father.

Don't take it personally, Alan told her. Most of the time, Tim doesn't answer questions. Not mine, either. He handed Tim the cookies. Your mother made them, he said. Oatmeal raisin.

Tim set the cookies on a shelf next to his bed, which was made perfectly. There was a picture of the *Challenger* on the wall next to the bed.

It blew up seventy-three seconds after launching, January 28, 1986, Tim said.

The other thing he had was an aquarium. Wendy walked over to study it. There was a plastic figure of a skin diver on the bottom, sitting on a bunch of multicolored pebbles, raising and lowering his arms over a plastic treasure chest. There was a mermaid with a tail that moved, and a plastic anchor, and a fake frog with bubbles coming out of his mouth when he opened it. No fish.

He doesn't like fish, Alan said.

Fish make the water dirty, Tim said. When they die, you have to flush them down the toilet.

It's nice the way you have it, Wendy said. You've got a good-looking setup there.

Tim was studying the pictures on the box of Legos his father had brought. Next time, I want the rocket ship, he said. Model number seven nine eight eight.

I brought the laundry, Alan said. You think we can handle all this?

Tim looked at the bag. Yes, he said. I can do it.

Well then, Alan said. What do you say we get to work?


They drove into town, Wendy in the backseat, Tim next to his father. You could see a certain resemblance in their faces except the expressions were so different it changed everything.

Wendy moved here recently from New York City, Tim, Alan said. She's like you. She likes to read a lot. She's a really good artist, too.

New York City is not the capital of New York State, he said. It's Albany.

What do you like to read? she asked.

*The Farmer's Almanac.* The dictionary. *Everything You Always Wanted to Know About Sex but Were Afraid to Ask.*

That's an actual book, Alan said. He found a copy in my store one time. He carries it around with him all the time.

I like novels, she said. I also read a lot of Japanese animation comics. Have you ever seen those?

*The Farmer's Almanac* says we can expect areas of high pressure and temperatures in the low seventies this afternoon, he said. Picabo Street broke her ankle recently, but she was back in time for the Austrian National Slalom Competition.

I wish I had a name like that, Wendy said.

Maybe we should think up a nickname for you, Alan said. What do you think, Tim?

They sell Tide at the Laundromat, but last time they were out of bleach.

This is his favorite thing, Alan said when they got there. He likes sorting the clothes and having a few different loads going at one time. Sometimes we take a walk while we're waiting, but he's just as happy to sit here. Then we put the clothes in the dryers, and that part we always stick around for, because you can look through the glass windows on the front and see everything spinning around.

We had a lot of stuff this time, Alan said. Your mother was gardening.

Bleach wash, Tim said.


Tim liked putting the quarters in the machine to buy the little individual packets of detergent. He had a pair of scissors in his pocket that he used to open them. He scattered the contents of one packet into each machine, one for dark clothes, one for whites, one for lighter colors, and one for delicate cycle only. In the white wash, he poured a packet of bleach in, too.

You have to be careful with bleach, he said.

One time, Tim put a shirt of mine in the bleach wash by mistake, Alan told her.

It used to be green, huh, Tim?

Used to be green, Tim said. For a second there, he got a very sad look on his face.

That's okay, Tim, Alan said and put an arm around him. Now when I wear my greenish white shirt, I always think of you.

\* \* \*

They walked around downtown Modesto a little during the spin cycle. You could tell Tim was uneasy, though. He kept checking his watch.

We should go back now, he said.

We've got thirteen more minutes, Tim, Alan told him. I was thinking I'd buy you guys an ice-cream cone.

It's good to be on time, Tim said.

When they got back to the Laundromat, Tim put the wet laundry in the dryers. They had used four washing machines but only two dryers. Tim put the quarters in. Then he plunked himself down in front of the machines. He sat very straight, his blue eyes fixed on the glass windows as the clothes started to spin.

This is his favorite part, Alan said. Isn't it, son?

Tim wasn't talking. He was staring in the windows.

I try to imagine what goes on in his brain, Alan said. He's in some other place we don't know about. I don't suppose we can imagine. I just hope it's nice there.

When my little brother was a baby, my mother set him down on top of the dryer sometimes and turn it on just for the sound and the vibrations, Wendy said. She'd hold him so he wouldn't fall off. It used to calm him down.

A bomb could go off right now, and Tim would still be sitting here watching for the one red sock in the window, Alan said.

They left a little after three o'clock, two hours after they got there. Tim helped carry the laundry out to the car. When Alan brought it, everything was jumbled into one big laundry bag, but now it was folded in baskets.

After Alan set the laundry in the backseat, they stood by the car a minute.

I'll be here again next week, he said.

Okay.

Anything special you'd like me to bring?

Lego model seven nine eight eight. The rocket ship.

I'll see what I can do, Alan said.

It's going to be cloudy next Tuesday. Temperatures between seventy and seventy-five. Chance of showers.

I'd better bring my rain jacket.

It was nice meeting you, Tim, Wendy said. Maybe I'll come back sometime.

I could call you Picabo. If you wanted a nickname.

Alan put his arms around the boy. Tim did not resist, but he didn't hug back, either.

I don't like it when the fish die, Tim said. It's better just to have the decorations.

I know how that is, she told him.


On the drive back they were quiet for a while. Around the time they got onto Route 5, he spoke.

That was a lot for Tim to say—what he told you about the nickname and the fish.

I like him, she said. He reminds me of my little brother in certain ways.

He probably likes Legos, too, huh? said Alan. Only for him, it would be age-appropriate.

As he said that, she imagined what it would be like if Louie never stopped playing with Legos and sucking his thumb. If he turned into someone like Tim, who Josh would have to spend the rest of his life visiting, and taking someplace like the Laundromat.

It's understandable that your brother would be having a rough time, Alan said. And you, too. Who's to say what normal behavior is in a situation like that? The usual rules just don't apply.

I wish I could see him, she said. It doesn't work, talking over the phone. I feel I have to be there in the room with him.

And then you've got someone like Tim, he said. You can be right there in the room, and you still can't get through. You should have seen him as a little boy, Alan said. Not just the usual kind of energy and alertness. More even. He used to come to the bookstore with me on slow days. We had a high stool for him so he could sit up at the front and color. He loved talking to customers.

This one woman, Mrs. Meehan. She'd cut jokes out of the newspaper for him. Not that he could read, but she'd tell him the joke and then he'd re-member it. All day long when people came in, he'd want to tell them the new joke. Sometimes he'd get it a little wrong, but if it was one of those jokes where there's a talking frog or something, he could make great voices. All my customers loved him.

I'll always remember this one joke he loved telling. What did Humpty-Dumpty say when he fell off the wall?

What?

Ha-ha. The yolk's on you.

The changes started happening a little before his fourth birthday, Alan told her. He began to be afraid of certain things. He wouldn't wear clothes with buttons. If a person came in the store carrying a backpack, he thought they had a bomb. He started rocking back and forth a lot, and he had to carry a tape measure at all times to measure things. None of it made any sense. When his mother would take him grocery shopping, if she walked behind a display of cereal, he'd be afraid he'd lost her forever, and even after she came back, he didn't calm down.

The doctors couldn't do anything. Nothing anyone could do. It was as if our little boy had been stranded on an iceberg that broke off from the main-land, and all we could do was stand there and watch him float away.

It was hardest on Linda. She couldn't get past the idea that it was her fault. The books and doctors tell you it's some kind of chemical imbalance. Nobody knows why. Plenty of really good, loving parents have autistic children. But to my wife, it was a sign she'd failed at the most important thing.

She spent years trying to get through to Tim, working with him, reading books, taking him to specialists. Five years ago, I finally convinced her that we should take him to Homewood. I thought it might be better for her, but I'm not even sure which has been harder on her—having a son around she had to watch every minute, or not having him there and just thinking about it.

Does she work in the store sometimes? Wendy asked him.

Hardly ever. I think being there reminds her of the old days. She gardens mostly. Plays the recorder. She tutors French a couple of times a week at the college. Maybe some people know how to get beyond a thing like this, but Linda never could.

When I realized my mom wasn't coming home I didn't know how I was supposed to keep on doing the normal things, Wendy said. It felt like nothing mattered anymore.

But then it started to, didn't it? he said. You didn't stop living after all. Which is how your mom would have wanted it.

The part I don't understand is where I belong now, she said. My old life just sort of disappeared.

It's still there, Alan said. People's lives just keep changing. That would be so even if your mom hadn't been in that building that day.

I want to see my dad and my brother, she said. She meant Josh when she said that.

I miss New York, she said. But in some ways, it's good being here.

You'll figure it out, he said. It seems to me like you're doing the right things. Though it might be a good idea if you didn't play hooky forever. An education comes in handy. Not that you aren't getting one, in a manner of speaking.

I just wanted a little while to think, she said.

I can appreciate that. I won't tell anyone. At least I'm glad nobody's hitting you. That's what had me worried before.

I'll take the number of the person you told me about in Sacramento, for my friend, she said.

Let me know if you need help, he told her. I know you want to take care of things yourself at the moment, but everyone can use a hand on occasion.


Garrett was late coming home. I've been at Carolyn's, he said. She got a call from her son.

It took Wendy a second to remember about the baby she'd given up.

He's living up in Oregon, Garrett told her. Tracked her down through some kind of adoptees' rights organization. She got a call today. Not from the boy himself. From his girlfriend. Wanting to know if she'd had a baby on this certain day. Everything matched up.

How'd she take it?

She'd always wanted this to happen, but once it did, she wasn't sure what to think. Never having had any other kids, she's worried about what he'll think if he meets her. She's going on a damn diet, just on the chance he might come down and see her. As if what he'd care about is whether she's a size eight.

If I'd been adopted and I'd tracked down my birth mother and it turned out to be Carolyn, I think I'd be pretty happy, Wendy said.

That's what I told her, said Garrett. A person could do a lot worse. Look at you. All you got was me.

That's fine.

So what's he like? she asked him. Did he end up with nice people?

The girlfriend didn't fill her in on a whole lot, he said. I guess she was the one who was kind of pushing the whole thing, and now she's going to tell her boyfriend that she and Carolyn talked. His name is Nate. Twenty-five years old.

What's Carolyn going to do now?

Write him a letter, I guess. Hope he decides to come down here. Paint the entire house inside and out, knowing her. I told her not to worry so much. You are who you are, I said. It's every kid's job to work that part out and learn to deal with it.

Still, Wendy said. I can understand how she'd be kind of worked up.

What can you do? he said. There's no changing the past. All you can do is move on from where you're at now.

Wendy and Garrett worked on their fishing flies for a while. She wasn't sure she'd be into fishing, but she sort of liked making the flies. The long, quiet evenings bent over the table with his tackle box, tying the knots and constructing the perfect little lures to fool a trout into thinking he was catching a piece of food in the water instead of a hook.

Soon as spring comes, Garrett said, you and I are heading up to the Sierras, camping. We'll catch ourselves a big old fish dinner, and sleep under the stars. Maybe bring along some art supplies and do a little sketching. I've been realizing how I've been missing out all these years, not spending time with you. Kind of like Carolyn and her son, in a way.

*　　*　　*

Then there's a person like Alan, Wendy thought. Driving the sixty miles to visit Tim every Tuesday, dependable as the sun. Sitting in the Laundromat year after year, watching the tumble dry cycle.

She thought of her mother's words: Your idea of parenthood, Garrett, is to drop in when you're in the neighborhood.

You do what you can, Garrett said. Sometimes you do the right thing. But sometimes you make mistakes. One thing's for sure. Hardly anybody actually means to screw up their kid. Not even my parents probably.

Why would I ever go back to Cleveland? Todd had told her. At least whatever mess happens from now on, I did it to myself.

# Twenty-Seven

Chief and Amelia were kissing now. He had also put his hand inside her bra. Not that he found anything.

We were in Washington Square Park, she told Wendy. We'd spent the afternoon looking at CD's. He bought me the new Michael Jackson for my birthday.

Oh my God, I can't believe I forgot, Wendy said. Amelia had turned fourteen right after Thanksgiving.

It was getting dark, she said. We were sitting by the fountain, and he just reached over and did it.

How did you feel?

At first, it was weird when he put his tongue in my mouth. Then I got used to it. He's pretty experienced.

But he didn't try to do anything else, right? Wendy asked her. They had decided to stay virgins until they were seventeen, and not do anything with anyone until they'd discussed it with each other first.

We talked about it, she said. He explained to me how it is for boys. The sex drive and so on. He did it one time already with a girl at his old school.

He said next time he wants it to be with a person that he's really good friends with first, like me.

Listening to her, Wendy got a depressed feeling, a little like how it was when her mother and Josh would be in the kitchen dancing to *Clifford Brown with Strings,* and it was as if for those few minutes she wasn't even there.

Carolyn had come for a sleepover. Before, Garrett had just gone over to her house on his own now and then—the times Wendy figured they wanted to have sex. But this time, she showed up around nine-thirty, when he was reading and Wendy was working on one of her storyboards.

I was so wound up, she said. I figured you and Wendy wouldn't mind me dropping by.

Any port in a storm, huh? Garrett said. But he looked glad to see her.

They had a beer, and Wendy went to bed. She fell asleep, but later, lying in the dark, she could hear them in the other room. Not very loud, just a little. The sound of the bed creaking and low, soft whispering. A faint moan just once.

Wendy had heard her mother and Josh like that sometimes, too. It made her feel lonely, knowing there was this thing that happened between them that had nothing to do with her. There was this part of her mother's life that she didn't know about or understand. Something she couldn't imagine and didn't want to.

My mother never talked to me about sex, her mother had said one time. She gave the impression it was something bad. I never believed that. But I was definitely embarrassed to talk about it. I wouldn't want you feeling that way.

Okay, Wendy said. She was twelve at this point.

So anytime you're wondering about anything, she said, you shouldn't feel like there's any question that would be too dumb to ask.

Okay, Wendy said again.

For instance, her mother said. Some people talk about sex like the only reason to do it is having babies. People have sex because it feels good, too. That most of all.

But you shouldn't ever do it until you want to. A lot of girls end up having sex before they're ready because some boy puts a lot of pressure on them. They want the boy to like them, so they do it. That was probably me at first.

I'll remember that, Wendy said. She wanted this conversation to be over.

Another thing is, you should know all the parts of your body. It's a good idea to take a mirror and just look at yourself carefully so you know what's there. Even Anne Frank did that, all those years ago. It's in the diary.

A woman's body is actually very beautiful, she said. There was this woman artist named Georgia O'Keeffe who painted flowers all the time, but most people think it was actually women's bodies she was thinking of. We can get one of her art books out of the library.

Wendy couldn't imagine taking a mirror and studying her body the way her mother was saying. She had studied her breasts a lot—or the one that had started to grow, which at that point was still a hard little lump on her chest—but that was all she'd really looked at.

I guess you don't really want to discuss this at the moment, huh? her mother said. Don't worry. We'll talk about it more another time.

Only they didn't. Carolyn had told Wendy that she could talk to her anytime. But even though she liked Carolyn a lot, it was hard to imagine bringing up sex with her. Then there was Violet, of course. But just because a person had a baby didn't necessarily make them a sex expert. It could be that Violet's having a baby meant she didn't know that much. How not to have one, for instance.

Now she lay in her bed, hearing the hushed sound of her father and Carolyn in the next room. She thought about Amelia kissing Chief, and Violet with the boy who looked like Brad Pitt but hit her sometimes. She wondered if, before he hit her, he had kissed her. She thought about Tim, with his copy of *Everything You Always Wanted to Know About Sex but Were Afraid to Ask*. Todd in the Fairmont Hotel bathrobe, sitting on the chair next to her bed, eating cashews. I hope this doesn't weird you out, he said. I wouldn't try anything.

She wondered why not. She probably didn't seem all that attractive.

Though sometimes lately when she looked at herself in the mirror after she got out of the shower, she thought she looked sort of nice. Definitely better than she used to.

You look like your mother, Garrett said. If that was true, it would be good.

My son might look like me, Carolyn said. If he's unlucky.

From the next room now, she could hear the sound of Carolyn's voice, low and drowsy. Not worked up anymore, the way she'd said she was when she first got there that night.

Wendy unbuttoned the front of her pajamas. She put her hand on the bare skin of her chest and felt her breasts, her heartbeat. She slid her hand slowly down over her ribs and the flat place that was her stomach now. Then she moved it farther down, the place her mother called beautiful. She touched very lightly, imagining how it would be if it was some boy's hand there instead of hers.

Violet and Wendy were at their usual table in the food court at the Almond Grove Mall, having Cokes. Wendy had brought the brochure Alan had given her about the teen counseling center, where there were people Violet could talk to about getting mad at Walter Charles.

How did it happen that you got pregnant anyway? Wendy asked her. She figured if they talked about that for a while, the conversation might come round to the other part. Violet feeling like hitting Walter Charles and maybe even doing it.

I was dumb, she said. I didn't know anything. My mom never told me word one about sex. Everything I know, I picked up on Maury Povich or Ricki Lake.

When I started doing it with Evan, I asked him if I should be worried, but he said no. He told me he got this case of mumps when he was eleven that made it so all his sperm was dead. When I told him he still had to use a condom, based on a show Ricki did about girls that got AIDS in high school— he said I was the first girl he'd actually done it with, so he didn't have to use a rubber. It feels better without, he said. I should've asked him how do you know if you never did it before, but I only thought about that later.

I didn't even notice in the beginning when I missed my period, because they were never what you could call regular in the first place. The throwing up part was the giveaway. My mom heard me in the bathroom in the mornings. You and me need to have a talk, young lady. Oh boy, I thought, here it comes. Turned out all she thought was I had bulimia, which she'd just seen a show about on TV. Sometime in May, I got one of those home pregnancy tests.

I could've come up with the money to get rid of it. But I just blocked it out, like it wasn't really happening. Every time the thought came into my head, *You're pregnant,* I'd zap it out. I'd make my brain start playing some song off the radio. If I was home, I'd call up one of my friends and say, Want to go shopping? Loose clothes, that was the ticket.

By the time school started up again at the end of August, some people were wondering, even with all the layers I had on. Mostly what I did was keep to myself. I moved through my classes, answering questions when they called on me, but I didn't volunteer. Just don't attract attention to yourself was my motto.

Evan had already dumped me a long time before this. I was mad at him for telling me that stuff about the dead sperm but the only way to tell him I knew that was a crock would have been to tell him I was having a baby, and I wasn't about to tell him that. He was going with this other girl by this time. I could've written her an anonymous note not to believe him if he told her some story about getting the mumps in his balls, but I never liked her anyway.

Didn't your mom ever notice that you were looking pregnant? Wendy thought of her own mother, who could tell if all you'd done was go to someone's apartment to see their home theater setup. Just by the look on your face. Who could tell if Wendy was coming down with a cold—before Wendy knew it herself.

You'd think, said Violet. The weird thing was, after that one remark about me throwing up, she never said anything. Maybe she blocked things out, too. Then one day when I was going out the door to school, she said, You're having a baby, aren't you? That was like two weeks before Walter Charles was born.

At that point, I was still planning on giving my baby to the San Francisco people. But before I even had a chance to tell her that part, she was screaming at me how she wasn't going to be stuck taking care of another kid and if I was thinking that, I had another thing coming.

I wasn't thinking anything like that, I said. As a matter of fact, I'm moving out.

I had over a thousand dollars saved up from my waitress job. I bought my furniture and the boom box. I went back to my mom's apartment once to get a few clothes and some CD's and that was it.

Then it hit me. Here I was this person that never had anybody that really cared about me. Not my boyfriend that lied to me and hit me for no good reason. Not my father that I never even knew or any of my mom's boyfriends. Not my own mother. Now along comes this person that's my blood relative, and he'd love me more than anyone in the world. Why would I give him away?

I told the lawyer in San Francisco the deal was off. And I went out and got the crib on the installment plan and the stroller.

But your mom must have called you or come by to find out how you were doing, right? Wendy couldn't imagine how there could be a mother who wouldn't love her child more than anything. Or at least enough to go see her when she had a baby.

They aren't always like that, said Violet. I got one of those moms that never read the rule book on how moms are supposed to act. Violet sat there playing with her straw for a minute. Tapping it in front of Walter Charles, in case he might like that maybe. He was fussing, as usual, but the straw didn't help.

The problem is, she said, when you have one of those moms that didn't get the rule book, you don't know how to act yourself. You want so bad to do the right thing. You just never saw what it was except maybe on some TV show like *Family Ties*. So you keep screwing it up, too, same as she did.

Carolyn was working on her letter to her son. She must have been working on it for a while, because there were a number of pieces of paper on the table that she'd started and then crumpled up.

The funny thing is, Carolyn said to Wendy, when your father decided to go see you in New York after all that time, he didn't sit around thinking up what to say to you. Just got on the plane and flew out there, like he was running down to the hardware store. He might have looked like an idiot, but odds are no more so than if he'd spent three days scratching out a couple of introductory remarks on a notepad.

Why don't you just tell your son a little about yourself? Wendy said. Like about your cactuses, and how you can read palms.

That might not go over so big, she said. *So, Nate, let's take a look at your lifeline, see what it indicates. Oh right, abandoned by your mother at age thirteen hours. There's a good start in life.*

Wendy had never seen Carolyn like this. Before, she'd always thought of Carolyn as such a laid-back person. Now she was a wreck.

I bet he can understand perfectly well why you gave him up for adoption, Wendy said. This girl I know that has the baby is having a really hard time with him. Sometimes I think he might do better if she gave him up. She never seems to know what he wants, and he cries all the time.

He's picking up on her vibrations, probably, Carolyn told Wendy. Babies know a lot more than we give them credit for. He probably knows his mom's in a tough situation.

Wendy looked at Carolyn's kind, freckled face, her hair falling out of her braid as usual, her worn gardener's hands, so different from Wendy's mother's, with their pink nail polish.

You should put a picture of yourself in the letter, too, she said. He'd probably like that.

Carolyn didn't have a camera, but Wendy had one that made miniature Polaroid pictures the size of a sticker to give your friends to stick on their notebook. She bought it at South Street Seaport one time when she and Amelia were fooling around together trying on clothes.

While Wendy went to get the camera, Carolyn went into the bathroom. When she came back out, it looked like she had brushed her hair, and put on some makeup.

He's going to love it, Wendy said. She snapped the picture. She counted to thirty and peeled off the adhesive backing. The pictures her camera made were only about the size of a postage stamp but Carolyn looked good as much as you could make out. They stuck it on the bottom of her letter.

Did the girlfriend tell you what color hair he has? Wendy asked.

Strawberry blond, same as me, she said. He probably has the devil of a time at the beach, too.

When Carolyn went back to her cabin, Wendy called home again, but Louie still didn't want to talk to her.

The therapist says maybe we shouldn't push it right now, Josh told her. It may be his way of dealing with loss.

He hasn't lost me, Wendy said. I'm here.

For a four-year-old that's hard to understand, Josh said. To Louie, you being in California feels as cut off as your mother not being here anymore.

Then we need to make sure he knows I'm alive, she said.

I'd put him on if he'd do it, Wen, he said. But when I talk about you, he gets angry. The only people he'll talk to these days are me and Kate, when she comes over.

She thought about before, just after Labor Day. The first day she'd gone back to school that fall, when Josh and Louie had walked her to the bus stop. Louie with a strip of fake fur their mother had given him pinned to the back of his pants to be a tail, skipping alongside her, though really it was more like hopping. He had started to climb the steps of the bus with her. Josh had to remind him it was just Sissy going to school, not him.

We discussed this last night, Lou-man, he said. You know it's a big kids' school. Us two guys will stay home and build a fort.

Just let me come one time, Sissy, Louie said. I'll stay home tomorrow.

I can't take you, Louie, she said, kneeling down next to him. But I'll be home in a few hours and we'll play.

Not a few hours. Now.

I can't, Louie. The bus is waiting.

Take me, take me, he said. Like Frankie in her book, wanting to go off with her brother when he got married.

She got on the bus. From the window, she could see them standing there, Josh in his green sweatpants, same as always. Louie in his arms. She waved, but he hid his face. The bus pulled away.

# Twenty-Eight

It was starting to be Christmas. If this was an ordinary year, they'd be making plans to take a trip out to Connecticut to cut down their tree. You could buy one right on the street near their apartment, but Josh liked tromping through the woods in the snow and cutting it down with an ax. On their way home with the tree on the roof of their car, they always stopped at a diner that served the best macaroni and cheese.

Maybe this year we should only put white lights on the tree, instead of multicolored, her mother would say. Remember how pretty Kate's tree looked last year?

What do we think about that idea, guys? Josh asked them.

Bad, said Louie. We want colored lights.

Next thing you know, you're going to tell me when we get home that you want to put on Alvin and the Chipmunks' Christmas album.

Al-vin, Al-vin, Al-vin, said Louie. He banged his spoon on the table the way Josh did when he was listening to some really cool drummer.

Someday, her mother said, I'm going to live in this really tasteful house where they only play the *Messiah* and the Joan Baez Christmas album and the Christmas tree has only white lights, and the ornaments are color-coordinated blue and silver.

Boo, said Josh.


Louie would be wired about Christmas, but her mother always said Louie wasn't even the most excited one. It was Josh. Her mother explained to Wendy one time that Josh's family was Jewish, and even though they weren't religious, they hadn't celebrated the holiday when he was growing up.

So now it's like he's making up for all those years, her mother said.

Josh wanted to do everything—stockings, Santa's footprints on the rug, like he'd stepped in the ashes of the fireplace and tracked them all over the place. Corny presents for her mother, and the red vest he always put on Christmas morning. Christmas dinner he'd make a bûche de Noël and set poppers next to their places.

I don't know how you survived all those years without Christmas, her mother said to him.

I was just waiting till I located people who'd know how to get into the spirit. No point doing Christmas until you've got yourself the right kind of crowd to do it with.

We're the right kind of crowd, right, Poppy? Louie said.

Are you ever.


It was a Saturday, but Garrett had some odds and ends to attend to over at the job site he was working at. He already had the truck loaded with his tools, and Shiva, when he called out to Wendy.

Why don't you come along, Slim? he said. I'll show you what I build.

She'd been reading *The Butcher Boy*. She could tell something bad was going to happen to the boy in the book, so in a way she was glad to be interrupted.

When I was young, Garrett said as they headed out, I thought I was going to be an artist. But not the kind my mother would have liked, that did portraits of rich people.

So you gave up art? she asked. Living in Brooklyn with her mother, and imagining his life in California, she had pictured him painting.

I didn't stop loving to draw and paint, he said. I just got a little more realistic about making a living at it. That was something your mother and I always argued about, as a matter of fact. At the time, I thought she was unreasonable, but I came to see her point.

But art was your passion, right?

I would have said that when I was twenty-five, he told her. Now if I'm honest with myself, I think it was partly the idea of being an artist. Living in a loft back in the days when it was still actually the artists who lived in lofts in New York City. Sitting in bars in the Village, going to openings, telling beautiful women I wanted to paint them. Even the part about never having any money kind of appealed to me. It was such a slap in the face to my father, who always cared about that more than anything.

But what about the actual drawing part? Making the artwork?

That part was real. I still keep a sketch pad in my truck, and anytime I go off camping, there'll be one day where I just sit on a rock for a few hours and draw. But that whole thing about making a name for myself, having these big angry paintings hanging on a wall someplace, stopped mattering so much. I go to San Francisco now and then, take a look at what people are doing these days, or, more likely, the old stuff, the work that's stood the test of time. Once or twice a year I might make some little drawing that feels good enough to hold on to. But it started to feel more important, having a life that worked, instead of making art that didn't. There's more satisfaction than I would have known in going off to a job in the morning, framing a house really well, knowing it's going to be around a lot longer than most of the stuff my friends and I used to turn out in our studios back then.

He had pulled the truck to a stop in front of a partly finished house, situated on the rise of a hill, a few miles outside of Davis. The walls were mostly up, though there was only plastic covering the doors and windows, and the roof was only half-shingled. Shiva jumped out of the truck. Garrett began unloading some boards from the back.

My mom used to want to play Peter Pan on Broadway, Wendy said. When she was growing up, that was her dream. She used to say she was going to fly.

A person should have those kind of dreams, Garrett said. But you don't have to see your life as a failure if it doesn't end up taking the exact shape you originally pictured. You might hang your art on the walls of a museum. You might make the best damn trout lure anybody ever cast into the Merced River. You might build cabinets or grow cacti. That might be your art. Who's to say?

They walked into the half-finished house. The smell of sawdust hung in the air. At the far end of one room, a stone fireplace was under construction. Not yet finished, but Wendy could see it would be beautiful.

I made that, he said. I gathered all the stone in riverbeds. He ran his hand over the mantel.

My mother doesn't like to tell her friends her son is just a carpenter, he said. I have a feeling she tells them I'm an architect. To me, the only shame in building houses is if you do it badly.

She was in her room drawing. The phone rang. It was Kate.

Josh says maybe we should leave you alone out there to get into your life, she said. But I just had to call. We miss you so much.

Hearing Kate's voice after all that time gave Wendy a dull, empty feeling, like walking past a house you used to live in a long time ago, and they've changed the paint and the stone lion that used to be out front is gone. She thought about the old days, not just before September but before Josh and Louie, too, all those nights when she and her mom and Kate would curl up on the couch together watching Shirley Temple movies or old musicals and eating popcorn.

Sometimes she would lie in bed and listen to her mother and Kate in the other room, talking late into the night about their jobs or their dream of opening up a little bed-and-breakfast together in Maine. They told each other stories of horrible dates they went on that always made them sound funny even though at the time they probably weren't.

Then Wendy's mother met Josh, but Kate had stayed single all these years. Maybe I'm just supposed to be this Auntie Mame–type person to Wendy and Louie, Kate said. Which isn't so bad.

Now she was calling from New York. Josh fills me in on what you're up to out there, she said. But I just wanted to hear your voice.

I have to admit, when you went to California, I was really down on the idea, she said. But maybe it's turning out to be a good thing for you after all, huh?

In some ways, it's better here, at least for now, Wendy said. But I miss everyone back home a lot. And I'm worried about Louie.

I've been spending a lot of time with him lately, Kate said. We go to play Skee-Ball every Saturday, and he seems to like that. I think it's partly that I remind him of your mom. Last week when I went by to pick him up, he wanted me to wear that red jacket of hers. The week before, he wanted to give me her boots.

It's a good thing he gets to see you, Wendy said.

Next weekend, I'm taking him to see a magic show, Kate told her. Maybe we'll go check out the tree at Rockefeller Center.

How would you say Josh is doing? Wendy asked her.

Oh, Josh, she said. She was silent for a moment.

We talk on the phone a lot. He's just so lonely. He's got all his musician friends, but the truth is, your mom was everything to him. He came over to Kate's mother's house for Thanksgiving, and I'm hoping he'll do the same for Christmas, but I know he wishes he could just go in a cave somewhere. Only he can't because of Louie, which is probably a good thing.

Do you think it would help if I came home? Wendy asked her. She had been thinking about it more lately. In her original plan, Davis was just going to be a getaway.

You do what's best for you right now, honey, Kate said. Your brother and Josh will work things out eventually. All Josh wants is for you to be okay. You and your brother.

When I talk to Louie on the phone, his voice has this dead sound, Wendy said. He won't tell me anything about school. Most of the time he doesn't even want to talk to me.

He doesn't talk about it, but I know he thinks about your mother all the time, Kate said. Just because a person's only four years old doesn't mean he can't get depressed.


Then suddenly Louie seemed better. He called her the next week around dinner time.

What are you doing up, Louie? she asked. It's got to be nine-thirty.

Me and Kate went to a magic show, he said. All the kids got balloons, but I got to go up on the stage with the magician. He spoke in a hushed whisper, like just the thought of it was too much to repeat.

You were a lucky duck, huh? she said.

He wanted someone that was really brave, because it was a hard trick. He said you should only raise your hand if you weren't afraid to go in a box, and if you did, Miss Sparkle, the helper, had a special treat. I was afraid, but I raised my hand anyway, because I wanted the treat.

And he picked you.

I was worried he wouldn't see me on account of Kate and me were sitting behind a tall man, but I got up on my seat and I was waving and sending energy beams, so he would pick me. He said, How about that boy in the Yankee jacket, Miss Sparkle? And that was me. And Kate said, Think you can do it? And I said, Yes!

The magician had asked him his name.

Louie, he said. For Louis Armstrong, the greatest trumpet player of all time. Josh had taught him to say that when people asked.

The crowd had loved that. They clapped for me, Sissy, he told her. Then the magician had explained how he was going to put Louis Armstrong's namesake inside a special box and close the lid. Little Louie, the magician called him.

And I was scared, he told her, but Miss Sparkle gave me a special flashlight to hold while I was in there.

The magician said he was going to saw the box in half then. I sure hope we don't lose Little Louie, he said. I was starting to like that kid.

Then Louie told her some things she couldn't follow about spears coming through the box, but in certain places where he knew they wouldn't stab him, and a secret passageway with Miss Sparkle inside. She had jelly beans.

Then the magician was opening the box again and Louie came out, only he was wearing a silver cape and holding a wand just like the magician's. Everyone started clapping and Louie bowed the way their mom taught him this famous dancer used to do named Mikhail Baryshnikov that was her favorite. They didn't even tell him to do the bow. That part he just thought up.

Since you did such a great job here today, Louie, I'm thinking maybe we should give you the special magic wand to take home. Let's see if the audience agrees.

They did. So he got to take the wand home with him. Before he walked back off the stage Miss Sparkle had bent down close to him and whispered in his ear.

There's one special wish in every wand, she said. If you save it till your birthday and you're a very good boy and close your eyes and wish very hard, it could just come true.

Neat, Wendy said. And then I bet Kate took you to see the tree at Rockefeller Center, right? With all the skaters.

She did but he didn't have so much to say about that part.

So what did you ask Santa for, she asked him. Every year, he and Josh wrote the letter together.

Some Legos and the Tonka crane, he said.

Wendy knew that other years his list had been much longer.

How's school going? she asked.

Okay, Louie said. We're learning about when letters say their own name.

Before you know it, you'll be reading, Wendy said. And then you can read *Curious George* to Josh and me.

This was where, in the past, he would have asked her when she was coming home, but he didn't.

Louie, she said.

Yes, Sis. His voice sounded very small and far away.

Even when I'm not there, I think about you every single day.

Okay, he said.

Who's your only sister in the whole world?

You.

And who's my only brother?

Me.


A letter came for Carolyn. She had used their address because her mailbox had fallen down a while back and she hadn't gotten around to fixing it. When Garrett came home and saw the letter he called to let her know.

Postmark Bend, Oregon, he said. Looks like your kid wrote back. I suppose that means you might be moseying over here one of these days to find out what he's got to say in his letter.

She was there a half hour later.

He said he'd received her letter. Received was the word he used.

The whole letter was a little like that. Written in the kind of language Wendy's Connecticut grandmother would have approved of.

"It was gratifying that you would invite me to pay a visit to your home," he said. "After consideration, I have decided to accept. I will be coming with my future wife. We are planning a trip to visit her parents over the Christmas holidays. Assuming your schedule could accommodate us, Sharon and I could stop through on the morning of the twenty-fourth. If this is satisfactory, please send confirmation and directions to your home. Yours truly."

Then came the signature. *Nathan Lowry* in small tightly formed letters. Underneath it was a P.S. "Sharon asked me to express appreciation for the photograph. Due to the size, it was hard to make out much of your appearance, but evidently we share the same color of hair."


He doesn't sound all that friendly, Carolyn said.

Some people aren't the letter-writing type, Garrett told her. He's taking it slow. Doesn't want to get too hepped up till he gets here. Smart kid.

They'll never find my place, she said. And then there's that old car out front, and all the mess of my plants. You think we could have them over here instead?

*Mi casa es su casa,* said Garrett.

It'll be the Long-Lost Children's Christmas, he told her. All we need to make the festivities complete is my mother.


They did hear from her oddly enough, but not the usual Christmas package, the Brooks Brothers shirt and monogrammed blouse. She was going into the hospital, she told him on the phone. They'd found a blood clot. You don't need to worry. Not that you would.

*    *    *

How's Tim doing? she asked Alan when she stopped by the store. Does he like Christmas?

Christmas is hard on him, said Alan. Tim likes a nice steady routine. When we went to the Laundromat last week, he got upset because they had all these decorations up.

Do you and your wife go up there to spend the day with him? she asked. She had been thinking about Josh. People who might be alone on Christmas. Violet being another one.

Linda goes to an ashram up north every year for the week between Christmas and New Year's, he said. And Tim does better if I keep to the schedule and only come on the usual visiting day.

If you're going to be alone, you could have dinner with my father and his girlfriend and me, she said. My dad's girlfriend's son is coming for a visit the day before, but Christmas Day, it's just going to be us.

Garrett wasn't the kind of person you had to check things with. She knew he'd be fine about that.

I might take you up on the invitation, Alan said. I make a Christmas pudding every year, first week in October, so it has plenty of time to age, let the rum really sink in. I'll bring it.

I never had Christmas pudding before, she said. My dad always made a bûche de Noël. My other dad, I mean.


At Garrett's house, you wouldn't have known the holiday was coming.

I'm not so big on all this Christmas hullabaloo, he said. Christmas was still a week away, but he was complaining that he couldn't turn on a radio anymore without hearing carols.

You shouldn't be such a grinch, Carolyn told him. Maybe your daughter would like to get a tree.

That's okay, Wendy said. Maybe we could just put a few lights on one of your cactus plants.

She sent a package back home to Brooklyn. For Louie she had bought a bunch of little things—Silly Putty and a really great bubble-blowing wand, and a baldy wig and three Matchbox trucks. She got Josh a book Alan had recommended about a jazz singer named Billy Tipton, and a shirt Carolyn helped her pick out at an imports store in Davis, with hand-embroidered designs around the neck and sleeves and wooden buttons. Drawing them a card, she realized that this was the first year there would be no family Christmas card photograph of the four of them.

Violet was going to spend Christmas with her mother.

She stopped over last week, Violet said. She brought a sleeper suit for Walter Charles. She was nicer than I expected.

That's really great, Wendy said. I couldn't believe she'd just let you disappear out of her life like that.

She thought Wally was cute, Violet said. It turns out I had that same way of wrinkling my nose up when I first got a taste of the bottle, like he does.

So you're going to have Christmas dinner at her house? Wendy asked.

Don't get the wrong idea, Violet said. It won't be like your old hometown, Neverland or anything. We're going over to her boyfriend's place. They like watching all the parades on big-screen TV.

What are you giving her? Wendy asked.

There was this pendant I saw in Long's. A heart shape, with fake diamonds and a fake ruby in the middle. Twenty-nine ninety-five, but you only get one mother, right?

Four days before Christmas, Amelia called. Listen, she said. I wasn't sure if I should tell you this or not, but if it was me, I'd want to know.

It would be about her mother. They'd found something. One of the red shoes. Or worse.

I went over to your apartment the other day, she said. My mom and I wanted to drop off some Christmas cookies for Josh and Louie. It was kind of early in the morning, because we were on our way out shopping.

Listening to her, Wendy felt a creeping sense of dread.

Josh came to the door, Amelia said. You could tell he'd just gotten up. He hadn't shaved or anything, and he was in this bathrobe. I asked if I could see Louie so we could give him this special gingerbread man. He told me Louie spent the night at Corey's house. I said that was good news, remembering how you'd told me before he wasn't doing that for a while. Figuring he must be feeling better.

I was asking him some other things. How you were doing in California. What his plans were for the holidays. But you could tell he wasn't in the mood to do a whole lot of talking.

He's probably having a rougher than usual time right now, Wendy said. He loved Christmas with my mom.

That's what I was thinking, too. Okay, I said. I'll just copy down the address really quick. That's what I was doing when she came out of the bedroom. In your mom's robe.

Who? Wendy said. But she knew.

Kate.

Carolyn, she said. I know you're probably busy. But I was just remembering how you told me that time if I felt like it, I could talk to you.

I was just going out for some fencing wire, Carolyn said. Why don't I stop by? We can go get ourselves a cool drink.

Carolyn and Wendy sat in the diner drinking lemonade—Christmas carols playing, the two of them in T-shirts. In New York that morning, Amelia had told her, it had been snowing.

So, Carolyn said. Let's review the situation.

Back in September your dad got his heart ripped out of his chest and torn to pieces, right? She was talking about Josh.

You don't have any doubt he loved your mother, right? From the sound of it the man was nuts about her.

Yes.

So he loses the woman he loves more than anything. And if that isn't enough, you go away, too. Then he's got this four-year-old to take care of and for a while there it's almost like he's losing him, too.

He tries to do the right thing. Take care of his son. Leave you to do what you need to sort out your own problems. Earn a living maybe, while he's at it. But as far as he's concerned he might as well be dead himself. Only what's worse is, he's not. He's got another fifty, sixty years of living to fill up on this planet, and at this stage I'm guessing one day feels pretty unbearable.

He said he wished he could die, Wendy whispered.

Of course he did. For a while.

The thing is, he's not someone who gives up on life forever. Any more than you are. This is a guy that plays music for his job and goes around riding roller coasters with you guys and making all this great food. He loves life way too much. He just hasn't quite figured out how he's supposed to keep on living either.

Same as me, Wendy said.

Another cactus person from the sound of it, Carolyn said. Stick one in the middle of the desert where there's not a drop of water for a hundred miles. Not only does the plant refuse to die, it keeps growing. May even throw out a bright red blossom now and then, who knows?

Listening to her, Wendy began to feel a little calmer. She took a sip of her lemonade.

So there's this woman, Carolyn said.

We're not talking about some kind of husband-stealer. This is your mother's best friend. Someone else who happens to be missing your mom pretty badly and feeling this big, awful empty space of her own.

Kate and my mom talked on the phone every single day.

And all that time Kate and your mom were friends, did you ever get the feeling Kate wanted to take Josh away from her? Let alone wish she was dead.

No.


It gets to be December, said Carolyn. Three months have gone by with the guy, your dad, alone in that bed he used to share every night with your mother. It's coming on Christmas to top it off—the time when it seems like everyone in the world but him is hunkering down with their family.

Kate's been coming by now and then to help out with your little brother, and he really likes her, right? She's the one familiar thing that didn't go away. So when the friend's over, he can feel like that even though things aren't normal, they're not so bad anyway.

And just like you out here, brave enough to move forward with your life instead of throwing in the towel, that's what Josh and Kate are doing. It doesn't mean they didn't love your mom or miss her any less badly, any more than you being willing to give it a try out here with Garrett and me is some kind of indication you didn't really care about your mom. When you get down to it, that's about the best way you can honor a person you loved that died. To keep on with your life and do the best job you know of living it.

Then there's this other part, she said quietly.

You'll probably have to be a little older to understand this. But it has to do with physical affection.

Maybe you don't even have to be older, come to think of it, she said. Because it's not even about sex so much, is my guess. It's about something you've experienced plenty of times, which is just how good it can feel when a person puts their arm around you now and then. Particularly when you're having a hard time. The simple ordinary comfort of having this other warm body lying in the bed next to you.

Wendy did know about that. She thought of Anne Frank, and how she'd written about lying on the bed in their little prison of an apartment with the boy, Peter—how happy it made her just to have his face next to hers. Louie, climbing into her bed in the mornings. How she and her mom used to go Rollerblading along the West Side Highway, arm in arm, pretending to be Ice Capades Girls. Josh's big bass-player hug, when she came home that night after the memorial service for Billy Flynn. *My God, I was going crazy.* She remembered the feeling in the fitting room at Macy's when she and her mother had just stood there in nothing but their bras and underwear, holding each other.

*What would I do if I didn't have you for my daughter? I'd have to kidnap you.*

Sometimes you just want someone to put their arms around you, Carolyn told her. Even Garrett, who grew up never getting that kind of thing and sometimes has a hard time giving it—even someone like him needs it. Sometimes I think a person could give up food more easily than affection. Maybe that's why cactuses have prickers all over them and people don't.

Do you think now they'll get married? Wendy asked her. What would she be then? My stepmother?

Oh, God, I don't know, Carolyn said. I've never even met these people.

Though if I were guessing I'd say it wasn't likely. There's a kind of mending that happens from deep inside that probably takes years. These people are just getting through the days for a while, then getting through the weeks and maybe one day finding out they've managed to get through a year, which at this point would be about as far as anyone would try to look ahead under the circumstances.

This might be a lot to ask of you, Wendy, she said. But the day may even come when you could manage to feel a tiny little bit of happiness for Kate and Josh. Not like how it was when Josh and your mom got together and everyone was probably throwing confetti or rice or some damn thing over their heads and dancing around all over the place. Not the ten-piece band and the full moon and the sky lit up like Disneyland.

Just a small scrap of something good is all. This is more like a harmonica tune and one small star shining down on them. You've got two good people who've had a crushing load of grief lately, and if they can find some way to give each other a little comfort one of these days, who'd begrudge them?

A telephone call came for Garrett from a hospital in Greenwich. Didn't like delivering news this way. Fairly routine procedure. Complications. His mother had died that morning.

The surprising thing was how he took it. Wendy might have thought from the way he was with his mother back at Thanksgiving that it wouldn't be that bad when she died, but he sank into the chair, weeping. Now it'll never be any better, he said. As long as she was around I could always hope things might change someday, and now I know they never will.

He wore a suit jacket and one of the shirts she'd given him, for the trip back east. Before he left he stood in front of the bathroom mirror and cut his hair. No more ponytail.

So it turned out to be just the two of them, Carolyn and Wendy, for the visit of Carolyn's son and his future wife. Wendy tried to locate some sadness about her grandmother, but mostly who she was sad about was her father. Driving off in his truck that afternoon he had looked a little like Louie staring at the TV that wasn't on, or Alan's son Tim staring at the clothes dryers. Blank and haunted at the same time.

All day Wednesday, Wendy and Carolyn cleaned the house in preparation for the visit of her son. Wendy made brownies, the Josh method. They're not exactly a traditional Christmas food, but they're so good, she said.

If he's really my son, he'll love chocolate.

Carolyn got her hair done. She had been hoping to drop a few pounds, but with all the stress about his coming she couldn't stop eating chips, she said.

They had written they'd be at the house around ten o'clock that morning, the twenty-fourth. At exactly ten o'clock the car pulled up. A tall, thin young man got out and came around the side. The young woman stepped out very slowly, feetfirst, in lace-up Hush Puppies, followed by the rest of her, which was pregnant. She looked as if she might give birth any minute.

What do you know? said Carolyn, watching them come up the path. I'm going to be a grandmother.


Their greeting reminded Wendy of when her dad's mother had gotten out of the elevator in the Fairmont Hotel, and for about one second Wendy had been getting ready to give her a hug, but it turned out the idea was a handshake.

Pleased to meet you, he said. I'm Nate. This is my fiancée, Sharon.

We were only expecting two visitors, Carolyn said. Looks like we might end up with three.

We would have gotten married before now, but it's important to us to have the ceremony in our church, and our pastor believes in a six-month counseling period first.

Make yourselves at home, Carolyn said. This is actually my boyfriend Garrett's place. His mother died and he had to go east for the funeral.

Sorry to hear it, Nate said.

This is Garrett's daughter, Wendy, she told them.

They sat in the living room. They had put his fishing tackle away and the pile of old towels he kept out on the floor for Shiva to lie on.

So, she said. How many hours does it take to drive from Bend?

We stopped in Springfield to attend a youth ministries service, he told her. If we were driving straight through, eight or nine.

It's great you came, she said.

We were coming this direction, Sharon told them. My parents live in Newport Beach. We're getting together with both our families for Christmas.

You two looked like Joseph and Mary getting out of that car, Carolyn said. Only there's room at the inn. Wendy had never heard Carolyn's voice sound like this. Higher than normal and when she said that she made a laughing sound.

We can't stay that long, he told her. We still have a long drive to make, and I'm stopping off in Glendale to see my mother's cousin.

Wendy looked at his face, trying to see a resemblance to Carolyn. His red hair and the freckles on his arms, that was about it.

I've got to tell you, said Carolyn. When Sharon called, it was like a dream come true. I never would have forced myself on you, but I was always hoping the day would come when you'd want to find me.

It was Sharon's idea, Nate said.

Not that I'd expect anything, Carolyn said. You have parents. I just hope they gave you the love you deserved.

My folks are wonderful people. I was raised with faith.

How about brothers and sisters? she asked him.

Two brothers and one sister. My brothers are doing missionary work at the moment and my sister's a computer programmer back east, but they'll all be out here for the wedding this spring.

Wendy waited to see if he was going to suggest that Carolyn come, but he didn't.

There's a reason I was so anxious to locate you, Sharon said. She reminded Wendy of an insurance salesperson who came to their apartment back in New York one time. Who spent a minute asking Josh about jazz and then, just like a timer went off at the sixty-second mark, switched over to actuarial tables.

We felt we should find out if there were any genetic abnormalities to look out for, she said. With the baby coming.

Carolyn looked blank for a minute. At Wendy's suggestion she had brought over from her place a couple of her rarest and most interesting cactus plants to show them, and a set of tarot cards in case they turned out to be interested in a reading. She had gathered up a collection of pictures of her mother and sisters from back in Iowa for Nate to look at—his grandmother and aunts. She hadn't been thinking about genetic abnormalities.

You mean like my blood type and so on? she said slowly.

More along the lines of medical problems that might run in your family, Sharon said. Mine doesn't have any, but I told Nathan I wanted to know what we were in for with yours. Mom and Dad Lowry understood and agreed it was worth getting to the bottom of all that.

Something changed in Carolyn's face.

I get sunburned real easy, she said quietly. But you probably already figured that one out, didn't you, Nathan?

He told her he didn't spend that much time in the sun.

Other than that I can't think of a damn thing, she said. Wendy wondered if she said the damn part on purpose, but more likely it was one of those times where the one word you knew you shouldn't say in front of certain kinds of people was the very one that popped out.

Well, that's a load off my mind, Sharon said. Wendy got the feeling she would have liked to get up and leave right then and there but she knew to be polite they should stick around another few minutes.

I made brownies, Wendy said.

Thanks, said Sharon. But our families are likely to have a big meal waiting for us.

They sat there for a moment. Wendy imagined all the crazy things she could say here. Hey, want Carolyn to read your palm? Look on the bright side. You should see my friend Violet who kept her baby. He cries a lot, so she keeps hitting him on the head with a straw. Oh, Carolyn. When is it that your three autistic nephews are due to show up for Christmas dinner? Is that before or after your uncle who never grew any eyebrows?

I just wanted you to know, Carolyn said. I can understand, now that you're about to have a baby yourselves and all, how it must be for you, imagining me giving you away like that. But it didn't mean I didn't want you. I was trying to do the best thing. Nothing else I ever did in my life was as hard as that.

Only God can judge, he said.

You could tell she'd been thinking about saying this for days. She spoke as if every word mattered so much.

After they took you away, she said, I felt like running out of the building and chasing after the car. I wanted to say, Wait a minute. I can't go through with this.

Well, it was good you weren't one of those people who kill babies, Nate said.

Carolyn looked blank for a moment.

Abortion, said Sharon, as if just speaking the word was more than she liked to do.

You might have been wondering if you had a brother or sister, Carolyn said softly. But I never had any other kids. Just you.

I hope, he said, that you have accepted Jesus Christ into your heart as your personal savior.

Drive safely, she told them. And congratulations on the baby.

# Twenty-Nine

Then it was Christmas.

Wendy and Carolyn got up around eight-thirty. No need to be out of bed at the crack of dawn the way she would if Louie had been there, padding into her room at ten to five. *Is it time yet, Sissy? I peeked and you should see all the presents. Santa ate every single cookie.*

It was strange having such warm weather on Christmas Day. When Wendy got up, Carolyn was out in the yard setting up the barbecue. She was preparing the turkey from a recipe she'd cut out of the paper, cooked on the grill. A man on the radio was saying the temperature could get into the seventies.

Merry Christmas, Carolyn said. She gave Wendy a quick hug.

You, too.

They hadn't talked about Nate's visit, but evidently she'd found a flyer they'd left for her, with the words on the front NOT TOO LATE TO REPENT.

I guess I don't need to start knitting booties, Carolyn said. Wendy wasn't sure what she meant.

Their baby, she said. I don't get the impression they have me in their plans.

Nate didn't seem much like you.

No. I guess not.

There's probably lots of people who would really love to have you be their mom.

It doesn't matter, Carolyn said. The good thing is, now I don't have to go around anymore, wondering who my son turned out to be.

Anyway, you've got me. Wendy hadn't intended on saying something like that but looking at Carolyn standing there in her too-tight cutoffs and T-shirt, scrubbing the grill, she felt an unexpected wave of affection. There wasn't one single thing about Carolyn that reminded Wendy of her mother. Four months ago they hadn't even met. Now it was Christmas morning and here they were.

I got you a present, Carolyn said. A couple, actually.

Me, too.

Hers, for Carolyn, was a book about a woman who traveled on her own, on a raft, along the Amazon River. I picked it out at Alan's store, she said.

She had also gotten Carolyn a beaded hair clip, turquoise and green, because she figured it would look good against the color of Carolyn's braid.

Carolyn had tied a purple bow around a cactus pot. It was her special Scarlet Ball cactus that Wendy had admired at Carolyn's cabin, the one she dug up in Death Valley.

She had also picked out a pair of pants and a sweater from a store in Sacramento. Not a lot of people know how to shop for thirteen-year-old girls, her mother used to say. Carolyn did.

Garrett called this morning, she told Wendy. The funeral went okay, I guess. He said he's flying standby back home. He'd gotten as far as St. Louis when he called. He figures he'll make it back today or tomorrow.

How did it go? Wendy asked.

He didn't say much. I guess there were about four old ladies there and some man who'd been her lawyer. She'd asked to have this poem read, by Robert Frost. The big surprise was this black woman that used to take care of your dad when he was little. She came all the way from Boston with her son and got there right in the middle of the service. It turned out your grandmother paid for the son's whole college education and now he teaches at some private school in New Hampshire. The man's mother got pretty emotional about your grandmother evidently. Called her the most generous woman she ever met.

Your father never even knew, Carolyn said. Just goes to show.

The package had arrived the week before, but she had waited till now to open it. There was a CD of Miles Davis and another one of another trumpet player she hadn't heard of before called Lee Morgan. Someday in the future, Josh had written, when there's some very cool guy you really want to impress, show him you have this in your collection and he'll treat you with nothing but respect.

He had bought her a pair of sneakers with retractable wheels in the soles—for sometime when you need to make a quick getaway, the note said on the box. Josh always put Post-it notes on his packages. There was another larger box, also with a note, but a longer one:

*I spent two days walking around the city looking for a different kind of present.*

*I wanted to find some incredibly precious thing I could put in a box and send you that would tell you all the ways I feel. How much I have treasured every minute I've gotten to be part of your life. If there was any doubt in your mind as to how it might affect things, that I am not your blood father, I wanted to find you something that would tell you the answer to that one. The answer being: No difference, Wendy. However it is that you'll come to see me over the years, whatever place you end up finding for me in the life you go on to have, I wanted to make sure there was no question in your mind who you will always be to me. My daughter.*

*I decided it was stupid to think there was any object I could send that would say all those things to you. Where's the store a person goes to shop for an item like that?*

*But of course in the end I had to try a music store, my favorite one, over on Forty-eighth Street.*

*For me the only thing that ever came close to bringing me the kind of joy*

*I've known with your mother and your brother and you has been music. I honestly don't know if it'll be that way for you. Could be you'll find your big joy in a musical instrument. Could be you'll find it in your box of colored pencils, or books. Or something you haven't even discovered yet.*

*But whether or not the clarinet becomes for you what the bass is for me, I wanted you to have the most beautiful clarinet you could be playing at a moment when you've got to take your joy where you can find it.*

*I saw this in Manny's window and had to take a closer look. I liked the tone of the thing. I loved the thought of how you'd look playing it. You, who always gets that really serious expression when you're playing a piece of music—the concentration you have when you play, like nothing else is there at the moment but you and the notes.*

*I thought about how your mother would have loved to see you with a clarinet like this one. Her having been a somewhat flashy dresser, as we know. You being a more understated kind of person, but I'm thinking maybe you're about due to bust out with something a little flashy yourself.*

She opened the case. It was a cherry red clarinet.

Carolyn called her mother and sisters in Iowa. Wendy called home, too, but nobody was there. She figured Josh and Louie must've gone over to Kate's. She felt sad not to be hearing Louie's voice Christmas morning, getting the rundown on what he'd found in his stocking. But it was good they'd gone out. She thought again about Josh and Kate in the bathrobes that morning Amelia came over. She wondered if they would do that when Louie was there. Whatever happened, it wouldn't be so terrible. Josh would know what Louie could handle.

She and Carolyn weren't making a big meal. Turkey with store-bought cranberry sauce. Frozen peas, baked yams, corn bread. In addition to the Christmas pudding Alan was bringing, Carolyn had picked up a pumpkin pie at Shop 'N Save and vanilla ice cream and a bottle of champagne.

A little after two o'clock, the phone rang. Wendy could hear Carolyn say, You must have the wrong number. No Kitty here.

Wait a second. I think that's for me, Wendy said.

It's kind of my nickname, Wendy told Carolyn as she took the receiver.

I hate to call you on Christmas, Violet said. But I had to talk to someone.

That's okay, Wendy told her. Things are pretty low-key around here.

I wish I could say that. My mom and her boyfriend got in this god-awful fight over at his house. It started because I set Walter Charles's bottle on Ed's big-screen TV and it left a mark. You and that precious TV, my mom says. All you ever do is watch TV.

Next thing I know, he's calling my mom a tramp that's probably fooling around with her boss. She said, Maybe I am? Who could blame me given your performance in bed lately? In front of his sister and everything.

His kids came over. He was drinking out back at this point. They started eating all the food my mom brought and acting like she was the maid. She said, Come on, Violet, let's get out of here. I was almost thinking, Good, now it can be just her and me, and we can have our own little family celebration back at her place. Only in the car she starts in on me how it's all my fault. If it wasn't for me and my baby, none of this would've got started in the first place.

I still had the heart necklace wrapped up in a box in my diaper bag. I hadn't even got a chance to give it to her and here she is saying all this stuff about how I always wreck her life. Then Wally starts crying and she says, Isn't that perfect? Join the club. You'll see what I mean about kids.

I was trying to quiet him down. Only he wouldn't let up.

Look at you, she says. You can't even get your own baby to quit hollering.

I can, I say. He's just got a touch of colic.

But he keeps on wailing in the car. Like someone put tacks in his Pampers. And I'm stuffing the bottle in his mouth and waving his rattle at him, but nothing makes any difference. It's like he knows she's a witch.

What did I tell you? she says. You should've given him away while you had the chance.

I don't want to give him away, I tell her. I'm his mother. He loves me.

Kid's doing a pretty good job of concealing it, she says. We're stopped at a light at this point. Walter Charles is screaming so loud now people are looking in the car at us like I'm committing murder.

Face it, she says. You don't know what you're doing. Just because you know how to spread your legs doesn't make you Mother Teresa.

Walter Charles, I'm saying. Stop it now. I'm trying that thing you do where you make the little noises in his ear, but it's hard with him in the car seat.


Good luck getting some guy interested in you now, she says. Guys love it when they see a chick with a kid. Let alone a screaming one. Take it from me. I had to deal with you since I was seventeen and it didn't exactly do wonders for my social life.

Oh boy, I tell her. You mean I might have to do without some prize like Ed over there? Him and his TV.

Stuff it, she says, at least he had a Christmas dinner all set up for us. We were having a good time watching the parade till you and Little Mr. Life of the Party there showed up.

Walter's screaming so loud now, his face is the color of the cranberry sauce. I'm scared he's going to bust a vein. I figure it's probably half her fault he's having this fit in the first place. He can pick up the tension.

Let me out of the car, I say. Just pull over right here and let me out.

Just remember I was the one that tried to mend the fences here, she says. Got the kid an outfit and everything.

She pulls over. It's in the middle of no place. A muffler shop and a 7-Eleven, that's it. I unbuckle his seat belt and lift out the car seat, not that I know how I'm going to haul it home all that way. My hands are shaking so bad I can hardly undo the buckles, with Walter Charles wailing the whole time.

Merry Christmas, she says. Slams the door shut and lays rubber. She's out of there.

Then it's just Wally and me standing by the side of the highway with the diamond heart necklace still wrapped and everything in his diaper bag. Down to my last diaper, too, if you must know.

So what happened then? Wendy asked.

That's where I'm calling from, she said. The 7-Eleven, side of the highway out by the entrance to I-5. Wendy realized then that she could hear Christmas music playing in the background, and the sound of cars.

I know this is crazy, but I was wondering if someone there can pick us up?

In the car on the way over Wendy explained a few things. Violet's heard a slightly different version of things, she told Carolyn. She got the impression my dad died in a plane crash, only that was my stepdad. She thinks I've got this mom that's pretty broken up about it.

Something tells me this girl isn't going to be giving anyone the third degree about their family tree this afternoon, said Carolyn.

Hey, she said when they pulled up in front of the 7-Eleven. I'm Carolyn.

I'm Violet, and this is Walter Charles.

Well, Merry Christmas, you two. Hope you've got an appetite, because we've got a twenty-pound bird roasting back home.

Carolyn got out of the car and came around the other side while Violet set the car seat in back. She reached for the baby as if she'd known him all her life.

Walter Charles, who had been crying nonstop, looked right into her eyes. The crying stopped so quickly, it was as if someone pulled the plug. He reached his small hand out toward Carolyn's finger, that she was holding out to him, and grabbed on tight. Then he smiled.

Carolyn laid him against her shoulder. He had his head against her neck. He was looking around, but not with that worried look for once. More like, *It's about time.*

Carolyn was rubbing his back. Her big hand, worn from all the cactus work, made circles on his small, bony back. She held him very firmly. In a second, a sound came out of him—a surprisingly loud burp.

There, she said. She handed him back to Violet. I think he'll be fine now. What do you say we get ourselves home and make the stuffing?

\*     \*     \*

Alan showed up at four o'clock, just as Wendy had suggested, but there was a change of plan.

I know I said it would be just me, he told Carolyn. But they got an infestation of fleas up at Homewood, and everyone had to leave for a few days so they could fumigate. So Tim's with me. He's out in the car. I could understand if it's more than you want to handle, having someone like him in on your Christmas dinner.

What are you talking about? said Carolyn. How many people would I ever have over for dinner if I limited my guest list to the normal ones?

Tim was wearing his same outfit, the too-short corduroy pants, belted high, with the shirt tucked in, only now he was sporting one of those plush Santa hats with white fake fur trim. He had on bowling shoes, red leather, with black and green stripes and a number on the heel, ten and a half.

They had this bowling tournament at Homewood one time, Alan said. Tim didn't like the bowling part, but he loved the shoes so much, he didn't want to take them off after, so finally I just bought them from the bowling alley. He only wears them for special occasions.

Nice shoes, Violet told Tim. I always wanted some of those.

You can have my hat, he said. He handed it to her.

The thing that helped was they had all this dirty laundry. What do you know? Carolyn said when Alan told her that his son would be more than glad to do it for her. There really is a Santa Claus.

The washer and dryer were in the basement. They didn't have the little individual packets of Tide he favored, but he made do with the regular-sized box. Violet went down to help supervise, since she also had some baby shirts in her bag that could use a wash.

Carolyn said she'd hold the baby while Violet was attending to the wash with Tim. The minute she took him that same look came over his face as if he was thinking, *Where have you been keeping this woman?*

In addition to the Christmas pudding, Alan had brought all sorts of interesting things: paté with fancy crackers, smoked almonds, the makings for eggnog, which he began whipping up in the kitchen, with fresh cream and egg yolks and nutmeg grated on the spot. He poured a little rum into his drink and Carolyn's.

You got that bookstore over on E Street, right? she said. I've been meaning to stop in there. I should read more.

Do that, he said.


Carolyn put on a record. Sorry to say we don't have any Christmas music, she told him. It was a very old album of female blues artists. A woman was singing about how all she could do was cry.

Etta James, Alan said. Now you're talking. Too bad we can't follow up with a little Sugar Pie De Santo.

That's the next cut, she said.


From down in the basement they could hear the washer going, his second load. The dryer kicked off. Maybe I should go check on Tim, Alan said.

I'll go, Wendy told him.

Violet and Tim were sitting on the floor. Tim was folding baby shirts. Violet still had the hat on.

Smell this, she said, handing Tim one of the baby shirts. You might not have noticed, but I put these little fabric softener sheets in with them that make everything smell like lemon.

You know Picabo Street? he asked her.

Is that over by the mall? she said.


Dinner was ready. Alan said Tim probably wouldn't eat anything, but not to worry. He'd brought along his Wheat Chex.

They had set up a table in the yard with a tablecloth and a cactus in the middle with white lights. This looks beautiful, Alan said, pouring the Wheat

Chex in a bowl at Tim's place. My wife goes up north every year for Christmas. This is the first real holiday meal I've had in five years.

Violet and Tim came up the stairs. Violet set Walter Charles on the table in his infant seat. One of his booties had come off and Shiva was licking his foot. He looked happy.

You can sit here, Tim, Alan told him. I brought your cereal. I'll sit next to you.

Her, he said, meaning Violet.

You want me to sit next to you? Violet asked.

Well, sure.

Know what Humpty Dumpty said when he fell off the wall? he asked her.

No.

Too bad. The yolk's on you.


Carolyn was just setting the turkey down when they heard the door open. You expecting any more company? she asked Wendy.

No.

Ho ho ho, he called out. Her father.

It's Santa and his elf, he said. Better late than never.

They were standing in the doorway then. Not just Garrett, but the boy too, with a backpack over his shoulder and his skateboard under his arm, holding a straggly poinsettia plant. Todd.

The phone rang. Wendy picked it up. Josh on the line, and Louie on the extension, singing "Jingle Bells."

I want to talk, but something amazing just happened, she said. I'll call you back.

Tell me this isn't some kind of cosmic alignment, Garrett said. I'm just getting off the highway for our exit when I see this kid standing there with his thumb out. I've been traveling ten, eleven hours by this point, mind you. Flying standby on Christmas Eve out of La Guardia is not exactly a mellow experience. So I've got an above-average amount of sympathy for my fellow holiday travelers by this point. I figure I'll give the kid a lift into town, if that's where he's headed.

You have yourself a destination? I ask him. Or were you just planning on taking in the sights of downtown Davis, Christmas Day?

There's a girl I thought I'd look up, he tells me. She said I could drop in on her if I didn't have a place to go for the holidays. He shows me the piece of paper with Wendy's name on it. My own damn address.

I was remembering what you told me about how a person shouldn't be alone on Christmas, Todd said to Wendy. He handed the plant to Carolyn.

They were throwing this away outside a McDonald's I stopped at. I don't know if it's any good, but I figured I should bring something.

Some people have no patience with plants, she said. Just because the foliage might be looking a little funky one day they toss it. Imagine if we were that way about people.

You should meet my mom, Violet told her.


They set two more places. Garrett came over to Carolyn and put an arm around her. Hey there, he said.

Good to have you back.

Good-looking bird you girls cooked up. He reached out a hand to shake Alan's.

I'm Garrett, he greeted Violet and Tim, not that Tim looked up. Tim was working on a Lego set Alan had set at his place next to the Wheat Chex.

Sorry to hear about your mother, Alan said. Don't mind my son. He isn't used to gatherings like this.

Name me one person who would be, said Garrett.

Just then the baby let out a little hoot—happiness, from the looks of it. His foot, hanging out over the edge of his infant seat, had collided with the bowl of peas and now a bunch of them showered down over the table like it was Mardi Gras.

So how does it happen that a kid your age is traveling around on his own at five o'clock in the afternoon on Christmas? Carolyn asked him. If that isn't too personal.

I was up in Truckee, Todd said. Thought I'd look up this old friend that works the ski lift at a mountain there. A bunch of snowboarders this guy knows were renting a house for the week. It was going to be a big party scene.

But it didn't work out? Alan asked him.

Oh, it did, he said. There must've been eighteen, twenty kids up at that house. Cold cuts, beer, weed, you name it. You walked in the door and there's snowboard boots lined up like you'd landed at Santa's workshop.

Don't any of these kids have parents? Carolyn asked. They just take off like that on Christmas?

These are the kind of kids, Todd said, whose parents give them a check the week before Christmas and a gift certificate for a new board and bindings, the keys to the Land Cruiser and their ski house. *Take your friends to Tahoe. Happy holidays.*

It's guilt, see. The holidays roll round, these kids' parents take off for the Caribbean probably, or Hawaii, with their own little stash of mind-altering substances, just a different variety. They liked their kid when he was little but for the last ten years or so the only thing they can figure out to do with him is get him expensive stuff and hope he stays out of their hair.

Treats make trouble, Wendy's mom would have said.

One kid's father owns some computer company in Mountain View. He's got his own plane and a bunch of different houses, the Truckee place being one of the smallest. The parents split up a million years ago, and now the dad's with some real young chick and they've got a couple of little kids, still in the cute stage like him.

When he said that, Todd pointed at Walter Charles.

So the kid takes off on some ski trip to Switzerland last year, and he ends up traveling all over the place. When he comes home, his whole face is tattooed blue and he's had one of these balls the size of a jawbreaker inserted under the skin on his forehead, which is a thing they do over there in Berlin evidently. Where it looks like you've got a tumor only it's actually a decoration, if you want to call it that.

What did the father do when he saw it? Wendy asked. She thought about her and Amelia and the hidden rose tattoo they were planning when they turned sixteen. One small bud. Imagine if your whole face was blue forever. And wherever you went for the rest of your life, that would be the thing people would think about you first.

The father told the kid he'd buy him a Porsche if he'd have the ball taken out of his forehead. While they were at it he wanted the kid to remove a couple of studs he'd put in his tongue. There wasn't much to be done about the blue face. I think they sent him to some kind of dermatologist where they lightened it up a little. He used to be bright turquoise. Now he's more that color the sky gets when it's going to snow.

They had all stopped eating at this point.

And my mom thinks she's got problems with me, Violet said. That rich dad would probably love it if the only problem he had was one little baby that cries a little more than average.

This is a great baby, Carolyn said, stroking his head. This baby isn't what I'd call a problem.

Tim looked at him then, his blue eyes locked on the face of Walter Charles. Do you like Wheat Chex? he asked.

Wally doesn't talk yet, said Violet. He's still a little young. She said it in this matter-of-fact way, as if the idea of someone addressing a question to her two-month-old wasn't so unusual.

Hey, said Garrett. I forgot for a minute. The boy came over yesterday, right? From Oregon. How'd it go?

Wendy gave him a look. *Not now* was what she was trying to say.

Oh, he said. I guess we can discuss it later.

Let's just say we're a lot better off with the crowd we have over here today, Carolyn told him.


So how come you left Truckee? Violet asked. If there was this great free house with all the food and everything? I bet there was even a hot tub.

Also a sauna, he said. Surround sound in the family room.

Some people's idea of heaven, said Violet.

They were partying last night, same as always, he told them. Everyone was wasted. Music playing so loud you couldn't hear yourself think, so I went onto the deck, where you could look out at the mountains. And I'm thinking how it's Christmas Eve and even though I'm not religious, it always seems like this special magic night to me. Like you should do something different from what you would normally. Or at least not play some CD at top volume where some guy's yelling about how he wants to have sex with his mom.

There was this house a little ways away from the one I was at, he said. I could see in the windows. I saw the Christmas tree with all the lights on, and the mom and the dad putting together this dollhouse. Arranging all the little furniture in the rooms. Getting ready for morning.

All of a sudden I just wanted to be out of there. I didn't want to go to bed in that guy's house with the blue face and wake up there on Christmas with a bunch of people throwing up in the bathroom.

I had one of those fathers, Garrett said. The kind who writes you a check when he doesn't know what else to do.

At least you didn't have a Ping-Pong ball inserted in your forehead, Carolyn said.

In a manner of speaking you might say I did. I did a lot of pretty crazy things when I was younger anyway. Where the main point, looking back on it, was probably hurting my parents.


From the kitchen they could hear the sound of Carolyn taking the store-bought pie out of the oven. On the stereo, Laura Lee was belting out a number called "Dirty Man." Wendy thought about home, with Ella singing "What Are You Doing New Year's Eve" and "Moonlight in Vermont." Alvin and the Chipmunks doing their version of "Santa Claus Is Coming to Town." Josh in his red vest setting the bûche de Noël on the table, with the meringue mushrooms and the sparklers stuck in the frosting and little flashes of sparks lighting up their faces. Her mother slipping off one ballet slipper and resting her foot in Josh's lap the way she did at the end of a meal.

Wendy looked across the table at Todd, his plate piled with turkey, stuffing, and yams. I can't believe all this great stuff, he said. I feel like I'm on *The Waltons*.

Eat hearty, John-boy, Carolyn said. There's plenty more where that came from.

I didn't get a chance to go shopping for you, Slim, Garrett said. I was going to and then the call came about your grandmother. But I brought you something from Greenwich.

He reached in his pocket and handed her a gold cameo pin of a woman's face in profile. She remembered her grandmother wearing it that time she and her mother had met her grandmother for lunch in New York, and her mom saying how she'd always wished she had a cameo.

Her grandmother had said it used to be her mother's. I have no one to pass it on to, she had said. Only having a son.

I made you something, Wendy told Garrett. She went to her room and came back with a colored pencil drawing of him holding his fishing rod, with Shiva next to him, and a fish on the line. She had studied the photograph he'd sent her of him in front of Carolyn's cabin for reference, but the part about the fishing rod and the fish was from her imagination.

What do you know? Garrett said. It would appear I just caught myself a twenty-pounder.


Alan set the Christmas pudding on a platter.

It never looks like much when you take it out of the mold, he said, and he was right. The pudding sat there like an old log. Not a bûche de Noël kind of log. More like something you'd find at the bottom of the woodpile.

It's one of those things where the good part is concealed, he said.

He explained to them how you make a Christmas pudding, starting with nuts from the farmer's market, and currants and raisins and dried apricots soaked in whiskey. There was a certain kind of cherry that grew outside of Modesto. He picked those himself in the fall. His wife had helped take out the pits, even though she was never into Christmas pudding. Then he soaked those, too, in a different kind of liquor—kirsch.

There's flour and butter and sugar, naturally, he said. Nutmeg and cinnamon, cardamon and allspice. A little orange peel and candied ginger.

You've got some patience, man, said Garrett. From the sound of it, you might have a future as a fly fisherman.

To me, it's a kind of therapy, Alan said. Some people wade into a trout stream. I bake.

When the batter was all assembled, you poured it in the mold. You set the mold in a pan of water in the oven. After the pudding was baked, you set it aside and forgot about it. Till Christmas, when you took it out and set it on a good fireproof platter like this one. Whipped up a batch of hard sauce with cream. Doused the thing with rum. Struck the match.

\*      \*      \*

It was dark out now. On the Sweet Soul Sisters record, Fontella Bass was singing "Rescue Me." Garrett turned out the lights, so there was only the string of bulbs on Carolyn's cactus. Even Walter Charles looked up.

Alan touched the lit match to the rum-soaked pudding. Blue flame leapt up around the platter, high enough that for a second there Wendy wondered if the house might catch on fire, and she could see Carolyn reach over to shield Walter Charles's face. But the fire stayed only on the Christmas pudding, dancing around the edges of the platter. Wendy had never smelled anything like this before—spices and liquor and something burned but in a good way. Then the fire went out and Alan reached over to scoop the warm pudding onto their plates, with a puddle of hard sauce on the side.

I don't suppose anyone here would be a big enough fool to choose pie, Carolyn said.

I would, said Tim.

It's only store-bought, she told him.

I want pie.

After, when Tim was licking his plate to get the last crumbs of the Shop 'N Save pumpkin pie, Alan said he'd drive Violet and Walter Charles home. I hate to see this baby go, said Carolyn. Not that we haven't enjoyed your company, too, Violet. I just meant it's good to have a baby around the house.

I could come back, she said. She reached into her diaper bag.

This is for you, she said to Carolyn, handing her the small foil-wrapped package. It was supposed to be for my mother, but you turned out to be more of the mom type.

It was the pendant in the shape of a heart.

Man, Garrett said. You're really making me look bad here. I even had it on my shopping list. Ruby necklace for Carolyn. I just ran out of time.

I love you anyway, she said.


Tim wanted to check the laundry one more time to make sure they hadn't left any socks in the dryer. Alan packed up the empty pudding mold and platter and the box of Wheat Chex.

I hope you'll stop by the bookstore, he told Carolyn.

Maybe you'd want to go fishing sometime, Garrett said.

Sounds good.

Carolyn handed the baby back to Violet then, looking like she wished she didn't have to. Violet still had her Santa hat on, though it had started to slip down over one side of her face again. She straightened it. Carolyn, with her pendant on now, put her arms around Tim, who stood very still, arms at his sides, his blue eyes staring into the night.

Todd said he'd do the dishes. That was always my specialty back in Cleveland, he told them. Wendy said she'd help him.

Looks like we lucked out, Garrett said to Carolyn. What do you say you and me take a little stroll around the neighborhood with this dog of mine?

Then it was just the two of them, Wendy and Todd, in the kitchen. The pile of dishes, the sinkful of warm soapy water. Todd's sleeves rolled up. The Sweet Soul Sisters still blasting about men who did them wrong.

You have a great family, he said.

It wasn't exactly the one I started out with, she said. Or who I thought I'd be spending Christmas with.

Me neither.

She thought about the night back at the Fairmont Hotel, Todd in the bathrobe.

You look different from that other time, he said.

It's probably just my hair, she told him.


You have a boyfriend?

No.

I don't have a girlfriend, either, he said.

Where are you going after this? she asked him.

Colorado. A kid I bumped into in Truckee said he heard my brother might be out there working at a restaurant. It would be the greatest thing to see him again.

That's how I feel about my little brother.

I could write to you. I don't write letters all that much, but sometimes I do.

That would be nice.

You look pretty with your hair like that.

Thanks.

I guess you're still just thirteen, huh?

It's my birthday in three weeks.

When difficult things happen it makes you seem a lot older, he said. A lot of people take me for older than fifteen.

Me, for instance. This whole time, I thought you were sixteen.

Some kids I know force themselves on a girl, he said. I wouldn't do that. It's not like I wouldn't want to, but I just think it should be the girl's decision, too.

That's what my mom used to say.

You must be missing her a ton today.

Yes.


If you felt like it, we could go take a walk, too, Todd said after the dishes were done. He put his hand up to her cheek, and for a second, she almost felt scared.

You had a little soap there, he told her.

They heard the door open, and Garrett and Carolyn and Shiva coming back in.

We're calling it a night, her father called out to her.

I set out a couple of blankets for you, Todd, Carolyn said from the other room. You can make yourself comfortable on the couch. Wendy heard the sound of their feet on the stairs, the bedroom door closing, the dog settling herself on her towel.

It was a perfectly clear night. They walked to the end of her street, past the house with the Santa display on the roof and another with a couple of reindeer set up in the front yard, white lights blinking. Inside the window they could see a man washing dishes and, in another window, a boy playing a video game.

They walked without talking for a while. She could feel every inch of her skin.

That first time I saw you, I noticed you right off, he said. Down at the Embarcadero, when I was skating.

He took her hand. Is this okay? he said.

Yes.

I would kiss you, he said. If that was all right.

Okay.


When she had pictured kissing in the past, she had imagined it was more something a person would do at one precise moment, like sticking a stamp on an envelope. But Todd kept on kissing her for five minutes without stopping. He stopped. He didn't pull all the way away from her but enough that she could see his face again.

Are you all right? he asked her.

Yes.

He started kissing her again, but a little harder this time, with his tongue in her mouth. He'd had both his arms around the back of her the whole time, stroking her hair and her shoulders and sometimes her neck, but now one of his hands moved to her breast, the one that had been slower to develop. His hand wasn't inside her shirt, just on top.

I would touch your skin, he said. But I don't want you to get scared.

She would be scared, though partly she wanted him to. Nobody ever touched me there, she said.

It probably has to happen sometime.

I guess you could.

He touched her cheek first. I like you a lot, he said. I wouldn't ever want to hurt you.


His hand, when he touched her skin, felt rough for a person his age. He must have known it. Your skin is so smooth, he said. It was just her belly he was touching. The space between her belly button and where her bra started.

You might think I do this a lot, but I don't, he said. She felt his breathing, deep and slow. From somebody's house she could hear Christmas music. Nat King Cole.

His fingers had reached the front of her bra, the one she and her mother bought that day they went shopping together, though when she'd first gotten it, she still had to stuff Kleenex in the one side.

Oh, he said, as if he was discovering something he never would have known was there. Very slowly, he moved his fingers over the lace edge and under the fabric. His hand was on the skin of her breast now. Then her nipple.

She hadn't realized it, but he must have been holding his breath, because now he let out a long, slow sigh. Oh, he said again. She must have been holding her breath, too, because now she could feel the air leaving her lungs.

They stood that way a long time. He only touched the one breast—the smaller, newer one. Part of the time while he was touching her, he was kissing her, but most of the time he just looked at her.

Some time passed. The Nat King Cole record was over. The people in the house with the blinking reindeer had turned off their lights.

I guess it's late, he said. He looked back up at her. Very slowly, he removed his hand from underneath the fabric and drew her shirt back over her bra. I wouldn't want to go too far, he said. I wouldn't want you to do anything that made you feel bad after.

She didn't say anything.

All through dinner, I was thinking how much I wanted to do that, but I didn't know if we would, he said. I was just hoping.

She had not been thinking about it during dinner. For her, the kissing had come as a surprise, like the cameo pin and the special cactus.

They started walking back to her father's house. That was probably the first nice Christmas I ever had, he said when they got to the door.

She thought about all the things her mother wouldn't know about her now, all the things that had happened already, and her life was only starting.

After, she stood alone in her room and looked in the mirror. She thought she'd look a little different, but she didn't.

She hadn't realized, until it happened, how much she'd wanted someone to put his arms around her the way Todd did.

Wendy set the cameo pin in her jewelry box and folded up the note from Josh and put it in her drawer. She opened the clarinet case, and took out the pieces of the red clarinet, put them together. She wet her reed and slid it in the mouthpiece. Soft as she could, she blew one long low note, just to hear what it sounded like.

She had forgotten to call Josh and Louie back. The whole of Christmas had passed without talking to them.

They were all getting on with their lives, she figured. The best they knew how.

Her brother called in the morning. We had a sleepover at Kate's, he told her. Poppy said it would be better than driving home in the dark with all our dishes and presents.

He had probably seen them in their bathrobes together then. But it didn't sound as if he was upset about it.

I got the Tonka crane, Sissy, he said. Also a game called Operation where you have to take the parts out of the man and not make the buzzer go. Also Pokémon cards, and the Lego fishing trawler, and a book about whales, and smell markers, and a CD of music from Africa and a stuffed hedgehog. Kate gave me a tape of *Thomas the Tank Engine* and a kit for building pulleys.

Wow, Louie, she said. You made out like a bandit. After she said that she remembered where she learned the expression. Christmas night when she was tucking them in, that's what their mother always said.

Who else was at Kate's house? she asked him.

Just us guys, he said. Me and Poppy and Kate. Poppy made the turkey. He says Kate isn't that great of a cook, but not to tell her because we don't want to hurt her feelings.

Good idea, Louie, she said. Did he make that special dessert? The one in the shape of a log?

Louie must not have remembered the other years. We didn't eat any logs, silly, he said. We had pumpkin pie.

Josh got on. I meant to call you back, but there was a lot going on here, Wendy told him.

That's the way it should be on Christmas, Josh said. Hey, that's a great shirt you got me. I never would have thought to get myself something like that.

But you'll wear it?

Absolutely. The book looks good, too.

I love the clarinet, she told him. All the stuff. The sneakers and the CD's. But especially the clarinet. It's got a great sound.

How about that color? Kate was a little worried you might think it was too flashy.

I'll definitely have the only red clarinet in Davis. Send me some sheet music, would you? she said. I'm in the mood to start playing again.

So you're doing all right? I figured it was going to be a tough day for you.

I was thinking the same about you, she told him.

Mostly I'm just so glad to have it over. I was dreading Christmas.

Well, we did it, huh? she said.

I'm not sure which is harder, he told her. When you feel like you can't go on any more, or when you start to realize you will.


Louie mentioned you stayed over at Kate's after the meal, Wendy said.

It seemed like a good idea. I had a couple glasses of wine. Not that I was drunk, but I didn't think I should drive.

There was the faintest sound in his voice, like how a kid gets when he's talking to his parents, and a subject comes up he doesn't want to discuss.

It's good you slept over, she told him. And Louie's sounding more like his old self.

I'm not even sure what changed, Josh said. I know he's still dealing with plenty, but he's got this kind of peaceful attitude like things are going to be okay eventually.

I'm doing okay, too, she said. Except for missing you two.

We're right here, he told her. Anytime.


Garrett told Todd he was welcome to stay on with them as long as he wanted, but Todd said he figured he should get going to Colorado. He didn't want to risk missing his brother. He was catching a train from Sacramento to Denver. Garrett said he'd drive Todd to the station.

Wendy and Todd stood outside the house. He had his backpack and skateboard, and an old army jacket rolled up under his arm for when it got colder in the mountains. She stood there with her arms at her sides. Now that they had kissed each other, it felt strange not touching him.

I hope I get to see you again sometime, he said.

Me, too.

You think you'll stay out here?

I don't know, she said. I hardly know anything anymore.

It looks like your dad's really happy you're here.

I hope you get back with your brother, she said.

You, too, he told her.

She heard the screen door slam. Garrett, with Shiva following behind.

What do you say we quit this stinking burg, you and me, Todd? he said in a cowboy kind of voice.

Carolyn had come out with him to say good-bye.

I made you a little packet of turkey for the train, she said to Todd. You know what they say. The leftovers are better than the actual meal.

That's hard to imagine, he told her.

# Thirty

The days passed. Carolyn kept sleeping over at Garrett's house. Nobody said anything, it just seemed to happen. Then she started bringing plants over. Not all, just certain of her favorites.

Wendy was spending her days around the house more often now, drawing and playing her clarinet mostly. It was school vacation, so Wendy didn't have to go through her usual routine of heading out every morning in the truck with her father or taking off on his bike. She had liked her adventuring days, but she liked staying home, too. She'd lie out in the yard with her colored pencils and her sketch pad, or her book, or fool around on her clarinet.

She finished *The Butcher Boy*, and, as she had expected, things didn't go well for the boy. First his mother died. Then his best friend got sent away, and everyone started treating him like a crazy person, which he wasn't. But finally he snapped. He went to the house of a terrible woman, Mrs. Nugent, who had been tormenting him through the whole book. He murdered her, and the amazing thing was, by the time he did it, you could sympathize. You could actually understand how he'd got to that point. You were hoping he'd get away with it and knowing he never would. The next thing you knew, it was forty years later and the butcher boy had been locked up in a mental institution all this time. Now, instead of everyone just treating him as if he was crazy, he actually was.

How can it be, Wendy asked Alan, that you'll be reading this story that's so sad, it almost hurts to look at the words on the page? What happens to the characters practically tears your stomach out—and then the book is over. And the first thing you want to do is find another book like that.

Sometimes it's almost a good feeling, hurting that way, he said. That's what the blues is all about.

But maybe you should take a break from all this tragedy, he told her. He handed her a hardback copy of a book called *A Tree Grows in Brooklyn*. This girl, now, he said, she's a survivor, like you.

Alan had asked her when she was going to tell her father and Carolyn the truth about school. She'd been thinking about that. When she started not showing up at school, she hadn't really known them that well that it hadn't felt bad lying to them, but now it did.

They had finished dinner. It was the day before New Year's. Garrett was working on a drawing—something he'd started doing again since Carolyn had been around. Carolyn was sitting at the table drinking tea and reading her book about the woman going down the Amazon.

So, her father said. You looking forward to getting back to school?

She looked around the room, at his fishing poles and toolbox, Carolyn's half-finished macramé plant hanger, Shiva on her towel, the dishes on the counter, the painting he'd made from years ago. Things that had seemed strange when she got here and seemed familiar now. Comfortable, even.

Actually, I don't go to school, she said. I've been meaning to tell you.

Neither one of them said anything.

After that first day, I just stopped going, she said. I didn't have a plan or anything. I just walked away.

I see, Garrett said. He had been working at a table over by the window, but now he pulled out a chair beside her and sat down.

At first I probably thought someone would do something about it, she said. Way back when it started, I sent them a letter, pretending I was you. I didn't think it would work, but it did. Nobody ever noticed. I found other things to do instead.

Like what? he asked her.

I walked around. I rode your bike. I drew. I rode the bus into Sacramento sometimes and helped Violet with her baby. A lot of the time, I went to Alan's bookstore and just read.

He knew about this?

Not at first, but later. I made him promise not to do anything about it. But he wanted me to tell you.

It's not like I pictured myself being a dropout forever, she said. I know I need to learn things like geometry and U.S. history. I just wasn't in the mood at the time.

Carolyn had gotten up. She reached for another mug and poured tea for Wendy. She looked over at Garrett.

Fact is, we knew this, he said. Not right off the bat, but for a while. It was Carolyn who figured it out, he said. I wish I could say I knew enough to see what was going on, but I didn't. She kept saying it seemed like you had other things on your mind besides school. Which was understandable, of course.

From what I could see, you're the type of person that if they were going to school they'd be doing it up right, she said. Writing reports and going to the library and so on. Also, you'd be the type that would be making friends. Which you did, of course, just a different type.

But you let me keep skipping school? Wendy asked.

Hey, he told her. I trust you. I figured you'd talk to me about it when you were ready, and look. You did.

I called the school, though, Carolyn said. I told them there'd been a change of plans and your father had made other arrangements. That was evidently enough for them. By the time they got that letter you sent, they'd probably already heard from us.

So what do you want to do now? Garrett asked her.

I guess maybe I should start going to eighth grade, Wendy said. I'll be really behind.

Nobody said you had to turn up on the honor roll.

* * *

He drove her again. She told him he didn't need to come inside with her, but he wanted to.

It's not that I don't trust you to stay. There's just certain times a girl should have a parent around.

At the office, he explained that his daughter had been doing a home-schooling program. The guidance counselor said they'd understand if it took her a while to get caught up.

They gave her the same schedule she'd had in the fall. I guess this is where I'm supposed to take off, Garrett told her.

I'll be fine this time, she said. The bell had rung for first period.

Hey, a girl said to her—the same one who'd told Wendy back in the fall that she'd tell Wendy which were the cute boys.

You look different, she said.

It's probably my hair, Wendy told her.


They were reading *Lord of the Flies* in English. In history, they were studying the Spanish-American War. In gym it was basketball now.

Then came band. She'd brought her clarinet, figuring it might be a band day. Opening the case at the start of the period, as she took her seat in the woodwinds, she felt a little embarrassed at what the other kids would think when they saw her instrument.

The thing about a clarinet player, Josh had said. A clarinet player is low and thoughtful and crucially important to the sound of the band without making a big show about it. Very subtle and deep.

Nothing subtle about a red clarinet. Then again, there was that other part about the clarinet. Playful at times, Josh had said.

She took out the clarinet and started putting the pieces together. Assembled, it looked redder than in the box, and more so in a band full of wood-colored woodwinds.

That's the bomb, a boy said sitting next to her, also a clarinet player. I never saw one like that.

My dad gave it to me for Christmas, she told him. He's that type of person.

My dad's more the black clarinet type, the boy said.

You want to give me an E flat? she asked.

She put her instrument to her lips.


School was fine, she told them when she got home. I don't have a clue what's going on in geometry, but history's interesting, and I kind of like basketball.

Who did you sit with at lunch? asked Carolyn.

A boy from band. Henry. We might go bike riding together tomorrow if I can borrow your bike, she said, looking at her father.

Would this be during school hours or after? asked Garrett. Not that I want to cramp your style.

After.


When she heard about Wendy going back to school, Violet sounded sad.

I'll still see you and Walter Charles, Wendy told her over the phone. Just not on school days.

Now I'll probably turn into one of those people that sits around their apartment all day watching soap operas and Maury, she said.

You should call that number I gave you, Wendy told her.

Maybe next week, Violet said.

Listen, said Wendy. Why don't you and Walter Charles come over for dinner Friday? If you took the bus over, my dad or Carolyn would drive you home.


So they did. Garrett barbecued chicken and Carolyn made a salad. She held Walter Charles during dinner to give Violet a chance to eat without having to worry about him for once. He seemed to remember her from before.

I really like this baby, Carolyn said. You get the impression he's going to be one of those people who takes things slow but does them right. He'll be the type that doesn't have a million friends, but with the ones he has he's true blue. He doesn't need to be off at some bar all the time partying. He's happy to just sit there looking at the stars.

You can tell all this from a baby? Garrett asked. To me they're all pretty much the same.

I suppose now you're going to tell me all cactuses look alike, too? she said. Then, to Violet: But try telling him it doesn't matter which lure he uses for trout fishing.

Carolyn told them about the cactus garden she was working on, in the atrium of the office building outside Sacramento.

I'm thinking about getting a job, too, Violet said. My mom's old boyfriend offered me work hostessing at his bar. You're supposed to be twenty-one, but they hardly ever check.

I was just thinking, Carolyn said. I could use some help with the planting, if you wanted to come over someday.

I don't know how much help I'd be, with the baby, Violet told her. I'd probably have to stop a lot to pick him up or change him.

Or I could do that sometimes, said Carolyn. We could take turns.


After dinner they played poker. They had pulled a drawer out of Wendy's bureau and laid some blankets in it for Walter Charles. All through the game, even when someone forgot he was there and got a little loud with a bid, he slept quietly. Now and then they'd hear a soft murmur from the drawer beside them, as if he was having a nice dream.

You know, it doesn't really make sense driving all the way to Sacramento tonight, unless you're bound and determined to get back to that apartment of yours, Garrett said. Otherwise we could put you two up here.

That sounded good, Violet told him.


In the morning, it was Carolyn who dropped her off. I could get attached to those two, but I'd better not, she said.

What do you mean? Wendy asked.

You can do your best, Carolyn said. But a person can't always fix everything.

I was thinking you were going to read her palm, Wendy said.

Sometimes I'd rather not know what the future has in store, Carolyn told her.

Wendy had planned on going up to Homewood again Tuesday with Alan to see Tim but now she told him she couldn't because of school.

I think Sunday would work fine for the trip, if you were interested in coming along, he said. Tim seems to be getting a little better about my changing the schedule now and then.

Alan was quieter than usual on the drive. She was talking about *A Tree Grows in Brooklyn*. The girl, Francie, lived in a different part of Brooklyn from where Wendy came from, and she was very poor, but Wendy could just picture sitting out on the fire escape the way Francie did, with her package of peppermints and her new library book, losing herself in the story.

She also told him about the book they were reading in English, *Lord of the Flies*. The boys in *Lord of the Flies* went crazy, too, a little like the butcher boy. But unlike the butcher boy, who was also named Francie, oddly enough, it seemed as if the writer was saying that when you put people in a bad enough situation, they would do terrible things to one another, because that was their true nature. That was the difference about the butcher boy. Even after he'd killed Mrs. Nugent, you could still believe that he was a good person. The boys in *Lord of the Flies* were just plain bad. Wendy didn't want to believe life was really that way, but maybe it was.

Normally Alan would have observations of his own about the books, but he mostly just listened.

My wife isn't coming back from the ashram, he said. She decided to stay up there.

Forever? Wendy asked.

Who knows? She said it feels better living there now. Being away.

She might change her mind after some time passes, Wendy said. How about you? What will you do now?

I'll probably carry on pretty much the same as I always have, he said. What else can you do?

On the porch at Homewood, the younger children were playing Picture Lotto. One of the teachers would hold up a card with a picture on it, and whoever had that picture on their card got to put a bean on it.

*House,* said one of the teachers. The girl with the house on her card was sucking on the collar of her dress.

Look at this, Lily, the teacher said. You've got the house. She placed the bean on Lily's card.

*Bunny,* said the teacher. She held up a new picture.

I got it, said another girl, who had been rocking in her chair, winding thread around her finger.

No, Davia, that's a toaster, said the teacher. That's what we put your bagel in at breakfast, remember?

I got the bunny, said a boy, the one who knew so much about shipwreck disasters.

We had a bunny one time, said the boy. My mother forgot to feed it carrots, and its teeth got so long, they curled all the way out its mouth like elephant tusks. One day, they poked through our bunny's neck and he bled to death.

That's a very interesting story, Jacob, she said. I hope next time if you get a bunny, you'll feed him more carrots to keep his teeth from doing that.

We don't get bunnies anymore, he said. We don't get anything.

They got to the room marked TIM AND BRIAN. Alan knocked. I'm here, he said. I brought our friend Wendy again.

They waited. Silence.

We're coming in now, he said. Here we come.

Alan opened the door. Tim stood there in his turtleneck and high-belted pants. His piercing blue eyes locked on Wendy.

Picabo Street, he said. I call her Picabo Street.

I used to call her Kitty, myself, Alan said. But her real name is Wendy.

They had brought the laundry, but no tin of cookies this time, only store-bought. The Lego set was a man on a horse, a jousting knight.

Number 6043, he said. I have that one already.

I guess I forgot, Alan told him. Sometimes it's hard to keep them straight.

Wendy went over to the fish tank. The scuba diver was bent over his treasure chest, same as always, lifting the string of pearls up and down, up and down, as, all around him, bubbles rose from the mouth of the plastic frog.

I was thinking maybe we should try a fish or two in that tank again, Alan said. Something along the lines of an angelfish. Those hardly ever die. What do you say, son?

Tim didn't answer.

Not this week, maybe, said Alan. Just something to think about for the future.


They drove to the Laundromat. Only one load of laundry this time, probably because his mother was at the ashram. No gardening clothes.

He took the handful of quarters over to the detergent dispensing machine. Bought one packet of Tide and one of bleach.

I don't actually have a bleach wash for you today, Tim, Alan told him.

They got ice cream. Tim was worried about getting back in time to start the dryer, but Alan said they'd be fine.

Then they put the wet clothes in the dryer. Wendy had brought along a couple of the fabric softener sheets they had at her house that made the wash smell like lemons.

The girl with the baby, he said.

That's right, she said. My friend Violet used these, didn't she?

We had pie, he said. Someday that baby won't be little and cute anymore. They might put a ball in his head.

You don't miss a trick, do you, son? said Alan. It only seems like it.

If we put a fish in my aquarium, it could die, he said. We'd have to flush it down the toilet.

Everything dies someday, Tim, Alan said. But probably not for a long time.

*     *     *

I have a joke for you, Tim, Wendy said. What's white and wanders through the desert?

He didn't answer, but he looked up, as if he was trying to think of something.

A flock of yogurt, she said.

Normally, his face had a haunted look, as if there was a movie playing in his head, or a piece of music that nobody could tune in to but him. His blue eyes seemed so vacant, Wendy wondered if they saw anything at all.

Now, though, an odd thing happened. Not all at once but slowly, like time-lapse photography, a small look of pleasure came over his face. First nothing more than engagement, the sense that her words had actually gotten through. Then an actual smile.

A flock of yogurt, he said. *A flock of yogurt.* Get it? A flock of yogurt!

What's blue and hangs from the trees? she asked him.

What? he said. A flock of yogurt?

No, that was the last one. Tarzan in winter, she said.

He looked at her blankly. Whatever small moment of connection they'd found, it had passed over like mist over the Golden Gate Bridge. Or maybe it was the opposite: For just a second there, the brilliant red towers of the bridge had shown themselves against the sky, but then the mist had rolled in again, obscuring the towers until you wouldn't even know they were there anymore, or that there was a bridge, or a bay below it, or a city on the other side, full of buildings and people, Japanese gardens and cars, men pushing shopping carts and men sleeping under cardboard boxes, doormen and skateboarders and ballerinas. Nothing but fog.

They got back to his room at the home earlier than usual, due to the light laundry load.

So I'll see you next week, son, Alan told Tim. Tim stood straight to receive his hug, arms at his sides as usual.

They didn't say anything, the first few minutes on the road, but she could tell from Alan's face that he was feeling unsettled.

Something like what happened there with the yogurt joke, he told her as they reached the entrance to the highway. I can live all week on a moment like that.

＊　　＊　　＊

Amelia called. So, she said. Any new developments in the saga of Kate and Josh?

Words like that—*saga*—she picked up from her mother. I would never tell that woman anything, Wendy's mother used to say, if I wasn't prepared to have it broadcast across Park Slope.

I'm fine about them, Wendy said.

You are so amazing, Amelia said. All the things that keep happening to you, and you stay so brave and upbeat all the time.

Good things happen, too, she said. It's not all terrible.

Does this mean you're never coming back? Amelia asked. Because if so, I may just slit my wrists, it's getting so incredibly boring here.

What about Chief? Wendy asked.

We broke up. I found out he had this other girlfriend from his old school. The one where he said it wasn't really intense like with me. Then it turned out the whole time he was having sex with her.

*I don't believe men.* Her mother talking. Wendy on the couch, five years old.

What don't you believe?

*Anything.*

At least you didn't have sex with him, right? said Wendy.

Silence on the other end. Not exactly, Amelia said. But sort of.

What are you talking about? said Wendy. I thought we were going to discuss it before we did anything like that. You were the one who was saying fourteen was too young. You could get pregnant, Wendy said. That happened to a friend of mine out here.

He told me all these things. About how hard it is for a boy when he really wants you and he can't get this physical release he needs. It can actually be bad for his health.

We didn't exactly do it the way you can have a baby, Amelia said. We did it the other way.

Did you like it?

I liked having him for my boyfriend. I liked it that he liked me. Only it turned out he didn't, even.

On the other end of the line, Wendy was looking at her picture of Madonna on the wall, thinking about her song.

Life used to be a lot simpler, huh? said Amelia. Everything got so complicated.

It was probably always complicated, Wendy said. We just didn't know before.

# Thirty-One

A letter arrived for Wendy, postmarked Steamboat Springs, Colorado. From Todd.

*Dear Wendy,*

*The first place I went after I got to Denver was Telluride.*

*This guy told me the name of a ski resort he saw my brother working at back in the fall. Oh yeah, I remember him, the manager says when I got there. He took off back in November.*

*I wouldn't admit this to a lot of people, Wendy, but I started to cry. Not right then and there, but after, when I was outside. Out on the street of this dumb ski town full of all these happy-looking vacationers, families, parents and kids, guys with their girlfriends, me feeling like I don't have anyone in the world anymore.*

*Man, was it cold in that town. A girl comes over to me. This may seem like a dumb question, she says. But you wouldn't have a brother named Kevin, would you? Because you look a lot like this kid I used to know.*

*Turns out she worked at the same lift as him back in the fall. He told her he was heading to Steamboat, she said. Someone knew of a restaurant there that was hiring.*

*This girl Brittany knew a guy that was driving there and he gave me a ride. Dropped me right in front of the restaurant.*

*I walk in the door. Who's the first person I see, standing there in this Wild West–type getup, cowboy hat and chaps and everything? My crazy brother.*

*Ultra-bro, he says. Gives me a bear hug. Who knew why, but I started in crying all over again. Worse than the first time, only now it was on account of being so happy to see him, I thought I'd burst. Him too. The two of us were standing there in the middle of the restaurant, pounding each other on the back, doing this dance we made up when we were kids, where we used to pretend we were part of* Riverdance.

*Hey, everyone, he's yelling out. This is my little brother. You gotta meet my brother.*

*So this is where I'm writing you from. My brother Kevin's place in Steamboat Springs, Colorado, where I'm working as a busboy at Big Bob's Old West Tavern, the breakfast shift, seven A.M. to three. Not doing as much skating as I'd like, considering every inch of potential sidewalk is covered with snow at the moment, but I'm working on my GED, if you can believe it, and if I keep up at this rate, I'll be a high school graduate in a year, max. Kevin and me got an apartment together, a couple of wild and crazy bachelors in a town full of snow bunnies. Just joking.*

*Really it's more like we get up, go to work, stop by the deli on the way home to pick up something for dinner and maybe a video. I might put in a couple hours on my homework while he's doing his assignments for this correspondence course on mechanical drafting he signed up for. Six-thirty, seven we grill ourselves a couple of steaks or what have you, put on the video, maybe split a beer. My brother gets us a cigar once in a while to share. We might sit around, smoking and shooting the breeze about the old days. Days off, we get to go snowboarding free at the mountain where his friend works, but it's a rare night we haven't hit the sack by ten-thirty. Funny thing is, I was never this happy in my whole life.*

*I wanted to write and tell you, Wendy, how much it meant to me spending time with you Christmas, and I think you understand without me going into the particulars of what I'm referring to. If I never saw you again in my whole life, which I hope is not the case, I will never forget that night. I am not just referring to the kissing part either.*

*I want you to know I also am thinking of you on this cold winter night and many others besides.*

*Yours truly,*
*Todd*

At first when Wendy picked up the phone all she heard was breathing. Then a small voice she knew saying, Now, Poppy?

In the background, Josh's voice. Now, Lou.

She heard the sound of his xylophone then. Josh must be playing, because it wasn't random notes; it was the tune of "Happy Birthday."

Happy birthday to you, Louie sang. Happy birthday to you. Happy birthday, dear Sissy. Happy birthday to you.

Hey, Louie, she said. I was just thinking about you.

It's your birthday, Sis, he told her. Did you know that?

I did, Louie.

Did you have a party?

No party, but Garrett's taking me into the city to a museum this weekend and out for Chinese food after. To Louie, she spoke of him as Garrett, though more and more lately she was calling him her father.

And pretty soon it's going to be my birthday, too, Louie said.

I know, Louie, she said. Just one more month. Have you decided what you want?

I already know what I'm getting, he said, in a low, serious whisper. But it's a surprise.

I wish I was going to be there.

I'm being a very good boy, Sissy, he told her. The best I ever was.

You were always good, Louie.

But even better.

Have you been over to Corey's lately?

Not so much, he said. But Kate and me go to the park a lot. Sometimes even on school days, when she gets out from work.

That's good, Wendy said. But I hope you don't give up on Corey. He's been a really good friend.

Corey says there's no such thing as magic.

And what do you think, Louie?

There is.

Well, she said. It's okay for friends to disagree. Amelia and I disagree sometimes, too, but she's still my best friend.

He said magic was dumb. I told him it was real. He said I was dumb if I said that. He hurt my feelings.

Maybe you can just not talk about magic so much with Corey, knowing you have different ideas on the subject, she said. Hearing herself saying this, she got an odd feeling, as if she was hearing her mother's voice.

But it is real, right, Sis? he asked her again. Sometimes magic is real.


Josh had sent her a package. She read the letter first.

> *I could have sent you this at Christmas. But I decided it might be better if it came when there weren't a million other things going on.*
>
> *You know how your mother always loved getting you presents. Truth is Jan started shopping for one holiday the day we finished with the last one. Two weeks after Christmas, she was bringing home things for you again and showing me. All year long, she was setting things aside on the top shelf of our closet for you. You probably knew that.*

She didn't. Though sometimes, opening a package Christmas morning, she would recognize some item she'd admired in a store from months ago and wonder how her mother managed to remember and track it down.

Treats make trouble, her mother used to say, and it was true she was never one for things like buying you candy at the checkout, or video games or expensive clothes at department stores that hadn't gotten marked down yet. But tell her about some funky pair of cowboy boots in a thrift shop or some great old ring in an estate sale, and she'd be there.

Other kids got those toys they advertised on Saturday-morning TV when their birthday or Christmas rolled round, or board games, or Hello Kitty accessories. Wendy got a rabbit-fur muff for skating and a real treadle-operated sewing machine, not some toy version. One time, for her birthday, her mother gave her a whole box of interesting buttons and flower appliqués to sew on her overalls. Another time it was a complete set of every eye-shadow color made by Estée Lauder that she'd talked some woman into giving her who worked at the makeup counter, when they got their new line in. A music box that you kept bath powder in, and every time you lifted the top, it played "Somewhere Over the Rainbow." An antique Victrola and a set of old 78s, mostly Al Jolson. Red sparkle shoes like in *The Wizard of Oz*. A night-blooming jasmine plant to set by her bed, that really did bloom only at night, so when the blossoms opened, her room would be filled with the most wonderful smell.

After September, Josh wrote in the letter, I found all kinds of stuff on her top shelf. Some things for your brother and one or two little items that must've been meant for me. But most of them were for you.

He hadn't wrapped the things separately, he said. He wanted her to find everything the way her mother had left them in the box.

Carolyn was there in the kitchen while Wendy read Josh's letter. It's from my mom, she said quietly. Things she bought me a long time ago.

Maybe you'd like to take the box into your room, where you could be private, Carolyn said. I can see how it might be kind of a big thing.

I think I'll wait till later to look, Wendy told her. I'm not quite ready yet. She set the box under her bed.

Her birthday fell on a Friday. Garrett had told her to save Saturday, when he was off work. They were heading to San Francisco again.

Carolyn wanted to go, but she only had a week left to get her cactus garden finished before the official opening of the office building. Even with Violet helping—Violet and Walter Charles, was how Carolyn put it—she was going to be working right down to the wire. So it was just the two of them, Wendy and her father, driving to San Francisco again.

He took her first to the Palace of the Legion of Honor to look at art. She might have thought, if they were looking at art, it would be modern, but what he wanted to show her were the sculptures by Auguste Rodin—big bronze figures, some inside the building, some arranged in gardens outside.

When I was a kid, my mother took me to Paris, he said. We did all the usual things, the Louvre and the Eiffel Tower, and we rode a train out to see the French Open for a couple of days even, this being the period when my parents still had high hopes for my tennis career.

But my favorite place in Paris, though you might not have expected it, was this smaller museum they have there of Rodin sculptures. You could walk around the garden and actually touch them all. In a book, you only get to see the one view, but the great thing about seeing them in real life is how you can walk around taking in all the different angles. How different the work looks, depending on where you're standing.

He's a classical sculptor, he said. These works were cast more than a hundred years ago. But the thing that knocked me out then and still does was how totally wild and modern the guy was in certain ways. What an absolute madman, but in the best way.

They were standing in front of a sculpture called the *Burghers of Calais*. Six large figures of men draped in flowing robes that even though they were bronze looked real as fabric.

Wendy knew, from all the sketches and drawings inside the museum, and what was written in the explanation, that Rodin had spent months sketching the hands and feet, the expressions on the faces of the men. He had studied the placement of muscles and tendons and bones, the same way she tried to when she drew. He definitely knew anatomy.

First he learned what the rules were, Garrett said. Then he threw them all away. Look at the feet on these characters. And the hands. They're twice the size of how a normal person's hands and feet would be in proportion to the rest of the body. Here, they look totally right, and if all of a sudden someone changed it and gave them normal feet, you'd probably wonder what was wrong. Because the big feet just work. But what gave him that idea? How in hell did he know the usual rules just didn't apply to his sculptures?

\*     \*     \*

Look at the expressions on their faces, Garrett said. There's nothing handsome or beautiful about them in the ordinary sense. Some of the people in Rodin sculptures are downright ugly. Still, for a hundred years now, people have been knocked out by this sculpture and calling it beautiful. Which is true. It's just that none of the conventional standards of beauty apply. With Rodin, beauty can mean big old ugly feet and these twisted, tortured faces.

It was like what Josh used to say about jazz, that the most exciting music, for him, was never the melodic stuff. It was Thelonius Monk and John Coltrane, Ornette Coleman taking it outside on his saxophone, Art Blakey smashing out a drum solo as if what he was really trying for was to destroy everything in his path, and when he was finished, he might just have succeeded, too. The skinny maid in the Mark Morris version of *The Nutcracker* pirouetting across the stage in her black toe shoes and maid's uniform, only she wasn't really a ballerina at all—she was a man.

It's the moments of dissonance that stay with you, Garrett said. Then he began talking about artists she didn't really know—a photographer named Diane Arbus, who took pictures of people in mental institutions, a painter named Robert Rauschenberg, who made a beautiful image, and then, for the final touch, tore a giant gash down one side. And another one whose name she knew, Jackson Pollock, who threw paint across the canvas as if it was blood.

Making art isn't about creating something pretty, he said. Any more than life is. It's about telling the truth.

After, they went out for Chinese food, to a place that had the best dim sum in Chinatown, he said. She hadn't had dim sum since he came to New York that day when she was little and took her to F. A. O. Schwarz.

Now they sat facing each other across the table under a red-and-gold wall hanging of cranes. He poured her green tea.

Fourteen, he said. Good age. Of course, I thought you were fourteen already, for a while there. But now I can see you were more like thirteen then. You're definitely more of the fourteen-year-old type now.

I do feel older, she said. Not in a bad way. She thought then about the note her mother had slipped under her door the spring before, telling her things would look different once she wasn't thirteen anymore. She could never have imagined.

Take a person like me, he said. Being forty-nine instead of forty-eight could be stressful. And we won't even talk about the number that comes after that. But going from thirteen to fourteen is definitely a good thing.

They ordered. She let him do the choosing. Trust me on this, he said. Dim sum is a specialty of mine.

It arrived on a bamboo platter, arranged like flowers. He must have talked to someone in the kitchen, because there was also a special dumpling in the middle, larger than the others, with a candle.

So I was thinking it would be good to check in right about now and see how you're doing, he said. He sounded a little uncomfortable, like someone who's been reading the *Understanding Your Teenager* book.

Fine, she told him.

I mean nobody would expect you to be totally fine. A lot has happened.

I'm doing okay, she said. When she wasn't, he couldn't have done anything about it anyway.

Some people would say you might want to go talk to a therapist or something, he said. I was never that type myself, but I could understand if you did. Just say the word.

That's okay.

He paused. He reached for another dim sum. So did she.


The other thing I wanted to let you know is, I talked to Josh. I called him up. I thought it might be a good idea if the two of us were in communication.

Wendy tried to imagine the two of them, her tall, thin, gangly father with his wisps of gray hair—less wild-looking since he'd cut off his ponytail, but still not exactly Friendly Farm material—and the broad, stocky figure of Josh, with his love handles and the bit of a belly that was the badge, he said, of a man with an appropriate attitude concerning chocolate. Her jazz-loving dad, who knew the names of every character on *Sesame Street*, even the minor ones, who couldn't let a day go by without leaving her mom some Post-it note to say how crazy he was about her. Her other father, who may have been happiest alone in a trout stream—there or in a bar with a bunch of strangers. A man who owned every recording Bob Marley ever made, whose romantic gesture for the woman he no doubt loved was having her cactus spade sharpened.

He's a good guy, her father said. He thinks the world of you, of course. So we agreed on that for starters.

Wendy couldn't say anything. The thought of these two men who had loved her mother in their different ways, at different times in her life—the one who had screwed everything up, by his own admission, and the one who had picked up the pieces after—made her feel a great, hollow sadness. These two men would never in a million years know each other, if it wasn't for the woman who had loved each of them. Now they had each other's phone numbers—they had discussed the Yankees even, Garrett was telling her now. He had asked Josh if he'd ever run into this old friend of his from the Village, a sax player by the name of Ronnie.

Now they were talking to each other. Josh and Garrett: her father and her other father. They didn't hate each other. They might even become friends. Except that the person who had brought them together wasn't there. Like someone who sends out party invitations, only when the guests arrive, she isn't there, and they stand around eating the food without her.

We both agreed that all we want is what's best for you, Garrett said. In Josh's case, it's not just him that misses you, but the little guy, Louie. Though according to him, your little brother's doing a lot better than he was for a while there.

I told him about school. I thought he might look at me as a total jerk for letting you bag eighth grade that way back in the fall, but he understood. I don't think it bothered him that much, though he was glad to hear you're going on a regular basis now. Playing in the band.

For a moment she imagined she might not even be part of this picture. It could just be the two of them, Josh and Garrett, off at a ball game somewhere, reminiscing together about what a terrific person her mother had been and then getting around to who was the greatest ballplayer of all time, Ted Williams or Babe Ruth. She felt mad without knowing why, but maybe it had something to do with the thought that they had been talking about her life without her there to participate. Deciding what was best, the way adults seemed to so often.

So what we came up with was that you should finish the school year out here and after that we'd evaluate. We figured Josh and Louie could come out here and visit sometime near the end of your term, maybe when they're putting on a concert at your school, so he could hear you play with the band. If he stuck around till summer vacation, you could go off camping, and if you wanted, you could go back to New York with him for a visit. Take it from there.

He was chewing on a dim sum as he said this. The crab is my own personal favorite, he said. You've got to try one of these. He held the dim sum out to her between the gold-lacquered chopsticks.

For the last several minutes, a feeling had been overtaking her. It was so unfamiliar, she didn't even recognize it at first. For so long now—since her mother died—she had kept these kinds of feelings to herself. Even when it was just her, by herself, she never let them out, or recognized that they were there, even.

There had been times in the past, with her mother, when fury had exploded out of her. Even Josh—though he tried so hard to keep the peace and made whatever adaptions were necessary to ensure it—had found himself on the receiving end of her anger, especially one time, when her mother had talked about the idea of Josh adopting her. But ever since September, she had been careful to contain strong emotion. She let herself cry now and then—not even much of that. She had felt grief and desolation, loneliness, and certainly confusion. But not one time in five months had she felt pure rage rise out of her, as she knew it was about to now.

\*     \*     \*

Did it ever occur to you? she asked. She spoke quietly, but she knew she was summoning her energy for the next. Did you ever for one moment consider the possibility that I might have some opinions about my life?

She could feel her body stiffening, her spine locking, something flooding into her, different from grief this time. A kind of fierce, resolute power, like the girl in the canoe in Maine in the picture her mother liked best, who got that boat to shore.

I only meant, he said. We were thinking. I never had to deal with anything like this before. I'm probably not very good at it.

He had set the chopsticks down with the dim sum. She looked at his face, and the long-ago memory came to her of the night in the New Jersey motel. Her father, coming out of the bathroom with the towel around his waist. The girl with the tattoo on her breast. Her mother's ravaged face on the ride back to Brooklyn, and the next day, throwing their belongings in Kate's car, and all those days after that. His infrequent and unannounced visits over the years, and his calm, quiet look of bemusement at her mother's fury, which always left it seeming as if her mother was the crazy one—hysterical, even—considering all he'd done was show up at the door, Mr. Mellow, with a fish he'd caught or a spaghetti squash from his garden, and not a single ounce of bitterness or resentment.

She had said as much to her mother, many times. *Look at my father. He never says one mean thing about you. He's always easygoing. You're the bitter one, the one that can't let it go.*

He didn't have to let anything go, her mother said. He never held on in the first place. Of course he was easygoing.

*Easy gone.*

Oh great, her mother said. He buys a doll at F. A. O. Schwarz. Where was he when the bills came due for Montessori? Where was he for medical insurance?

I can't believe he actually managed to harvest a crop from his garden, her mother had said, the time he brought them the squash, after an absence of two years. Knowing he's the kind of guy who would water and fertilize like crazy, when the mood struck him. And then forget about it so long, the next time he thought to check there'd be nothing but a few stunted plants and weeds.

He'd be better off raising something like mold, she said.

Definitely not a child.

She saw her mother, back on the day she moved the last of the costumes out of her dancing school and sold the fixtures. Thinking of her as she was that day—the crushed look as she watched the truck drive away with the last of the mirrors—Wendy wanted to slap his handsome face. Partly for how he had abandoned her mother. More so for the way his endlessly alluring presence had brought about Wendy's own betrayal and abandonment of her.

To Wendy, it had always seemed as if her father's unexpected arrivals possessed a certain magical quality, like Peter Pan swooping in the window, though she had liked it less well when he swooped out. Now she saw him as her mother had—a man whose ease and charm was made possible by carelessness and lack of attention. The thought of it—most of all, the memory of their last terrible fights about the trip to California he'd proposed in his letter that fall—made her sick with regret.

You think a person can just drop their life and start being your daughter when it suits you, she said. You think you're the big hero, rescuing me. And what did you think you had to rescue me from? Josh, who was around all those years, looking after my brother and me? My life that you never even bothered finding out about?

I'm sure I deserve this, he said. If it makes you feel better, go for it.

In the last ten years I only saw you four times, Wendy said. That and a few phone calls.

I was wrong, he told her. I didn't know. I hated my own father for how absent he was, but I guess I ended up being more like him than I thought.

Then you come flying in, thinking you can change everything, she said. You don't bother to call first. Like you assume I'll be there whenever it suits your timetable. Like my whole life up to that point was spent waiting for you to show up. On Halloween, of all nights.

He wasn't saying anything anymore. Just nodding.

Here I am ready to take you to California, you say. My mother dies and you think it's like now everything she did over the years and the life we had didn't matter. Like just because her body isn't anyplace, nothing else about her is there anymore either. But it is.

She's everywhere, Wendy told him. Everywhere you weren't.

I knew what she did mattered, he said, so quietly she almost couldn't hear. I know how much she's a part of you. I see it every day.

You know the difference between you and Josh? It's like you think you're standing in the center of the universe, and all that matters is what you want. You probably can't even imagine how it is to love a person the way my mom loved me, and how Josh loved my mom, and how he's loving me now, which isn't about what might be best for him. He loved me so much he let me go, just because he thought that might be what I needed at the time. Same way Carolyn loved her baby enough to give him away, and Alan loves his son so much that he drives an hour each way every week to watch him put laundry in the dryer, knowing he won't even get a hug back.

I know I've been a selfish person most of my life, Garrett said. But I honestly thought it would be a good thing for you to come out here with me.

As it turned out, you were right, she said. Quieter now. It was a good thing.

So now you know me, he said. Including all the worst parts. Fair enough. The thing is, I'm not the same person I was when I left your mother and you the way I did. I'm not even the same person I was three months ago.

The whole time she'd been talking, she could feel the beating of her heart. Much faster than usual. Her face was hot. For a few moments, she was actually trembling, though her voice had remained steady.

She was starting to calm down at last. Her breathing was regular again.

Looking at him now, across the table, she felt an odd and surprising desire to rest her hand on his arm. He looked so sad. She didn't want to keep hurting him. She only wanted him to know how it had been, not just for her but for her mother, too.

I wish I'd been a better father all these years, he said.

She was silent for a moment.

You've been doing better lately.

I didn't know what it was going to be like, he said. All this time, I stayed away partly because I was just so sure I'd screw up.

The staying away was the screwing up, she told him.

I'm not experienced at this, he said. I guess I was kind of proud of myself for calling Josh. It seemed like such a take-charge thing to do, which isn't even like me.

I wish I could apologize to your mother, he said. I can understand why she would have been angry. She had every right. And I apologize to you for thinking it would be okay to decide how things should go without even talking to you about it.

Thanks.

Another minute went by. The waiter, who had stayed clear of their table for the last many minutes, had set the bill on their table now.

One good thing anyway, said Garrett. I can see no man is ever going to mess with you. I'm really glad of that, because there's always plenty ready to try.

He set some money on the tray. Let's get out of here, he said.


It was raining when they got outside. He took his jacket off and wrapped it around her.

You may need to skip school one more time, he told her. It's the other part of your birthday celebration. I'm taking you to Yosemite.


They didn't even go home first. Rare for Garrett, he had the whole thing planned. He had bought a sleeping bag and warm clothes, a day pack, fleece gloves, hiking boots in her size, even. All the gear was in the back of his truck.

*　　*　　*

It was late afternoon when they got out on the highway. The drive took hours. He put on a tape and handed her a stick of beef jerky. Somewhere along the way, she leaned her head back on the seat.

You can put your head on my shoulder, he said.

Now and then she'd wake up halfway, and when she did, she could hear the soft, laid-back voice of Bob Marley, the reggae beat. Mostly she slept.

By the time they got to the park, the stars were out. The truck had pulled over at the gate. She could hear her father rolling down the window to talk to the ranger.

Not a lot of people make it out here this time of year, he was saying. You two are going to have this place to yourselves pretty much.

He started giving Garrett directions to the Yosemite Lodge, but Garrett said he had a little generator-run heater in the back. They'd camp in Lower Pines and sleep under the pop-top in back.

They drove a little farther, along a stretch of road that wound through what her father called the valley floor.

He found them a campsite—empty except for one old VW bus. He got out a flashlight to show her where the toilets were.

We can get ourselves properly organized in the morning, he said. Main thing for now is to get a good night's sleep, what's left of it.

She had put on the new hiking boots, for the snow, which came up to her ankles. You couldn't make out much along the path, but she heard the sound of water moving over the rocks nearby. The moon was out, but the trees all around had mostly hidden it from view.

When she'd finished in the bathroom, her father was waiting for her on the path. He took her hand and led her the rest of the way back to the truck.

I don't know why more people don't come here this time of year, he said. Summer's amazing, too, but then you've got the crowds to deal with. To me, winter's the best time. I always feel like I'm entering this vast empty cathedral. If I was ever the type to go looking for a place of worship, this would be it.

He had set up an air mattress in the back of the truck, with their sleeping bags on top, and a blanket on top of that. The generator was humming quietly. He had lit the Coleman lantern.

I guess I never got us any dinner, did I? he said. We'll just have to make up for it with breakfast.

She slept so well the sun was already up when she woke, and she could hear the rushing of the water on the rocks. Her father had the Coleman stove going, and he'd set out cups and bowls. He must've stopped for provisions along the way the night before, while she was sleeping, because now he had hot chocolate ready, and a pot of oatmeal, a cup of orange juice, a banana and a bran muffin—set out on a picnic table, with his bandana for a cloth.

She stepped outside the truck. The light on the snow was so brilliant, she had to shield her eyes for a second to adjust. She looked up. Even with her head all the way back, it was impossible to see the top of the rock face beside them. Across the field, though, she could make out plainly the tops of other peaks, encircling the valley floor. If she had landed on the moon in the middle of the night, the scene that met her in the daylight would have been no more foreign and mysterious.

With her mother and Josh, Wendy had taken day hikes in the White Mountains of New Hampshire, but she had never seen mountains like these—a landscape that seemed built on a whole other scale, its peaks stabbing so high into the sky they seemed to belong more to heaven than to earth. After her old familiar mountains of Washington and Jefferson back home, the peaks of Yosemite seemed savage and unapproachable—scary almost, but also more beautiful than anything she'd ever seen.

He handed her the hot chocolate. She let the cup warm her hands first before taking a sip. She could feel the warmth of the liquid going down her throat. In this place, everything you took in—light, warmth, sound, taste, smell—seemed sharper and more deeply felt.

The first time I ever came here was with your mother, he told her. We took a road trip cross-country a few months after we met. Ended up right here.

I can't picture her as the camping type, Wendy said.

For starters, it wasn't winter, he told her. Then you've got to factor in the fact that we were nuts about each other. People do all kinds of things they wouldn't normally, when they're in love.

I don't know if this is the type of thing a person's supposed to tell his kid, he said. But your mother always said this was where you were conceived.


After they cleaned up, she took out her new things, cut off the price tags, and dressed. Once the sun was out, the air was no longer stingingly cold, especially when you started moving. He handed her a couple of Cliff bars and a bag of trail mix, a water bottle for her pack.

The trail wound, first, along a place called the Tenaya Lake, through the canyon. Looking up, she could see a strangely shaped peak—round on one side, sheer flat face on the other.

That's Half Dome, he told her. In the warm weather, you can hike up there. They've got metal spikes put into the sides of the rock, and cables set up to help people make it to the top, but in October, the park rangers take the cables down till spring. One day we'll tackle that one.


They hiked in silence, and that was fine. It wasn't really silent anyway. Wendy would never have known there could be so much to listen to, with no one saying anything. There was wind and moving water and melting snow. It turned out there were birds even at this time of year, and Garrett knew all their names and recognized their songs: nuthatch and Steller's jay, brown creeper, mountain chickadee, and, the night before, a great horned owl. He knew the trees, too, and pointed them out to her: lodgepole pine, California black oak, cottonwood, bay laurel, ponderosa, Jeffrey pine, incense cedar.

She caught sight of a group of deer, running across an open field and leaping over the brush back into the woods. Another time she felt the eyes of an animal on her and looked to the side. It was a coyote, off in the distance, staring right at her.

You wouldn't feel this so much in the warm weather, he told her, when the buses and the people are here. But right now, you get the feeling things have barely changed since the glaciers first made this place, eighty million years ago. It's only been in the last hundred and fifty years that anyone besides the Indians set foot in this place.

They were climbing now. Off to the west, she could see and hear the crashing waters of Yosemite Falls. See over there, he said. They call that one El Capitan. People actually climb down that one. It's more than seven thousand feet from the top to the base. Every summer there's always some crazy types to free-fall parachute jump from the top, too. Me, I'd just as soon keep my feet on the ground.

Studying the vast craggy granite face of El Capitan, the picture came to her of the Trade Towers as they'd been before September. Measured here, against the granite of the Sierra, even the tallest buildings in the world would have seemed small. She and her father, moving slowly along the trail to the lake, were only specks.

They made their way steadily up. I figure we can stop to eat at Vernal Falls, he told her. This time of year, they're really something.

All these months, her grief had taken the form, in her mind, of rushing water, and now here it was, cascading down the face of the mountain with force enough to wear down granite. Force enough that when her father spoke to her here, it was hard to make his words out over the sound of the falls.

When your mother and I drove out here back in '87, he said, we said how we'd come back one day. Neither one of us grew up in the kind of family that took their kids camping. We were going to do it differently.

And I did come back plenty of times over the years, he said. Just not with her. Or you.

But look, she told him. Here we are now.

At the top of Vernal Falls, the rangers had strung a chain across the trail with a sign, CLOSED FOR THE SEASON.

They always put these things up, her father said, handing her a granola bar and an apple. I never pay attention to this stuff.

Once Wendy would have. Now she just stepped over the chain.

The trail was becoming rougher, and there were no footprints ahead of theirs.

The snow was deeper here. Making her way up over the rocks, Wendy felt her foot slide a couple of times and caught herself on branches. One time, she fell. She thought of suggesting that they turn back, but from behind, she could hear Garrett's voice. I love this, he said. Wait till you see the view from the top. You'll think we're in heaven.

They were on a rock ledge now. On one side of the trail, the granite rose in a sheer, unclimbable face. On the other side, nothing. Wendy looked down, but only once. If you missed your step here, there would be nothing to catch your fall till you hit the rocks a hundred feet down, maybe more.

How much farther? she asked. I wouldn't want to try this in the dark.

They rounded a sharp corner. Where the trail had been barely wide enough for her two boots before, it suddenly narrowed to almost nothing. Snow on the rocks, melting and then freezing again, had covered the path. When Wendy tried to set her foot down, she could feel the ground give way. I can't get a foothold, she said. It's sheer ice.

Okay, Garrett said. Looks like we turn back here.

There was no room to turn around, and nothing to hold on to but ice-covered rock. Below lay a canyon of stone.

I can't move, she said. There's nowhere to go. Fear gripped her, then terror.

From behind her, she could hear Garrett unzipping his pack. I have a pick in here somewhere, he said.

I can't move, she said again. If I reach back, I'll fall. She had set her feet, one in front of the other, lined up as if she were walking a tightrope. Just in front of her, she could hear the sound of water rushing under the ice. Even the spot where she stood felt as though it might break away at any moment and send her shooting down into the canyon below.

I'm coming up behind you, he said. I'll hold on to you. All you have to do is step backward.

I can't see where I'm going, she said. I don't dare turn my head to look back. If I step wrong, I'll slip.

Reach your hand behind you, he said. Hold on to me. But she knew there was nothing steady about the spot where he was standing, either, and he must have known it, too. She heard him cursing.

I'm scared, she said. I feel like I could fall any second.

I've got to admit, I'm not so thrilled myself, he told her.

She thought about her mother on the eighty-seventh floor, standing at the windows, looking out as the offices of Mercer and Mercer filled with smoke. She thought of Josh wrapping his arms around her on the Tornado Coaster, singing "Love Me Do." More than anyone, the person she would have liked to see here now was Josh. Though if it had been Josh with her instead of Garrett, she never would have found herself in this position in the first place.

There was no going forward—that much was clear. Nothing for it but to step back, blind, and hope the ground held under her boot. She held her breath and backed up. One step, two. She was at a place where she could turn around, finally. She breathed again.

For a minute there, I knew what a person would feel, if they thought they were about to die, she told him.

I'm sorry, he said again. The second time in twenty-four hours he'd apologized. I'd hate it if you lost faith in me after this. A father's supposed to be someone you can count on.

# Thirty-Two

She hadn't dreamed about her mother for a while, but then she did.

It was the day the two of them had gone to see the matinee of *Peter Pan.* Wendy was six or seven, but they'd brought the show back, with a different actress playing Peter from the one who played him all those years ago when Wendy's mother made the final cut to be Princess Tiger Lily. Tickets were expensive, but her mother had gotten them two in the orchestra anyway. That way, she said, when Peter flies, it'll be right over our heads.

They were sitting in their seats waiting for the houselights to dim. In the dream Wendy was wearing her plaid taffeta Broadway dress. Her mother was dressed up, too. So far the dream was totally how it had been in real life. The two of them studying the *Playbill* the way they always did. Her mother giving her a rundown of the highlights of the show. We definitely got the best seats, her mother said.

Just then a man came out in front of the curtain. We have a terrible problem, he said. I hate to tell you this, but Cathy Rigby just got hit by a bicycle messenger crossing the street. There's nobody to play Peter Pan. Unless someone out there thinks they could do it.

My mom, Wendy called out. My mom can.

Where is this person? he asked.

Her mother had only hesitated a second before rising slowly from her seat. I guess that's true, she said, smoothing her hair in that way she had. I know all the words.

Not to mention the dances.


They brought her backstage, but Wendy stayed in her seat.

I'm named after the character, she whispered to the woman next to her. This is my mother's favorite show.

The houselights went out. The orchestra began to play pieces of all the familiar songs. The curtain went up. It was the scene where Wendy, John, and Michael's parents were going out to a party and telling their kids good night. The dog, who was really an actor in a dog suit, was looking restless, sniffing under the beds as if something was there. Darkness. Then came the little flickering light that signaled Tinker Bell was in the room. Then a *whooshing* sound as a small, nearly weightless figure landed on the windowsill. *Peter.*

Her mother's hair was short already, so they hadn't needed to cut it. She was wearing the green elf suit—green stockings, green slippers, a green cap. The way she moved through the air, it looked as if she'd been flying all her life. From where she sat in the orchestra, Wendy looked for the cables, but she couldn't see any.

I've lost my shadow, Tink, Peter said. What'll I do if I can't get it back?

In her seat in the fifth row, center, Wendy was whispering all the lines along with her mother. Now came the part where the children woke up. Now Peter Pan was telling Wendy his problem. Wendy was sewing the shadow back on, taking care of everyone, the way she always did. In a minute, they were all going to fly out the window together.

The dream got fuzzier after that. Captain Hook was in there somewhere, and the Lost Boys, and Princess Tiger Lily. There was that moment when Tinker Bell drank the poison so Peter wouldn't, and now she was dying. Peter stood on the edge of the stage, telling the audience that the only hope would be if they all closed their eyes and thought about how they believed in fairies. Slowly, Tinker Bell's light grew brighter. She was going to be all right after all.

It was the end of the show. The curtain calls: the audience cheering for them all, except for Captain Hook, who shook his hook hand at them when he came out, so everyone called out, *Boo.* Last came her mother, flying, but not just over the stage this time. She flew over the audience, too—right over the orchestra seats and up over the balcony, and then to the very highest, cheapest seats, the ones she and Wendy usually sat in on their matinee days.

Wendy had never heard an audience clap so hard. *More,* they called out. *Do it again.* Her mother was spinning and dipping like the most amazing bird, swooping low sometimes, then ascending to the highest part of the theater. She touched down on the balcony railing once, more like a bird than a person. Then she was flying again, but higher this time, clear up to the golden ceiling, the glittering chandeliers.

The woman in the seat next to Wendy leaned over to her. You must be so proud, she said. Even Mary Martin was never like that.

Then everyone was puzzled. Her mother hadn't flown offstage, but she wasn't there anymore. Like the Blue Angels, disappearing into the clouds over the San Francisco Bay that day, she had flown up to the ceiling and kept on going. Only she didn't come back.

That is some trick, a man said sitting in back of Wendy. I never even spotted the cables.

It's probably something to do with lasers, his wife said. What'll they think of next?

People were putting their coats on. Gathering up their *Playbills.* Heading to the lobby. Shaking their heads in amazement. Now it was only Wendy left alone in the theater, except for a man sweeping up candy wrappers.

Time to go home, he said.

I'm waiting for my mother, she told him. She was Peter Pan.

She's long gone, he said. Got to hand it to her. Not only could she dance. She could fly.

She's coming back, Wendy said. She wouldn't just disappear like that. She had heard the phrase before—*into thin air*—but never understood how that could be.

It happens, he said. There are no rules for these things.

How am I supposed to manage without her? she asked. How am I supposed to get home?

I guess that would be on your own two feet, he told her. Just like the rest of us.

They were putting on *Guys and Dolls* at her school. Henry, from band, had invited her to go with him. Not go exactly but meet him there.

He was standing outside the front of the school when her father dropped her off. He was wearing a dress shirt, tucked in, and a sport jacket. I guess this must be like a date, Garrett said when he saw Henry standing there. Just don't do anything I wouldn't.

What am I saying? he said. Never mind.

You like musicals? Henry asked her.

Yes, she said. She could have told him a lot more on that subject, but no need. *Guys and Dolls* is one of my favorites, she told him.

I tried out for Nathan Detroit, he told her. But Ira always gets the leads, and I didn't want a dorky part like Sky Masterson.

Nathan Detroit is definitely the cool one, she said. Same as I'd never want to be Sarah. I'd want to be Adelaide.

He had saved them seats near the front. Too bad they don't have a full band, he said. It was just Mrs. Thompkins, one of the music teachers, accompanying the singers on piano.

I saw this show on Broadway one time, she told him. Tonight she didn't feel like adding: With my mom.

This version might be a tad different, he said.

It was different, all right, but she loved the music so much, it didn't matter that much how the Redbirds performed the show. She had listened to the original cast album so many times she could substitute their voices for the seventh and eighth graders up onstage in their too-big suits and their dresses that looked like they'd been rooting around in their grandmother's closet. Except for the outfits of Adelaide and the Hot Box Girls.

The girl who played Adelaide was a full head taller than Nathan, with a body that wouldn't quit, as Garrett would have put it. Where Ira, the boy playing Nathan, looked like he'd be more comfortable playing one of the little brothers in *The Sound of Music.* Or the kid, Winthrop, in *The Music Man.* When he opened his mouth, though, you knew why he got the part. The boy could sing.

At intermission, Henry took her out to the hall and bought them both a Dr Pepper and a couple of chocolate-chip cookies.

So how do you like band so far? he asked.

It's okay, she said. I was never crazy about the theme song from *Titanic.* I'm more into jazz.

That's awesome, he said. Me, too. Who do you listen to mostly?

She thought about the CD's Josh had sent her for Christmas, what he said about how she could really impress some guy if she mentioned certain artists. She decided to save that for some other time.

Oh, the usual, she said. John Coltrane, Bill Evans, Charlie Parker. You know.

Wow, he said. I guess it's different in New York. I've got like one Kenny G CD and the soundtrack to *Sleepless in Seattle*, that's about it.

My dad says someone should take Kenny G and his saxophone someplace like Alaska and wait till it's really cold and make him stick his tongue out and put it up against the metal.

The dad she meant was Josh, naturally. Henry looked puzzled.

I think what he means is he doesn't like Kenny G's music that much, she said.

You really know a lot about jazz, Henry said. Maybe we could go to Virgin Records in Sacramento some afternoon and try out CD's at the listening station.

To Henry, it occurred to her, she was this very grown-up and worldly type of person. It was possible that, unlike her, he had never French-kissed even.

We could probably do that, she said. I have a friend who lives near there with her baby. I'd want to stop by and say hello to her, too.

She could tell this also impressed him.

You must think Davis is pretty much of a two-bit town, he said. After New York.

In some ways, she said. In other ways, it's sort of a relief.

Then it was act two, and Adelaide and the Hot Box Girls were coming out. It was the number she and her mother had worked up their routine for,

"Take Back Your Mink." She should have known it was coming, but when she heard the first chords of the song on the piano and saw the girl playing Adelaide sashaying onstage, busting out of her gold spandex bathing suit, it caught her off guard.

This girl was only thirteen or fourteen, tops, but she was a lot bigger than Wendy's mother had been, and with more of a Hot Box kind of look to her. Wendy thought about her mother dancing this number—her skinny body in her red sleeveless leotard, shimmying her top, even though she didn't really have much there, her slim legs in their fishnet stockings, tapping.

She had taught Wendy some steps for their number, Wendy being the other Hot Box Girl. Just basic tap steps—kick ball change, kick ball change. Mostly they wiggled their rear ends and flung their boas around.

The truth was, Wendy had always been a terrible dancer. Her mother worked with her a lot in the old days. When Wendy was little and they still had the Pocahontas Dancing School, she'd sit in on all the classes. But she never could get her feet to move the way her mother showed her. Even when she was very young—four, five—she knew she would never dance like her mother.

Maybe you won't be a ballerina or a jazz dancer, her mother said. But you've got all sorts of other talents I don't have, things you got from your father. Like how you can carry a tune. How you can draw.

When her mother said this, her father was gone already, and Wendy was used to hearing her mother say mad things about him. The idea of being like her father didn't necessarily sound like a good thing.

I want to be like you, she said.

Here's the great thing about when people have a child, her mother said. The baby isn't all from one person or all from the other. She's a little of both. The best parts of both, if you're lucky, which we were.

I thought you didn't like my dad.

I don't like some of the things he did. But I liked who he was when I met him, and I know those things I liked are still in him, because they couldn't just disappear. Just being around you all the time reminds me of the things that made me want to get married to him in the first place.

What part of you did I get? Wendy asked. Because she knew it wasn't the dancing and even at age five it was becoming clear, not the skinny little body, light as air, either.

I like to think I have a zest for life, her mother said. I know you do, and I like to think maybe you got some of that from me.

Up on the stage now, the Hot Box Girls were shimmying heavily offstage. A man in the seat next to Wendy was standing up with his video camera pointed at one of the secondary Hot Box Girls in the back row.

If you ask me, they were the Lukewarm Box Girls, Henry said. Maybe even the Cold Box Girls.

There was not a single good dancer in the bunch, that was true. But something else had been missing that he was picking up on, though he might not even have known it. The zest for life part, that would have made her mother a good dancer if she'd never taken a single class in her life or never heard of a timestep. The thing that came across when you watched her mother dancing was how much she loved being alive.

For Louie's birthday party, Josh was taking a bunch of kids from his class to Bowlmor Lanes and then out for pizza. He'd arranged a bunch of other stuff, too, he told Wendy. Right in the middle of the bowling, Roberto and Omar were going to come in dressed as pirates and act like they were going to steal the presents, and Josh would hand out pirate swords to all the kids and they'd fight them off, and the kids would win, naturally. Then they'd have cake, which would be in the shape of a pirate ship, with rigging and little plastic pirates on top for everyone to take home, with cocktail-pick swords.

Eight kids were coming to the party. Kate was going to help out. Later, back at their apartment, they would have a birthday dinner and Josh would give Louie his present, a train set with a bridge and a station and passengers you could put in the cars. There were special pellets to put in the engine that made steam come out. It was a more expensive present than they usually got him, but Josh didn't need to explain why he might be trying unusually hard to make this birthday go well.

Every morning, Louie asks me how many more days, Josh told Wendy on the phone. Way more than Christmas even, he's been gearing up for this one. It's like he thinks turning five is one of the landmark events in life.

Maybe it's just that Corey's been five for a while, she said. He's anxious to catch up.

Maybe, said Josh. But when he turned four, Corey was already four, and it wasn't like this.

Wendy had sent Louie a pair of pajamas she'd sewed for Pablo, his rabbit, made from rabbit-print flannel, with a carrot made out of felt stuck in the pocket, and a copy of *Runaway Bunny*.

The morning of the birthday party, she called their apartment before they left for the bowling alley. It was only six-thirty in California, but she got up early to catch him.

Happy birthday, big boy, she said, the way their mother always used to on his other birthdays.

Five is a pretty great number, isn't it?

Yes, he said. She could hear him breathing heavily on the other end of the phone and knew he was holding the receiver very tight.

I bet Poppy made you waffles this morning, didn't he?

Yup, he said. But I was too excited to eat any.

Remind me all the kids that are coming to your party, she said.

I forget their names he told her. He didn't seem focused on that part. He was thinking about the presents, probably. She could remember being five and feeling that way.

Is it going to be bumper bowl or regular? she asked.

I don't know.

Let's hope it's bumper, she said. You know how with some kids who don't bowl as much as you, the ball is always going in the gutter? They can get discouraged.

Uh-huh.

What flavor cake did Poppy get? Yellow or chocolate?

He didn't answer her. Sissy, he said, in that same husky whisper. I'm getting a very special surprise today.

I know, I told him. Wait till you see. You're going to love it.

I've been so good, he told her. The best I ever was.

They had to go. She said a quick hello to Josh.

Say hi to Kate, she told him. Good luck with the pirates.


It was a fairly big day at her house, too. The office building where Carolyn and Violet had installed the cactus garden was having its grand opening. Garrett and Wendy were heading over that morning with Carolyn to make sure everything was in good shape. They were picking up Violet and Walter Charles on the way.

Carolyn was wearing her jeans, on the chance that she might have to do a little last-minute work on the plants, but she had put on makeup and curled her hair. The front pieces were pulled back, held in place with the hair clip Wendy had given her.

You look really nice, Wendy said.

I got you a little something, Garrett said to Carolyn. This was unusual. He wasn't much on presents generally. He handed her a small box, unwrapped.

Garrett, she said. She wasn't the type to get worked up, but you could tell this really got to her.

He'd had business cards printed up. "Carolyn's Cactus World," they said. "Professional plantings for home and office. Just because they're prickly doesn't mean we'll stick it to you!" Then the phone number, which was his.

I figured it made sense, he said. Looks like you're going to be over here more than at your place. Not that we mind, right, Slim?

That's the most thoughtful thing, she said. I never would have expected.

Me neither, he said.


The opening went well. Violet also wore work clothes, and she had brought her own trowel. She had Walter Charles in a backpack, rather than the infant carrier she'd had at the beginning. This way, it's easier to work on the plants while I'm carrying him around, she said.

The garden was beautiful, so everyone said. At Harvey's Cactus World, the plants were stuck in a mostly random way in whatever patch of dirt seemed to be free. Carolyn's garden was like an artwork. Garrett said that looking at it reminded him of when he did acid back in the seventies. To Wendy, it was almost like something you'd expect to see at the bottom of the ocean—that strange and exotic. But dry.

Four different people came up to Carolyn during the opening, wanting to know if she had time to take on other jobs. Let me give you our card, she said. A little ways off, Violet was also answering questions about the plants.

This particular garden contains specimens that wouldn't react that great to rain, she was saying. But we have a lot of others back at our main nursery that would do fine in a space like what you're talking about.

Driving home, they didn't say much, but Carolyn couldn't stop smiling.

Violet, she said. I hope you're up for sticking with this for a while, because I could definitely use your help.

They stopped at a restaurant on the way home, not the diner this time, but more of a real restaurant. Man, I hope Walter Charles behaves, Violet said.

He did.


It was eight o'clock when they got home. Late to call New York, but she wanted to know how Louie's party had gone. Josh was up. He picked up on the first ring.

Oh, Wendy, he said. It's been rough here.

What do you mean? Did something happen at the bowling alley?

The bowling part went fine. Nobody cried, since we had bumpers up, so even the worst bowlers knocked down a few pins. Roberto and Omar were great. Kate, too. Everyone loved their swords, particularly the girls. They said nobody ever gave them a sword before.

The presents? she asked.

That went fine, he told her. Louie didn't seem to be all that much interested, like his mind was someplace else.

The trouble came later, he told her. Everyone had gone home. Kate and I took him back to the apartment to give him the train.

Close your eyes, Louie, they told him. It's time for your surprise now.

He was standing there in the kitchen, waiting for us to lead him into the living room, where we had the train set up. Walking him through the doorway, I could feel how his whole body was trembling.

When we got in the room and he opened his eyes, he just stared. Kate had turned the train on, so it was going around. Through the tunnel, over the bridge, steam coming out. He didn't even seem to see it, though. He just kept looking around the room.

Where is she? he said.

Who?

Mama.

What do you mean, Louie? I bent over to put my arms around him, seeing the look on his face, but I couldn't get to him. He started running all around the room, knocking the train down, flinging pillows.

He kept saying the same thing over and over. *My mama was supposed to be here. I was sure.*

Oh, Josh.


I never saw your brother like this before, he told her. Even after I got to him it took all my strength to keep him from breaking free of my arms. He was crying so hard he couldn't catch his breath. I never heard a sound come out of him like that before. Like some animal that's been shot.

Kate tried to comfort him, too, but that was even worse. He started screaming at her to go away. All this time, she's been so great to him. It seemed like she was the one person he was really happy with, more than me even. He kicked and threw things at her face. You're not my mama, he said.

I know that, Louie, she told him.

He told her he wished she was dead. I wish it was you in that building, he said. *Get away from my pop.*


She had to leave, that was all there was to it, Josh said. He was just going crazy. He was still very worked up after she left. All I could do for an hour—maybe longer—was sit there holding him. I could feel his heart pounding. His body was still shaking. He was burning up.

I finally got him in bed. I didn't try to put his pajamas on or anything. I just lay down next to him in the dark, stroking his head. After a long time, he could talk.

So what happened?

\*     \*     \*

It was that day at the magic show with Kate that got him started, Josh told her. That woman who helped him when he was in the box up onstage.

Miss Sparkle, Wendy said. They had all heard the story. The magician cutting the box in half, the flashlight and the jelly beans. Louie's bow. The magic wand.

It was the wand. She told him he should save it for his birthday. She told him if he was really good he might get his wish.

There was no need to ask what he'd wished for.

Wendy got home from school to find a note from Carolyn on the counter.

*Your mom's friend Kate called. She's on her way to Hawaii, but she's stopping to see you. She said she's renting a car at the airport and driving up tonight. She wants to take you out to dinner.*

An hour later Kate was on the doorstep. Like Wendy, she was thinner, and her hair had grown, but her face was as familiar to Wendy as any she had known, besides her parents and her brother.

Why don't we go someplace? Kate said. They got in the car.

Neither one of them was hungry, so they drove to a place Wendy knew from her days riding around on her father's bike—a field that looked out over the hills in the shade of a bunch of almond trees. They sat on the grass.

I'm moving, Kate told her.

Where?

Hawaii, for now. My brother has a place on the Big Island. I figure I can pick up a restaurant job for a while and see how it goes. I just needed to get out of New York.

You've lived there a long time, Wendy said. As long as she'd known Kate.

It was never a choice so much, she said. More of a habit. Your mom was there, and you guys. Which was basically my family. Only it wasn't completely, which is what I came to see. I was borrowing your mother's life.

We liked having you around. You were the best friend my mom ever had. Way more like a sister than Aunt Pam.

I know, she said. But your mother's not there anymore.


I don't know if I can talk about this with you, Wendy, she said. But I feel like if I don't, you'll never understand, and you might feel like I'd abandoned your dad and your brother just when they needed me the most.

I guess I fell in love with Josh. Or thought I did. Probably I fell in love with the whole package of your family. Going to the park with Louie, having meals together, reading to him. Feeling like someone really needed me for once. All those years of putting my energy into these dumb relationships with New York City bachelor types, and here I was now, spending my Saturday nights with Josh and Louie, watching *Herbie Goes to Monte Carlo* and loving it.

I swear it was never anything I thought about for one second when your mother was alive. I was just glad to see Janet happy like that, finally. Seeing Janet and Josh just made me feel hopeful that I could find someone like that, too, someday. But I never meant it to actually be him.

There's something about seeing a person taking care of a child, she said. I'd see the tender way Josh was with your brother, and imagine what it would feel like to have someone be that way with me.

She looked at Wendy, as if she was checking to see if it was okay to go on.

We were both so sad, she said. There was that most of all. There didn't seem to be anything that could ever make it better. And then it started to seem like maybe there was. This one small thing.

One small star shining down on them, Carolyn called it.

I didn't ever kid myself he would feel about me the way he did about your mother. I knew there were certain records they used to play, a restaurant they went to. Places I'd never go with Josh.

But I thought maybe there was enough left over to make something worthwhile out of, she said.

Remember that amazing cake he made for your mom last year when he threw that goofy party in honor of National Secretary's Day? The one holiday she hadn't celebrated yet. And right when he was setting it on the table, he dropped it. But Josh scooped up the layers and fitted them together on another plate. A smaller one. And slathered a bunch of leftover frosting on top to cover up the ruined parts.

It wasn't beautiful like the original one, she said. But it was still way better than average.


They didn't need to say more. Wendy might have told Kate that maybe it could still work out. Just because Louie said he hated her that didn't mean he really did. Look at all the terrible things she'd said to her own mother. Just because Josh might never write her Post-it notes or do fancy dips with her in the kitchen didn't mean they couldn't have a nice time watching old movies with Louie on the couch.

But she also knew Kate was right. Every time Josh looked at her or heard her voice he would know who she wasn't. When she pushed Louie on the swings, he would know the swing-pushing rhyme she wasn't saying.

I hate it that your brother got set up for thinking he could wish your mother back home, she said. I would give anything if that hadn't happened to him.

But maybe it's a good thing for me that I finally got to see things clearly. I probably should have left New York a long time ago.

After, Wendy invited her to come back to the house and have dinner with her father and Carolyn, but Kate had a plane to catch out of San Francisco at midnight. Tell Garrett not to take it personally, she said. The last time I saw him, I wasn't that friendly. It's probably about time to let all of that old stuff go. If you spend all your energy thinking about the past, what's left to put into the future, right?


Wendy had been getting her period for a year already, when September happened, but after, she stopped. Amelia told her she'd read in her *You and Your Body* book that sometimes when a person was under a lot of stress, that happened to them, especially if they hadn't been menstruating that long, where their body already had much of a rhythm established. Her period was just one more thing that went away, along with so much else.

It came back in March, a little while after Kate's visit. She woke up feeling something wet and looked on the bed: blood. The first time she'd seen it, a year and a half earlier, she'd felt scared, but this time she was almost glad. It felt like a small sign that some kind of natural order was coming back to her life.

She thought then of the day it happened, the first time. Her mother had been out at yoga. Josh and Louie were at the park. She was home alone, drawing.

When her mother came back she had felt shy at first, telling her. Even though this was her mom, it was hard getting the words out.

I guess it finally happened, Mom.

Her mother had put her arms around Wendy. Oh, honey, she said. This is a big day.

I don't know what to do, Wendy said. Her mother had told her a little before, but it hadn't seemed to apply until now.

Back when I got my period, we all wore sanitary napkins, she said. But really, it's so much easier if you can use tampons, and it's no big deal.

She and her mother had shut themselves in the bathroom until Wendy figured out how to put the tampon in.

You have to relax your muscles, her mother told her. Think of the nicest thing you can imagine.

That would be getting a dog, Wendy said.

Well okay then, think about a dog. What kind are you picturing? her mother said.

A Boston terrier puppy.

See what I mean? That was easy, right?

They went for ice cream after. Her mom had taken out of her purse the old paperback copy of *The Diary of a Young Girl* that she had read when she was Wendy's age. She opened the book to the part where Anne talks about getting her period.

"I think that what's happening to me is so wonderful," her mother had read, leaning close so only Wendy would hear. "And I don't just mean the changes taking place on the outside of my body but also those on the inside. . . . Whenever I get my period, I have the feeling that in spite of all the pain, discomfort and mess, I'm carrying around a sweet secret."

*A sweet secret.* Wendy knew her mother would have loved to have a real mother-daughter talk then, about sex, and boys, and love, but she didn't feel like it. She couldn't think of anything to say.

I never knew you wanted a dog that badly, her mom told her. I guess now every time you get your period for the rest of your life, you'll think of Boston terriers.

# Thirty-Three

She was playing her clarinet a lot now, sometimes by herself, sometimes with Henry, in the band room during study halls.

Maybe you could come over after school, she said. We can do our homework, and I'll play you some music.

She played him Louis Armstrong first. The starting point, Josh liked to say. Then they moved on to Miles Davis, *Kind of Blue.* Now they were listening to her CD of Stan Getz and João Gilberto—another of the all-time classics, without which, Josh said, a person couldn't claim to have a real jazz collection.

In the middle of "Corcovado," Henry looked over at her and set his pencil down.

You ever have a boyfriend? he asked. She could tell he had been preparing to ask her this for a few minutes, minimum.

Sort of.

I never had a girlfriend, he told her.

They drew a little more.

I was wondering if you wanted to be my girlfriend, he said. If you weren't still seeing that other guy.

I'm not exactly seeing him, she said. We're still good friends, but he doesn't live around here.

This is probably where the hero in the comic would sweep the girl up in his arms and carry her off someplace, he said.

That's okay. I might be a little heavy for you. Though the name Garrett had given her, Slim, actually fit now, to her surprise.

His kiss was more the way she had expected it to be the other time, with Todd. Sticking on the postage stamp. She saw that she would have to show him.

She moved her chair closer so it wouldn't be so awkward. She put one arm around his neck and put her mouth against his. Two clarinet players, she thought, working on their embouchure.

They kissed like that for a few minutes. My dad will probably be coming home soon, she said. Carolyn was getting home later than Garrett now, due to all her new jobs.

You know, you're the first girl I ever really got to talk to, Henry said. Not having a sister or anything.

A picture came to her then, as Henry was packing up his clarinet and zipping up his backpack. It was of herself and Louie, but years from now. She was in her twenties, living in some city, going to music school, or studying art maybe. She had her own apartment. Maybe she had a boyfriend, maybe she didn't.

Her brother would come to visit for the weekend. He would be fourteen years old, the age that Henry was now. His voice would have changed, and he might have started shaving once in a while. He would look a lot like Josh, but when he danced, which was often, the person he would remind her of would be her mother.

They'd be in her little studio apartment, listening to music, sipping hot chocolate, or who knows, she might even let him have a little beer. He would be telling her about a girl he liked. The first one. She would have had a number of boyfriends by this time, though not so many that she didn't remember, still, what it was like to be fourteen, and kissing someone for the first time.

If you ever have any questions, she would tell him, I hope you ask me.

*   *   *

*A Tree Grows in Brooklyn* was a wonderful book, but she didn't like *Lord of the Flies,* she told Alan. It could be true that kids would do terrible things like that, she said. But I myself believe more along the lines of Anne Frank. That people are basically good.

And how do you explain it when terrible things happen? Alan asked her. And it's the fault of some human being? Or a whole culture of human beings? The book he had given her most recently was called *Night,* by Elie Weisel—the story of the author's days as a young boy in a concentration camp. Of all the people in his family, only he survived. And there he had been, fifteen years old, with practically his whole life still to lead, trying to figure out whether it even made sense trying.

But he did in the end. Not only did he go on living. He wrote books. That one, and others. And though the books told of terrible, unbearable things, they were beautiful, too. Out of the most unspeakable horror, he had found something hopeful and good.

I'm still trying to figure it out myself, Alan said. How it is that for some people, a terrible tragedy can happen and it seems to make them stronger and more determined than ever to make their life mean something. And for other people it just flattens them. They never get over it. They aren't less good people. They're just missing some kind of survival instinct.

Carolyn calls me a cactus girl, Wendy said.

Linda is not a cactus girl, he told her. His wife had been gone two months now. It didn't look like she was coming home.

Luckily, he said, I'm something of a cactus man myself. If Borders doesn't kill me, nothing can.

Henry was coming over to Wendy's house regularly now, and bringing his clarinet. The best thing about him wasn't the kissing. He hadn't gotten the hang of that. The best part was playing duets.

Henry had been playing a couple of years longer than she had, and he was really good at sight-reading. He had a book of Beatles tunes that they worked out parts for, and another of old-time jazz ballads like Josh might play. They would sit side by side in the backyard for hours sometimes, flipping through the pages, picking out songs to work on.

Who would have thought? Garrett said one time, when he came home from work, a little after six, and found the two of them there, in the near darkness, leaning in to study the sheet music. That this is how I'd find my daughter and some boy, who'd been home alone all this time. Playing their clarinets.

She might have been embarrassed, but she wasn't. Henry had turned out to be more of a friend than anything else. They had long conversations, walking home after school, but the best part was definitely the music. When she played her clarinet, she discovered, nothing existed but the notes. There was no New York and no mile-high mountain of rubble, no flyers taped up in the subways, no Josh even, hunched over the photograph albums, no Louie, staring at the TV set that wasn't even on, no ache in her chest at the thought of her mother. The music filled her whole brain, and not just her brain but her body. Everything else might have changed, but the music hadn't.

I'm playing again, she told Josh one night on the phone. Not just for practicing and band. I play for myself.

You know something? he said. I wouldn't have thought I could, but I've started to do that, too. Times when I'm playing and I lose myself in the music, I almost feel like my old self. Your mother used to say the same thing about dancing—that no matter what was going on in the rest of her life, when she was dancing, she could always count on being happy. I don't feel that way yet, but I can begin to imagine the day might come.

Louie was not doing well at the moment.

He went to school, Josh told her. He even went over to Corey's now and then to play. Also, strangely enough, he had given up sucking his thumb. After all that time that she and her mother and Josh had worked on it—the chemical her mother had dabbed on his thumb to make it taste bad, the retainer they'd gotten from the dentist that made it harder to suck, all the talks they'd had, lying on his bed with him, about not wanting his teeth to grow in crooked, being a big boy now, getting ready for the first day of preschool—he just woke up one day and stopped. Right after his terrible birthday.

But in other ways, Josh told Wendy, he was worried about her brother. It seemed to him as if Louie was putting on a big act the whole time. Even when he would smile or laugh, it was as if he was trying to figure out how a boy might behave if he was happy. One time at the park, he had said to Josh, We sure are having fun, right, Poppy? We sure are having a good time, huh?

He had nightmares a lot. He didn't call out for his mother, but sometimes he said the building was falling down. When a plane passed overhead, he would look up and say, That's just a regular plane, right? The good kind?

Then there was this: He never dressed up in his costumes anymore. He never wanted to be a wizard or a pirate or a lion anymore. All he ever was now was Louie.

Josh had started taking him to the therapist again. He mostly just played with blocks there, but he didn't pretend to her anymore that his mother was off on a trip.

My mother is dead, he told the therapist. My mother's never coming back. It doesn't matter how good I am.


Louie, she said to him. It was their Saturday morning phone call. I have a school vacation coming up. I was thinking maybe I could come see you.

Okay, he said. His voice sounded flat.

We could play your new games, she said. I used to have Operation, but I forget how it goes. You'd have to teach me.

It's a dumb game.

Fair enough. She realized, hearing her voice talking to him, that she was sounding like one of those adults she always hated when she was little, who say things to kids that they don't really mean. The truth was she still knew very well how you played Operation. The truth was, it was a dumb game.

So maybe I'd come stay with you and Josh for a while. For a visit.

And then you'd go away again, he said. Weary.

My school's out here now, Louie.

I know.

*　　*　　*

Wendy hadn't been over to Violet's for a few weeks. With school now, it was harder. For a while there, Carolyn had been getting together with Violet and Walter Charles almost every day, to work on the cactus garden installation, but for the last week Carolyn hadn't been able to reach her, so they'd decided to drive over—Wendy and Carolyn—to make sure everything was all right.

When Carolyn pulled her station wagon up in front of Violet's building, there was a pile of trash on the street. A couple of Huggies boxes full of odds and ends, but something else: Walter Charles's changing table, and, hanging over the edge of the trash can, his musical mobile.

When they got to the top of the stairs, the door was open, music playing. The place was mostly cleaned out, except for Violet's boom box and a suitcase. She was sitting on the floor, doing her toenails.

What happened? Wendy asked.

Where's Walter Charles? Carolyn said.

Listen, Violet said. It's not like I'm thrilled about this.

Walter Charles, Carolyn said again.

There's so many great opportunities he could get with someone else, she said. You wouldn't believe what some people have in their houses. A TV set in the bathroom. Heated toilet seats.

Violet, Carolyn said. What's going on? She sat down on the floor next to Violet, who had finished one foot and started in on the other one. She put an arm around Violet, who was studying her foot.

I called up that lawyer in San Francisco, she said. I was just wondering if that couple she was telling me about might still be interested.

Nobody said anything. Carolyn had turned off the music. Now Wendy heard her let out a long, slow sigh, like wind over the desert, John Coltrane in the night.

*　　*　　*

How could you just do that? Wendy asked her. You didn't even call us. She had a million things to say, actually. It surprised her that Carolyn had not spoken a word.

You think you know everything, Violet said. But you only know how things work in your little world. Not everybody takes clarinet lessons and has a mother who dyes Easter eggs with them.

Wendy didn't have that either anymore. But she did once. That was still a lot more than Violet ever got.

There's more to this, isn't there, Violet? Carolyn said quietly. Rich people in San Francisco don't just drive up and take your baby away.

It was my mom, Violet said. She was over here, deciding to be all motherly again, only then she started in on me like always, and things got a little crazy. After she left, I just kind of lost it. Wally was screaming, and I guess I started shaking him. The neighbors called Child Protective Services. They took him this morning.

Her voice sounded like an answering machine. Up until now, she hadn't looked at them, but now she did, square in the eye.

See what I mean? she said. Things are different here.

It was very late when the call came, a time of night when it can only be bad news.

Wendy, her father said. It's for you. It's a boy, and he's crying.

She had thought it was going to be Henry, but it was Todd, calling from Colorado.

There was an accident, he said. Snowboarding. My brother.

It was their day off. His friend had gotten them passes like usual. Conditions were perfect. They'd just finished building a bunch of new jumps, and the half-pipe was packed down hard, glass.

We were on our last run of the day. Watch this, Kevin said. He wanted to try a three-sixty.

Kevin was never as good at snowboarding as Todd. He'd always been scared of the jumps. And that was the thing of it. Once you were trying for a three-sixty, you had better commit. The worst thing a person could do was get three-fourths of the way around.

He landed on his neck. Todd was at the bottom of the half-pipe, watching. He knew that first instant it was bad.

They took him down the mountain on a special sled that holds a person's neck in place in case they broke it. I can't move my legs, he said. Gasping for breath. I can't move my arms. I can't feel anything.

You're going to be okay, Todd told him. It was like he was inside his brother's body, they were that connected. He felt nothing—nothing and everything. He could hardly breathe.

They wouldn't let him ride with Kevin in the ambulance, but someone from the mountain took him in a car. The roads were very snowy. There must have been an accident up ahead. Nothing serious but enough to slow them down. He thought they'd never get there.

Finally, they were at the emergency room. Running through the halls. Lights flashing. Other people running. Sticking tubes in his neck. *We need oxygen. He isn't breathing.* Then it was still.

I'm really sorry, the doctor told him. It was his spinal cord. He couldn't even breathe on his own.


All there was on the other end of the line then was great gasping sobs. More tears than Wendy had known possible, she who had known plenty.

I wish I was there, she said.

I just got done finding him.

At least you were there with him.

In the whole world, he said, I only had one brother.


That night, lying in the dark, nowhere close to sleep, Wendy heard a sound on the roof, as if someone was throwing rocks. She got up and went into the dark yard. It was a hailstorm. Pieces of ice big as gum balls were pounding down on the orange tree, smashing against the hood of Garrett's truck. She stood watching for a while, in her pajamas, imagining Todd, alone back in his bachelor pad in Steamboat Springs by now, surrounded by pizza boxes and an ashtray full of half-smoked cigars.

Wendy remembered her own self, those first nights after her mother's building went down, wanting only to disappear. If you had given her a spoonful of cocaine then, or a pill to make a person go to sleep for ten years, she would have taken it. Now, though, Wendy knew, she would rather be in the world, even with all the sorrow that went along with that, than to miss what it felt like to be alive. She would rather feel the awful sadness of losing someone you loved than have it the way it was for her father, when his mother died: losing someone he never had in the first place—feeling, at the end, as if he never even had anything to lose.

At least you had a brother for a while, she said into the air, as the hailstones showered down around her.

Imagine if he hadn't. Imagine if you never knew how it felt to love anyone.

Sometime very late, Wendy made her way back to bed. In the morning, when she got up, the storm was over. Carolyn and Garrett were in the yard—Carolyn still in her bathrobe, barefoot, with her hair hanging loose and wild down her back. She was holding a couple of plant pots in her arms. Even Wendy could tell, the plants were past the point of nursing back to health.

I can't believe it, Carolyn said. All my favorites. Destroyed.

It turns out even a cactus isn't indestructible, Garrett said. Close, but not quite. He had an arm around Carolyn, more tender than Wendy had ever seen him.

We're going over to my place, Carolyn told Wendy. I dread seeing what it's like over there, but I might as well know.

We'll be back in a little bit, okay, Slim? Garrett said. When we do, we'll make sure we get some flowers sent to Todd in Colorado. I want him to know he's welcome here, if he needs a place to come and hang out for a while, where nobody will expect anything of him.

\*       \*       \*

After they left, Wendy sat in the yard, among the pots of hail-damaged cactus plants. Some were definitely goners, but a few looked as if they might, with time, survive. Even among cactus, some were hardier than others evidently.

She went back in the house and took out her clarinet, and a couple of pages of the sheet music Josh had sent her. The tune she picked out was one of his favorites. "Let's Call the Whole Thing Off." She had heard Josh playing this one so many times, she could almost hear the bass line, see his big hands wrapped around the neck of his instrument, his eyes focused on the middle of their living room. She saw him smiling as he watched her little brother and her mother doing their Fred Astaire and Ginger Rogers routine with the rug rolled up. She heard her mother's off-key voice, "You say tomato, I say tomato," and her brother's clear and high, the click of her mother's tap shoes, the low thump of the strings. Steady as a heartbeat.

*Home.*

Looking out at the almond tree, with Shiva licking her leg and the sun coming out from behind the low hills, Wendy felt clear, for the first time in months, where she was going. It had been right to come to California. But it was right now to leave.

# PART THREE

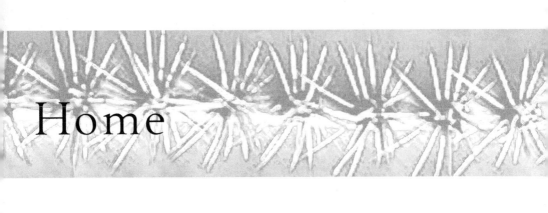

# Home

# Thirty-Four

When she told them she was going back to Brooklyn, they didn't argue. This is not about me feeling angry anymore, Wendy told Garrett. She was done with that. The weeks since her birthday had been the best ones they'd spent. She just needed to get back to her brother and Josh now.

Garrett said he'd buy her the plane ticket, but she didn't feel like riding on planes. She'd rather take the train.

Garrett said he'd drive her back east in the truck if she could wait a week or two for him to finish up a few things on his job. He could bring her to New York and then head on up to Greenwich, take care of some things at his mother's house, which he was selling.

Sometime I'd really like to drive cross-country with you, she said. Only I think I need to go now.

Some parents—most, and certainly her mother would have been one, and Josh would be another—would never let their fourteen-year-old ride alone on Amtrak from one coast to the other. That was Garrett for you, a guy who could leave his daughter alone in a hotel room in San Francisco in the middle of the night, to wander on the Embarcadero, a guy who could see a sign on a steep mountain trail in winter that said CLOSED FOR THE SEASON and decide to step over the chain.

But—this was the other part—he was also a guy who had let his daughter skip school for two months, trusting her to do other worthwhile things instead (as she had done) and to figure out, on her own time, when she needed to go back. He had made terrible, costly mistakes. He had also been willing to admit them. He might not remember to give Carolyn a Christmas present, but he would spend the next three days helping her dig up hail-damaged cactus plants and hauling them back to his house in the truck. He would never make it up to her mother—the way things ended between them, and after—but he would do better with the woman who loved him now. He was probably never going to change completely—never realize that most parents, even the ones fool enough to put their daughter on a train alone for a three-thousand-mile trip, would at least call ahead to let someone know on the other end that she was coming.

But he would remember, at least, to give her a package of beef jerky and a bunch of Bob Marley tapes for the trip and money for the dining car. He would have a book for her, his own ancient paperback copy of *On the Road,* and a set of yellowed postcards of artworks he loved, collected over the years, to study when she got tired of reading.

Anyway, he said, the really dangerous things that happen hardly ever come from the places most people think. As she well knew.

If anybody gives you trouble, tell the porter, he said. But your best protection comes from your own strong self.

The good part about Garrett was his belief in his daughter—his faith that, if he wasn't a totally reliable person, at least she was.

She went to school one more day to say good-bye to a few people—her band teacher and one girl she liked in English class, but mostly Henry. He didn't say much, but she could tell he was really sad. You're probably the only person I'll ever know who has a red clarinet, he said.

That could be true, she said. But think of all the other colors.

*       *       *

She went to the bookstore to say good-bye to Alan. I'll be out here to visit, she said. Keep a stack of interesting books set aside for me, okay?

Just remember these two words of wisdom, he told her: Picabo Street.

You were my one friend, Violet told her.

You could make a lot of other friends, Wendy told her. If you'd just call that number I gave you for the counseling center. She had tried discussing with Violet how it was for her, with Walter Charles gone, and what she might do to get him back, or see him sometimes anyway. Take parenting classes maybe. I bet Carolyn would help, she said. You don't have to give up on being his mom.

Violet didn't want to talk about it, though she had told Carolyn that once she signed the papers a few months from now, Walter Charles would be available for adoption. I just don't want them changing his name, she said. That's the one thing.

You can call me in Brooklyn sometime, Wendy said. Collect is okay.

Well anyway, I'll probably see you before too long, Violet said.

They're doing a Mother's Day show on Maury Povich about moms and daughters that get back again and mend their relationship, she said. My mom sent in a letter about her and me.

What are you talking about? Wendy said. Have you forgotten what you told me about Maury? Have you forgotten Christmas?

It's a free trip to New York, Violet said. They put you up in a hotel and give you money for a restaurant. Anyway, people change. Everyone deserves a second chance. Who knows, we might even stay out there. My mom has a friend with an apartment in New Jersey.

Wendy was going to ask, What about your job with Carolyn? What about learning about cactus gardening and going back to school?

She remembered what Carolyn had said then, how she'd better not get too attached to Walter Charles and Violet. Sometimes you don't want to know what a person's palm might tell you.

*　　*　　*

Wendy spent Saturday taking her posters off the walls and packing up her stuff. She'd accumulated a couple of new outfits and CD's since she'd been there. Some artwork, her books, her clarinet. Also the cactus, which she hated to leave.

I was thinking we could rig up a basket to put it in, Carolyn said. Just keep it on the seat next to you on the train. Then no one will mess with you either. That was the other great thing about a cactus.


All that time the box from Josh had been sitting under the bed, with the presents her mother had bought over the last year. Ready or not, she figured she'd better open it.

There were a bunch of little things, joke presents: a set of collector cards of the Backstreet Boys, who Wendy and Amelia used to make fun of. Day-of-the-week underpants.

There was a pair of earrings she'd admired that a woman was selling on the street in Nantucket—silver with real garnets. Also a shirt she'd wanted at Macy's that day, but it was expensive and not on sale. Unusual for her mother to buy at full price like that, but she had.

She had bought Wendy a glue gun for her art projects, and a special drawing pen she'd been admiring at Sam Flax but she didn't think she'd ever mentioned it. A pair of leopard-skin-print stretch velvet gloves. A matching bra and panties set from Victoria's Secret, the thinnest purple silk. A two-CD set of Ani DiFranco.

Two books. One was the same paperback edition of *The Member of the Wedding* that Alan had given her back in the fall. When she opened it, there was an inscription in her mother's handwriting.

"This was my favorite book when I was your age," she had written. "In certain ways, the girl in it reminds me of you. Her fierce, brave spirit and her hunger for adventure. Her zest for life."

The other was a book about sex for teenagers.

"We can talk about any of this stuff," her mother had written. "But I know that can be hard to do sometimes, even with your mom. So for those times when you might not be able to discuss something with me, this might help."

One more thing remained in the box. It was in an envelope. She opened it very slowly, undoing the top instead of ripping the paper, picturing her mother sealing it up all those months before. After this one last gift from her mother, there would be no more, ever.

Inside was a round-trip plane ticket, New York to Sacramento, with the dates left open.

"I shouldn't have given you such a hard time about this," she had written on the card. "A girl has every right to get to know her father."

He drove her to the train station. She had said good-bye to Shiva and Carolyn back at the house. No way to say good-bye to a dog, no matter how much you were going to miss them, of course, and the same applied to people, actually.

Garrett carried Wendy's bags out to the car. All except the cactus and the clarinet, that she managed herself.

Two nights and three days on a train, he said. You sure you're up for this?

She had expected Garrett to be a little awkward about telling her good-bye, and he was.

So, he said. I hope it turned out the way you wanted.

I didn't even know what I wanted, she said. But it did.

I'll be back there before long, he said. Attending to my mother's estate. And I'll get down to the city.

You can meet Josh and Louie.

We could even take in a ball game, he said. I'd really like to meet your dad.

My other dad, she told him.

*     *     *

It was good having you here, he said.

For me, too.

You're always welcome back. Goes without saying.

I know.

But it probably makes sense for you to get back to your life there with the family. The little brother. I never had one of those, but I can imagine what a good thing that would be. The one other person in the world who can appreciate all you had to put up with from your crazy parents, right?

He looked as if he was ready to hug her then. She set the cactus plant down.

You've got all the snacks Carolyn packed for you, right? he said. You'd think there wasn't a scrap of food to be had between here and the East Coast.

Well then. He put his arms around her. Still not exactly Josh's kind of embrace but firmer than it has been back when she met him in the fall.

I always liked a road trip myself, he said. That's the thing about a plane trip. You get to a place too darn fast, before you have a chance to take in all the miles in between. It's a long way from here to New York City in more ways than one.

He had gotten her a sleeper car, with a bed that pulled out from the wall, though for now she set out her things on the seat next to her. If it was her mother and Josh seeing her off, or just Josh, or Josh and Louie, they'd be standing on the platform waving till the last possible minute, but looking out now, she could see Garrett walking away, his gray hair—no longer in the ponytail—curling up around the collar of his jacket.

The train began to move—a slow lurching first, then picking up speed as it made its way out of the yard and out across a long, flat expanse, heading east. It had begun to rain, and the sky was a flat, dull gray. She was just as glad. Harder to leave California, when the sun was shining.

She took out the little packet of postcards Garrett had given her and studied them, one at a time. There was a painting of a wheat field by van Gogh, with a sun swirling overhead and a road winding off to a farmhouse. There was a painting by someone named Bonnard, of a woman lying in a bathtub, a portrait of a man by El Greco, a mother with a child on her lap by Mary Cassatt, a group of cartoony-looking figures that looked as if they'd been made out of cardboard, by a man named Red Grooms. The card said it was part of a larger work called *Ruckus Manhattan.* There was a black-and-white photograph of the rock face of El Capitan at Yosemite, taken by Ansel Adams. She flipped slowly through the stack, then went back to study them a second time. Across the seat from her, a woman had settled herself with a little girl young enough to still have a pacifier. She was reading to the little girl, but Wendy wasn't paying attention at first. Then she heard the words . . . "goodnight stars, goodnight air." *Goodnight noises everywhere.*

She fell asleep. When she woke up they were in the desert, a dry, golden landscape, and more sky at one time than she'd ever seen. Something about the sound the train made felt good—the steady, lulling rumble under her of wheels on the track. A few hours must have gone by like that, in which she did nothing but stare out the window. She thought of Tim at the Laundromat, and how, when her brother was little, her mother had sometimes set him on top of the dryer, if he was fussy. The vibrations, when she turned it on, had seemed to comfort him.

They were heading into the mountains now, out of Utah into Colorado, with the sun going down. Wendy made her way to the dining car and ordered a bowl of soup, that she sipped, alone, still looking out the window, though the view now in the near-darkness was jagged peaks and snow.

Sometime after Denver the porter came by to make up the bed. Wendy put on her rabbit pajamas and climbed in. She thought of Louie and how he would love this. She imagined his hot little body snuggled against her. *What do you want to talk about now, Sissy? Which do you like best, a fire engine or a Jet Ski? When we grow up, can we still have our same rooms?*

You might get married, Louie. I might do that, too. We'd probably have kids eventually.

But we can still stay in our same apartment, right? We'll just make some more rooms.

Your wife might want to go live someplace different. You might want to explore other places.

I won't. I just want to stay here.

Then it was morning, and they were in Nebraska, a man told her, when she went to the dining car to get her cereal. Nebraska looked flat and cold, but not as flat and cold as Iowa, and Iowa seemed to go on forever. She took out her postcards again, and tried drawing, but she wasn't in the mood. When she was back in New York, though, she would pay a visit to her favorite store, Forbidden Planet, and check out the underground comics. They had a book there she wanted to get, on how to draw different facial expressions. She had been thinking that she might want to sign up for a figure drawing class someplace, on the weekends, with a live model. Across the seat from her now, a man was reading a paperback book about how to keep from getting wrinkles. She studied his hand, resting on his forehead, and thought how she'd draw that.

In Chicago, when they had to change trains, Wendy hated to leave her little compartment. She had begun to like the feeling of being sealed up in the train, like a space capsule, but shooting over land instead of through the atmosphere. She made her way down the steps onto the platform and found the sign for the New York train, leaving in just a little less than two hours. She got herself a turkey sandwich and stood at a newsstand, reading *People* magazine. Jennifer Lopez had gotten married. Drew Barrymore was getting a divorce.

The second train was almost exactly the same as the first one. This is a pretty big trip for a young lady to make all on her own, the porter said. Some people would want to take the plane. But if you do that, you miss everything, right?

I like to see where I'm going, she told him. Even the parts that aren't all that beautiful.

It's all part of life, right? he said.


When she woke up, they were in New York State, heading to Buffalo, then Schenectady. Louie, if he heard that name, would probably say it over and over, or try to. Josh, if he was there, would do something like grab her mother and say, Run away with me, Janet. Let's run away to Schenectady.

*I would go with you anywhere, sweetheart. But please, could it be Paris instead?*


The porter came by. Forty-five more minutes and we'll be at Penn Station, he said. Just wanted to give you time to gather up your things.

Out the window now, there were just buildings, no more green. The area they passed through looked like the kind of place with more factories than houses. Gray smoke billowed out from some of them. Wendy could see highways and cars, and another train, on a parallel track, coming from the opposite direction. There was a little snow on the ground, still, but not much. Viewed from the train, the city—even with its permanently altered skyline—looked sparkling and beautiful, in a totally different way from the hills outside Davis, or Yosemite, or the Golden Gate Bridge. Wendy wondered where Carolyn was at this moment. And Garrett, and Shiva.

She put on her headphones and slipped in her Sade CD. She skipped to number seven—Sade's lullaby to her daughter, her mother's favorite. She didn't play this one often. Like her mother's dress, that she kept sealed in the plastic bag so the smell of her wouldn't wear off, she didn't want to use it up. As it was, if she didn't overdo it, she could imagine her mother with her, when she listened to the words. She could bring herself back to the two of them listening together that time, her mother saying, Just once more, okay? Her mother's voice singing out of tune, along with Sade. *I will always remember this moment.*

When I hear this song I want to cry, her mother said. But it's a good feeling.

*Listen, Mom.*
 *I'm here.*
 *I went to California.*
 *And how was it?*
 *Good.*

*I wish you could come back.*
 *But I can't.*
 *I know.*

When you have a child, an amazing thing happens, her mother told her once. The thing I used to fear most was dying. But once I had you, it wasn't that way anymore. The worst thing would be if something happened to you.

You don't need to worry then. I'm fine.

The train was slowing down. Out the window, she saw many other trains now, pulling into the station. The man across from Wendy picked up his suitcase. She reached for her backpack, then her cactus. The porter had already set her larger suitcase by the steps.

I hope someone's meeting you, honey, he said.

It's all right, she said. I know my way around here.

She got herself a cart to put her suitcase on, and the clarinet case and the basket with the cactus. She wheeled the cart out to the curb and found a taxi right off. Park Slope, she said.

As the taxi made its way across the bridge, over the East River, Wendy could see the buildings in Brooklyn Heights, where, last September, a swirl of paper and debris had drifted over from the towers like a freak blizzard. There was the Watchtower building, and the warehouses along the water, the stretch of road where she and her mother used to Rollerblade.

Back in California, Wendy had promised Carolyn that she'd call Josh and Louie to say she was coming, but she hadn't. She remembered what it was like being little and waiting for something that seemed to take forever, the way she'd waited for Louie when her mother was pregnant. Time will fly, her mother had said, but the days before his birth had seemed endless. Better to just show up. Call out to them, *I'm here.*

She thought Josh would be home when she got there but he wasn't, and his bass was gone, so she figured he was probably off giving a lesson. She set her things in her room, which looked exactly the same as how she'd left it, except for her Madonna poster not being up. The rest of their apartment looked pretty much the same, too, though a little messier than it had been before. Evidently they'd put away the train set for now at least.

She looked in the fridge. The crisper drawer was full of fruits and vegetables, and the fact it was made her happy. Hopeful anyway. The Spanish tapes were out on the counter, as if Josh had been listening to them again, though if so, he was still only on lesson three. There was a library book, *Choosing a Puppy*, with Post-it notes marking a couple of breeds. There was a cereal bowl and a plate on the table with a puddle of maple syrup on it still. They'd left in a rush, nothing unusual about that.

She walked into her parents' room. The last time she'd seen it his clothes lay in piles on the floor, but everything was put away now. The picture of her mother and Josh in New Orleans was still on the bureau, but when she opened her mother's side of the closet, the clothes were gone. There were a bunch of boxes on the shelf. *Janet*, they said.

She looked at their wall clock. Felix the Cat, with jewels in his eyes and a swinging tail, bought by her mother for Josh's birthday that time. If only you'd have more of these birthdays, you might get to be as old as me someday, her mother said.

Well, now he would.

She went to the closet. She got out her winter coat that was hanging right there, as if it was just yesterday she'd hung it up, instead of a whole year ago almost. Last March probably, the last really cold days of last winter.

Louie's school was five blocks away. She had only been there a few times, back in the fall, when she'd picked him up.

After all these months she still knew where to find his classroom. It was naptime when she got there. They were lying on their mats while a tape played of Native American chanting.

I'm Louie's sister, she whispered to the teacher.

He's got an appointment today, Wendy told her. I came to pick him up.

I thought you were gone, the teacher said. Louie used to talk about it all the time. California, right?

I was, she said, but I'm home now.

He's going to be so happy.

She walked slowly over to his mat. Even lying on his belly that way, with nothing but the back of his head showing, she would know him anywhere. She bent very low over him. His hand, that would have been up by his mouth so he could reach his thumb, in the old days, formed a tight fist at the side of his mat. He was asleep, or almost.

Louie, she whispered. I came to get you.

He opened his eyes and studied her face. He looked older, and not just because he was five instead of four.

Sissy, he said. I dreamed you were here.

Later they would go many places. If not today, then soon, she would take him where the towers used to be, as close as the policemen would let them get.

Is this where Mama is? he might ask her.

This is where she used to be.

That's a very big crane, isn't it, Sis? he might say. He might even know the official name for it. He knew all the names of the vehicles.

So this is where it happened, she would tell him.

The men are cleaning everything up now, aren't they?

Yes, Louie, she'd say. After a while, all this mess will be gone.

But Mama's building isn't there anymore.

No, Louie.

Or Mama either.


I used to think there was such a thing as magic, he said. I used to think if you believed hard enough, it might come true.

In a way that's so, Louie. Just not the way you might picture it. We won't get things back how they used to be. But if you think it's going to be okay again someday, it will be. If you believe in goodness, it's still there.

Sometime soon, she thought, they would send out invitations. They would find a place—not a church maybe, but a big beautiful room or, if they waited a few more weeks till the warm weather came, some outdoor spot—and maybe they could rent one of those portable dance floors. If she had her way Mark Morris would be there, but there would be someone to dance anyway, in a red leotard and a boa, with a zest for life. Josh would not have his bass that day, but there would be other musicians, friends of his probably, and he would know all the songs they should play.

Kate would come back from Hawaii, and probably even though they hadn't gotten along that well, her aunt Pam would be there. Amelia. And lots of other people, friends. She thought Garrett would want to come, too, and if he did, she would tell him, You should bring Carolyn.

She would not wear a black dress to her mother's service. She would wear a yellow one. She would sit next to her brother, and even though sometimes it was hard for him, sitting still, this particular time she believed he would manage.

They would be very sad that day, and for many days after. In certain ways always. They would also never be the same as how they used to be. But they would also be happy sometimes.

*   *   *

Aren't we lucky? she said to him now, as they walked out of his classroom and down the hall, out the big wide doors of his school into the sunny day, Louie shifting his backpack so he could take her hand.

What if I never got to have you for my brother? she asked. I would have had to miss you forever.

Did you know, Sis? he said to her. I learned how to skip.

# Afterword

In the first week of September 2001, I left my home in California, with the intention of spending the next six months in some remote place far, from the distractions of my life, to write a novel. I wasn't sure what I'd be writing about, but my mind was much occupied by the knowledge that for the first time in twenty-four years, I would have no child to care for. My nearly-grown sons and my daughter were all gone from home now—two out of the three of them on other continents—and no doubt my decision to take my leave was inspired, more than anything else, by the vast, empty space my youngest child's departure had left in my life. I was thinking a lot about parents and children, for sure—about my quarter-century-long project of raising my own three, my desire to see them safe, and the growing awareness that little I could do anymore, now or in the future, could shelter them from the risks that come with being a human being alive on the planet.

I was thinking about the scars divorce had left on all of us, the dream I had once held so dear of children growing up under the same roof with their two original parents. And I was thinking—as I watched my sons and daughter embrace one another at the various airports where we said our good-byes that September, on one coast and another—of the great gift that has been their huge and steadfast love for one another, in the face of so many other uncertainties.

Before leaving the country, I stopped in New York City to pay a brief visit to my son Charlie, who was a student there. Two days after my arrival, leaving a midtown coffee shop, I heard the news that a plane had hit one of the Twin Towers. Nothing was the same after that for anyone.

I ended up staying in the city much longer than I'd planned, long after planes had resumed flying. As grim and terrible a place as New York had become, in those early days after the attack, it also felt necessary—particularly as someone who has loved that city since the day I first laid eyes on its glittering skyline, at age ten—to bear witness to what had happened. I spent most of the next few weeks just walking the streets, taking in the names and faces on the flyers posted everywhere, listening to conversations on the street, standing in front of those heartbreaking altars that sprang up all over the city within hours.

Other people's tragedy and loss remind us of our own vulnerability, I think, and so I worried terribly about my younger son, off in Africa somewhere, and unreachable, and my daughter, in Central America. But I worried less for my children's physical safety, over the course of those days, than about the world they and the rest of their generation were fast inheriting. Where was hope to be found? How could a young person absorb the crushing news of what we had all just witnessed? Tragedy and disaster on an immense scale had taken place on shores beyond our own, but like most Americans, I had always enjoyed a certain comfortable remove from what went on far from home. That would never again be possible.

Perhaps because of the ages of my own three children, I found myself trying to fathom how, in the midst of so much tragedy and violence and uncertainty about the future, a young person could go on to build a hopeful life. I thought about the children and teenagers who had lost a parent that day. I wanted to know how a child goes on with her life—how anyone does—after huge and irrevocable loss of the most abrupt and senseless form. Lacking any clear answers, I decided to create a character who might help me to locate them.

I don't pretend that every child who has experienced huge losses will survive as hopeful and whole as my fictional girl has done on these pages. I only mean to offer a glimpse—for myself, and the young people I love, and others I haven't met yet—of what might be possible, of the light that remains, after a season of darkness, and the spring that follows even the coldest kind of winter.

# Acknowledgments

This novel came out of the desire to tell the story of how it is that a young person can survive great and terrible heartbreak, with a certain sense of hopefulness about the future intact. No voice has ever spoken more powerfully on that subject, for me, than that of the young Anne Frank, writing in her diary more than half a century ago from the tiny annex where she and her family lived for two years before their eventual betrayal and capture by Nazis. Her brave, optimistic attitude about life, in the face of great danger and imminent threat of death, was never far from my mind during the writing of this novel.

I am indebted, as well, to a number of real-life girls whose ideas and stories and feelings I tried to give voice to, through the character of Wendy. They are Giovanna Marrone and Nicole Monestero of Park Slope, Brooklyn, and the seventh grade of Grace Church School, in Manhattan, whose enthusiasm and willingness to assist me helped me to believe in the value of telling this story. The time I spent at Grace School and with Giovanna and Nicole, in September, offered an invaluable glimpse of the buoyancy and grit that a young person is capable of, even in the face of devastation and despair all around.

Eventually, though later than intended, last fall, I left the United States and settled in Guatemala to write this book. As has been true in the past, my freedom to work was made possible by the great generosity of my dear friend Jim Dicke II of New Bremen, Ohio. Another longtime friend, Mark Nemmers, owner of my all-time favorite bookstore, Bogey's, in Davis, California, made my absence possible by taking care of all the things a person can't manage herself when she's living without telephone, Internet, or reliable mail service—not to mention providing essential information and advice concerning Yosemite National Park and life in Davis during the winter of 2001–2002, and caring in the most loving way for my dog, Opie. To any reader who might suggest that the small independent bookstore described in this novel is too good to be true, I can only say, go visit Bogey's.

This novel was written in the small village of San Marcos, La Laguna, on the shores of Lake Atitlan, Guatemala. My first reader was Didier Verbrug, a gifted young writer who put aside the pages of his own novel in progress, many evenings, to switch from Dutch to English for the purpose of listening to mine. He was an unlikely reader but an invaluable one, as were—a little later in the process—the fourteen wonderful writing students who joined me in Guatemala last February, who stayed up late more than once, after long days of work on their own manuscripts, so I could read them portions of mine. They were my American (and Canadian) ears when I needed them most.

Josh Needleman—bass player supreme—informed me on the subject of playing stand-up bass. My friend Joe Heavey can always be depended on, when my computer cannot. Bridget Sumser reminded me of how it is to be a fourteen-year-old girl, when I forgot. Vicky Schippers—always a treasured reader—talked to me about Brooklyn, with the love and insight of a mother who has raised five children there. Graf Mouen, my brother of choice, collaborator and friend for thirty years, and the one with whom I traveled to Ground Zero, late in the middle of the night after that first terrible morning, has—all my adult life—provided me with mind-altering inspiration.

Charlie Bethel, my older son, saved me from grievous errors concerning the art of skateboarding. It was missing him as I did this year and thinking back on the child he once was that inspired me to conjure, on the page, the character of a four-year-old thumb-sucking boy with a dreamer's love of costumes, and unwavering devotion to his older sister. My daughter, Audrey Bethel, who is not the girl in this novel but who endured some of the same struggles my young character did, as a child of divorce, caught in the middle, taught me more than anyone ever has, over the years, about how it is to love two parents who no longer love each other. And if her brothers are the model, in this story, for brotherly devotion to a sister, she is the model for a sister's devotion, back.

I am indebted to Jan Weil, child psychologist with the Jewish Board of Family and Children's Services, who agreed to read my manuscript in its earlier stages and offered essential insight into the experience of children who lost a parent on 9/11, and to Kathi Morse, bereavement counselor with the North Shore Family and Child Guidance Center in Roslyn, New York, who also took the time not only to read my manuscript but to share with me so many important lessons that came out of her many months of counseling children and families of 9/11 victims.

At the time when I embarked on writing this novel, I could not have conceived of intruding into the private grief of anyone directly affected by the terrible events of that September day. Many months later, though—and recognizing that the story of every single one of those people remains utterly unique—I sought out the experiences and observations of people who had gone through some of what my fictional character does. I am indebted to Tara Feinberg, whose father, Alan Feinberg, was a fireman with Engine Company 59, killed in the line of duty at the World Trade Center, September 11. Another whose experiences and insight informed my story is George McAvoy, of Brooklyn, New York, a counselor and brother of John McAvoy, Ladder Company 3.

Three writers—one I never met, two whom I am lucky enough to count as good friends—offered crucial guidance and inspiration for this project. Judy Blume, who understands young people as well as any writer I know, was one of the first people with whom I talked about the idea of this novel. Jacqueline Mitchard gave my character her name, and so much more.

The gift, from Carson McCullers, was her exquisite novel *The Member of the Wedding*, which my daughter, Audrey, and I read aloud to each other over the course of ten irreplaceable days we spent together last fall. The love my character expresses for that novel is mine.

No editorial assistant has ever offered more support or encouragement to me than Nichole Argyres—a calm and reassuring voice at the end of the telephone on many hard and lonely days. I am deeply grateful to the time and thought given this novel by Stephanie von Hirschberg, a wonderful editor and, now, agent, as well as my fellow writing instructor on Lake Atitlan. Special thanks goes to Joanne Brownstein, of the Brandt and Hochman Literary Agency, and to Sara Sanchez, for help way beyond the call of duty in procuring the rights to the lines of books quoted in these pages, and for taking care of many other things besides.

My agent, Gail Hochman, remains unfailingly supportive and fiercely loyal, in addition to being a deeply perceptive reader and a voice of reason when mine falls somewhere short, and a true friend.

Once again, I want to thank my treasured editor, Diane Higgins, whose enthusiasm and support was present for this novel from that dark September day when I first told her my idea to this one, a year later. What Diane brought to our many-months-long dialogue concerning this novel—as she has in the past—is not only her perfect pitch for language and unerring sense of story, but an understanding of the lives of children and parents and what it means to be a mother, a sibling, a child, that mirrors and complements mine as closely as that of any person I have ever known.

To my last-born child, Willy Bethel, who looked out over the sea of parents one June day, eighteen months ago, as he delivered his graduation address, to find my face in the crowd, face me squarely, and say, "Now, Mom, go write your novel," goes the word that I take what he says seriously and always will. Fierce love and nothing but.

To Ken Munn, builder of the finest cabinets found in British Columbia, goes love as straight and true as old-growth timber.

And finally, my thanks to a precious young reader who wrote to me, from her tiny village in the northernmost part of Israel last spring, to tell me she had read and cared about my work, and—most important—that it made her feel less alone in a violent and uncertain world. Shani spoke, in her letter, of her love of Anne Frank, her dream of becoming a writer, and her hope that one day she might tell stories other girls would read, as she read mine. It is for a reader like Shani Boianjiu that I write.